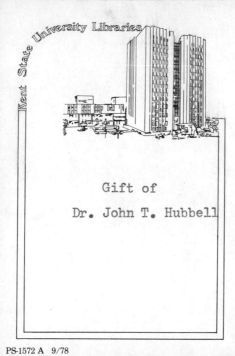

Song
of the
Pedernales

A Novel of Reconstruction Texas

by John L. Mortimer

MADRONA PRESS, INC. - AUSTIN, TEXAS

ISBN 0-89052-021-6
Library of Congress Catalog Card No. 76-40637
Copyright 1976 by John L. Mortimer

FIRST EDITION

Manufactured in the United States of America

SONG OF THE PEDERNALES

Brevet Lieutenant-Colonel of John Dunn MacAllan, one of

All over the South men were decamping without a mind
to it, by your leave . . . Yet, down there was Carterson Island,
a hundred miles away and they made a stronghold of a homesite

1

The darkest days had now come to Texas. Disaster was close, but nobody could forecast just when or where it would engulf the land.

Brevet Lieutenant Colonel John Levit MacAshen, late of Ross's Brigade of the Tennessee forces of Nathan Bedford Forrest, spurred his horse through the crowd of angry farmers around the bulletin board of the little Sabine River telegraph station.

Having just ferried over from Louisiana to Texas, he stared in disbelief at the message tacked to the wall. Good God! Didn't *anybody* have any judgment left? Reaching down from the saddle, MacAshen tore off the notice and held it closer to read it again.

On the morning before—the bleak and muggy morning of March 6, 1865—the Confederate authorities on Galveston Island again had executed one of their own soldiers, a Fayette County boy, on a charge of desertion. Another oath broke from MacAshen's lips. Did anybody think the inevitable could be staved off merely by killing all the deserters?

All over the South men were decamping without so much as a by-your-leave. Yet, down there on Galveston Island, a hundred miles westward, they'd shot a stripling of a homesick boy for that! This was the sort of thing that would blacken even the memory of the Confederacy. Turning the people against the army itself, it encouraged men in every state to think now of secession from the South, too. If these backwoods farmers were as bitter as they seemed, perhaps they had reason. MacAshen crumpled the paper into a wad and threw it into the dirt.

Wincing from the jab of his unhealed bullet wound, he pulled his horse around and forced a path back through the sullen crowd, pointing the stallion away from the center of the community. At a tavern where the road angled off toward Houston, MacAshen let himself down and looped the reins over the hitchrail, pressing a hand against the throbbing pain in his side as he did so. The journey had been rough but, if he could only stop and rest for awhile, he figured he could mend again.

Inside the tavern, he ordered whiskey. As the bartender set a glass before him and filled it, MacAshen gulped down the fiery potion. "Again." The man refilled and MacAshen swallowed half of that too, then sat staring at his reflection in the cracked mirror behind the bar. It had been a long time since he had stood before a mirror, and what he now saw startled him. He grimaced, scarcely able to recognize the steel-gray eyes that stared back from beneath black eyebrows and a forehead drawn by fatigue and pain. He was spare in countenance anyway, with high cheek bones in a visage that hollowed down to the chin. His face, reflecting strength when his natural stamina had not been sapped, was mile-posted now by lines and, though he was only in his middle twenties, his lank frame helped create an impression of greater maturity. The corners of his mouth bore a determined imprint, bred on the frontier and nurtured in war. Such a countenance, framed by a mass of unkempt black hair and a three-day stubble on the jowls and chin, were enough to chase the devils out of hell.

MacAshen's weariness would have been evident to anyone. When he leaned on the bar his six-foot-two body seemed to merge into it. There could have been a touch of fever about his eyes. In fact, he looked like a man who had passed into maturity without having known the exuberance of youth. He certainly was not handsome. But the half-rakish cut of his much-mended campaign garb, the scarred, costly leather boots, and the tailoring of the bleached butternut blouse beneath his *chaqueta* marked a class seldom seen at the tavern on the Sabine. Even the bartender dispensed with his usual small talk.

In the midst of his self-appraisal, MacAshen became vaguely conscious of three young women eyeing him curiously from a corner table, obscured by shadows. Saloon girls, he realized, like those in the fleshpots beneath the cliffs on the river at Natchez. Cajuns from Louisiana's back swamps.

Despite their suggestive glances, he gave no hint of invitation, which seemed unnatural for a soldier returning from the fighting. There was an air about this man that seemed to discourage casual relationships. His need exceeded what these girls had to offer.

He paid his tab and, as an afterthought, tossed another coin onto the bar, nodding to the girls in the corner.

Outside, he looked toward the people still clustered about the telegraph office, then down the road toward the west. He had planned to spend the night in this town, but the open road seemed better now, tired though he was. Slowly, he pulled himself into the saddle.

The temper of the people in the settlement disturbed him. Disaffection with the war, growing for months, had swelled suddenly into threatening discord. The Confederacy was tired, its bones scattered from Harper's Ferry to Louisiana's Sabine crossroads, the length and breadth of the Old South. MacAshen had encountered this rising belligerence elsewhere, but here in the Southwest he recognized it as resistance nourished on defiance.

Forrest had warned him. Rumors were everywhere, and nobody knew what they might portend. Even as far east as Tennessee, men spoke of a new plan of empire being hatched out here in Texas—the old Texas Republic, maybe, with whatever else it could latch onto. In fact, MacAshen had his orders in that regard—if he could make it home. "You report to Governor Murrah at Austin, when you're able, MacAshen," Forrest had advised. "He'll set you straight on what to do."

The bond between General Forrest and his junior officer had been well-known among the troopers. Forrest's driving force and his capacity for leadership were indomitable, and men observed the same qualities in the younger man. Forrest once had said to him, "You've got mesquite acid in your blood, Mac-Ashen. Anybody waiting out there for you? A gal, maybe?"

"No," MacAshen had replied.

"Well, then, you'd better find one."

Here on the road to Houston, MacAshen was seized by a fatigue he had never known. The sun was dropping behind the pine trees and twilight was close at hand, but he kept on for another half mile before pulling up to dismount under a dwarfed sweetgum. Most of the men back there at the battlefront had said he wouldn't make it this far with that hole in his side. He himself had doubted it at times. But Forrest had taken things for granted, once he had spoken his piece:

"The place for you, MacAshen, is back where you came from. You've done all you can here. You've got to make it home, where you'll get the care you need, but you'll just have to make up your mind on that. When you're fit again, you'll find plenty to do. Get that hole in your side closed up, then offer yourself to your own people."

So here he was, back in Texas. He actually had made it, at least to the state's border, hard as the journey had been at times. Now he had to light somewhere, and soon, to stay put until he could get back on his feet. For a week, at least, maybe two or three. Austin, he feared, was too far, and his ranchhouse on the Pedernales River beyond certainly was, even if Indians had not burned it down. Glad that Houston was not too many miles ahead, he laid out a small camp in the twilight dampness and ate from the meager rations in his saddlebags. Then, lying on his tarp spread on the ground, his head resting on his saddle, he slapped at mosquitoes and waited for sleep to overcome the ache in muscles and tendons.

As he gazed at the darkening sky, his reflection in the mirror came back to him, and he was startled by the feeling that he had seen not his own but his father's face. Four years of warfare had dimmed many memories, but not those of his father. From the moment of his mother's death, while he was still a boy, he and his father had experienced a closeness beyond the ordinary. Maybe that was because there was no other kin for either of them in the Southwest—or anywhere in America, for that matter. His father, as other Scotch-Irish adventurers, had come across the ocean long ago, settled in Texas, and built the ranch home on the Pedernales, even before the German colonists had taken up land in the upland hills and meadows. Into this land he had brought MacAshen's mother, too, arranging passage for her across the Atlantic to Wilmington, and then by packet around the Florida cape and through the Gulf of Mexico to Indianola. But Levit could not remember much about her—only the warmth and tenderness of fireside evenings in the big stone house on the Pedernales. As a child, the horror of her death had been almost more than he could bear, and he struggled even yet to put it from his mind.

The news of his father's death, when it finally reached Levit, had been a heavy blow, even in the midst of the violence at hand. For a moment, MacAshen lived again the parting with his father, and his mind wandered to the homestead in the Pedernales valley, northwest of the Bee Caves. The house itself probably was falling apart by now. He had never seen his father's grave, which the neighbors had placed atop one of the low mesas, and he feared it may have been desecrated by Indians. Then sudden determination took hold of him, dulling momentarily even the throbbing in his side. His passion was to carry on the task his father had begun—and to perpetuate the Mac-Ashen legend in the country of the green mountains and the sparkling rivers. With the South seemingly doomed, it was all he had left.

At last his eyes fell shut and sleep crowded such thoughts from his mind.

The Texas coastal plain is dank and marshy from the Sabine to the San Bernard and in the daylight of the third afternoon following MacAshen's departure from Louisiana, the landscape was changing. Not far ahead was Houston and, conscious of his appearance, he looked at his worn garments and ran a shaky hand across his chin stubble. He stopped at a creek to shave.

The road pointed southward. Black, uninviting pools shallowed close by and spread out toward the receding forests in the distance, but a line of dark green water oaks ahead marked the course of the bayou. That's where the town actually began, and he could see the first fringe of huts beyond.

The trail crossed the bayou over a long wooden bridge. Buffalo Bayou, MacAshen remembered, though the bison had long since been driven from the area. Crossing the bridge, he noted the dull, distant undertone of the city. The brash, metallic turmoil of the iron works came to his hearing. Down the bayou, after a time, showed the outlines of a mile-long wharf and, just beyond that, the smokestacks of a busy sawmill. But there were houses along here, too, where people lived.

Within the houses would be the women, left behind when their husbands went away to war. Haunted women, starved for love and companionship, struggling between hope and hunger. Eager women peering with burning eyes at every traveler coming down the road, then turning back somberly to overwhelming tasks, waiting for their men to come back.

There still were menfolk here, of course—frontier types, merchants, planters, traders, cattlemen—still in their prime, who had not gone to the war. As he rode on in thought, it aroused no particular bitterness in MacAshen. There had been good reason for many Texans to refuse enlistment, at least in the eastern armies. There had been troubles here at home, notably in the frontier counties, as great in proportion as those afflicting people in many parts of Virginia and Tennessee.

Levit caught the flash of a white face in a doorway. This was a soldier's home, he decided, for the stare directed at him held an indelible fragment of hope that he had learned to recognize. The woman was young, and pretty, and she was no doubt lonely. In his years with Forrest, the brigades had seldom bivouacked close to the settlements and when they did, the settlements had been largely abandoned. It occurred to him that he had almost forgotten what women were really like.

A waste-pit fire from a big sawmill marked the end of a street at the bayou. MacAshen recognized it as the main thoroughfare. He could distinguish the framework of a vast structure that evidently was a cotton compress, and nearby a sprawling cornmill with its outlying buildings. A distillery was close at hand, too, and now the clank of hammers from a structure across the bayou marked the location of the iron works. He could identify the dimly discernible sign above the roof, "Cushman Foundry." He wondered if they were still turning out muskets, and, if so, just what they planned to do with them.

The road curved on around a shack or two, where children idled beneath a magnolia tree. Tall pines still hid the town but when he rounded the trees, the road widened and business houses of both wood and stone began to line its course.

MacAshen had stopped only briefly in Houston in 1861 on his way to the war. It had been rough and dangerous then and, from the looks of the people who now appeared in increasing numbers, it might still be. On his previous visit he had bedded down at a stagecoach inn that had a bar on its lower floor, the same building he now saw ahead. It no longer appeared to have hotel facilities, but he pulled his horse to a stop before the hitching rail anyway.

A few steps away an old lady was talking with a younger woman. They were homey people, and he let his eyes rest on them. The girl was quite pretty and when she turned in his direction, MacAshen could see that her face, beneath a wealth of upswept red hair, was striking. The hair, he noted, was sometimes russet, depending on the way the sunlight struck it. A small sunbonnet, tied with a loose string, capped the back of the head.

MacAshen had found little opportunity in recent years to look at a pretty girl up close. For that matter, he'd had few such opportunities at his Pedernales Valley home before the war. She was vibrant and refreshing, and he felt he would just like to touch her, to feel the warmth of her soft skin beneath his hand.

She smiled momentarily at some remark by the older woman, and MacAshen sucked in his breath. Fleetingly, he could visualize himself touching the freckled nose, holding those smooth white cheeks in his palms, and planting a kiss on her apple-red lips. "Daydreams," he told himself.

As the older woman entered the store adjacent to the tavern, the girl idled in MacAshen's direction. Her white muslin skirt, falling from a full bodice over graceful hips, swung almost to her ankles. For all her twenty or so years, her body was firm and solid, and she exuded distinction.

As she moved abreast of him, he observed a small mesh of tiny facial lines. Though scarcely visible, the lines spelled out care of one sort or another, maybe for a husband or lover away at war.

Suddenly aware that she resented his gaze, MacAshen turned away uncomfortably and gathered himself to dismount, failing to observe at first the figure of a lounger who had stepped from the tavern doorway. An angry outburst from the girl startled him to attention.

"Keep away from me!" she cried.

"What's the hurry, sister?" The fellow who had emerged from the tavern had a hand on her arm. MacAshen turned in time to see her jerk free, raising the tiny parasol she carried, threateningly. The bonnet fell to her shoulders, and the fire that shone in her hair seemed also to be reflected from her hazel eyes.

"Now, now, baby doll," the man said with a coarse laugh, his arm upraised to ward off a blow from the parasol. "No need to be so uppity."

MacAshen swung out of the saddle, a bit too fast for his own comfort. "Let her alone!"

For an instant there was startled silence. The accoster rocked back on his heels, then turned to face MacAshen, who took in the man's attire, typical of the frontier farther west, and a black-butted gun, carried low, the man's right hand hovering near it. The hand was brown from the sun and wind, indicating it never wore a glove. With an empty feeling in the pit of his stomach, MacAshen recognized his plight. No barroom rowdy, this. He shot a glance at his own holster, still tied to his saddle.

"Well, I see we've got a soldier boy with us," the man said sardonically, eyeing MacAshen closely. "A soldier-boy dandy."

Over the man's shoulder, MacAshen vaguely saw another man take shape in the shadows of the tavern doorway and for an instant he thought the man was coming to his aid. But then the man's eye fell on the girl, and his expression changed completely. MacAshen apprised the reaction as surprise, mingled with anger. But the figure did not advance from the doorway. MacAshen's adversary shifted his stance, keeping his right hand close to his holster.

MacAshen, pondering his chances of getting to his own weapon in time to use it, did not see a third man enter the scene. The voice came from his left and behind him, near the corner of the building.

"Stand right where you are, both of you!"

Over his left shoulder, MacAshen glimpsed a tall, gaunt man, considerably older than himself, with a drooping mustache, cradling a shotgun. He advanced, shifting his gaze from one to the other.

"Storm," he addressed the man facing MacAshen, "we don't see no trouble around here till you show up."

"Put that shotgun down, you old galoot," Storm snarled.

"You all right, Miss Newcomb?" the newcomer asked, keeping his eye on Storm.

[8]

"Yes . . . yes, I'm all right, Mr. Fall."

Fall shot a sidelong glance at MacAshen. "Reckon you can relax, Mister, seein' as how you're not even packin' a gun."

He turned back to Storm. "I don't like fracases around here, and I don't like you, Storm, as I've told you before. Now just hightail it out of here."

Storm's eyes sparked, but the shotgun was still pointed at his belly.

"Don't try anything," Fall warned as the other began to back slowly off. "This gun ain't loaded with birdshot."

Both MacAshen and the young woman watched silently until Storm disappeared from view. Then MacAshen turned toward the girl, whose tilted chin held the hint of sharp challenge.

Replacing her bonnet and smoothing her skirt, she moved away from the wall and hurried into the store beside the tavern. "A pretty girl," MacAshen repeated to himself, wishing she had waited for him.

His thoughts were interrupted by the swarthy man in the doorway. "Storm's a reckless fellow," said the rugged, intent man. He came out onto the sidewalk now, and MacAshen looked him over, aware that the other had kept his distance until the air had cleared.

"Friend of yours?" MacAshen queried casually.

"An acquaintance." The man glanced cautiously at the shotgun in Fall's hands. "Only an acquaintance. I don't answer for what he does but I hope you won't let him worry you none."

"He ain't worryin' nobody around here, Devers," the older man spat out.

"Then I'll be moving on."

MacAshen turned into the tavern and Fall followed. MacAshen ordered whiskey. "Do you think he'll come back?" he asked Fall.

"Oh, he'll be around, all right, if not here then somewhere else close about. But I'm not afraid of the likes of him."

"It's lucky you happened by, Mister. And thanks for helping me out."

"I didn't just happen by. I'm the proprietor here. Name's Fall, as you probably heard out there. I see you're a soldier."

"Yes." The bartender had set a glass before him and MacAshen took a swallow. Tremors ran up and down his spine, and he felt icy cold in spite of the fiery draught. Some kind of a reaction, more weakening than at any time in recent days, was certainly setting in.

"Where you from son?" the older man asked suddenly. "I mean, before you went off to the war?" MacAshen, when he turned around again, saw that the other was studying him curiously.

"The hill country."

"Pedernales Valley, maybe?"

"Yes."

"Could have swore to it, the minute I saw you on the sidewalk. And your name's MacAshen, ain't it?"

MacAshen straightened. He looked the Texan over from head to foot. "Yes, my name's MacAshen. And how did you know?"

"I'd know the MacAshen marks on anybody. Used to trail with your dad in the early years, before I got too old for much of anything but bartendin'. I said 'your dad,' but you sure look older than anybody MacAshen could've had for a son."

"My father," Levit said, "is dead now. I didn't expect to run into anybody around here who ever heard of my people, or even my part of the state, for that matter. How'd you land down here on the bayous, Fall?"

"Guess I wasn't too partial to those mossyback Longhorns, 'specially when they holed up in the brush," the other laughed. "It was a long time ago, anyway. You just passing through?"

"I guess I am. I'd intended to stop in Houston a day or two, but I've already run into trouble here. I've had enough of that for a while, so I guess I'll keep going."

Fall stroked his chin uncertainly. "You don't look like you've been having it too easy. Are you headed for the Pedernales?"

"I don't know yet. I'm headed that way, but I don't know yet how far I'll get."

MacAshen finished his drink. He glanced once toward the corner of the room, wondering if he should plant himself in the chair there, at least for a little while. He moved toward the doorway instead. The tavern keeper walked beside him. "Glad to have met up with you, Fall," MacAshen muttered as they reached the threshold. "Sounds good to hear the Pedernales mentioned again." He almost stumbled as he reached the sidewalk but managed to recover his balance.

[10]

"I'd like to see it again someday myself," Fall answered.

As MacAshen reached his horse, the two women came hurrying toward him from the adjacent building. "This is the gentleman who rescued me, Auntie," the younger woman said.

"His name's MacAshen, Miss," Fall spoke up. To the soldier he said, "This here is Mrs. Newcomb, son, and her niece, Miss Karryl."

"I've been waiting to thank you for helping me out," the girl said.

"I didn't do anything." The twinges knifed at MacAshen's side, leaving a churning nausea in their wake. But the sound of her voice was soothing. Nodding toward the parasol she still carried, he added, "You did a pretty good job taking care of yourself."

"I'm grateful just the same," the girl said. Her eyes, which had flashed such fire during the episode, now were soft, more of a grayish-brown than true hazel, he noted, as she dropped long lashes over them for an instant. He sensed that she had been more annoyed than frightened by the incident on the sidewalk.

"I don't think . . . " MacAshen began again. But suddenly the older woman stepped in front of him, interrupting as she stared up into his face. "What's the matter?" she questioned. "You look sick."

"I . . . was . . . shot up some, over in Tennessee, Ma'am. It's nothing much."

"Shot up?" She studied him more closely. "Well, I guess you were."

Fall gently pushed her away and stood in front of MacAshen himself. "So that's it. I was wondering about you. What're you doing, trying to get back up on that horse?" You oughtn't to be thinking about riding anywhere, if you're as weak as you look. Let me think—this is a bad town right now for a wounded man, but surely we can figure something out."

Mrs. Newcomb took the bait instantly. "What do you mean, a bad town for a wounded man? At least I've still got a house, and a big one at that. You show this sick boy straight away down to it, you old outlaw!"

Levit MacAshen tried to raise his hand in protest, but even that effort was taxing. "I couldn't do that, lady," he argued.

"Don't be ridiculous, young man. You just stand still and

[11]

listen to what I'm saying."

MacAshen considered the imposition he would be placing on her. As one of Forrest's outfit, he might have a price on his head. Who could say where the Union soldiers, not to mention spies, were by now? The Federal army might be just off the Texas coast, for all he or any of these people knew, and it could move on Houston at any time. Harboring him could be an invitation to trouble.

But Fall intervened: "You'd better accept her invite, Colonel. I can't think of anything else right at the moment and, the way you look, you ain't got no other choice, no way."

MacAshen could scarcely argue the matter. "Oh, do come on, Colonel," the girl said, and there was insistence in her tone. Damn it, why did he have to crack up at a time like this! Sure, he would like to go home with her, but not like this.

Maybe, just for a night though. Christ, how he did need the rest! He groped for words, and then he was falling.

2

The stately old plantation home called Newcomb Hall lay a dozen miles out of Natchez, Mississippi, away from the river and on the road to St. Francisville, in Louisiana. Built in the early 1840s by Tolbert Newcomb, it was a typical antebellum structure of red brick built by slaves, in the midst of a grove of stately live oaks hung with Spanish moss. In the springtime, one could see, through picturesque dormer windows, beyond its huge beds of varicolored iris, clear to the grove of sweet olives lining the road from Natchez. Four great Tuscan columns supported a front gallery and the oaken roof above it.

Wide steps led onto the verandah, flanked by tiny plots of syringa, boxwood and Louis Philippa roses. Farther back were gardens of azaleas and japonica. Great masses of purple wisteria hung from arbors and trellises. In season, flowering peach trees cast a back drop of pink across the whole terrain toward the rear, and lazy farm animals grazed on lawns stretching out in front toward the gates on the Natchez-St. Francisville road.

Unique fanlights offset the carved entrance doorway. Midway inside, columned smaller doorways led to halls and reception rooms, and ultimately to an exquisite spiral stairway. Walls of polished walnut and pecan ran from shiny hand-scrubbed floors up to lofty ceilings, and the rooms were rich in furnishings of mahogany and rosewood. In the main drawing room, faced at either end with mirrors and the portraits of the earlier Newcombs, hung a select collection of old masters, including Barocchio and Coccanari.

Karryl Newcomb was born in that house and she grew into young womanhood there, laughing and playing on its lawns and in its corridors, and adding life and vibrancy to a normally languid existence. In more recent years the reception hall rang with frivolity as the young people from near about gathered to enjoy Newcomb hospitality. Many young men came to court Karryl, and once or twice she almost succumbed to their ardor. But then the war surged across the land, changing the whole way of life.

For a while, spontaneous gaiety continued to be the order of the day. During the winter of 1862, with Grant blocked in his effort to storm Vicksburg's defenses and Farragut sent scurrying back down the river, the romantic excitement was boundless. Each succeeding hour was more wonderful for Karryl, who even before she was eighteen, was acclaimed throughout the county for her comeliness and charm. Her rare beauty had a magnetic quality, inviting yet warning, and ambitious young swains knew to watch their steps. Actually, she never left a suitor long in doubt. But even those put in their places came back to her parties just as fast as they could get there.

She loved the Mississippians best, of course. But she fretted over them when visitors were around, because they were not as gorgeous as they might have been. The Mississippians had accepted the uniforms the Confederates prescribed, and sometimes they were pretty drab beside the others. But many of the soldiers who came from a distance were almost too marvelous for Karryl. She loved them all and tried to get every one of them into her home whenever she possibly could. Some of the newcomers were riotous in the hue of the distinctive attire. Musketmen and cannoneers from Mobile, wearing emerald green. Patterson's "Yellow Jackets," out of the Tennessee hills. The plantation Louisianians in shades of rarest blue.

And the Zouaves from New Orleans . . . well, they simply were the most wonderful of all. They came up the river road looking for battle in scarlet trousers resembling bloomers, blue sashes, jackets covered with lace, blue shirts, white gaiters, and headgear they called fezzes.

Exotic days, exotic evenings.

But the days raced by, and Karryl was subjected to the sobering realization that, much as she liked such things, the war would not always be made up of parties and dancing and young bloods who came courting. The thought brought a change to Karryl, accentuated by the appearance of some men from way back in Tennessee, and even from eastern Mississippi, who had known the drumbeat of the battle line and had seen Southern blood spilled on Southern soil. Even the uniforms of these hard-bitten men were different from those usually seen around Natchez. People called them butternuts for the color given the homespun fabric, provided by the soldiers themselves, by copperas and walnut-hull dye. Although Karryl disapproved of their garb too, she found a strange attraction in the soldiers themselves.

In late winter, 1862, the war was no longer in any sense a carnival. Even the thought of festivity was long past. The young men in cadet gray and emerald green and scarlet pantaloons were gone, some north to Vicksburg, some east to strengthen Lee and Stonewall Jackson. Romance and glamor faded as people began to experience fully for the first time the rigors of war. Yankee patrols, swinging wide to avoid Vicksburg, overran whole regions, and the stories of suffering in all theaters struck deeply along the river.

Karryl no longer went into Natchez. She wasn't going to let herself be intimidated by Yankee upstarts, even if the young men among them were as starry-eyed as her other swains had been. And so she hadn't even heard about the terrible epidemic of lung disease, spreading up the river from the Louisiana swamps and sweeping into homes and plantations far back from the turgid stream itself, until it actually struck around the Tolbert Newcomb plantation. In a single month more than a hundred field hands had died in the nearer farm lands, including many at Newcomb Hall.

The planters and their families fared no better. In June, as food-crop harvesting was just beginning, Karryl's mother and then her father collapsed and died within a few hours. Strangely, Karryl herself and the Newcombs' two house servants were untouched by the malady. Karryl remained in the big house alone, scarcely knowing for long days and nights what course to follow. But the great responsibility that had fallen upon her strengthened her in time, both in demeanor and in thought, fighting as she was against being completely overwhelmed by her sadness.

The servants depended on her, just as they had her mother and father. She now depended on them, and so the seasons ran until the winter of 1864-1865.

Tolbert Newcomb had sold off most of his cotton land before the war got under way, content with maintaining just his food plots and his pastures, and otherwise living off comfortable outside investments. Unfortunately, most of those investments had been converted to Confederate securities after the war began, and now Karryl could scarcely get by, since there was no way left to redeem the securities for Confederate money.

In late fall, 1864, there were stern auguries of what lay ahead. Union soldiers were said to be spreading out from the captured towns along the Mississippi, and stories of their depredations were frightening.

"Got to say, though," one neighbor told Karryl, "it's not the Yankee officers generally that do such things. Leastways, not when they're with the soldiers. It's mostly men in the ranks—riffraff from the big cities. They spread out in little squads and such."

"Doesn't matter if the officers are not with their soldiers," Karryl came back crisply. "They're responsible, because they could stop such doings if they wanted to. Somebody surely ought to put those Yankees in their place." She tossed her mop of red hair and raised her chin defiantly.

December arrived, warmer than usual. Karryl's two old servants, Clay and Phoebe Washington, eventually brought news from Natchez that could not be disregarded.

"You got to get out of this house, and stop staying here by yourself, honey," Phoebe admonished.

"Why?"

"'Cause of them Yankees, that's why, just like everybody's been telling you."

"They haven't bothered us yet, and maybe they won't even come this way."

"They's already coming this way. And when they get here it'll be too late to even hide."

"Fact is, Missy, them Yankees lately been rampaging pretty wild this side of Natchez. Not more than eight, ten miles from here," Clay Washington said.

"What kind of rampaging?"

"Stealing everything they can get their paws on. Burning houses and barns."

"I'm not afraid of them, Clay."

"It ain't just being fearful, Missy. We always knew you ain't that. But, Missy," his words becoming deeply earnest, "they could even burn this house down with you in it. They've burned a lot of others. And done some mighty bad things. They been telling folks they gonna burn down every plantation home a-round Natchez."

"Well, when they come in here trying to burn ours down, they may wish they hadn't. I'm not just going to sit here and take it. Or walk out the front door and leave just like I didn't want to try to do anything about it."

"Missy, you got to think about yourself. Them Yankees'll sure be thinking about you."

"You mean for me to go somewhere and hide? I won't do it."

Clay Washington scratched his head uncertainly. "Ain't you got somebody off somewhere else you could go to?" he queried. "Like a old auntie or somebody, a long ways from here?"

"Yes," Karryl replied thoughtfully. "My Aunt Betsy, at Houston. That's a long way from here, in Texas. She would let me come and live with her. But how in the world would I get to Texas now? Or even out of Mississippi? And across the river! And how could I go away and leave Newcomb Hall and all of you—well—to whatever comes, if things do happen to us here?"

"Missy, ain't nothing gonna happen to us farm hands an' house people. Yankees ain't paying no mind to black folks. The way we hear it, white folks been having homes and farms just took away from them anyway, and given to Yankee folks."

"We'll see about that, if they try it around here, even if I . . ."

"Missy, if you'll make up your mind and go, before something happens to you, I'll get you over that river. With the horse and surrey, too, And I'll go with you."

"You couldn't go away and leave Phoebe, and I wouldn't let you."

"Ain't planning on leaving her for good, Missy. Anyhow, she was the one who first thought about me trying to get you out

[17]

of here. And then coming back for her some day. But right now, Missy, you got to be getting out of that house, in case they come swarming in here."

"I'm not ready to leave home yet, Clay. And just let the Yankees have it. Tell me, if they are really working this way now, how soon do you think we should expect them?"

"Two or three days ago they was at the Hardemans', Missy. I'd say three or four days at the most, but it could be sooner, if they keeps coming down our road."

"Well, there just must be somewhere around this plantation where I would be safe, at least for a little while, if we did know they were near in time. Even an old shanty, or a half-filled corn crib." Suddenly Karryl spoke more excitedly. "There was a little underground room, a rock-walled place sort of like a grotto—father dug it out—down in those woods," she pointed. "He would never let any of us even go around the place. I haven't been there, I don't think, since he was building it. Ages ago. He said he had things there that children simply couldn't play with."

"Yes'm, it's down there. But you still ain't goin' traipsin' around there. The field hands sure don't, and me neither, less'n we're made to. That's where your pappy kept his kegs of powder we blowed up them stumps with."

"Powder?"

"Yes'm. Black powder. Maybe four, five kegs of it still down there. We ain't blowed up nothing in a long time now, so it's there, fo' sure. After the war started, your pappy said he was gonna give any he had left to the soldiers. But he never got around to it. But you sure couldn't run down there to hide out, Missy. Place is likely full of spiders now, and maybe snakes. 'Sides that, it's always had a big lock on it."

"Where is the key?"

"Your pappy kept it in the house, I guess. With his farm books, seems to me now."

"Clay," Karryl said after a long pause, "tell Phoebe to come over here tomorrow afternoon and start putting some things together for me to take along, if I do decide to do like you say and leave this place. Take them to your own quarters, where I might have a chance to get them."

"She done been doing that, Missy," he grinned. "But what you ought to do yourself is get together anythin' that's left that's worth anythin', or you could sell."

She turned away, but as he started to leave she said, "Clay, don't you have some of those dark lanterns, that you can cut off the light from, but still keep the wick burning? That I could use if something happened in the night, and I needed a light nobody could see?"

"Yes'm, they's two, three in the barn."

"Please get them for me and put them there in the kitchen before you go." Then she turned to look somberly towards the woods, and the place that had been forbidden to her.

When Clay and Phoebe came back to the main house the following afternoon, the old woman asked: "You ready to hightail it out of here yet, baby?"

"No, I'm not, Phoebe. I still have some things to do. Tomorrow I'm going back to the Hasslers' to try to help with those sick children. I may even stay there tomorrow night, that is, if I can get through here—." She stopped, but then spoke up again. "Clay, get one of our boys and put him on a horse and send him up the road toward Natchez. As far as he can go without somebody taking the horse away from him. If he sees any Yankees he is to get back here as fast as he can and tell us."

"Yes'm."

"Phoebe, this evening I want you to finish up the supper chores as soon as you can and go back to your own house." She added sadly, "I just want to be alone here tonight."

"Yes'm, honey chil'. I know how you feels. But if you hear anything anywhere, you come a-runnin'."

"I'll do that, of course, Phoebe."

The Hasslers lived about four miles away, and the closest route, as Clay had instructed, was on a dirt road through both the Newcombs' and the Hasslers' back pastures. It was sundown of the second day when one of the Hassler hands brought her surrey up to the door and helped her into it. She touched the mare with the whip, and started toward her own home.

It was dark when she reached the fence line, and she halted to open the gate, but found it already open. Clay Washington came out of the shadows into the middle of the road. "What's the matter, Clay?" Karryl asked swiftly.

"They is here, Missy."

"The Yankees?"

"Yes'm. And they already been pretty awful. Rode them

Yankee horses right up the steps into the front door. Three, four hours ago, now. Hackin' at everything, and tearin' down pictures and them window drapin's. Sure they went all through the house, and they knew who they was huntin'. They was lookin' for you Missy, and said so."

"What did you tell them, Clay?"

"Said you was gone into Natchez. Two, three days now. They wanted to know when you'd be back, and we told 'em maybe tomorrow night or the next day. An' they said they'd just wait. Missy, some things they said was pretty awful. You got to get away from here fast."

"How many were there, Clay? she said at last.

"Counted eight, Missy. But maybe nine, all told. Acted like they had some spirits from somewhere, and they was tearin' up things the last I saw, seein' if they could find some more in your house."

"Let's go, Clay."

"Go where, Missy?"

"Back home."

"You mean you want go back there with all them Yankees around?

"Not to the house itself. We will cut across the lower pasture and come up back there in the trees behind your cabin. I can get my things from there."

"I would do that for you, Missy, and you could go back to the Hasslers."

"No, I intend to see for myself."

It was an hour before midnight when they finally stopped in the trees behind the servants' cabin. "Clay, I don't want to talk with Phoebe yet," she said. "You go on in there and quiet her if she starts worrying."

"What you gonna do, Miss Karryl?"

"I'm going up to that side window where I can see in. I want to see for sure what they're doing to us."

"Let me go with you, Missy."

"No. You get my things. You and Phoebe. And Clay, one of those dark lanterns is under the surrey seat. Get it and go back there in the trees and light it, please."

"What you want that fo', Missy?"

"Just get it and light it. So that I can have a light coming back, if I need it."

[20]

"Miss Karryl, if you open that cover, them Yankees will see you and grab you up before you know it."

"They won't see me."

He did as he was bid, and then Karryl was gone in the shadows around Newcomb Hall. She slipped quickly up to the big side windows, gazing through the dormer panes into the reception room. She was appalled by what she saw. That which had been so beautiful, and which had seen so many gay and happy hours in the plantation home, was now completely wrecked. Violent anger overcame even her despondency.

"Not to me and mine you won't," she vowed savagely.

She went around the corner of the house and past the kitchen steps, hidden by darkness. Then she went on to the little cover at the base of the house where the opening for the cellar potato bins was located. Quietly she lifted the cover and laid it back, then she stepped down into the dark aperture, carrying the lantern with her. She pulled the wooden cover down, then opened the lantern shutter. In the glow from the wick she saw what she wanted—a bundle of heavy fuses of the kind used by farmers to ignite explosives for blasting stumps. Removing the cover from the light, she held it to the fuses, which sputtered violently, but she made sure everyone of them was lighted. Then she snuffed the lantern, pulled herself quickly through the little cellar entrance, and ran as fast as she could for the darker shadows.

Near Clay and Phoebe's cabin she swung about to fix her gaze on the big house as both came to her. "Take a good look, Clay and Phoebe," she said softly. "It was a wonderful home for us in our time."

"What you sayin', Missy?"

A blinding flash, lighting up the entire terrain, stopped the words in Clay's throat. A massive reverberation, then a roar like a thousand claps of deafening thunder, knocked them all from their feet.

Newcomb Hall seemed to explode upward, then buckled and caved in upon itself. An awful silence followed the great roar. Then came the crackle of flames, licking hungrily at the splintered timbers of the manor. Monstrous clouds of black smoke rose into the sky and swept out to the trio standing spellbound on the edge of the compound.

"God almighty!" Clay choked out.

Phoebe alone held on to her wits. She threw her arms about Karryl and held her tight. Then she pushed her away, in the direction of the rig still standing behind the cabin. "You run now, honey, and you run fast. You keep on goin' too, and the Good Lord and Clay Washington'll see you get a runnin' start on the way to your auntie's place. But don't you never try to come home again here to Mississippi!"

A tawny hulk of a man, well-dressed, but apparently uncomfortable in such attire, stood at the end of the hotel desk in the little port on the Atchafalaya, eyeing the scared people as they fought to gain the attention of the harried hotel clerk. They were frantic, trying to flee Louisiana ahead of the columns of Union troops advancing over the southern part of the state. He saw the red-haired girl as soon as she appeared in the swarm of panicky men and women. Unlike the others, she didn't look frightened. In fact, if she showed anything, it looked to him like just plain anger.

She was gorgeous, like the high-bred women he'd always admired from a distance—slender but fully formed, aloof—quite different from the kind of women that he had known in the saloons of brawling western towns. Her breeding was evident, but there was something else, too, that held his interest. Her expression bespoke more than just anxiety at fleeing the advancing Federals.

"I'm Miss Newcomb," she appealed to the hotel clerk. "Karryl Newcomb, from Newcomb Hall, Natchez. Stop that jumping around and listen to me."

In the instant, the watcher's mouth flew open, and he struck one fist into the palm of the other. Here was the very woman people back in New Orleans had been talking about. Right in front of him. Newcomb Hall. He knew the name well enough, even if the rest of the people around here didn't. As a matter of fact, when the Federal administrators had slipped him out of New Orleans it was about the only name on any of their lips. A whole squad of Union soldiers had been killed at a place called Newcomb Hall. They had ridden their horses right into the reception hall, hacking at the rosewood and mahogany and tearing up the rich tapestries, and somebody had blown them to bits, along with the rest of the house. The fact was that the Federals knew just who had done it, too, or they thought they did. Telegraph lines all over the Mississippi River country were alive with messages about that fugitive. And the quarry was a red-headed woman named Karryl Newcomb. If she was not as famous—or infamous—here as elsewhere, it was because Union troops still hadn't moved in on this town. But the patrols were pushing out everywhere now. There would surely be a squad or two, if not a whole outfit, showing up soon, and maybe just on this red-haired woman's account. This was one fugitive they wanted, and wanted quick.

"Can't you really help me?" she demanded of the man behind the desk. "You said there would be a ship leaving today."

"The packet's sailing, for a fact, later on," the harried clerk answered. "It'll be on down the river after it picks up some cargo upstream a ways. Reckon by noon. But it's jammed already to the rails, miss. Like I told you before, I wish I could do something, but I don't know what it would be. Why don't you go on into the dining room and wait? Maybe something will turn up sooner or later; right now I don't think they're even talkin' to any more passengers."

The girl was elbowed back by others trying to reach the desk. The dark man saw her stare go from person to person, but obviously she knew no one. Men and women were scurrying about, children wailing, frenzied country folk wrangling over baggage. She was confused, maybe even dubious, but she wasn't daunted. At least not yet. And she did as the clerk had urged—she forced her way into the dining room, finding a vacant place finally in which to sit down. Casually the dark man followed, making his way across the dining room also, and ultimately halting in front of her.

"Mind if I join you, miss?"

"Mind if—what—who are you, anyway?"

"Name's Devers."

"What do you want?"

"I understand you're trying to get to Texas."

"Well—"

"I heard about your little sociable up at Natchez, Miss Newcomb, the explosion and all that."

"You heard about what?"

"That blow-up at Newcomb Hall. Everybody along the river knows about it, in fact, by now, and maybe around here too. At least they will before long."

[23]

"Why are you talking to me?"

"I thought maybe I could help." He grinned. He did sit down. "Are you hungry?"

"I guess I am."

"Then you'd better eat."

She stiffened, but Devers quickly added, "I'll pay."

"I've got money."

"I doubt if you've got very much, at least if you're like the others." He touched a passing waiter's arm. "Bring the young lady some breakfast," he said. "And bring me some coffee." Then he pulled a cigar from his pocket. "I've been watching you. I heard you talking to the clerk." He lit the cigar.

"Why do you . . . ?"

"I said my name is Devers."

"Well, Mr. Devers, just how would you propose to help?"

"Wait a minute." He struck another match. "You must take things as they come."

"What do you think I've been doing? Look at my face, my clothing!"

"Never said you'd maybe not been havin' a time of it. But so has everyone else. Settle down now and wait for the food." She simply stared at him. "Guess what's making you so panicky this morning is that you've heard about the soldiers they're sendin' out everywhere to try to run you down. Or if you haven't heard it before, then you know it now. Truth is that when I left New Orleans I thought there was a patrol already on its way right to this place. And likely there was. If anything, they're stopped up somewhere, making side trips into the towns along the way."

"Then why are you still here?"

"Me?" He grinned again at her. "Oh, they're not interested in me. 'Specially since I've got friends among them in New Orleans."

"And you're going to sit around here and just wait until they do get here?"

"No, not that either. I try to keep out of their way as much as I can. But that's why I'm talking to you. As I said, I thought I might help."

"You mean you'd really help me get away—from here—before some Yankee soldiers do show up?"

"Yes."

[24]

"Just how could you do that, Mr. Devers?"

He glanced toward the throng in the lobby, then back to her. "You can go with me if you want to," he suggested brazenly. "There's no other way to leave the Atchafalaya now except by boat. And after this one goes today, there won't be another one. It's full up, just like the clerk told you. But I could take you aboard with me, if you really want to get away from here as bad as you make out that you do."

"You mean—*travel with you?*"

"Yes, that's what I mean. Maybe the idea upsets you. But these are strange times, and right now you haven't got anywhere to light. Besides—and maybe this will make you feel more comfortable—people look on things differently these days, or maybe more honestly."

She dropped her stare to the tablecloth, closing her eyes tightly, and twisting her handkerchief in her hands.

"That packet will be down at the dock by noon, and it'll leave just about as fast as it can after that. You'd better make up your mind if you want to go, because time is running out. I've got a couple of things to do at the stores, then I'm pickin' up my baggage and getting down there. And you'd better be there before that, if you're smart, because these people who ain't got passage are going to have to be fought off, before that packet pulls out from the dock."

He rose, put on his hat and started to leave. Then he looked back at the girl. "Just one other thing, Miss Newcomb," he said in a hard voice. "The party who fills those Union people in on who you are and where you are now will be set up in high cotton for the rest of his life with the Federals all over this swamp country. I'll have a letter in my pocket, Miss Newcomb, when I get on that packet; if you're not there waiting for me, I'll just hand it to one of my people here who'll see that it gets to the right parties when they ride in."

In later years Karryl would remember every detail of that first interview with Devers, how he had come into the dining room and sat down beside her, how startled she had been in the instant, and then a moment later how hopeful. But how insulting, even appalling, his real proposal had been. Her angry, horrified stare had followed him as he went out. The vulgar, depraved fool! Everything that was good welled up inside her— the training of her childhood, her whole way of life. She forced back the tears that tried to jump into her eyes.

The waiter brought food to her table. When she tried to pay him he shook his head. "The gentleman took care of it," he said. For a second she could scarcely restrain herself. But God, how hungry she was! That was the way it had been ever since she and Clay Washington had galloped down the road from Newcomb Hall, how it had been while he worked along the river bank until at last he had located an old flatboat, long tied up but still solid, that once had been used to haul lumber down the river. Across in Louisiana, it had been just as bad as in other places. People were afraid even to talk with travelers.

In a few places they had been able to buy a bit of food. And sometimes a frightened family would give a place to sleep for the night. But her little store of money had about run out now, and she was determined to see that Clay Washington got what she did have left, to help him along on his own way back home. She took a small wad of bills from the little bag on her wrist and spread them out in her lap. The bills were mostly of small denomination, with the image of the Confederate, Miminger, staring upward from the engraving. "Blue Williamses," the tradesmen called them. There were a few $10 notes, pitiably few, displaying the likeness of the South's vice president, Stephens. But Karryl had discovered even before crossing the Mississippi that this money was not worth even twenty to one now, in Louisiana or anywhere.

What would happen when the Yankees did come? Would they drag her out into the streets and hang her from a tree, as she had heard they had done Confederates in other places? Or shove her before some Yankee judge to cart her off to one of those sordid prisons somewhere?

Maybe not even any of those things, she thought, her blood chilling. She remembered the whispered stories of what had befallen other young women who had run afoul of the soldiers.

A sudden impulse swept through her. Who was this man who had so shamelessly approached her, threatening exposure to the Union soldiers if she did not accede to his haughty overtures? He was no better than those others back there who had ravaged Newcomb Hall—maybe even worse. Her brow meshed in thought as she dug into the repast. "I'll eat his food, too," she lamented angrily.

Outside, she looked at the throngs milling up and down

before the hotel, eventually picking out Clay crouched on the low roof of an abandoned building. His eyes were watching her, and she motioned him to join her behind the hotel.

When they were together she said, "Clay, on this piece of paper I have given you the right to sell what's left of the surrey. Maybe you can swap it for a saddle, at least an old one. Then you get on the mare and get back to Phoebe."

"What you gonna do, Missy?"

"I'm going to be on that packet when it leaves here," she vowed.

"But Missy, that boat done been sold out two times over."

"Nevertheless, I'll be on it, that is if I can count on you one more time."

"Sure you know you can do that, Missy."

She touched his elbow and led him farther away from the hotel. In a low voice she began to tell Clay what had been said to her, revealing her plan.

"I'll kill him!" he blurted out.

"No, that wouldn't help any. But what I want you to do is see that he is the one person who does not get on that boat. Clay, this money is for you. I was going to give it to you anyway, but maybe you can get a little more for the rig and buy some food or whatever you need that way. And with at least some of this money maybe you can get one of those boys down on the dock to help you and, between the two of you, overpower that man when he comes back to the hotel and hide him away somewhere or somehow until the boat is gone. If anything worse happened to him, and he was found before we could get away, they might not let the boat go. Do you think you could do that?"

Clay Washington took the small packet of bills in his hand and ran through them. "Powerful few," he said thoughtfully, "and they ain't worth much now, anyway."

Just then a ship's bell sounded. The packet was warping in to the shore toward the dock.

"I'll find somebody," the Negro vowed earnestly.

"Then you must hurry. I'll get my things from the surrey, and I'll be waiting for you here at the side of the building, so I can point him out to you when he comes back. You can tell anyone who asks that you are there to pick up his valises to carry to the packet."

[27]

"Miss Karryl," Clay said as he started to turn away. "Don't come close to me no more now. You just be where I can see you when that man comes back, and you point him out. Then you go away, so's nobody would know we was together, if things didn't go right."

Karryl's eyes filled with tears. She threw her arms around the old retainer and sobbed brokenly. "Clay Washington," she whispered finally, "you go home just as soon as you can and take care of Phoebe."

"I do that, Missy. But Phoebe and me, we gonna follow you."

"No, you must never leave Mississippi. It's your home, and you love it. And you would never be happy far off across the country from there." She dabbed at her eyes, then ran toward the distant grove where the mare and the surrey had been left.

The packet's mate stood athwart the vessel's gangway, barring the unauthorized. "You got passage, miss?" he asked as Karryl stopped before him, a valise in each hand and bundles under her arms. "Yes. But I don't have the ticket with me. I will have though. Someone is bringing it."

"What do you mean by that?"

"Someone I'm traveling with is bringing it."

"Who, miss?"

"Mr. Devers."

The man was abruptly silent. He looked her over from head to foot, whistling a little through his teeth as he did so. Then he called a deck hand. "Block 'em off till I get back," he said. He turned to Karryl. "You come with me, miss." He led her up the deck to a doorway forward, rapping on that portal when he reached it.

A large man, beginning to gray at the temples, opened the door and stepped out, pulling his jacket together and a button or two as he did so.

"Says she's supposed to be travelin' with that fellow Devers," the mate informed the other in a low voice.

"Is he aboard?"

"No, sir. He still ain't showed up."

The captain turned now to stare at Karryl, too. "Well, it ain't the first time. But he's shore travelin' in better circles now." To Karryl he said, "You'd better wait in my quarters here till he shows up, miss."

Karryl stepped inside. The captain looked at the big watch he carried in his upper shirt pocket. "Gettin' to be time," he said to the mate. "Tide'll be runnin' now before we clear the mouth."

"Yessir."

"Let me know when Devers shows up."

The mate went back to the gangway, and the captain stepped off down the deck checking the masts above, the cargo, and the location even of the deck passengers where they had found places for themselves. When he had satisfied himself he returned to his cabin. "You been down the coast before, miss?" he asked Karryl, seated near the door in the cabin's only casual chair.

"No, I haven't, Captain. This is the first time I have ever been on a boat this big."

"It's a ship, miss," he smiled. "We call it a packet. Where're you from?"

"Natchez."

"Natchez, huh? Well, I guess your friend Devers has been spreadin' out some. He's usually just for New Orleans and back, if he don't have to get back out by way of the delta. No packets workin' that way now since the Yankees moved in."

She did not answer, and he busied himself at his desk with the last-minute chores and the waybills. Eventually he took out the watch again and looked at it, and almost as he did so the mate knocked at the door again.

"Time to weigh," the mate said, "and Devers still ain't showed up. You want me to send somebody to look for him, bein' as he's a reg'lar passenger?"

"No. That don't make no difference now. Give him ten more minutes, then slip the lines."

The captain finished with his papers and put them away, then he turned slowly back toward the girl. "You'll have to go back too, miss, if he don't show up," the captain said gently.

"Captain," she spoke up, "couldn't I—that is—Captain, I can't get off and go back up there into the town. The Yankees—well, they have been doing some bad things to us at Natchez, and now they're trying to arrest me and take me back there. They will, too, unless I can get away from here this very day."

"Is that—would that be why a girl like you would be travelin' with a man like Devers?" the captain asked curiously.

[29]

Her eyes fell as she silently nodded her head. But then she started up again. "I—I haven't been traveling with him," she said slowly. "I just met him this morning, and he offered to take me to Texas if I would go this way with him."

"If he don't get aboard, have you got money for passage, miss? There're whole families out there beggin' even to be allowed to pay just to sit on the deck till we make Galveston."

She shook her head sadly. "It took every dollar I could scrape up just to get this far," she said. But then her chin went out stubbornly. "I've got something else though."

She opened the little bag on her wrist and took out a folded paper. Unwrapping it, she extracted a beautiful gold ring and handed it to the captain. "That's all I have left," she said.

He took the ring, and turned it in his hand. There was no question of its value. It was mounted with a large diamond surrounded by emeralds, but he laid it back on the table at Karryl's side, then stepped through the cabin door and to the rail. "Have you seen Devers yet?" Karryl heard him ask.

"Nope, he ain't showed, Cap'n."

"All right, forget about him. Have you got a single down there on the dock tryin' to ship with us? A woman, maybe?"

"Plenty of 'em, Cap'n," the mate answered. "Woman with a kid over there, beggin' to git back to Galveston. Kid's about four or five. An' she was the earliest."

"Let them aboard. And cast off."

Karryl sat stiffly in her place. "Thank you, Clay Washington," she sighed to herself. She heard the captain's directions as they warped the vessel out into the channel, then the orders that got the vessel under way down the river. Eventually the captain returned to the cabin. He walked to the table and picked up the ring again, shaking his head as he did so.

"Miss," he said in a kindlier voice, "you know it's worth a lot more'n passage to Texas?"

"Yes. But I thought that if you did let me stay aboard maybe you'd speak to someone down there at one of those Texas towns where you dock about my getting to Houston."

"Why are you going there, miss?"

"I have an aunt in Houston. She's the only living relative I have left in the world."

He smiled. "I'll see to it. The best way to get to Houston is by Anahuac. All overland from there to Houston, maybe forty miles. It's the last port we dock at before tyin' up at Galveston."

"Captain, I'm so grateful. I'd just about reached the end of my endurance."

Now he laughed. "A woman with hair the color o' yours?"

3

A nightmare disturbed Levit MacAshen's sleep. There was his mother's face agonized in death. His father had pulled a lance from her body—a lance of the Quohada Comanche, stained vermillion-red. He tossed restlessly as the dream coiled through his sleep.

It was long ago, and he was on the northward trail that ran from the Pedernales to Red River, a child futilely pursuing the Indians who had slain his mother. In his sleep his muscles racked to the movement of his steed.

Now they had reached the Magill Mountains, and his father called a halt. They climbed to the shelves above, searching the trail northward toward Cherokee Spring and the San Saba River for a sign of the fugitives.

"We've lost them," his father was muttering. "But they'll come back. They always come back. And this is the way they will come." He pointed up the depression toward Wolf Mountain. Behind them, to the south, lay the country of the Enchanted Rock. "When they come back they will come right down this valley," his father said. "White men must stop them here if they are ever stopped, for this is the Comanche war trail. It points straight as an arrow toward the Pedernales. They call this valley their 'Lost River.' If I am not here, Levit, make sure

[32]

the Comanches never get through this pass again. Or the rest of the women and children will die—as your mother died."

MacAshen opened his eyes to a realization of the white and flowered wallpaper above him, feeling at the same time the cold perspiration on his cheeks. His head hurt; the horror of the nightmare left him jaded and drawn. He turned his head and saw an old lady of strictly homespun stock staring soberly at him. Her thin locks were bound into a neat white ball on the back of her head. She was plump, and her dress was of a faded calico.

Suddenly it all came back to him: the encounter in the street, the scene at the tavern, the relief at having a place to rest again. But what was going on here? He tried to raise himself on an elbow, only to discover he lacked the strength.

He said, "You must have got me down as an invalid, Ma'am, and I've no call to impose myself on you like that. I thank you for letting me come here, but if you'll just step out of the room, I'll get dressed now and be on my way."

Her hands flew up. "On your way? Boy, you talk wilder now than you did when you were out of your head."

"Out of my head?"

"That's what I said. Why, the very idea of you traveling down that long road when you were fit to be in a hospital!"

Again MacAshen tried to lift himself, and again he failed. His consternation knifed as deeply as the pain. "How long have I been here, Ma'am?" he asked, glancing toward the sunlit window. "It was almost dark when we came."

"Ah," she murmured, "that was nights ago. You've been out for a spell, but, Lord, you must have marrow in your bones. At first we thought you were gone. You're much better now. Fall said he never figured you were so done in, and surely the rest of us didn't." Her eyes sparkled. "I've got a mighty fine kettle of chicken broth cooking on the hearth in there." She nodded toward the door. "Just waiting for you to come to. I'll get you some."

"Ma'am, I couldn't expect you to—"

"You aren't beholden to me, boy." She scurried through the door, to return in a moment with a steaming bowl. She held a ladle to his lips. "Now you try to swallow, son."

When MacAshen could get his breath again, he said, "I

[33]

was—I am—a soldier, Ma'am, and the Federals could come any time now. If you'll just give me my clothes—"

"I lost two sons at Pea Ridge, myself, boy." Then, belligerently, "And I'm not afraid of anybody, Yankees or otherwise. You just lie still and don't try to think. And don't be taxing yourself—or any of the rest of us, for that matter—with silly talk." Again she clucked at him, almost reprovingly.

The sun was slanting low through the tall pines by the window when MacAshen heard his next visitor approaching. A hearty laugh accompanied the entrance of the tavern keeper, Fall. "It's good to see you perking up, Colonel," the old man boomed.

"I've made a hell of a mess for everybody, Fall."

"Oh, you don't need to spell it out that bad. Beats living on parched corn and meat skins and raw turnips, don't it? An' that's what you was headed for, most likely."

"Maybe it was. But that doesn't mean these people should be bothered with a shot-up soldier. They must have their own troubles."

The old man grinned. "Nobody ever gits so many troubles he can't take on part of somebody else's. Leastways, that's how Mrs. Newcomb figures it."

Another step sounded on the threshold, and he turned his head to see Karryl Newcomb standing in the doorway.

"You look alive, Colonel," she said, halting beside his bed smiling. "I'm glad to see you're better today."

"I've made a nuisance of myself, Miss."

"Not at all. You're welcome here. As a matter of fact, my aunt likes having you. You give her something to stew about. My name is Karryl Newcomb, in case you've forgotten."

"I haven't forgotten." MacAshen saw that her face was delicately shaped, with curving lips and eyes you couldn't read too quickly. "I told your aunt she should send me on," he apologized halfheartedly.

"Why, how on earth could she? You're not even able to get out of bed. You're a very sick man, Colonel MacAshen."

"Maybe I am. But I've been sicker, and I still got along."

"Fiddlesticks, Colonel! Men like you always prattle that way, even when they can't raise a finger. You're about as flat on your back as anyone I ever saw."

Fall chuckled and MacAshen glared across the room at him.

[34]

The girl straightened the cover on the bed, then went about tidying the rest of the room. "There now," she smiled. "This room looks better. And you look a great deal better, too, Colonel, in spite of your temper."

Fall got up from his chair. "I'll be mosey'n on," he said. "But I'll be around, Colonel, if you need any errands run."

MacAshen recovered rapidly. Joshua, Mrs. Newcomb's old servant, dressed his wound every day, and Mrs. Newcomb herself generally came along to see that the job was done properly. Karryl visited him regularly too, teasing him even as she comforted him.

On one such of her visits—his fast progress by that time having made him restive—he flipped around too quickly as she entered the room. There was a momentary pinching in his face. "Is it still that bad?" she asked.

"Well—" He forced a grin. "I get a kink now and then, but it never amounts to much."

She came close and placed a hand on his forehead. "You'll feel better soon. And don't jump so when someone comes to see you."

"Thanks, young lady. You make invaliding a lot more attractive than it would be otherwise." Her cheek dimpled, and MacAshen added, "I'd like to stay on the sick roll permanently, with treatment like this." She smoothed the sheets on his bed, reaching down once to brush a lock of hair from his eyes.

"Your hands are gentle," MacAshen said.

"I helped in the hospital for a while."

"They're naturally gentle."

She smiled. For just an instant she was coy. "You have talents, Colonel MacAshen, besides soldiering."

"If I have, I've never had much chance to develop them."

"Well, you'll be going home soon and you can begin to try again. Your home is a ranch, Mr. Fall told us."

"It was once."

"Haven't you kept in touch?"

"Not very well. My father died just after the war started, and the hands drifted on, I guess. Nobody around to run things."

"And you've heard nothing since then?"

"I had a letter from an old neighbor down the river, a man named Elledge, about a year ago. Things were pretty bad then.

[35]

Indians and renegades. Where was the hospital you served in, Miss Newcomb?"

"Natchez. In the very first months of the war."

"Couldn't you find a place closer to home?"

"Natchez was my home. I'm from Mississippi, Colonel." A sober note touched her voice as she added, "I've not been here in Houston very long." She turned away, picking up a bunch of early-blooming flowers she had brought to arrange them in a small bowl. She handled the delicate plants tenderly.

"I've been to Natchez," he said. "It was early in the war, and that was some time back, but I'd mark you as being from there."

"How, Colonel?"

"The way you talk. You don't—well, you don't sound quite 'Texas.' "

"What's different about me?"

"Oh, I don't know. Lots of things, maybe." He mused for a moment. "Natchez—yes, I remember Natchez. It was a lively place. Parties, and that sort of thing, though I didn't get to join in them."

She was silent a moment. "Parties? Yes, there were parties in Natchez—music and flowers, and all the folks happy and laughing. But I don't really remember much about such things now. So much has happened."

"Why did you come to Texas?"

"To stay with my Aunt Betsy. She's the only relative I have left in the world."

"I don't mean to pry, Miss Newcomb." He was silent a moment himself, then he said, "That's a long road from Mississippi. I just came over it myself."

"I came by packet boat." An odd resentment seemed to enter her voice for an instant. She turned and walked to the window.

She's no doubt had her troubles, MacAshen thought, like lots of other folks. But somehow she was different. For one thing, she was mighty attractive. And her skin was soft. Again, he just wanted to touch her.

Suddenly she turned around. The way he was looking at her must have been bolder than he'd realized, for instantly she was back at the bedside, an even stranger expression in her face. "Something bothering you, Colonel?" she inquired.

"Why—no," he answered.

"Then don't gawk at me. Just lie there and concentrate on getting well."

"I'm sorry . . . I didn't mean—."

"We're trying to help you here and I'll expect you to keep that in mind, that is, if you really do want to get your strength back and be on your way."

"I'll remember, miss," he responded quickly. "And, believe me, I'm sorry if I've done something to offend you."

She went toward the door, and MacAshen gazed after her in wonderment.

At the threshold she halted momentarily, and he thought she was about to say something more. But if she intended to, she changed her mind. To his surprise, almost a spark of coquetry suddenly colored the smile she cast back over her shoulder as she went through the door.

Toward the end of the month MacAshen was entirely fit. Mrs. Newcomb said, "A big, husky fellow like you just can't be killed off by one bullet. What's more, you can see to it when you get out again that you don't get in the way of another."

"I'll certainly try, Ma'am."

Fall inquired, "Have you ever thought about sinking your roots down this way, Colonel?"

"No, I haven't. And even if I had, I couldn't. I've got to get to Austin. I figure I'm still under orders, Fall. General Forrest told me to report to Governor Murrah—when I was able to, and to stay with him as long as he wanted me."

"If you're just thinking about tryin' to stay busy, Houston's likely to have a full shake out of things. The soldiers here ain't been paid for months, and you can't expect 'em just to sit and twiddle their thumbs. But worse, the town's fillin' up with strangers now—bad-looking hombres, and sure they'll stir up trouble sooner or later."

"Oh, I guess things are about as bad in one place as another."

Fall did not argue. He himself had brought MacAshen word of what was going on in other areas as well as Houston—when he heard. But the old man did persist in one regard. "Houston's still not a bad town, MacAshen, any way you look at it," he said. "Near eight thousand people living here now."

MacAshen glanced out the window. The city was a sprawling, muddy place, almost without a beginning or an end. Its homes seemed to surge away into the forests. But he answered, "The bayous are not for me, Fall."

"The Confederates—even in Texas—ain't apt to hold out much longer, anywhere you are."

"Maybe not. But bringing the scrape to an end won't mean the world is all pretty and quiet again. The facts are, Fall, that it's really after the white man's war is over that the real trouble will start down here. I figure I'd better get close to my own stoop while I can."

"Well, I'll hate to see you go. I've come to feel right attached to you, son."

On MacAshen's final morning in the Newcomb house, breakfast was announced early. Both Karryl and her Aunt Betsy were already seated when he entered the room.

"I'm sorry I'm late," he apologized, "but I didn't realize you'd turn out so early. I'm a little slow, anyway, from lying up in bed most of the past month, I guess."

Mrs. Newcomb's cheek dimpled as she said, "Fiddlesticks, Colonel. You weren't really too bad off when we brought you here. And you haven't been at any time since."

"I knew that better than you did," MacAshen grinned, "but I kept trying to make things look their worst."

"Before you came, it had been a long time since the Newcomb house boasted a man," Karryl interjected. "We won't have anyone again now but ourselves to look after—ourselves and old Josh." Then, to MacAshen's surprise she added, "We'll be sorry not having you around."

"I'm glad you said that," MacAshen responded, "for I've come to feel pretty much at home with you here."

"Do you think you'll ever come back?"

"I don't know. But I'll try. Then, almost impulsively, "Of course, I'll come back."

When the meal was over, Karryl said, "Josh is bringing your horse to the gate. You can leave this way when you have your things." MacAshen nodded. He rose to follow Mrs. Newcomb. The old lady pulled him down and kissed him on the cheek as he reached the door, then scurried off into another part of the house.

Karryl waited in the parlor, and when MacAshen returned with his gear, she said to him, "Goodbye, Colonel, and I hope things go well for you."

"Thank you, Miss Newcomb. I would say the same to you. I'm grateful—more grateful than I know how to say—for what you folks have done for me here. You've been mighty good to a shot-up maverick."

"We've tried to be, and I'm sorry if I seemed testy the other day. Sometimes things upset me. Tell me, Colonel, do you think the end of the road is close? For the South, I mean?"

"I don't know, Miss Newcomb." The fire in the grate crackled up, then died to a glow. "Will you stay in Houston with your aunt?" he asked.

"I suppose so." She spoke the words uncertainly. In spite of the red hair and stubborn chin, she seemed for a moment almost like a lost and lonely little girl. He felt the urge to take her in his arms and give her comfort and assurance, but that would have been risking impropriety, as well as her wrath. He said, "I'll not forget you here."

"We won't forget you either, Colonel." She took a tiny step toward him. "And I hope you will come back some day."

Then she turned quickly and went out of the room, leaving him standing there alone.

The fact that he had been shanghaied even before he could leave the hotel for the packet boat had dug at Devers ever since. He couldn't be absolutely certain, but at least he was pretty sure.

When he finally had worked his way free in the closet of the hotel room on the Atchafalaya, he hurried down to the lobby only to find that the packet already was at sea. "Just what in the hell has happened?" he stormed. But he had no answer, nor did anybody else. He had not been robbed, or hurt—except for a light blow on the head—but missing the ship had cost him three weeks' time. He stayed on at the hotel because he had no choice, there being no such thing as a saddle horse for hire or sale now.

When he looked for Karryl Newcomb and failed to find her, he was even more put out. The very thought of this beautiful, cultured, plantation girl—a kind he had seen only at a distance, surrounded by escorts—stirred a hunger inside of him. More, she was the most vulnerable woman he had ever encountered, with the threat of apprehension by the Federals hanging over her; he had anticipated something better than he was getting. How did it happen that she, too, had disappeared in the same hour that the packet boat had left? That ship had been booked solid for days. He kept his suspicions to himself, however; the Union soldiers that had showed up since she left would have laughed him out of town, even if it was a girl they were searching for.

The situation continued to gnaw at Devers until he learned of a Mexican bark, working its way along the coast trading for muskrat skins. For a day or so it stood near the mouth of the Atchafalaya. He hired a boatman to take him to it and bought passage to Texas. By the time the trader put him ashore on Galveston Island, more than a week later, he had decided to make his own investigation of the whereabouts of the wily Miss Newcomb.

At Galveston he found the packet, as he had expected, tied up for the war's duration. But the crew had scattered, and Devers could not even locate the captain. He did eventually find the mate and bought some answers from him. Yes, the red-haired woman had sailed with them. Yes, she had disembarked either here or at Anahuac. Sure, she had said she was traveling with Devers, but she hadn't been put ashore when he failed to show up. And that was that, as far as Devers could add it up.

If Karryl Newcomb had engineered a deal, she had done it well, and quickly, though there wasn't much chance he would ever be able to prove any of his suppositions. But the sprightly lass was still in the same hot water she had been in back in Mississippi, and she'd better remember it if he should find her again.

Eventually, the sight of his quarry, when Storm accosted her on the walk in front of Fall's grogshop, had sent a new surge of anger and desire through him. The Union soldiers weren't here yet, and until they were—well, he would have to handle matters carefully, and perhaps privately.

After the incident at the tavern, Devers had hurried back to his lodgings over the stable at the lower end of Preston Street. His quarters were rough but they were clean enough, and they suited his purpose. The sight of the Newcomb girl had changed his plans a bit, and he stayed off the street for a time. She evidently did not know of his arrival in Houston, and he didn't want her to find out until a few matters had been taken care of.

Three weeks later, that time had almost arrived.

Vanner Storm, seated behind the only table in the room, his chair tilted against the wall, was sullen today, as he had been since the episode with MacAshen, Fall, and the girl.

"You've had plenty of time to salve your feelings, Storm," Devers told him. "Why don't you shut up about it and put your mind to more important matters? This run on the border will put more money in your pocket than you've ever seen."

"I've already got money in my pocket, Devers. Pushing longhorns through to those Union buyers in New Orleans and hauling cotton back to the Yankees across the Rio Grande has paid well enough both ways."

"But all that will be done with after this trip, Storm, and money won't come easy after that. Just stay with what I'm saying to you, and don't let an old man like that innkeeper get your goat."

Storm lit a cigarette. "All right, Devers, I'll forget it for the time being, anyway."

Devers smoothed the map spread out on the table. "You want to stay high on the coastal plain here above Victoria, Storm. Too many troops around to take chances."

"Where'd you say the stuff is now?"

"Half the shipment, with wagons and teamsters, is waiting on the far side of the San Bernard. You take on the rest at a ford five miles above Wharton. The route's laid out to throw you into the back trails. Maybe there'll be some Lipans, but you'll be traveling the worst stretch during the dark of the moon. Cross the San Antonio thirty miles above Goliad and hightail it south. It'll take you two weeks to get to the river from the Goliad crossing and, chances are, when you get back the war will be over. I've got my mind on something else after that, but you can decide then if you want in."

Storm looked at his lean, muscular hands, turning them from side to side. "You think you'll still be around here if I do come back, Devers?" he asked.

"Of course I'll be here. What made you ask that?"

"You've been dealing under the table a long time, tied in like you've been with the Yankees. Bein' a Texan yourself, I know these people around here won't take kindly to you, once they find out where you've stood."

"Does that mean you're afraid to come back, Storm?"

"I can look out for myself. But no sense in ridin' in here just to stick my neck in a noose. I'd rather tangle with a Kiowa war party than a mob of these south Texans with their dander up."

"I don't think it'll be too bad, once the Yankees have taken over."

"Usual like, maybe not. But in your case, maybe yes, Being a Yankee agent is one thing, hard as they'll take to that when they find out. But being a Yankee agent with blood in him, like you, is something else."

"You're really wild, Storm."

"No, I'm not. I know too well what's eating you. You're part Cherokee, or is it Comanche? And you're afraid for people to know."

Devers flushed, but Storm went on. "You don't look too much like a Redskin, but you let it drag on you like poison."

Devers had risen to his feet. Deep anger was in his eyes, but he held it back. "Stick to your end of the business, Storm," he ground out.

Storm threw up his hands in mock resignation, then bent over the map. "Go on with what you were saying."

"Cross that last stretch right here between Roma and Rio Grande village, but at night—and put the stuff down at Camargo. Now, anything else you want to know about it?"

"The teamsters. They can talk."

"You know what to do about them. But be sure it's on the other side of the river."

A cold smile touched Storm's lips now. He glanced at Devers, then looked at his hands.

Colonel MacAshen, after his departure from the Newcomb house, rode west from the bayous, camping the first night in a small grove of pines. Later he crossed the Brazos, then the San Bernard, following the insweep of the coastal plain almost to Alleytown, where he forded the Colorado to the west bank.

He put the river between him and the village of LaGrange and held to the western bottoms until they slid away into a long ridge of red cliffs. In the river here the water was low, almost green in color. The setting reminded him of the Sakatonchee, back off across the Mississippi. But there was no thunder of guns here, no brigades of wan horsemen in gray. Only the low, sad note of the southwest winds, bending grasses and caressing the leaves.

Above and across the river he entered the Lost Pines, tuning his ear to the far-away melody of the breath upon the slopes. He spread his tarp near a stock farm, on the road from Bastrop to Austin. A small black boy came to lead his horse to a watering trough that stood in the great shady backyard. "Can you tell me, sir, how long 'til Christmas?" he asked.

"Christmas!" MacAshen repeated in surprise. "This is only March. Why do you want to know?"

"'Cuz I'm goin' home at Christmas," the boy sighed. Then almost belligerently: "I ain't belong to these people. I is only hired to them."

"Don't you like it here?"

"I wants to see Mammy, and Missis Opal and all the folks, and I'm goin' back home Christmas."

MacAshen watched the boy lead his horse away, then built a fire between two stones and unwrapped his food. When he had eaten, he spread his blanket on a sandy spot and stretched out. The halting query of the young boy stayed with him. A little boy whose only dream was a distant Christmas when he could go back to his mother again—a child torn from home and family. These were signposts of a ruthless world, but one, too, that fast was changing.

In the cloudless morning the great red stallion, Old Warrior, moved at an easy walk, carrying Levit MacAshen toward Austin. It had been an almost impossible feat, Warrior's survival through all that long journey eastward and back, and through the carnage of battle.

The day turned hot. Although it was not far into spring, summer seemed to have descended with all of its sultriness. The dull hum of the bees and the occasional call of a field lark lulled the senses. Here in the narrow lane, dry spirals of dust touched MacAshen's face, like the white and powdery clouds that had hung above Chicamauga on that grim and terrible Saturday, the 19th of September, 1863. He had been little more than a youngster then; today, not two years later, he was a wiry, mature-looking man, his thick black hair tinged with gray at the temples.

At midmorning he sat for an hour watching Warrior feed upon the green carpet beside a bursting spring. There was winecup in the eroded flecks of the draws, and frescoes of Indian paintbrush upon the hillsides. Strangly, the paintbrush brought to mind a young man he had left behind him in Forrest's army in Mississippi. This man, named Ord, had ridden stirrup with him. The youth had sometimes seemed part Indian, and MacAshen supposed now that just the name of the flower, Indian paintbrush, stirred his recollection. Ord had a matchless skill with a pistol, and suddenly—in contrast to the mood stimulated by something as delicate as a wildflower—the recollection of Ord's talents also brought back to MacAshen the sinister individual he had confronted at Houston. A kind of lethal quality seemed characteristic of both Ord and Storm.

Ord had carried a heavy dragoon Dance gun low on his thigh, just above his hand. He never wore a glove on his right hand. It was powerful and brown, but delicate as a woman's; and so was Storm's.

Ord and MacAshen had grown close to each other as men do when they are far from home. But all of that was long ago, on the eastern battlefields. And the Houston incident with Storm was a month behind him.

Austin, which MacAshen reached without incident, was a rugged frontier capital town. He noted few changes as he crossed the river. The buildings and the homes were of stone, for the city was, in fact, a place of homes and fortresses at once. The courthouse and jail were near the river, and the capitol stood at a far distance up the avenue. There was a hospital upon the northeastern corner of the city, and the armory—probably now Austin's most important meeting place—lay on the eastern edge. Off near the western outskirts was a private academy for the sons of the more affluent residents of the community. MacAshen recalled his own schooling there.

At the Mansion House, he found accomodations still available, and he slept soundly in an old four-poster bed, opening his eyes for the first time only when the sun came through his window on the east. His room was directly above the hotel entrance—a big room that was clean and airy, furnished with chairs of scrubbed, unpainted wood. The seats were of rawhide, but the bed was wide and cool, and there was a strong flavor of wholesomeness and comfort all about.

He dressed and made his way downstairs. In the dining room an East Indian punkah, draped with clean towels, hung above the table, and two small Negro boys kept it in slow motion to circulate the air. He breakfasted on pork, eggs, and cornbread.

Afterward, from the steps of the hotel, MacAshen could look off across the river toward the bluffs of the Colorado, the strange geological formations where the chocolate-colored sands of the prairie ended. Behind those prairies rose the familiar mountain ranges, limestone prominences covered with live oak and dwarf cedar. In that direction, too, lay his home on the Pedernales.

Along the sidewalk, as he idled northward on the avenue, he noticed a drygoods store, apparently still stocked with at least some type of merchandise. From where MacAshen stood stretching as far as the next thoroughfare, the big Eclipse Stables appeared quite active, even at this hour. Men were scurrying about, assembling goods and saddling animals. MacAshen halted a man at the entrance.

"Howdy, Miller," he said.

The man looked him over, from the faded cloth of his uniform to his dark penetrating eyes. "Well, bless my soul," he said, "if it ain't Levit MacAshen." He looked at the worn uniform again. "Should have knowed it. You been a-soldiering, and from the aspects of things, right smartly, too."

MacAshen laughed and clasped the outstretched hand. "Yes, I've been a-soldiering," he responded.

"What're you doing here, Levit?" the other asked. "You going home for a spell?"

"Who knows, these days? But I'm still in the army—not a deserter."

"Well, now, I wasn't meaning anything like that," the livery stable owner assured him. "Reckon I've knowed you that well, and your daddy before you. I was just about to remark that the brakes outside this town are full of drifters these days. Giving us trouble, stealing horses, and anything else they can get. They may be thick up Pedernales way, too."

"These are bad times, Miller. Bad for us, and bad for them." Glancing about, MacAshen said, "However, you've done all right here during the war, if I remember what your stable looked like before."

"Sure have. We've got departments now. Transfer, mail, boarding stables, livery—even got an undertaking department."

MacAshen laughed. "Well, you're in the best business then.

[45]

Everything sooner or later turns to undertaking."

"Reckon I'll be about the most important man in town." Miller also chuckled. "At least, if the Yankees try to come in here."

They shook hands, and MacAshen continued northward up the street. There was a church off that way and he remembered the pastor well, The Reverend Mr. Josiah Whipple. He had come across the hills to the Pedernales to offer solace on the death of MacAshen's mother. Levit would visit with him, and perhaps with one or two other people, before making further plans.

Scores of men idled under the pecan trees in the plaza. Beyond, from the churchyard, came the fragrance of wild honeysuckle, just beginning to bloom. Sweetgum and chinquapin and magnolia and tulip trees lined the pathway.

Mr. Whipple was old. He had suffered in the trying days, but he welcomed MacAshen. "I remember when you came by here on your way to the war," he said. "I see that it has gone hard with you. Are you starting home now?"

"I'd like nothing better, Reverend, but I'm still a soldier."

"The people up there in the hills have suffered while you were away. The Comanches have been cruel."

Leaving the pastor and his wife, MacAshen directed his steps toward another home he remembered well. Before the war, his father had done business with the Raymond Bank. Nat Raymond, he had learned, was now the state treasurer.

"Well, by God!" Raymond exclaimed on seeing Levit. He gripped the colonel's hand and slapped his shoulder. "I knew you would be back. You MacAshens have always been a hardy people." He locked his arm in MacAshen's and led him into the study, just off the entrance hall. MacAshen wanted to know about the ranch.

"Haven't been able to keep track of things back in the hills too well," Raymond answered. "Maybe the house and barns are still standing—if the Indians left them alone. It's not likely, but I don't know. The red cutthroats are all over."

MacAshen disclosed his own situation, including his wound, and his temporary furlough.

"Then what'll you be doing, now you're up and about again?" the banker asked.

"I'll see it out," MacAshen answered. "I don't know just

what that'll add up to, but maybe nobody else does, either. The way I got it, Forrest planned to write out an order transferring me—if I was ever able to report in again—to the military here in Texas. What part of it, or what for, I don't know. Maybe he never had a chance to do it, but he told me to talk to Governor Murrah if I mended in time."

"I'm glad you're not quitting yet, Levit," the banker said. "Sure, we know the Confederate cause has about collapsed. But here in Texas we're still trying to hold on—God knows for what!"

MacAshen went on, "I'm wondering what's left of the things my dad had, Raymond. Like money, I mean. He never told me much when I was a kid. Then he died, and it was too late."

The banker paced slowly up and down. "I'm glad to be able to tell you, Levit—and you're one of the few I can—that you're in pretty fair shape. About your cattle—the livestock, horses and so on—I can't say. Likely, they're gone. And maybe your house and barns, too, as I said. But your dad died before the Confederate money and securities were issued. His deposits with us were in United States dollars.

"Now, my bank has always had accounts in foreign tender. Money used to be mighty scarce on the frontier. We accepted money in the form it came. Frequently our customers converted, according to their interests at the time. But unless they gave us the right to convert, we've tried to protect deposits the way they were received. And to do that we've been lucky enough to hold onto a reserve in our vault made up of many types of currency.

"So, your father's deposits are still of record in United States dollars. I guess you'll want to keep it that way?"

MacAshen gazed into the fire. "Yes, I suppose I do. Did it amount to much?"

"You aren't a rich man, Levit, but you're comfortable. And with everything in ruins in the South, maybe moving that way in Texas—financially, I mean—the money you have will be worth many times its normal value. I guess you'll be wanting it now?"

"No, not yet," MacAshen answered slowly. "I'll have to find out what's set up for me in the rest of the business still ahead before I can even think of my own affairs. But I'm glad to know something is still left at least."

[47]

Karryl Newcomb tried to keep busy. Like everyone else, she was simply waiting, though she didn't know what for. Sometimes she vexed her aunt's friends, especially the more gossipy, when she refused to talk about what had happened before she came to Houston. But she couldn't, even though that was hard for them to understand. "Don't they have enough anxieties of their own?" she asked once, when Mrs. Newcomb chided her gently on her reserve.

"Of course, they do, honey," her aunt responded. "And they don't mean any harm. It's just that people here have been a long way away from the kind of things you went through back in Mississippi, and they just—well, they just want to know how it was."

Karryl did not respond for a moment. When she did, her voice spirited. "Better if they never found out," she said shortly. "Especially from their own experiences."

Instantly, Aunt Betsy was contrite. "Now I've upset you myself, and I didn't intend to do that," she exclaimed. "Nobody's been happier than I have to see you settling your troubles behind you, and to see you lighthearted again sometimes," she dimpled, "like you are when that Colonel MacAshen is around. We all know you've been through lots of the bad things in this war and—well, of course, we shouldn't talk about it. You and I won't, either, anymore, will we?"

A tear moistened Karryl's eye, but she brushed it away. Her aunt's instant commiseration made her feel almost like a little girl again, wanting to run to old Auntie Newcomb for assurance and protection. But that would never do if she was to rely on herself at all. "I know I'm hard to understand, Aunt Betsy," she whispered. "But I'm trying not to be. I'm trying very hard, in many ways, and I'm already a good deal better off than I was when I came." She stepped back to an arm's length. "You've not heard me crying in my sleep lately, have you? Like you said I did when I first got to Houston?"

The days followed rapidly, one upon the other. Despite the mounting tension in the streets, Karryl asked Aunt Betsy to let her run all errands and to do the marketing, and Mrs. Newcomb was happy to do so. The big house itself was hard to look after with just one servant left, Joshua, and there was always something to worry about in connection with the hundred acres of cotton land up-county, the last of the several plots Mrs. Newcomb's husband had left her.

In the market place Karryl could divert herself. The double galleries and the highly decorated window openings were reminiscent of Vieux Carré, back in New Orleans.

And, strangely, the stores continued to shout their wares. Townspeople could have their pick of poplins, linens, and even exotic textures in valentin, zenobia, and Sicilian cloth. The stocks of pantaloons, merino undershirts, and satin and casinet vests seemed to increase hourly, too, even as the homespun army cloth on the garrison troopers wore thinner and thinner.

Most of the goods continued to come overland by way of Mexico. The Rio Grande traders could supply almost any need. Into Houston they even brought mousselines de laine and merino. Karryl watched excitedly for the caravans that brought in the goods. The great prairie freighters required from eight to twelve span of oxen, and the drivers sweated and cursed and prodded at the beasts as the wagons creaked heavily over the long bayou bridge into the city.

Near the wharves at the foot of the town's main street the vegetation was lush—laurel and rhododendrons offset by bay and fir trees, and arbutus and cistus on every hand. White and gray cranes stalked amid the shallows. Great pelicans often rested there too, and sometimes she could even observe a brilliant red flamingo.

"You're a young woman and an all-fired pretty one," her aunt had lectured her. "I'm glad to see you getting out like you are, and I sure don't want to see you pining. People here in Texas don't pine away over anything."

"I'm not going to pine away, you can rest assured of that, Aunt Betsy."

Later Karryl recalled her aunt's remark. "As if I'd let myself," she scoffed inwardly. Would a person who'd made her way to Texas—for the reasons and in the manner she had—do so? "Not this young lady!" she vowed.

"Prince John" Magruder—Major General John Bankhead Magruder, C.S.A.—came back to Houston, where he had been assigned once previously, to take command of the Texas Department. Mrs. Newcomb was one of those with whom he had been acquainted during his previous stay, and he lost no time in paying his respects. He met Karryl, too.

Some people—like the old tavern-keeper, Fall—were not impressed by Magruder's return. "Enough fancy dans in sashes and clean officer uniforms around here already to set up a full division, the one General Lee could use, if they really wanted to fight," he snorted.

But others among Houston's residents—the more affluent of them, at least—felt differently. They liked General Magruder, despite his less-than-brilliant war record in the East. A short while after his return they set up a reception at one of the homes to welcome the general back officially. Present when Mrs. Newcomb and Karryl arrived were a score of persons, visiting with each other in a manner suppressed by war weariness.

"Howdy, there, Betsy Newcomb," a voice boomed at them. It was Thorn Revelow, the merchant-broker, who also pulled forward a companion. "This here's a newcomer to our town. He's been wanting to meet Miss Karryl," Revelow said.

Karryl turned to accept the greeting, and as she did—Good God!

"His name's Devers," Revelow went on.

"How do you do, ladies, Mrs. Newcomb, Miss Newcomb." The man bowed low.

"It cannot be; it simply cannot be!" churned through Karryl's mind.

"I understand you're a newcomer here, Miss Karryl." Devers said to her.

"Yes, she is, Mr. Devers. She's making her home with me," Mrs. Newcomb replied for both of them.

Revelow took Mrs. Newcomb's arm. "A glass of punch, Betsy?" he invited.

Mrs. Newcomb and Revelow started off and Karryl tried to follow. But Devers' hand stayed on her elbow. "Turn me loose!" she ordered through clenched teeth.

"I'm afraid you'd run away again, if I did. I only want to talk with you."

"I remember the kind of talk you make, and I find it despicable."

Devers grinned nervously, glancing over his shoulder to see if they were being watched. "Looked like a proper offer at the time, Miss Newcomb," he said. "And it would have taken you out of the trouble you were in. As it is now, you may still be in a lot of trouble.

"That's no affair of yours. It makes no difference here, anyway." Raising a hand to her bosom, she fingered her brooch, trying to make the motion appear natural.

"But the Yankees will come," he said. "You've left a mark on me, and I'm not forgetting."

The brooch came loose and she quickly lowered her hand. Devers, with a muffled gasp of pain, released his grip on her arm, pressing the pin prick on his wrist against his side. Karryl scurried away to join the others, leaving a gawking Devers.

Overcoming his perplexity, he turned toward a group clustered near the refreshment table. General Magruder was there, and Devers got close enough to listen. The general's comments were interesting, but Devers' mind was too full of anger and embarrassment to give his full attention.

"Cotton speculation is a most serious situation, gentlemen," Magruder was saying. "It is uncontrollable and it is eating the heart out of the Confederacy. Many of our leading citizens take part in this pernicious business—some of our Confederate officers, too, though we have tried to stop them. It is pernicious because it defeats our war policies. There are literally hundreds of speculators in the Mexican town of Matamoros today. Four, maybe five, thousand bales are moving through there every month. Much of that cotton starts right here in Houston."

"That's because there's plenty of money in it," someone observed.

"Oh, yes, there's plenty of money in it. The Yankees will trade us anything for cotton. General Bee says he can buy weapons for the Confederate posts in south Texas right from New York if he pays with cotton. Some people feel the Federals could do more for themselves by capturing Fort Brown than by defeating Lee's army."

Devers set his glass down. Glancing once more in Karryl's direction, he saw that she was purposely keeping her back to him. He drifted slowly across the room and out into the hall. Retrieving his hat from the hall-tree, he strode then toward the exit.

Outside, a fog was settling, and the street lamps blinked dimly through the mist.

4

A council was staged in Austin as rumors from the East became more and more ominous. The meeting was momentous, not so much in the action it took as in that which it failed to take. In the declining hours of the Confederacy, Texas alone still had the resources to engender new resistance.

But Texas was not happy with the manner in which the war had been conducted. It did not particularly approve of Jefferson Davis, or the military direction at government level. Soon now, the Texans might well stand alone again, or at least some of their leaders thought so. They had been alone before. At the Alamo and at San Jacinto. Throughout the long years against the Comanche, and the Comanche's allied minions of the plains. The question was not whether they could still fight, but whether they would fight for the Confederacy. Some people envisioned an empire of their own again, under the Texas flag, drawing to their standards the disillusioned from the Old South and the disenchanted beyond the Rio Grande.

The state was well victualed. It still had the nucleus of an army. It had ammunition, stocks of modern European arms constantly arriving from Mexico, and quartermaster warehouses bulging with supplies. And something else: a thousand miles of open border with a nation theoretically neutral, a line the

Yankees could not assault without precipitating a European war.

Colonel John Levit MacAshen's arrival in Austin at a moment when the proposition of increased resistance, still unresolved, lay heavily upon the minds of the state's guardians was only a coincidence of the erratic hour.

"I talked to the governor about you, Levit, and he did hear from Forrest," the banker Raymond said. "He wants to see you personally. He's asked that you come to my house tomorrow morning." Noting MacAshen's look of puzzlement, Raymond added: "We meet in the homes of various citizens now. The capitol is no longer weatherproof."

MacAshen arrived at Raymond's house early the next day. Raymond, receiving him at the door, informed him that the governor was already present. "He's met for an hour with his council, and they've finished most of their business," the banker said. "But they've seen several other persons, too, and there's still one man ahead of you."

MacAshen, going out to the patio to wait, found a cavalry captain from DeBray's regiment stalking up and down. Recognizing MacAshen's insignia, the officer introduced himself. He himself was just in from San Augustine with reports for the governor, and to turn back a shipment of guns.

"Turn back a shipment?" MacAshen repeated.

"That's what I said. I've got more than I can say grace over now. A whole storehouse of new Enfields, boxes of small shot, sabres, pistols, trays of guncaps that nobody's using. Plenty of cannons, too."

"I haven't heard of anything like that since the war started," MacAshen said. "Where do you get it?"

"Oh, the mule trains bring it in from Mexico. The French can get you anything in Mexico."

"Not even General Lee has such a depot left," MacAshen said.

"No, I guess not. But then, there's a larger army under muster today in the Trans-Mississippi—and better equipped—than General Lee ever commanded."

Called shortly in thereafter, the captain remained with the governor only a few minutes, and then MacAshen was called.

The governor was standing near the head of a long oak table. "I'm glad you're a Texan, sir," Murrah said. "General Forrest wrote to me of you some weeks ago, but he wasn't sure you'd make it home. I had forgotten about his letter until Mr. Raymond told me you were here."

"It took a while to get back," MacAshen confirmed.

"You have come to Austin at an opportune moment. We are always shorthanded here. My own adjutant has had to leave and very likely will not see service again. Typhoid. There are other duties, also, for able men."

"I take it, then, you will want me here in Austin?"

"Very possibly—at least for a time. We'll speak of it later. The fact that you've just arrived from the East with a knowledge of the way things are there could be quite useful to us here. Very few in Austin have actually seen the fighting back there."

Now the governor turned to face the others seated around the table. "This is Colonel MacAshen," he told them. "I knew his father before the war, back in the Pedernales Valley. Colonel MacAshen was wounded with General Forrest. Forrest has sent him home to try to get well, and has told us we may use him here, if we need him."

Cleburne and Guy Bryan sat at the governor's left, Burleson and two others at his right, and there was Stockdale, the lieutenant-governor, and Raymond—men whose faces were lined and hard. The governor's pale, angular face seemed almost ghostly among theirs.

MacAshen had known Murrah was a tubercular, but he had not realized the seriousness of his illness. Even though he was thin and colorless, Murrah's vibrant personality was at once apparent. "Take the seat in the corner, Colonel MacAshen," the governor instructed. "I will not have time to talk with you privately, but will arrange to do so in a day or two. The issues we are discussing here now are of a general nature but they relate to our present circumstances."

Murrah coughed as he shuffled through the papers before him. "This overture by President Davis that we were discussing aims at withdrawal back this way across the Mississippi for a stand based on Texas. The purpose is to keep up the fighting while efforts are continued toward an alliance with France. With shortened lines and an open border, the president thinks we could hold on."

Stockdale remarked, "You said nothing further had been heard from Maximilian."

"Correct. And I do not think anything else will be. As a

Texan I can say that I would just as soon have it that way. Help from Maximilian would only make us a dependency of France."

"Let's get back to the main issue, Governor," Raymond prompted.

Murrah glanced toward MacAshen, silently listening from his chair in the corner. "Many people feel the Southern cause is lost. There is considerable discussion in Texas now of a plan for a new government here, divorced from the Confederacy, and flying the Texas flag. It would try to restore the failing ardor of our own troops and attract new men to service. We have about fifty thousand men, we think, to start with; at least, there are that many in the Trans-Mississippi Department, and most of whom, we believe, are Texans.

"You are originally from the border country, Colonel Mac-Ashen," addressing himself now directly to Levit, "and so you will grasp quickly what we face, if we do try to fight on. This is the dilemma we have been trying to deal with. There have been many Indian attacks along the frontier during the war. Some of these we repelled, some we lost.

"Recently, we tried to inspire another pow-wow at Camp Napoleon. We wanted to put up whatever it took to get the tribes to cease their murderous attacks on our settlements. But none of the really dangerous bands showed up. And since then they've simply increased their savagery."

"They've got to be stopped," another man broke in. "And our war with the Union must go on at the same time."

The words sounded blustery. MacAshen looked at the speaker, wondering whether the fellow realized how much he was taking in, and suddenly he understood that indeed he did. "A stubborn man," he thought. But the trait was infectious.

"Perhaps we must," the governor said. "But let's keep one thing in mind at all times: It is for all our people that we must make the decisions." Turning his eyes toward MacAshen again, he continued. "There is another alternative, tragic though the admission be. When Lee and Johnston have been ground under, we could end the war, seeking the best we can get out of capitulation. God alone knows what that would mean, but we may have to consider it shortly."

The governor rose. "At least I have had the opportunity to see you here this morning," he said to MacAshen. "Now I must go, but I will send for you when I have time to discuss your situation—and to examine our own a little further."

Leaving the Raymond house, MacAshen walked down a path that led away from the heart of the town. He quickened his footsteps, striving by vigorous exercise to shake his heaviness of thought.

Just then, the bell sounded in the steeple of St. David's, the second oldest Protestant church in all Texas. A melancholy refrain, he thought, in a melancholy hour.

MacAshen had no way to keep abreast of major events after his meeting with the governor, but he did hear what everyone else heard of the upheavals in many places. Impatient at Murrah's failure to call him immediately, he tried to keep busy. As he drank in Austin's beauty, its hills crowned by woodlands, the river winding in and out before taking a grand sweep to the south, he wanted more than anything else to go home. But he could not do that just yet.

Strolling about the streets, he remembered the gracious hospitality and friendliness of the Newcombs back in Houston. The nighttime thought of Karryl aroused in him a heady restlessness. On his return to the Mansion House one such evening, he found a black messenger waiting. He had brought the summons MacAshen awaited.

The governor's residence was an imposing structure, two stories high, with a little stoop at the front door and a balcony above. A large room with four windows looked out upon the capitol. MacAshen followed the servant into the house. In the lamplight he could see that the ceiling of the great room off entrance was unplastered. A few embers glowed in the big fireplace. Through another door he observed a smaller back room that he took for the governor's study, and there was an exit into the rear garden.

The servant beckoned him on. "De guv'nor, he sho' am ailin' tonight," the old Negro warned, as he led MacAshen up an unpainted stairway. There were two big rooms on the upper floor and MacAshen was ushered into the larger one, where the governor, propped by huge pillows, lay in a great four-poster bed. Nearby was a night table covered with medicines, and in the far corner, a trundle bed. Spread before the ailing man was a mass of documents, in which he was deeply engrossed, his effort punctuated with a hacking cough which he tried to stifle behind a cloth. But he looked up as MacAshen entered, motioning him to a chair by the bed.

"Busy hours, Colonel," he declared. "And there seems to be no end to our troubles." He indicated with a sweep of his hand the mass of papers. "Everything is confused. Our own house is divided. I have decided to keep you on here in Austin, in spite of the fact that as yet I can assign you no specific duty. Much depends on how things go during the next few days in the Deep South, and it would be foolish to think of other things until we know more of that. But I wanted you to know at least that I had not forgotten you.

"There has been new intelligence in the past few days, and something may come of it on which I will need some assistance. If so, I will assign you as my personal aide. President Davis has written several of our people, including General Smith and General Shelby. The president continues to speak of a bastion in which Texas would be the anchor, and covering huge sections of northern Mexico, if they could be brought in."

"What shall I do, Governor, until I hear from you?"

"The best you can," the other came back spiritedly. "That's just about all any of us can do right now. But stay in the city. I'll send for you sooner or later."

"Very well, Governor."

"The servant will show you out. I apologize for the hours in which I have to see you, but I have so many things to think about."

MacAshen nodded. There was little more that he could do, anyway, even though the governor's orders gave him nothing to go on. There were serious decisions to be made, and he supposed Murrah was the only man who could make them; little reason to bother with a mere colonel's personal impatience. Upon Murrah's thin and wasted shoulders rested the responsibility of the hour.

Fall, having added another job to his routine in Houston, arrived in Austin that night. A group of tradesmen had hired him as an express messenger between the two cities, and on this first trip he had arrived late, stopped at the Mansion House and gone to bed immediately. Now he found MacAshen in the dining room, intent on a plate of pork and corn cakes until he felt the heavy hand on his shoulder.

"Howdy, there, Colonel," the tavern keeper boomed. "Figured to find you close to the kitchen door."

MacAshen came to his feet and grasped Fall's hand. "You old vinegaroon," he exclaimed. "What brings you to Austin?"

"I've got me something new to do, something that'll put more money in my jeans, and that's why I'm here. But wait a minute." He looked MacAshen over. "Let's talk about you first; 'pears you're wearing well. Getting plenty of rest?"

"I haven't had anything else to do, Fall."

MacAshen led Fall to his room upstairs, then asked eagerly, "How are the Newcombs?"

"Well, Colonel, they were right cheerful and sprightly three days ago. Reckon you'll be pleased to know that Miss Karryl asked to be remembered to you."

"That I am. I think of them a lot, Fall."

"Then you'd better get back to see them."

"I wish I could. But I haven't even been home yet."

After visiting with MacAshen for almost an hour, Fall said, "I'll get going now." He explained that he had laid out his trip so he could make the first half by rail, the train taking ten hours to get from Houston to Alleytown. After spending the night in the log inn at the rail terminus, he hired a powerful horse to take him over the prairies to Austin.

"Be careful," MacAshen advised. "That's a rough, dangerous trip to Alleytown."

"Reckon I'm still middlin' capable," the old man said, patting his shotgun.

"I guess you are too," MacAshen agreed. He laid a hand on the other's arm. "Take care of the Newcombs, my friend," he said. "Nobody knows what's ahead."

In the Deep South, the swirling tumult called "the War Between the States" approached a climax in the early days of April. The tattered remnants of Longstreet's Corps fell back on April 6 toward Lynchburg. General St. John was at Amelia Springs. There were bridges to burn, but in the confusion of retreat they fell intact to the advancing Federals. A delaying action at Farmville gave little relief. A successful skirmish with Gregg's cavalry buoyed the Confederate hopes for a while, but at Cumberland Church the Union infantry thrust forward. A night passed. Then began the race to cross the headwaters

[58]

of the Appomattox toward Lynchburg. In the early afternoon, the Federals overran Prospect Station, cutting the Confederate line of retreat. Thereafter, matters were resolved quickly in the woodlands of northern Virginia.

On the morning of April 9, General Lee laid down his arms. President Davis received the news of Lee's surrender on April 10, at Danville. In his nervous haste, he grasped at straws, conferring with Beauregard and Johnston. But there was nothing anyone could do, for the Confederacy was in its death throes.

The news was long in reaching the Southwest. In Texas, hopes still soared on occasion, to falter a moment later. There were rumors of disaster, rumors of sudden victories. Politicians scurried about trying to dispel the rising gloom, but the spectre could not be dissipated. There were two persons, at least, in Austin and Houston, who were less misguided than the rest. They were MacAshen and Karryl Newcomb, for they had seen firsthand the way of the war in the East, and the final result, as each now realized, was inevitable.

Some days after the reception for General Magruder, Karryl was startled, on answering a knock at the door of the Newcomb home, to find Devers standing at the threshold. As she started to slam the door in his face, he thrust out a heavily muscled arm to keep it open and moved aggressively into the entrance hall.

"Now that's no way to welcome a friend," he said.

"You get the idea," Karryl bristled.

"I don't know why you should be so reluctant to talk with me, when I only want to offer you and your aunt my services."

She motioned him into the parlor but made no move to seat herself.

"Services, Mr. Devers? Really?"

"The town is filling up with rough characters—hard, mean men who aren't too choosy in their methods of getting along. I thought you might need somebody around sometimes . . . ."

Her eyes blazed. "Now you listen to me!" She kept her voice down to keep Betsy Newcomb from overhearing, but her words were nonetheless cutting. "I'd have to be in a pretty fix to need protection from the likes of you, now wouldn't I?"

But Devers was in control of himself. "You really ought to get that chip off your shoulder, young lady. In times like these you never know when you're going to need a friend. When I saw you in Louisiana, you weren't so choosy about the help you took before you thought of that way to have me shanghaied."

She stepped around him into the hallway. "You may leave now," she said coldly. "And don't bother me again."

A frown passed over his face, then deepened. "All right. But just remember, the Yankees are going to march in here, and then you may not be so high and mighty. I have my pride, too, you know." He passed through the door that she was holding open for him. Karryl stood alone for a moment in the hallway, trembling with rage.

The unpleasant memory of this encounter was erased from Karryl's mind a few days later by an occurrence that was both pleasant and heartwarming. Passing the Hutchins House with a package of groceries in her arms, she caught the uncertain notes from an old piano in the lobby coming through the broad front windows. Someone was struggling to pick out the proper chords, and a girl was giving the lyric to the melody. The voice was thrillingly familiar and, impulsively, Karryl turned into the entranceway. She stared in disbelief at what she saw.

Margaret Wayne! The little girl from Wayneleigh, near her old home in Mississippi. She hurried toward the girl.

"Karryl, Karryl Newcomb!" the girl cried, leaping up from the piano bench.

"Where in the world did you come from, Margaret?"

"Oh, we're on our way west," the girl exclaimed delightedly. "All of us in a big wagon: Father, Mother, and brother Burrell!"

"Brother Burrell!"

"Yes, he came home just in time; wasn't it lucky? And we're all going out where the Indians are and hunt some of the wild cattle."

"Wild cattle? The Waynes going west for wild cattle?"

"Of course. We're going to be ranchers."

Just then they were interrupted by a loud shout. "Great Jehoshaphat! Karryl Newcomb!"

Burr Wayne, descending the stairway, lurched toward Karryl in amazement. Karryl met him eagerly, uncontrollably happy, throwing her arms about his neck and kissing him soundly.

"Oh, Burr!" she cried. "It's been so long since I have seen

anyone from home."

"What in heaven's name are you doing here clear across the world from Natchez, Karryl?" he demanded.

"It's a long story, Burr."

"Well, it must be! But you're still a sight for sore eyes, wherever you came from!"

She was crying and laughing at the same time. "So are you, Burr, so are all of you!"

"Let's sit down, over here by the window, and talk. I want to look at you, Karryl."

"Oh, and I want to look at you, too. No one ever looked so good to me."

Margaret said, "Don't you forget I'm here, too. And I saw you first!"

"Indeed, I won't forget you're here," Karryl laughed. "I feel as though I'd just like to hold you close and talk to you forever." She threw her arms about the girl again. "You've grown so much, Margaret, I scarcely recognized you. Let's see now, it's been a year—no, almost two years—since I saw you last."

"At least two years, and maybe more," Margaret corrected her. "Of course, I've grown some in that time, Karryl. But who'd expect you to know me, anyway? You never paid me much mind in the old days."

"I did, too. But you were such a little child then, and now you're almost a woman!"

"You hear that, Burr Wayne—you never say such nice things to me, your own sister."

"Oh, come, Sis! This is no time to pick an argument." He tousled her hair, stopping her short. Then he said in a more serious tone to Karryl, "You're the last person in the world I ever expected to run into this far from home."

"I guess you haven't heard, but everything is gone, back at Natchez . . . Father, Mother, Newcomb Hall. Everything."

He took her hand in his. "I'm sorry, Karryl, so sorry to hear. But it's happened to a lot of people. Yes, I did hear about Newcomb Hall. But it happened to the Waynes, too, you know. Wayneleigh was burned, and everything we had in it." He changed the subject abruptly. "Don't stand there gawking, Margaret," he said. "Run and bring Mother. And Father, too."

"The last I heard, you were in the East with the army, Burr,"

Karryl murmured. "I understood you were still there or . . . or . . . well, nobody had had any word from you for so long."

"I was taken prisoner," he said. "Grant let some of us out on parole in the exchanges right after Christmas." He was suddenly grave. "When I got home," he went on, "I found that Father was getting ready to take Mother and Margaret west. There was really nothing else to do, so here we are." He turned for a moment toward the door, and Karryl studied his face. His high cheekbones and long chin reflected a hollowness that spoke of prison fare, but his head was still crowned with a great mop of chestnut hair. "It's hard to picture the Waynes migrating west from Natchez in a covered wagon, but I know you're proud of your father. He would have done just that, headed west, I mean, even if you hadn't come home," she smiled.

Burr grinned, too. "Yes, you should have seen him with a faded old tin-type he picked up somewhere. Two gentlemen living in San Antonio—they had on floppy white-linen coats and black string ties. Fine sets of sidelocks, too, just like his. He said to me: 'I presume I will look very well on the frontier, Burr.' While everything was lying around burned out, and nobody was even sure we could get away."

"Oh, I wish they would hurry," Karryl exclaimed, "I'm dying to see them."

Just then Burr's mother, Robella Wayne, came down the stairs, followed quickly by the elderly planter. Robella was a pleasant, matronly woman, who appeared short beside her husband and son. Her brown curls were straightening now, and she wore them parted over her forehead.

She opened her arms and folded Karryl into them, and a moment later Standifer Wayne did likewise.

"This is a wonderful surprise for us," the elder Wayne exclaimed. "We have felt almost like foreigners it's so strange to us here."

Karryl told them something of her own flight, omitting portions related to the start and to the conclusion. Then Standifer and Burr reviewed their own experiences.

"You're settled now, though, it would seem," Burr said, "and happy, too, as happy as you can be, considering all of these things."

"I guess so, Burr. But even here in Houston, it's pretty bad right now."

"I suppose the excitement will die down in time, and I wouldn't mind staying in Houston myself if we had some way to make a living here," Standifer said. "But we haven't. We're going on west."

"I know you'll do well," Karryl said. Then she put her arms around the older woman. "I'm so glad to see all of you," she said earnestly. "I wish I could just sit here and visit with you from now on. But I've got to hurry on home now, or Aunt Betsy will be out looking for me. You come and visit with us soon."

"We certainly will, Karryl," Burr accepted for all of them.

In the days that followed, Karryl and the Waynes made the most of each other's company. Karryl did what she could to show them all the things she'd learned about Houston. Texas was far from the war zone; its shops were active, and there were many things to see. After a time, however, Standifer Wayne excused himself from further expeditions. He called on a banker named Mellett instead.

"Are you open for business?" Standifer asked.

"Yes, of course we are."

"Then you must be managing to keep up your foreign contacts?"

"To some extent," the banker answered. "The mail goes far around, and sometimes it falls into enemy hands. But we hold onto a fair communication."

"Before the war I shipped my cotton down the river, and through a New Orleans brokerage to Europe. Those people had an agency at Havana. When the war broke out, I still had a small credit in English pounds with them, based on Manchester purchase records. I believe these credit memoranda are negotiable, sir. Would you be interested in buying them?"

"For Confederate money?"

"No. Good government tender only, Mr. Mellett. My entire fortune back across the Mississippi has already gone the way of the Confederacy. So I feel I've done my duty in that direction."

The banker nodded. He took the credit documents and studied them thoughtfully. After a time he excused himself, going into his accountant's rooms. When he returned, he confirmed: "It's good paper, all right, and under our present

[63]

circumstances I'm not averse to parting with some of our specie for it." He wrote down a figure on a piece of paper and handed it to Standifer. Standifer considered it.

"Very well," the latter accepted. "I suppose it's as good as I could do under the circumstances, and it will be enough to set me up in a homestead."

The banker arose. "If you will join me at the tavern next door, we will drink to your success," he said.

They went out the door and into the saloon adjacent. When the glasses had been placed before them, Wayne said, "I have the feeling you're not too sure of your situation—your banking house—here in Houston just now, Mr. Mellett. Otherwise, you wouldn't have been so willing to part with your specie."

"You're right about that."

"If the Confederate cause back East is lost, do you not think Texas might still fight on alone?"

"No, I don't."

"That's strange. I'd heard the people here favored a Republic of Texas again."

"They might have once. But that was when old General Sam Houston was still alive."

"President Davis has spoken some thoughts recently about establishing a new bastion out this way."

The banker frowned. "I don't think he'd get much encouragement from Texans," he declared. "Most of us feel, as Houston once remarked, that 'Jefferson Davis is proud as Lucifer, and cold as a lizard.' Besides, we've always had a war going on out here—with the Indians. I don't know of anybody who wants another one."

5

Soon after Karryl's meeting with the Wayne family, a sudden turnover occurred in matters at Houston. Vaguely, she wished someone—like Colonel Levit MacAshen—might be here to tell them what to do.

The stores, which had been loudly proclaiming full-stocked shelves of trader goods from Mexico, startled everyone by a-bruptly announcing auctions of everything they had. Broad-sides were thrown about the streets. The whole conglomeration of goods was dumped on the market at ridiculous markdowns. Anything was obtainable—printed flannels, alpacas, ladies' gauntlets, fine cotton hose. There was shoe thread, and men's undershirts and great stores of Irish linen and organdies. But the people who were without money—and the hungry soldiers—milled ominously in the streets.

"What does all this mean? I thought it was pretty steady here," Burr asked Karryl. "Certainly, the merchants."

"They're scared over the news from the East, and they're afraid the Yankees will take the goods away from them, I guess."

"Maybe so. But lately I've been hearing some things that put another light on it. The way it looks, people are really afraid now of their own soldiers—and maybe even the folks who live

[65]

right here in Houston."

"Oh, Burr, I hope not."

He was implying the possibility of a savage outbreak of rioting. Riots could be horrible for everyone, and the observation Burr made was a good deal nearer to the real state of the country than even he realized. Nobody was able to forecast what the threatening crowds eventually might do. The worried merchants suddenly adjusted their sights, and the goods that had been so prominently displayed disappeared overnight. In the space of a few days, there was nothing whatever to be purchased, even in the food shops.

"Just as I said, they've decided they can't take the chance even with their own people," Burr concluded. "There'll be violence and looting in this town before long. The place is like a powder keg, Karryl. Maybe you ought to get out of here—go on west with us—at least until the fever dies down."

She halted in the street to stare up at him. Go on west with the Waynes? Oh, if she only could! She forced herself to realistically answer, "That's a generous thought, Burr. But you have enough to look out for now, and I'll simply have to stay on here with Aunt Betsy."

The first stages of panic began on April 14. The newspaper reported northern rumors that Federal officers, including Lincoln, were aboard the *River Queen*, at City Point, discussing peace terms; that General Lee had received overtures aimed at his surrender. The editor tempered his report with the usual denial: "The Yankee dispatches are all gossip. The desperate condition of the enemy forces him to whistle up such balderdash."

But the next morning Editor Cushing had to admit that the stories of Lee's evacuation of Richmond and Petersburg were indeed true. Karryl read the account in the sheet brought to her by old Joshua. "The house is beginning to fall in on us now," she murmured sadly.

Fall, the tavern-keeper, brought more grim tidings: defectors from Hardeman's and Gould's commands near Cypress Creek were committing outrages upon woman wagoneers forced to that duty by the conscription of their menfolk. On April 18 the newspaper despondently admitted that the late news did, indeed, portend disaster, although the editor could not refrain from the final hope that the scope of the tragedy was being greatly over-estimated.

But the South was finished, and only the slowness of communications delayed the bitter admission of defeat. On April 21, Mobile surrendered to General Granger, and the Juggernaut moved on. The Confederate armies were collapsing everywhere.

At Averysboro, General Joseph Johnston entrenched, but Sherman sent a brigade circling through the marshes to break the rebel left. Johnston had seventeen thousand men left, but he was pushed back now upon the sea, and hemmed in by an army six times as large.

For General Hood, the conclusion was more tragic. Wilson's Yankee cavalry swept up from the rear, and Schofield drove against his forward wall. The Confederate line collapsed. Only nine thousand Confederates out of an army of fifty thousand were able to muster beyond the Tennessee. For all of them, Hood's men as well as Johnston's, the curtain had fallen.

The shattering impact of the disasters swept beyond the Mississippi. But wild rumors, one as late as April 7—that Forrest had captured Eastport—kept men in turmoil. Ashbel Smith took command of the garrison at Galveston on April 18. On the same date Wharton's old command at Hempstead, stripped of all encumbrances now, reported ready for action.

DeBray's brigade had been stationed at San Augustine, in the East Texas forests, during the late winter of 1864, as a reserve against the possible movement once more of Federal forces up from New Orleans against the Red River country. Now it was at Hempstead, too, fifty miles above Houston, and as the tension increased, the brigade occupied the military barracks in Houston.

On April 24, Editor Cushing conceded the surrender of Lee, though still pinning a forlorn hope on Johnston. In the same edition he reported the assassination of the President, ten days earlier.

The month of May arrived. From the west came intelligence of a savage battle in the post-oak brakes of Wise County between detached Confederate cavalry units and a vast band of deserters, branded now as outlaws.

In the towns, women busied themselves valiantly trying to keep their minds from the uncertainty before them. A fair at the Bagby home in Houston exhibited needlework, and fancy foods contrived from substitutes.

On May 9, the bark *Ida Carter* was at Dog River bar with a cargo of ice—strange traffic when the fortunes of war were tumbling the columns about men's heads. But Editor Cushing conjured visions of "sherry cobblers, mint juleps and other tipple of that like."

Fragmentary reports of a Federal advance from New Orleans, from St. Louis, from everywhere, echoed and reechoed, and Cushing took the not ill-advised opportunity to publish an article on the attractions of residential life on the Island of Java.

Far away, on the Rio Grande, Confederate troops from Fort Brown and Union soldiers from Point Isabel met in battle near Taylor's plain of Palo Alto. The news of the developments in the east had not yet reached them. The Confederates drove the Unionists back; the engagement ended in the evening, and with it the last of the organized hostilities in the long and tragic conflict.

General Lee had surrendered his paladins more than a month before.

Reports of bitter unrest appeared from every direction now. Austin was still trying to recover from the shock of General Lee's surrender when word came of Johnston's defeat, too; then Hood's. Oddly enough, concise reports on the rioting at Houston did not reach Austin immediately, and Levit MacAshen had about decided he might as well go home to the Pedernales when a summons came at last from Governor Murrah.

"I suppose you know as much as the rest of us do about the panic everywhere," the governor said when MacAshen reached the mansion. "Now I have a communication here from General Kirby Smith at Shreveport. He has been approached by the Federals for immediate surrender of his forces to General Pope in New Orleans. He has asked the governors of Texas, Louisiana, Arkansas, and Missouri to join him at once in Marshall. Unfortunately, I am not well enough to go. Colonel Bryan will represent me. But I want you to go along, too. Report to the military. Help Colonel Bryan where you can. All depends on the events of the next few days. Our last hope, I fear, is General Smith. Only one officer, I am told, is still afield east of the Mississippi—Bedford Forrest."

The skies above the little East Texas town of Marshall were

heavy, the air warm and humid. MacAshen, arriving on May 13 after an arduous ride from Austin, felt the perspiration on his brow. Standing at attention before the last of the ranking Confederate officers, he said, "Governor Murrah ordered me to report to you, sir. Colonel Bryan, of course, speaks for the state, but I rode here with him. He will be along presently. For myself, I come here as a soldier to return to duty."

Edmund Kirby Smith, full general in the Confederate Army, had fought valiantly with Taylor in Mexico. He had campaigned with Lee in the west, suffering grievous wounds in the wars with the Apaches. Smith had been one of those to whom the Rebellion called early, sustaining wounds again at Manassas. In 1863 he had come out to the West to muster the defenses of the frontier states.

"I thank you, Colonel," the general said. "The governor had written me of you. I am glad you are here."

General Smith looked at the calender on his desk. May 13. He made no effort to go through the disarray of papers, thrown untidily on his desk. There was a knock on the door, and he turned to heed the orderly sergeant. "They are here, sir."

Smith nodded. He looked about to see if there were enough chairs. "I don't know what will happen at this meeting, Colonel," he said, "but I would be glad if you would return to me when it is concluded." MacAshen saluted. He turned to leave, but the general stopped him.

"There will be a second conference in this town today," Smith further informed MacAshen. "My district generals have come in, too. I believe they have certain proposals to discuss among themselves. You may, or may not, wish to attend their meeting. Suit yourself, Colonel."

MacAshen went outside. Out in the public plaza he looked at the sky and mopped the perspiration again from his brow.

The final war council of the Confederacy was convened by General Smith in the old public building at Marshall. The last man to enter saluted and held out his hand.

"I am Colonel Guy Bryan, sir," he said. "As Colonel MacAshen informed you earlier, Governor Murrah is ill and he asked me to represent Texas at this council."

"Yes. I am sorry to hear of Governor Murrah's continued ailments. You have met Governor Reynolds here, of Missouri, Governor Flanigan of Arkansas, and Allen of Louisiana?"

Bryan shook hands silently with the trio; the general then motioned them to chairs.

"I am grateful that you could come," Smith said. "I think the situation is of such gravity, gentlemen, that a determination must be reached here and at once on our future course. From the intelligence just received at headquarters of the Trans-Mississippi, it appears that all organized resistance east of the Mississippi has ended." General Smith spoke faster. "On May second, I made a last appeal to the Emperor Maximilian for aid. There was no reply. At first I thought President Davis might join us here to help bolster the declining resolution of our people. Now, I know that cannot be."

The Missourian leaned forward. "Cannot be?" he probed.

"That is correct, sir." The general stared sadly out upon the landscape. "We have just learned that Mr. Davis already has fallen into the hands of the Federal troops. As far as the South is concerned, gentlemen, the government of the Confederacy no longer exists."

"It appears, then, that we must now make our own decisions."

"That, also, is correct." He drummed upon the table for a moment. "I have a communication, as you know, from the Federal officer Sprague in New Orleans, a colonel on General Pope's staff, dated May 5, and it demands the surrender of this department on the same terms offered to Lee and Johnston. The question before us is whether we shall accept these proposals or organize further resistance."

His listeners sat quietly in their chairs.

"I think our supply is not unduly alarming," he declared. "We can call up no more than seventy thousand troops as of this moment, but I think we might still offer an effective stand."

He launched into a review of geography and detail and of organization and strategy that stretched from minutes into hours. Occasionally the discussion was punctuated by a sharp question from one of his listeners.

Finally, the monologue was broken emphatically by the Louisianian. "Let us be realistic, General," he said. "The South is defeated. We can only bring additional sorrow and suffering to our people if we continue. The land areas of three states out of four represented in this room today are under Union domination already."

Bryan and the Arkansas governor nodded. General Smith looked from face to face. "Then there remains only an effort to arrange the best terms possible," he said.

Across the square, the meeting of generals was under way. From the bayou country had come Hawthorne, and Preston; Walker also, from Houston, and Buckner from Shreveport. From his temporary station at Fulton, Arkansas, had come Major General Shelby—Joe Shelby—and with him an escort of cavalry.

MacAshen paid his respects to Shelby, and the officer invited him to the conference, which opened on a depressing note with Walker declaring that no commander remained in action east of the Mississippi.

"Nobody still fighting east of the Mississippi?" MacAshen asked. "I thought there was at least one commander still in the field."

"And who would that be?"

"Bedford Forrest." The room was instantly silent.

"I'm sorry, Colonel," Shelby informed him quietly. "I thought everyone knew." He opened a newspaper on the table, and handed it to MacAshen. The colonel saw it was dated May 10. The story before him was the report of Forrest's last address to his command:

That we are beaten is a self-evident fact [MacAshen read] *and any further resistance on our part would be justly regarded as the very height of folly and rashness . . . . The cause for which you have so long and manfully struggled . . . and made so many sacrifices, is today hopeless. The government which we sought to establish and perpetuate is at an end. Reason dictates and humanity demands that no more blood be shed. It is your duty and mine to lay down our arms, submit to the powers that be, and to aid in restoring peace and order throughout the land . . . .*

You have been good soldiers, you can be good citizens. Obey the laws, preserve your honor, and the government to which you have surrendered can afford to be . . . magnanimous.

In later years, MacAshen could marvel at the welter of confusion, cross-purpose and independent action that erupted on the morning of the final war council in Marshall. Beginning with that moment no person knew from hour to hour who

[71]

commanded in the Trans-Mississippi, who was at war and who had surrendered, or who still retained authority to act for the people.

First, Smith's secondary generals urged him to step down so that new plans might be drafted for a continuation of the war under different leadership, and he agreed. But on the following day, the governors and General Smith dispatched one of the officers to New Orleans with a statement of terms under which they would surrender the Trans-Mississippi. At the same time, General Smith rushed off to Shreveport to muster his command.

MacAshen saw him as he prepared to depart.

"You can join me in Houston, Colonel," Smith said to him, hurriedly.

"Can you tell me, then, what we will do?" MacAshen asked.

"We will resist to the end," the general declared grandly.

By the time General Smith reached Shreveport, a new demand from the Federal commander for surrender lay on his desk. There were telegrams, also, from the governors he had just left, counseling surrender on any terms. Smith ordered Galveston evacuated, sent out couriers to all points to fall back upon Houston for a last-ditch stand. On May 22 he received an offer of modified terms from the Union general, Pope, and immediately telegraphed his representative to complete the arrangements. Even while these latter preliminary documents were being signed, though, Smith—apparently without reason—moved off down through the piney woods. He traveled toward Houston, notwithstanding the fact that, in effect, he had surrendered. He was fired again with the hope of continued action.

At Galveston, General Magruder had received telegraphed orders from General Smith to evacuate the island and fall back on Houston. The order bore profound effect on Magruder's troops. In the early-evening darkness scores of soldiers crossed over the bay and disappeared into the prairies, carrying their arms and supplies with them.

Early in the morning of May 22, as Smith was receiving Pope's new offer at Shreveport, the main movement from Galveston got under way. The remaining troops kept good order, but it was no secret that even these units were holding on only until they reached Houston, which was closer to their homes.

Houston itself was grim with anticipation of mob violence, or of Federal intrusion. Reports that troops from Galveston were on the way provided no comfort, for word of the real nature of the evacuation preceded them. The streets were deserted except for loiterers, drifters, and the riffraff of the garrisons. Houston waited in fear.

As the tension mounted, Vanner Storm returned to Houston and found Devers in his room above the livery stable.

"Devers," he said, "the cotton went mighty smooth across the river. And things don't look like they've gone too bad for you here. Are you ready to move on, maybe while you still can?"

The big man rose and stepped away from the table, hands thrust into his pockets, his eyes on the floor.

"No," he answered heavily. "I'm not going anywhere, now. Among other things, I've got an idea, Storm, that a lot more can be made out of this breakup than we ever heard of in either cotton or cattle. Before you left, I spoke to you about some other matters I was looking into. Well, one of them is a ruckus the Federal agents would like to stir up here in Houston. Something to speed the collapse, as they put it. You're back in time. Do you want in on this, too?"

"I'm not hepped on stopping at Houston again. But I always like to kick up my heels a little before I head for the brakes, Devers."

"This won't take long." Devers filled a glass with whisky and drained it off. "How many of your cronies around Houston, Storm?"

"Lotta," Storm counted. "Dog Behring and Summack. The Mexican didn't come back with us."

"That'll be enough. And when it's over, you can get on toward the Uvalde and wait for me." Storm nodded. "All right, then. Now for the details," Devers said.

Fall, back in town from his run for a few days, went to sleep early the night of May 22, on his cot in the room behind the saloon. Next morning he was just beginning to stir when a tap came on the window sill. "Who's there?" he called out sharply, rousing himself in the shadow. His hand gripped the old shotgun.

"Wake up," a whisper came through the window. "It's me, Tab Grotte."

"What the hell's going on?" Fall asked his barman.

"Well, I guess nothing as yet, but it looks like plenty'll be poppin' before long. I figured maybe you might want to be in on it."

"What're you talkin' about, Tab?" Fall queried, opening the door.

"Those soldiers who haven't been paid for a coon's age—and the deserters, too—they're aiming to help theirselves to what they can pick up."

"You mean they're gonna raid the town?"

"That's what they're planning."

"I'll be with you in a minute, Tab. Don't know if there's anything I can do but I'll go along, anyway."

The gray shafts of light cast strange shadow patterns among the pine trees as they hurried toward the heart of the town. About them was the sound of an awakening village. Roosters set up a contest from far and near. A cow mooed in the underbrush, and a donkey brayed energetically. "Where are the patrols, Tab?" Fall demanded.

"They ain't here," he answered. "In fact, they ain't been here since 2 A.M."

Fall stopped in amazement. "Why in hell not?"

"Can't say. Orders, I'm supposing, from somewhere, as they went out at the same time."

"You mean the town's wide open?"

Tab nodded grimly. Fall took a firmer grip on his shotgun and moved closer to the early shadows beside the building. The sun inched higher. He detected a sudden rising noise from the pines toward the southeast. It had a dull, abrasive note that gradually became more audible. "Sounds like people," Fall whispered.

On Texas Avenue they saw the mob. "Hell's fire!" Fall crouched at the corner and watched the huge, milling crowd, two or three blocks away, moving north.

"Where they going?" Grotte wondered.

"They're making for the ordnance building. Come on!"

They ran down the alley, the clamor rising with each second as they neared the mob. A square distant from the huge building, Fall halted beside a high board fence enclosing an equipment yard. He reached across to stand his shotgun inside and hastily clambered after it. Tab was right behind. Hidden from

[74]

view, they waited while the throng surged onward.

At the ordnance building, the mob wasted no time. A log was pushed forward and eager hands gripped it as a projectile to smash against the doors. In a second the portal was broken, and the crowd was inside.

"Somebody's calling the shots in that outfit," Fall muttered. "They know just what they're doing."

It did not last long. Suddenly the forward elements of the mob were battling back out into the street. There were shouts and screams and curses.

Then he could see the supplies—blankets, bolts of domestic, flannels, shoes, mosquito bars—anything that could be carried out. The men and women in the back were fighting to seize upon the goods their comrades had just pillaged. Those who carried loot were struggling to make their escape. He saw a side of leather go by, armloads of hammers, gray uniform cloth; even a shower of buttons fell in the street.

Then the crowd began to scatter and some milled around the hiding place of the two men. Through cracks in the fence, Fall could distinguish individuals. There were drifters and deserters—many drunk on salvaged whiskey—slaves, black women, even small children. He smacked his thigh in sudden amazement. "Tab," he almost shouted. "There's townsfolk in that mob, too."

"Sure are," Tab confirmed. "I see old Slaughter, and Bevins, and the Thacker boys. Old Lady Bevins, too, Yep, I recognize plenty of 'em. There's that fellow, Storm, too!"

The mob suddenly re-formed and then descended upon a warehouse across the street. It was a duplication of the earlier strike, and it was over shortly. Tab pointed to a man with a bale of rope in his hands. A Negro laborer had a string of new tin cups tied around his neck and was attempting also to shoulder a couple of heavy saddles. Close at hand a Negro woman cursed a drunken black because he would not hurry off to her shanty with a sack of flour. A small boy ran by with an armful of cotton cards, and from the bulging pockets of his jeans he dropped a package of Epsom salts, which spread upon the street.

"What do you make of it, Fall?" Tab asked finally.

"Got to think, man, got to think," Fall replied. "We better get back to the tavern."

The street was empty as they hurried along, but Fall had a feeling that people were watching from behind shutters. They entered the tavern through a rear entrance, and Fall dropped heavily into a chair. Tab reached onto a shelf and brought forth a bottle.

"Way I figure it," Fall said finally, "those people just went a little loco. But they've been in the act, and now they've got to stand the consequences."

"How do you figure there's going to be any consequences, Fall?"

"Marshal Ford will have his vigilantes out pretty quick. Or at least I hope he will."

On the afternoon of May 23, the Galveston troops began pouring into the city, without discipline, insistent that their duty to the Confederacy had ended. The mob revived suddenly, joined not only by the new soldiers, but also by throngs of local residents, half-insane it seemed, as they burst from their homes to join the mad debauch.

The throng moved next morning on the building where Marshal Ford at last had set up his command post, the Galveston troops in front. A huge blond sergeant stepped forward and stated his complaint to Ford: The goods previously pillaged from the warehouses rightfully belonged to the soldiers. "It was government property, and we haven't been paid for months," the sergeant claimed. "We're taking our pay, one way or another. If those goods aren't back on the market square by noon, we'll burn this town to the ground."

Ford bargained for time for his men to pass the word among the townspeople and got two hours. Under the threat, the goods came back, from homes throughout the city, from slaves' quarters, and deserter camps in the pines. The troops were satisfied, and the city again was quiet.

On May 29, Union General Philip Sheridan assumed command in New Orleans, unaware of General Smith's die-hard ambitions. But he need not have worried, for when Kirby Smith reached Houston he found that his army had disappeared. The Confederacy had, at last, come to an end.

These were the circumstances that created the unimaginable confusion in which the last bastion of the South completed its disintegration. MacAshen recognized the futility of further effort, even as he turned Old Warrior again toward the bayous. During his journey he learned that the telegraph wires between Shreveport and Houston had been cut, and there was no news from the coastal country. MacAshen rode hard. Reaching Houston in four days, he dismounted late in the night before the Hutchins House, where he considered himself lucky to find a bed.

6

MacAshen arose late, the hard journey from the East Texas pinelands having left him weary. After breakfast he sent a boy for his horse and rode to the Newcomb residence. Joshua answered his knock.

"Well, bless my soul," the old servant exclaimed. "If it ain't the Colonel! Come in the house, sir."

Mrs. Newcomb bustled from the kitchen. "Now, isn't this a real treat," she cooed. "You sit right down now, Colonel MacAshen, and tell us all that's happened since we saw you last. And how you've been, yourself."

"I'm fine, thank you—healthier than I've ever been before, thanks to you folks here. Is your niece still with you?"

"Of course she is. In fact, she's right here."

MacAshen turned to see Karryl already descending the stairs. The girl hurried across the room, her hands outstretched.

"It's wonderful to see you again, Colonel MacAshen," she said.

"Well, thank you, Miss Newcomb. You're kind to say that. I'll be trying for a relapse. You spoiled me here, you know."

"Did you come back just to see us, Colonel?"

"Sure," he laughed.

"Are you through with soldiering?"

"I thought I was, but suddenly I found myself haltered a-gain. Now I don't know." He related his experiences with General Smith, told her how the man still sought to hold onto his command. "I haven't the slightest idea what he will come up with," MacAshen explained.

"I'll be glad when everything is over, Levit. Glad for you, and glad for all of us. Maybe we could begin to think of other things, too. Tell me, will you know soon?"

"I can't answer that. But Smith had better move fast, if he wants to get here before the Yankees do."

She grimaced, but then the smile broke forth again. "Stand up and turn around, Colonel," she commanded.

"Do what?"

"Stand up and turn around!"

Wonderingly, MacAshen got to his feet. "Truly, you're a different looking person," she said, after eyeing him thoroughly. "You've filled out again, and you've got a man's color back in your face, too. I can say all of that because I saw you when you didn't appear as well."

"I guess you did, at that."

Mrs. Newcomb said, "I'll look toward something for our noonday meal. You'll eat with us, won't you, Colonel?"

"Of course he will!"

Mrs. Newcomb left the room. "You must be strong, Levit MacAshen, to have recovered so quickly," Karryl said.

"I guess I'm pretty hard to turn under."

"I wish I was too." She smiled at him again, then said, "Tell me, Levit, are women out in your prairie country as strong as you men from there?"

"I never thought to ask. Those who were around—well, I don't remember any complaints. Settlers kept 'em busy, so I guess they were strong."

"The young women, Levit?" she coaxed.

"You mean—your age? There just weren't any."

"Now don't tell me there isn't someone waiting for you."

"No, there's no one."

She tossed her mop of hair, looked out the window a moment, then said, "You're anxious to get back home anyway, though, aren't you, Levit? It's written all over you."

"Of course. I've been gone a long time now."

"We see a great many people passing through—going west—

leaving their old homes behind. Wagons—some of them loaded with women and children.''

"I know.''

"Do you think that's good?''

"Some of it, maybe. But the prairies are unsafe right now. The Indians have been burning and killing all up and down. Castoffs from the war are everywhere, too.''

"But you're trying to return to that.''

"I was raised out there, and ranching is all I know. Our range has been lying vacant, empty of stock I mean, for four years now. The thing about it is, if I don't get back, and quick, somebody will grab up everything we had.''

Instantly, she was serious. "I know what it means to lose a home,'' she said, "and I don't blame you for wanting to hurry on.''

When the noonday meal had been served, Karryl said: "I'm glad you came back to see us, and I hope you'll make the Newcomb home your own, as much as you can while you're here.''

"Thank you, Karryl. I've wanted very much to see you again. And I'll do that.''

He walked his horse all the way to the hotel. In the short moment in which he had seen her again, he realized Karryl Newcomb was more of a woman to think about than he had ever been aware of before. Suddenly he was aching for her.

In the next few days MacAshen saw a great deal of Karryl. On one occasion, when he arrived at her home, Burr Wayne was there also.

"Oh, come in, Levit,'' Karryl said when she answered the door.

"I didn't know you'd have company.''

"This is Mr. Wayne,'' she said. "He's an old friend—from Natchez, too—and he's on his way west with his family. Colonel MacAshen, Burr.''

"I'll go on back to town,'' Levit said.

"No indeed. I'd like for you to know Burr. He's someone I grew up with.'' She turned for an instant toward Wayne. "The colonel stayed with us for a while, here,'' she explained. "He was hurt in the fighting, and Aunt Betsy cared for him.''

"You're still in the army?'' Wayne inquired.

"I guess you could say that.''

[80]

"I was too, once. Mississippi volunteers. I'm out of it now—a parolee."

"Where are you headed for?"

"I haven't the slightest idea. It was my father's idea, and I just got home in time to come along. But nowhere in particular, I guess. Just west. We'll light somewhere, sooner or later, though." Wayne turned to Karryl. "I was just about to leave and I'd told Karryl that she ought to come along with us," he said back over his shoulder to MacAshen. "However, she wouldn't listen to me. She's changed," he grinned. "In Natchez she listened to me."

"Burr's sweet," Karryl smiled. "But I have my Aunt Betsy, and I wouldn't want to leave her."

"Well, I guess there's nothing left for me but to get along, then," Wayne said. "Father will be chomping at the bit unless I hurry. So good luck to both of you."

"Good luck to you, too, Burr."

Levit and Karryl went with him to the verandah, watching him go. Karryl raised a hand once in answer to Burr's wave as he passed beyond the pines. Then she went back into the house and Levit followed.

Kirby Smith finally arrived in Houston. He had left Shreveport with the remnants of an army, but it had scattered along the road. Now his hopes were to be shattered by the hard realization that the garrison at Houston also had disappeared.

MacAshen met him on the verandah when he reached the Hutchins House. "Ah, Colonel," Smith recognized him. "This is a dark hour, but I am glad you made it here."

"I'm glad you did, too, sir."

The general appeared tired. He turned to stare up and down the street, surprised, it seemed, that people in these moments could go on about their business as they were doing. "Do they not realize here in Houston that there is a war?" he wondered aloud.

"I doubt it," MacAshen answered. "In fact, I don't think Houston has ever realized there was a war."

Smith took the campaign hat from his head, and ran an arm across his brow. "This city was our last hope," he said.

Next day, General Smith released MacAshen. There was scarcely another officer to be found anywhere, anyway, and

[81]

that quickly became clear even to the general, since the civil authorities were gone too.

MacAshen had finished breakfast when Smith descended the stairway. He followed the general out onto the verandah.

"The war is over," Smith said to the few stragglers there. "Your future duty is plain. Return at once to your families, and resume the occupations of peace. Yield obedience to the laws and labor wherever you can to restore order."

Smith turned back into the hotel and sat down at a writing desk. MacAshen and a few others trailed to stand beside him. "I am composing a message to Colonel Sprague in New Orleans," the general said dejectedly. "I will tell him that the Trans-Mississippi department is now open."

MacAshen got his horse and rode back to the Newcomb house. He found Fall with Karryl on the verandah.

"It's over now, isn't it, Levit?" Karryl asked.

"Yes."

"The Yankees will come soon."

"Likely they will, and I will have to be gone before they do so, or I might never be able to leave at all."

Fall stepped forward. "Have you seen this?" he queried, shoving a newspaper at MacAshen. "Take a look, MacAshen. It just came out. Hell of a thing to happen, now that all the shootin' everywhere else is over."

MacAshen read the account handed him. Major General Jo Shelby, still armed and deadly, had struck out across the state. On June 2, the Iron Brigade was still intact—men who had campaigned up and down the length and breadth of "Bloody"Kansas and Missouri since the earliest days of the war.

MacAshen remembered Shelby from the conference at Marshall. "The Brazos River in Texas, gentlemen, is the new defense line," Shelby had said. "It is a line we can always hold." Apparently, Shelby meant to keep on trying. From a new bivouac at Stone Point, near Kaufman, he had moved southwestward.

"He'll draw Yankees like bees to a plundered hive," Fall said.

7

Wild rumors now swept through Houston. Trials for treason, the arrest of all persons who had ever favored the Southern cause—these were the fears prevailing everywhere. No less a dignitary then Colonel John Baylor purchased space in the newspaper: "Would the soldier who 'borrowed' my bay team and ambulance please return the outfit?"

Flake's *Bulletin* at Galveston reported many important people were in flight, usually for Mexico. Even General Magruder was believed to have been seen in a boxcar headed west toward Alleytown. For those who had no other place to go and no means by which they could flee the bayou city, there was small comfort in any of this.

"What do you make of it?" Mrs. Newcomb asked MacAshen.

"Some people always panic at first. But I don't think Houston has much to worry about from the Yankees."

"With Sheridan coming this way? Go along, Colonel! I wouldn't be too sure."

Karryl, seated in the big arm chair, spoke up too. "This wild general from Missouri, Jo Shelby . . . what about him, Levit?"

"Oh, I don't know. With the war itself over, soldiers carrying guns in Texas could stir up a ruckus, I guess, if they tried to.

But Shelby must realize he can't do anything useful by himself."

MacAshen had gone back to the hotel late in the day, and there he learned that Governor Murrah had suddenly arrived in Houston. MacAshen called on him immediately.

"I'm here to see to it that any terms to which we agree are complied with," he told MacAshen. He also said that a Federal warship would be in Galveston in a day or two, to settle things. "You heard about Shelby?" he asked suddenly. MacAshen nodded. "He worries me," the governor said. "And as soon as I'm through here, I intend to find out what he's up to. I want you to go back to Austin with me to help."

"But I couldn't do anything about Shelby," MacAshen protested quickly.

"Somebody's got to put some sense into his head. It's probably more than a mere civilian like myself could do, but he might listen to a soldier—somebody who'd been in the fighting, too. You could tackle that job, MacAshen, and I want you to try."

MacAshen stood once more in the Newcombs' parlor. "I've come to say goodbye," he said.

"So soon?"

"Yes. Governor Murrah has levied on me again—just because I was close—and available, I guess."

"In heaven's name, what for?"

"General Shelby—the man we were talking about. Murrah wants me to go to Austin to try to argue him out of whatever he's got in mind. Most likely he'll have me shot, instead."

"Levit, don't say that."

"Oh, it won't be that bad, of course, but I'd just as soon not be saddled with any part of it."

"After you've talked with him, what will you do then?"

"Head for home, I guess. I've got to find out what's happened there."

"Will I see you again?"

"Of course, you will." He threw his arms around her, drew her close. "You'll see a lot of me again." Then he kissed her red lips.

Shelby was bivouacked across the river on the damp, ominous night when MacAshen and the governor got back to Austin.

MacAshen saw the encampment as they rode into town.

The attendant at the Mansion House filled MacAshen in on how things had gone since the latter left the city. Austin was in a turmoil. The man said a certain Captain Freeman had been called on to enroll a small force to try to protect public property, but there hadn't been much he could do.

By the time MacAshen had finished supper, it was growing late. The governor had told him to come to the Mansion that evening. As he walked up Congress Avenue, a clock struck ten. Suddenly the sound of firing broke out in the direction of the capitol. MacAshen started to run. At a corner, he almost collided with a man.

"MacAshen!" the latter exclaimed. It was Captain Freeman. "Something doing up there. Are you with us?"

"Yes, Freeman."

They ran toward the capitol grounds, and others joined them as they ran. Then the huge figure of a man blocked their path. "Where do you think you're headed?" he yelled.

The little group halted. "What's going on here?" someone asked.

"Nothin' to concern you, fellow." The big man moved menacingly.

"Get out of the way!" Freeman shouted.

Levit caught the glint on the barrel of a gun. He jerked at his own revolver. The burst of the explosion lit up the spectacle for a second, the report echoing against the trees. The man before them fell and Freeman gratefully glanced at MacAshen. But Freeman wasted no words. They ran on toward the capitol.

A blast from within now rent the air.

"Good God! They're blowing the vaults!"

From ahead the gunfire also increased. As they reached the first levels, MacAshen could see people emerging from the doors of the structure. Acrid fumes poured out after them. The men around MacAshen worked their own guns, the reports puncturing the night in sharp, staccato notes. He heard the whizz of flying balls and he, too, shot at random, a figure here, another there.

Suddenly, it was over as quickly as it began. From the streets behind came the noise of pounding hoofs, dying away in the night.

Murrah raged. "By the saints of heaven!" he stormed. "That

Shelby has raided my own state house." He halted his swift stride before MacAshen. "What'd you say they got?"

"Looked like thousands, Governor," the colonel answered. "They left a trail of specie behind them. Then they crossed the river."

"Come on, Colonel," the governor said angrily. "We'll call on Shelby."

They hurried out the door. Murrah did not wait for a carriage. He stalked down the avenue toward the river crossing. They passed men in the fitful light of the streep lamps, but neither Murrah nor MacAshen replied to their salutations.

The ferryman rowed them across the stream in his little boat. They alighted on the far bank. "Now we'll see Shelby about this raid," Murrah ground out.

"Governor, I think you're on the wrong track," MacAshen said. "I don't believe Shelby had anything to do with it."

"You don't?" Murrah looked at him in surprise.

"No, I don't. Shelby never impressed me as a raider."

They climbed the path. Before them the campfires of the soldiers sputtered. Most of the men were still awake, the noise of the conflict across the river in the city having roused them. A challenge stopped Murrah and MacAshen.

"Who's there?"

"Two men, one the Governor of Texas," Levit answered.

Several men came forward from the circle of light. A few low words were passed, and one of the men turned immediately and hurried into the camp. Another said: "Follow me. Men, go back to your posts."

A corporal led them straight across the central clearway, toward a big tent. As they reached it, a man stepped out, followed by the soldier who had risen from the campfire.

"Governor Murrah!" the man exclaimed. MacAshen recognized him. It was, indeed, Shelby. "You come at an odd hour."

The governor wasted no time. "Shelby," he demanded, "did you raid my state house tonight?"

The cavalryman's jaw dropped. MacAshen saw the lines tighten in his face, and even in the firelight the recession of a healthy tan into the dusky white of complete anger was visible in Shelby's face. "What do you mean, Murrah?"

"I mean the state treasury was blasted tonight, and I want the men who did it."

For a long moment MacAshen feared the Missourian would strike Murrah, break him down. But Shelby appeared to control himself. "I guess you're in a bad way here, Governor, and I won't take offense at your remarks," he said evenly. He raised his voice. "Sergeant, come in here."

A soldier strode immediately into the circle and saluted.

"You in charge of the guard detail tonight?"

"Yes, sir."

"Have any men passed through?"

"None going out, sir. Had eight volunteers come in about sundown."

He turned back to Murrah, studying him for a time. "Does that answer your question, Governor?"

Murrah fidgeted, but Shelby was magnanimous. He recognized the strain under which Murrah had acted. The governor clasped and unclasped his hands. Shelby laid a hand upon his shoulder, and Murrah turned about to stare thoughtfully at him.

"Reckon I was wrong, General," the governor declared. "I had you down for a raider. Just can't tell what's going on around here now. I apologize."

A dull, angry murmur rose from the men nearby. Shelby looked at them, then he held up the flap of the tent and motioned Murrah and MacAshen into the shelter. "My men are tough," he said, "and bitter. But they're not bandits."

The governor said: "I've been worried about you, Shelby. What do you plan to do?"

The general clenched his hands behind him as he strode slowly up and down before his guests. "The men have voted," he declared. "The Iron Brigade will not surrender. But your problem here tonight shows clearly we must move on. Mexico, I guess."

The governor sighed in undisguised relief. He rose from the camp stool and turned toward the entrance, raising the tent flap. As he prepared to step through, he turned back toward Shelby. "I've a much different opinion of you, General," he said, "and I'm glad I came. I'll be in touch with you again." He went on down the river path, MacAshen following.

Next morning, from his window in the hotel looking off across the river to the west, MacAshen saw them ride away. The

Iron Brigade was gone. He felt a sadness for them, for in their going he knew he had witnessed the last disciplined effort in the sequence of the Confederacy. The column was too far distant to make out Shelby, but MacAshen knew he would be up front somewhere with his black plume and his standard.

A summons from the governor's residence came early to MacAshen. The black butler met him at the door, and as he was let in, Levit saw deep gravity in the old man's eyes. Something tragic had occurred during the night. The servant led MacAshen to the study. Fletcher Stockdale was there. "I'm glad you're still here, MacAshen," he said.

"Trouble?"

"Trouble, yes. But something more than that. Murrah has fled."

"Murrah, too!" he ejaculated. "Where has he gone?"

"To Mexico, I guess. He went away sometime before dawn, joining up with Shelby beyond the river. Smith, Magruder, Governor Reynolds of Missouri, Allen of Louisiana, Lyon of Kentucky—all the men who should be here to speak for the people."

"Well, some of us will have to stay, that's sure."

"I'll stay, MacAshen. I can tell you that the job won't be one a man should seek, but I took an oath when I accepted the office of lieutenant governor, and I'll see it out."

"For whatever it's worth, I'll be around, too, Stockdale."

The latter walked to the window and looked out. "You were one of Forrest's commanders and I've heard you might be wanted," he said after a time. "You wouldn't do us any good in a Federal stockade. Stick on here for a while longer, until I check into a few things. Then go back to that rancho of yours and keep your eyes peeled."

Fall rode into town again a few days after Murrah had left, and met MacAshen in the hotel lobby. After he had conveyed his usual salutations, along with Karryl's good wishes, he said: "There's something I want to post you on, MacAshen. Just before I left, I was tending shop when two Rebs ankle in and belly up to the bar.

"'Just passing through?' I asked them.

"One of these Rebs was a middle-aged man, kind of broken-down. Looked like he'd been sick and maybe in a Union prison.

The other was a boy about nineteen. Black hair, about five feet ten, or eleven, eyes like a cat.

"'Yes, just passing through,' the older guy answered me.

"'Been over around Tennessee or maybe Alabama, and through there, haven't you?' I went on.

"'Yep, been over in Tennessee and Alabama.'

"The Rebs finished their drinks, then it was the boy who asked me, direct like—and he was the kind you don't keep waiting too long for answers—he asked me slow an' easy if I'd seen a feller around with a hole in his side, a soldier from the Tennessee fights—named MacAshen.

"I allowed as how maybe I had and maybe I hadn't. I did not seem to remember. But this boy wasn't the kind you could fool too easy.

"They rode on, and I figured you ought to know about it, just in case it was important."

MacAshen slapped a hand across his thigh. "Ord!" he said.

"Ord?"

"A man I knew in the army back in Tennessee. A man I've been through a lot with. Did he say where he was headed?"

"No."

"Well, watch out for him. If he shows up again, tell him I asked for him."

"Sure, Colonel, sure. But he didn't show no signs of sticking to the bayous."

"I'd like to have a man like Ord around in the days ahead," MacAshen reflected, as if to himself.

When the news of Murrah's flight reached Houston, Devers especially was interested. "It smooths things some," he said to one of his men. "Murrah's always been a hard nut to crack. I'm just as glad he's out of the way."

"When do you calculate to hear from New Orleans?"

"Not before the Union soldiers move in. I put what I had to say down on paper while that ship was at Galveston to get Smith's surrender, and sent it along."

"Maybe the Feds will want you for another chore somewhere else."

"Well, it's in the government end, not soldiering, that the money lies now that the war is over."

While he waited to hear from the Union officials at New

Orleans, Devers went back to the Newcomb house.

"Not you, again," Karryl bristled.

"Yes."

"Why don't you let me alone?"

"Because thoughts of you don't let me alone, Karryl Newcomb. There's a concert by the colored people down at the opera house tonight, and I thought maybe you'd let me take you to it."

"Well, I won't."

"Why hole up here, like you're doing? You ought to be getting out in the whirl of things. It would do you good."

"I'm not holed up. I just don't want to have anything to do with you."

"Think you're entitled to be so lofty with me? Take my word for it, you'd be safer here if you tried to be friendly."

"You're wasting your time. Why don't you leave?"

"Because I've heard that people change sometimes. This isn't Mississippi out here—it's Texas."

"I'll never change the way I feel toward you."

"All right," Devers finally said. "I'm sorry if you're still of that mind. You know why I didn't show up to sail on that packet better than anybody. I don't hold grudges, but since you're planning on staying like you are, I've got just this much to say: You won't make me out for a fool and get away with it."

Now his black eyes bored into her and she sensed something new behind the needle stare. He was suddenly angry, angrier than she had ever seen a man. Now, mixed with her disgust for the first time was fear. Previously, she had thought of him only as a bad experience in her life, and one she could handle. But the possibility that he was really venomous had not occurred to her. A sense of panic displaced her feeling of disgust. She could not stay here in Houston, for Devers would reveal her to the Yankees. She had to go. But where to?

There were flooding rainstorms for the next two days. Even the people who normally had business outside were forced from the streets while they waited for the torrents to lessen. A week slipped by before the sunshine dried the mudbanks once more.

Although foreboding obsessed Karryl, it was not until Devers again stalked up to her, in the garden by the house, that she realized the validity of her misgivings. He seemed propelled by some kind of savage impulse.

"I want to talk with you, Miss Newcomb," he muttered.

"I told you to stay away from me, and there's nothing more you can say that I want to hear."

"Oh, maybe there is. At least, I can try. I've never had this kind of an experience before, but I can't keep my mind on anything else." His words were ponderous, almost belligerent. "I plan to be important in these parts. You and me, we're a pair, Miss Newcomb, and you'd realize it if you tried to reason a little. All you've had you've lost, but I'll not be one to suffer from the war, and neither will you if you'll listen.

"I've got interests here and other places. I could be good for you—we could be good for each other. I'd like to ask you one more time to unbend. I'm not above getting married, if that's what you want."

His outburst left the girl aghast. "He's been drinking, she thought desperately.

Devers towered over her, only a step away, his feet apart and firmly planted in the garden soil, his fingers outstretched, sinewy, and raised a little.

"Do you really imagine I'd marry you, Mr. Devers?" she cried out.

"I'd think you might." A defensive quality diluted the leaden voice for an instant, and just a trace of something else seemed to touch the corners of his mouth. But then both were gone, as he added, "And it might be the best thing for you that you ever did."

All she could read in his face now was the warning of great danger. She backed hurriedly toward the steps. "Stay away from me," she cried as he clasped and unclasped his burly hands.

She fled, leaving him standing there. As she passed the door, she saw old Joshua backing away, his hand upon the muzzle loader behind the drapes. "No, Josh!" she said.

Karryl did not wait for Fall to come to see her when he got back to Houston that night. She sent for him.

"Mr. Fall," she burst out, "I've got to leave Houston. Can you take me west with you?"

"West, miss? Where to in the west?"

"Anywhere, Mr. Fall."

"Austin, maybe?"

"Yes."

"When do you want to leave?"

"As quickly as we can. I've got to go quickly."

"We'll need horses. Can you ride?"

"I can ride. Do you want to know what's happened?"

"Later. I figure something special, and you just tell me everything on the road. We'll get out early tomorrow. Fix some vittles. I'll rustle horses if I have to shoot somebody."

Next morning the two of them—Fall and Karryl—rode out of the stable behind the house, and down the San Bernard trail toward the Colorado. Karryl was clothed in the old garb of a Confederate soldier.

8

Almost at the same hour that Karryl Newcomb and Fall depart-
ed Houston, two men in Confederate uniforms forded the Brazos River some miles to the west, scarcely realizing that they,
too, were now fated for roles in a rapidly tightening drama related to many people, most of whom were yet unknown to them.

These were the two men Fall had mentioned to MacAshen.
They hurried along a trail flanked by the plantation homes of
early Texas colonists. They had waited several days before
moving farther west from the bayous, resting in a small community on the outskirts of Houston. Now, as they rode along,
they observed the landmarks, establishing the direction of their
journey. To the north, the log outlines of Orozimbo, prison
place of Santa Anna, stood out; and far below the road, the
green fringe of the coastal marshes diffused into the skyline.

"Ain't Matagorda that way, Ord?" the older man asked finally. His companion nodded, and they corrected their direction.
Throughout the region the twisted branches of the trees de-
noted the influence of the prevailing winds that swept in from
the Gulf of Mexico. They crossed the Navidad, richly luxuriant
with its clumps of hedge roses and vast clusters of wild mustang
grapes. North of Lavaca Bay, they reined back again toward
the western ranchlands to avoid the possibility of encountering

any Federals that might have landed in the harbor.

At sundown, as the heat of the summer day began to wane, the man Ord knew as Salado Joe Garner pointed out a small campfire near a meandering stream. A stranger beside the campfire rose on their approach.

"Evenin', boys," he called.

Ord looked the man over carefully. He nodded and Salado waved a friendly greeting.

"Get down and pull up a chair," the camper invited. "Was just working up a few vittles. Guess there's coffee enough, and I'm a real hand at sourdough, but you'll have to furnish the bacon."

The two Confederates prodded their horses up to the campsite, noting that the stranger's dun mare was hobbled in a small grove of cypress nearby.

"Thanks," Salado responded heartily, swinging to the ground. Ord followed, but he kept a careful, practical eye on his host while he dismounted. His action was not lost on the man, nor the way in which Ord carried his right hand close to the big black gun on his thigh. The camper chuckled.

"You've got nothing to worry about from me," he assured the new arrivals, while he busied himself stoking the fire, "and I figure I've got nothing that would interest anybody else. Spread your tarps and make yourselves at home."

His free and easy manner was assurance enough, and Ord led the horses away to the cypress grove. Salado and the camper were in high conversation when he returned.

"Meet the 'professor,' Ord," Salado said. Ord accepted the outstretched hand.

"Like I was saying," the man resumed cheerily, "either one of you fellows might be Shanghai Pierce, or even Pendleton Murrah. It's all the same to me; I'm glad to see you." He tapped his chest. "I wander around because of my health, and it gets mighty lonesome. Always pleasant to meet someone to pass the time of day with."

Their host had a stooped posture and a pale, though freckled, countenance, bearing out his admission of ill-health. But the quick, dancing sparkle in his brown eyes contributed an air of honest tranquility.

"Guess you fellows have done a mite of soldiering," he observed, as he went forward with preparations for the meal.

"See quite a few former Confederates now, most of them headed for the border. Getting to be quite a populous country, that
borderland. Of course, it's some piece from here. And nothing
between here and there—in the Brasada—but mesquite and
chaparral and thorns. And, of course, the Lipans. But most
people make it, finally."

"Sounds like you get around," Ord remarked. "Still plenty
of open country down there?"

"Most ranges are open hereabouts. There's Indians around
sometimes, but the Indians aren't the main threats a man has
to face these days, at least in south Texas. To raise cattle, or
sheep, or even to farm the bottoms, people have to be on the
lookout for Mexican bandits and just plain white cattle thieves
and killers, too."

"Where are the Rangers?"

"There are no Rangers now, and so there's not much chance
of policing the gun-throwers. Just have to find a better man
with a gun. Not many like that for hire."

He paused for a moment, then continued.

"But it's not just the gunmen, either. Trouble's growing fast
in Texas. The war's done things to men. Every settler, every
cowboy, wears a pistol on his hip. And they use 'em, often on
each other. People are worried, and I guess they're nervous,
times being what they are. Honest settlers, ranchers, will throw
down on their own neighbors for little or nothing, often just a
matter of opinion. Texans don't even count the killings among
the border counties any more. Everybody's leery of the man
he meets—that is, if he's got anything to lose—and he'll reach
for his gun before he even weighs the consequences. It's a
tragic thing, considering the other enemies most folks have to
face."

Afterward, as the stars came out, they lay back on their
tarps and rested. The "professor's" heavy breathing soon indicated he was asleep. Ord stared upward at the stars. Salado
stirred on the ground beside him.

"Reckon you better be cutting loose for the Killeen country
soon," Ord said. Salado sat up.

"You mean, run out on you?"

"Guess that's what I meant."

"What were you plannin' for yourself, Ord?"

"I'll keep on, close to the mesquite for a while, at least until

[95]

I find out if the Federals are tailing me."

"What makes you think they'll run you down, Ord? The war is ended, remember?"

"I'm not thinking they'll run me down, Salado, but I intend to be careful. They won't think well of the way that Yankee sergeant was shot, just as the Confederates surrendered."

"You didn't know you were being surrendered, man. And they didn't know you were such a slick hand with a gun—when you could get your paws on one. Get it off your mind."

"I'll keep on for a while, anyway."

"What about the colonel? You were thick with him."

"MacAshen?" Ord turned his head aside. "I don't know," he answered finally. "Told me once he'd like for me to ride for him, if I made it through the war. He was good to me. Guess he got back to that ranch up in the hill country. Leastways, he got as far as Houston. But I won't go on there yet. If they've got me on the list, I wouldn't want to draw the Yankees down on MacAshen, too."

He rolled a cigarette and lighted it.

"I'd like to have somewhere to go, though," he muttered.

They pushed on early the next day, moving southwest in the direction of the old mission town of Refugio. It was a typical south Texas community, with sprawling houses of logs, offset by stores with high board fronts. On the edge of the community they came to a restaurant and saloon. "Get a drink and order food while I put the horses around back," Ord told Salado.

The scene inside the saloon was typical of the border country. Booted, vested riders milled in the smoky room and a few shuffled cards on a table near the door. Two men were seated behind a table at the far wall, their clothing identifying them as one-time soldiers. Salado was waiting for Ord at the end of the bar. And as Ord joined his companion, he noted various eyes about the room on him.

A tall, sandy-haired man, narrow of face but boasting a high forehead, ambled slowly toward them, his milky blue eyes a trifle sad. A dull star shone on his vest. Salado had only a moment to give Ord a look that clearly urged caution. He cast a fleeting glance at the stern, taut faces of the riders clustered down the bar.

"Mawnin', son," the marshal greeted him.

"Howdy."

"You a stranger hereabouts, ain't you?"

"Yes. Passing through."

"What's your name?"

"Ord. My partner here is mostly called Salado."

"Been soldiering?"

"Reckon so. Leastways, we thought we were."

The marshal grinned. "Where you headed?"

"Nowhere in particular. Just planned to keep on going."

"Uh-huh. Guess that's what most people coming through here hope to do," he agreed. At that moment, the bartender stepped from the rear door with two plates of food. He set steaming mugs of coffee before Ord and Salado. The marshal turned back to the crowd at the other end of the bar.

Ord began to eat. Beyond him Salado's eyes spoke eloquently.

The discord of broken conversation was heavy in the room. The men at the opposite end of the bar were particularly noisy.

"I tell you, Lockett," a strong voice said, "it's the riding renegades that are stealing us clean. What're you marshal around here for?"

The rancher was evidently testy from hard traveling and over-indulgence. Ord observed that the marshal faced him calmly but respectfully.

"Take it easy, Calder," he said. "Lots of boys slopin' for the river these days. That don't mean they're thieves."

A companion tried to restrain the rancher, but he gathered support from two hands with him, boys in their teens, who backed him up. He turned to stare at Ord and Salado. His eyes were dark and threatening. Then he filled his glass again. The clamor continued to rise, frequently punctuated with a curse.

"Reckon nobody'll be able to keep anything till we run these drifters off the range." To Ord, the words seemed to grind out. The whiskey had whetted the rancher's venom. He whirled around again.

A fourth lanky rider with Calder laid a hand on his arm, but the rancher shook it off. He shoved out of the little group and stalked toward Ord and Salado. The Confederates continued their meal, but Ord was keenly watchful now.

Here, apparently, was one of those Texans of whom the "professor" had spoken a short while ago. He had something on his mind and apparently Ord and Salado's arrival gave vent to anger.

"Saddlebums ain't welcome in these parts," Calder snapped. Ord ate silently, standing at the bar.

"I said saddlebums ain't welcome around here. Maybe you've already seen a few horses you could pick up."

Still Ord did not reply.

"You hear me, fellow?" Calder shouted. Ord stepped clear, his back to Salado, at the end of the bar.

"I hear you, Calder," he answered slowly. "And now you listen to me. We came in here to eat, not to bother anybody. We're not looking for trouble and we're hoping you won't bring any on."

The big pasty-faced man recoiled. Ord's response to his outburst seemed to startle him. He shook his head as if to clear it. Who did this tramp think he was? Suddenly Calder froze into a muscular crouch. Ord knew that stance. The man had started something and now he wanted to make it good.

"Keep away from that pistol, you fool!" Ord snapped.

But the man clawed downward, and even as he did so Ord pivoted and drew. The muzzle of the big Dance gun jabbed deep into Calder's belly before the rancher could even get his own weapon from the holster.

"Wait!" the marshal yelled.

"We came in here peaceably," Ord clipped out, his voice penetrating to the far corners. "But we can change that."

The marshal jerked Calder's gun out of its holster. He threw the pistol on the bar and spun the pasty-faced man around. "You're bad medicine when you're drinking, Calder," he snapped. "You most nigh got it that time." He turned to Ord. "Why didn't you kill him, fellow?"

Ord slowly returned his own gun to its holster. "Maybe I should have."

"But you didn't."

A vast curiosity seemed to permeate the room. "What'd you say your name was?" the marshal asked.

"Ord."

"Well, Ord, hope I never meet up with you again myself except on friendly terms. Fastest draw I ever saw in my life."

It was a compliment, by men in a country where speed with a gun was a man's best introduction, but Ord was in no mood for compliments. He shoved through the door and off the verandah.

Fifty miles to the west, Ord and Salado halted. They encountered a trader's wagon train on the ford of the Nueces. The wagonmaster was alert and suspicious, and Ord noticed guns in the hands of the teamsters. They appraised Ord and his companion at length before inviting them to dismount.

It was a big convoy, traveling fast, up from the Rio Grande toward Houston. "Guess you're heading for the river," the wagonmaster observed. He poured a steaming cup of coffee for each of the riders.

"Yes," Salado agreed.

A meal of fried steaks was popping on the campfires. The teamster invited them to eat.

"Seen anything of Shelby?" Ord inquired. The teamster raised his bushy eyebrows.

"You figuring on joining him?"

"Maybe. Heard he was headed for Mexico with an army."

"Well, you can turn around and go back. On the day we cleared Eagle Pass, he sank his flag and his black plume in the Rio Grande. Sold his guns and his cannon to the Mexicans. And his men are scattered. Some gone across the river as colonists. Some back to Missouri or East Texas or wherever they came from."

They left the wagon train when the first streaks of dawn appeared, riding up the east bank of the river now. Later, they passed the ruins of the crumbling Mission Nuestra Señora del Rosario de los Cujanes. In the distance the outlines of the Presidio de la Bahía were visible. Ord and Salado camped that night in a grove of elms, and early the next day moved on, northward still, toward the cattle country. In the back of Ord's mind, that name, the Pedernales, kept arising. He said little, and the prospect of the future weighed heavily upon him. But he could not even seek out his friends here in Texas, if any such remained, until he knew that he could do so without endangering them.

But he didn't want Salado to become involved in anything that might prevent him from returning someday to a peaceful life on the Texas frontier.

Suddenly Ord squared his horse around in Salado's path. "I'm moving on to the Sabinal, Joe," he said. "But you're going north, straight for Bell County, where you came from."

Salado started to remonstrate, but Ord silenced him with a gesture.

"Bad luck's started trailing with me, Salado, and anybody who rides along is bound to have some of it wear off on him. So far, you're clean and you're getting along home while the getting's good. Travel with me and you'll be an outlaw before you know it."

"Aw, Ord!"

"Never mind that now." Ord extended a hand. "The war's over, so far as you're concerned, and you're going home. Now move on without making it worse," he commanded.

Salado swallowed. There was a long trail behind the two of them. But the pull of his homeland was written all over his face. Slowly, Ord turned the head of his own mount west. "So long, pard," the black-haired youth called, and waved. Then he was gone, leaving Salado gazing silently in the roadway.

9

Far to the north from such scenes as Ord's parting with Salado—
as far north as the villages on the Cimarron River—there was
great sorrow in those weeks. But it was a sorrow unrelated to
the white men. To-Hausen, venerable chief of the Kiowa and
senior warrior among all Plains tribes, was dead. Lone Wolf, already infamous for cruelty and depredations along the frontier,
was chosen to succeed him. As a result, the Comanche quickly
met at Cottonwood Grove to select new leaders for their own
bands. One was a tall, hook-nosed savage who answered to the
name of Tosawi. Another was called Quee-Nigh-Tosav, White
Eagle.

Months before, White Eagle had done his hours of solitude
on the Medicine Bluff in the Wichitas, preparing himself for this
chieftainship. He had waited there for a vision—for the revelation from the spirits beyond—and out of that vision he had
drawn his *puha*, the power to lead others.

Parro-o-coom, the old war chief of the Quohada, had encouraged White Eagle in the consummation of this ritual, for Parro-
o-coom was nearing the end of his own days, and the Comanche
must have a strong, commanding war chief to succeed him.

White Eagle had sat four days there on the slope of the Medicine Bluff, oblivious to the beauty of the crescent or the music

of its rivulets below. He had prayed for power while he smoked and waited. He had fasted, too, and felt the penetration of loneliness. Each dawn had brought him to his full height, staring off toward the rising sun, seeking the power of this father of the Comanche while it warmed his body, but the sun had not provided his *puha*.

At last, when his quest had begun to appear fruitless, he had heard the scream of the mountain eagle for which he had been named. It was a predatory eagle, and it came to him as the thunderbird had come to the Comanche, bearing the lightning in its claws and the storms of the heavens upon its wings. From this bird he claimed his vision. From the vision he claimed the *puha* of the thunderbird—the power to lead others.

Then he had started back to the Palo Duro. He crossed the vast sweep of the South Canadian. Tricklets of water laced the dunes before him, eventually merging into one broad, shallow silver expanse; and there was sand blowing on the bed of the river.

Afterward he came to the canyon country where he lived. The tipis were behind the distant pinnacles, protected from the winds that still blew cold from the northwest.

His mustang stepped slowly around the base of a loaf-like mound, a thousand feet high. The course of the creek turned southwest, the walls of the canyon narrowing momentarily; then the gorge opened wide, to effect a grand bend toward the north. Here the floor was broken, and rising in its center was a vast, eroded red mound, like a buffalo sleeping upon its hooves, its head to the south, protected from the snows. Quee-Nigh-Tosav's home was close.

He could hear before he could see: the snarling, snapping howl of the spotted dogs; the brash, though modulated, undertone of village life. From the cover at his side rose the wild unseasonal call of the chachalaca, and from beyond the low scudding rises of the canyon sounded the sudden ruffle of mating grouse.

The tipis were on the creek below the mound. White Eagle studied them carefully as he approached. His young squaws would be glad that he had returned. There would be fresh meat from the hump of the buffalo, and perhaps even a great trout from the stream.

He wondered if Parro-o-coom had sent new war parties back

along the Concho and into the Lampasas country during his absence. If so, how far had they ridden? To the San Saba? To the Llano? Perhaps even to the Pedernales? The end of the white man's war was anticipated, he had heard, and soon the Texans would be sweeping across the Comanche hunting grounds again. White Eagle scowled, meditating upon whether he might not have been elected by the Great Spirit to stop these intruders once and for all.

But all that had been months before. Spring had succeeded winter in the Palo Duro and had passed. Now summer was at hand again. The Comanche were restive, as they always were at this season of the year. They had met in tribal council to elect new and more vigorous leaders. White Eagle's thoughts lay impatiently now upon the line of guarded cabins where the rivers knifed through the country called "the hills."

While white men lived and prospered in those regions, there could be no peace for the Comanche. He must never give the white men time to feel they were secure in their tiny settlements, or they would sweep out across the Quohada hunting grounds. The Quohada feared this enemy but would never show it.

Fear and uncertainty were not burdens exclusive to the Indians. For the very white men who stirred Redskin alarm now had some ominous matters of their own to worry about. For one thing, the Yankee general, Gordon Granger, arrived at Galveston on June 19, bringing with him eighteen hundred Union soldiers and Houston was occupied on June 20.

The bayou people feared the Yankee occupation troops more than they did the Indians and many of them had loaded into their wagons and started west.

Standifer Wayne, luckily, had gone on before this new exodus developed and, although the Waynes were pointing directly at the country which had most to fear from Indian atrocity, Standifer had been told just about how far he could go in safety. His easy confidence was accompanied by relief at having escaped the coastal lands before the Yankees' arrival.

At Gonzales, Standifer Wayne asked questions.

"You'll find the land beyond this county open," he was informed by an old gentleman who introduced himself as Judge

Stapleton. "The cotton ends here and the range begins. Many nationalities in these parts, farming or ranching. Poles, Germans, even Irish. There are Alsatians at Castroville, and Bohemians in many places. Italians, too, south and east, toward Houston. Most of them came in through Copano, or Indianola.

"You won't have any trouble," the judge added, "unless the rustlers hit you, but I'd still look for something close, now. Indians have been staying north of the Comal Springs, but you never know where the renegades will turn up."

The ranch land Standifer finally chose lay some fifty miles above Gonzales in a rolling prairie region between the Guadalupe and San Marcos rivers. The little village of Seguin was some fifteen miles to the west. An equal distance to the north, across the San Marcos, lay the tiny community of Prairie Lea. Beyond was the basin of the Blanco, and beyond that, the Pedernales.

"Reckon we're lucky to be able to sell," the former owner told Standifer Wayne. "Me and my old lady, we're about played out. Been here since the early forties. We had a boy and hoped he'd take the place and make a home for us on this land; but he died at Shiloh, and we haven't got anybody left."

The old couple, whose name was Gardner, took temporary quarters in a nearby cabin while winding up their affairs, and the Waynes moved into the old ranch house in time for Margaret's sixteenth birthday. Burr had patched up the roof and the things they had brought made the place livable and homey. There were peaches on the trees and soon they would be ripe and sweet.

Across the prairie a score of miles away also lay the little cow town of Luling, and Burr went there in search of ranch hands. He had found two: a gnarled old range product by the name of Adam Grippa, and a gangling, freckle-faced boy named Possum Wear.

Gardner, his affairs settled, came by for a last goodbye. Now familiar with the ranch, Burr told him, "I think we can make a pretty good home here, Mister Gardner."

The old man agreed. "It used to be a fine ranch, son, and I'm mighty glad to see somebody come in who has the feel of the land." Then he took Burr aside. "Just one word of advice, though," he said. "This is still a wild country and it'll be more so, especially for young bloods like you, though by your looks you've had a bit of weathering yourself. Riding outfits come by often—hard men, just out of the war. Usually they don't make trouble. Treat them civilly, but don't cotton to them. Give them a beef when you have to, or swap them a horse if they need it. But keep them traveling, or you'll never last to enjoy it here."

10

Karryl's exhaustion, even before her arrival in Austin, was matched only by one thing—her relief in having escaped Devers in Houston. She was sure that she had fled Houston not a moment too soon.

Fall took her to the hotel and arranged a room. He had food brought in. "Sleep," he instructed her. "Sleep a long time. I'll be around right on the spot till you wake up and we have a chance to talk again, so don't you worry none."

She did sleep—from that afternoon through the evening.

Morning roused Karryl. Aching, scarcely able to touch a finger to her skin anywhere, she climbed from the bed. The old Confederate uniform she had worn on the trail was piled in a corner. The saddle pack, containing what few articles she had been able to bring along, lay on the floor unopened. Karryl limped across the room, and stared out the window at the rows of little fortress-like stone houses threading off into the distance, then raised her eyes to the far hills.

"Thank God," she murmured fervently and almost unbelievingly, "I've made it this far."

She went back to the bedside. Bending down in spite of the jabs in her back she lifted the saddle pack onto the bed and opened it. For just an instant, she picked among the few womanish things there, wondering just what she could possibly do now.

"I'll do whatever I have to," she decided finally, tossing her red hair. The little bag of silver pesos Aunt Betsy had given her would support her personal needs for the time being. She simply would not let the thought of the future unnerve her. What other experiences could anyone possibly anticipate more complex than the ones she'd left behind?

"But dear God," she murmured humbly, "just let me be for a while."

She sat on the side of the bed. "At least I should try to look my best." She spread the garments out and made a selection, and quickly dressed. She combed her hair into a red knot on the back of her head and pinched up the color in her cheeks.

Levit? What would he think of her—running off across the country like this, apparently to live all by herself. Would he feel, because he had held her in his arms and kissed her, that she . . . Karryl sighed. This, too, was something that would just have to take care of itself.

Perhaps he'd already left Austin. She finished her preparations and went out into the hall. No, Levit hadn't left the city yet. He was waiting for her, at the foot of the stair, and Fall was at his elbow. "I brought somebody to see you." The old man grinned.

"You certainly did," Karryl murmured. She walked on down. "You didn't expect to see me here, did you?" she said to Levit.

"Well, I can't say I did. But I'm mighty pleased to do so."

She smiled at him. "I'm terribly hungry."

"I can imagine you are. And so am I. We've been waiting for you."

MacAshen took her arm and led her across the lobby to the dining room. Inside, he turned her gently in the direction of a table on the far side. "That's my place over there," he said.

She wondered if he'd ask her exactly why she'd come. And if so, should she answer him? But, instead, he said: "I'm glad you left Houston, Karryl. I was worried for you there."

She glanced at Fall. The old man obviously had told Levit only as much as he needed to tell him. "I decided, all at once, that perhaps it was best, at least for me."

Breakfast was served. "I guess you're pretty sore from

[107]

bouncing around on that horse Fall got for you." MacAshen grinned.

"I've got some aches, all right."

"Well, taking care of the inside may cut down on the trouble from the outside."

"I've not lost my appetite," she said. "I thought you'd be gone, Levit. Why are you still in Austin?"

"Murrah ran out on us, as I guess you know by now. There's a new man in the governor's chair, Fletcher Stockdale. He asked a few of us to stick around for a little longer. Just to bolster his nerve, I guess."

Fall said, "We've been trying to make some plans for you, young lady."

"I don't want you to do that. Honestly, I don't. I can look out for myself, and Levit here must certainly look to his own affairs out west. Aunt Betsy gave me a little money—Mexican silver she'd been able to save—and that will take care of me for a while. After that, I'll simply have to find some way to provide for myself."

"You mean work?" Levit asked.

"Of course."

"I didn't mean that the way it sounded," Levit came back instantly. "Certainly you'll get along. More than that, I'd like to take you on to the Pedernales with me. But right now, you're far better off in Austin. One thing, though, I can do for you is find you a place to live here. A place among friendly folks, and away from the hotel."

"I would be glad to have you do that much, Levit."

When the meal was concluded, Fall pushed back his chair. "I was waiting for you to make it down the stairs, Miss Karryl," he said. "Now I've got to hit that trail back to the bayou." Karryl nodded silently.

"You take everything easy and gentle-like for a while, miss," the old man admonished her. "Sooner or later, I'll be back."

"I'll make out," she assured him.

Levit and Karryl rose with Fall. Fall gathered up his things near the door and the three of them went onto the verandah. "Let me know how it goes," Fall said to MacAshen.

"I will."

Levit and Karryl watched Fall disappear down the road. From the verandah she looked about her at the things close by.

"Are you worried?" Levit asked.

"Well, a little, of course." She turned to him. "Levit," she said, "I hope you'll not let my coming to Austin influence in any way at all whatever you have to do."

He put an arm around her, holding her tightly beside him. "Your coming to Austin is about the pleasantest thing I can think of that's happened to me," he said truthfully.

Stockdale gave him his leave.

"The Yankees will be here soon now, Colonel," he said. "I had thought maybe we could get together and figure out some way to square off a stop-line somewhere out your way beyond which the Indians couldn't come. Something to try to keep you folks alive till things settle down again. But it's too late for any of us to try to do that now. The Yankees would just put a halter on us."

Stockdale handed a yellow notesheet across the table to Mac-Ashen. "I don't have to tell you how things are, where you're going," he said. "But maybe the good Lord will come up with something. This report came in no more than two hours ago. The Redskins have hit again near the mouth of the Concho. That's your country."

Levit nodded.

"The frontier will fold up like the leaves in a book unless something happens," the governor said.

"Maybe not, Stockdale."

"Get back to your home, MacAshen, but keep in touch with us. There's work ahead."

"I'll do that."

Levit left the man then, who was to fill the role of chief executive of the state for only a tumultuous fourteen days.

On the verandah of the Mansion House he told Karryl of his parting with Stockdale. "I'll have to go quickly now," he said to her, "or I might never get the chance again. And I've got to find out at least what's happened to what I had on the Pedernales."

"I've been expecting that, Levit," she answered.

"I've found a place for you to live, Karryl—if you think you could accept my suggestion. Get your bonnet and I'll take you to see it. If you do like it, move your things in.

"All right, Levit."

[109]

The home he took her to was the little white cottage on the hill. There she met The Rev. Mr. Whipple and his wife. "This is the young lady I was telling you about," Levit said to them.

Mrs. Whipple put her arm around Karryl. "We're glad to have someone like you coming to live with us," she said. "We don't see many young people anymore. You'll find we don't live extravagantly, but we're comfortable."

"Thank you Mrs. Whipple, and I'll be grateful if you'll take me in."

At midnight, on the verandah of the Mansion House, Levit kissed Karryl goodbye.

"I don't know exactly what to say to you," he confessed slowly. "I know what I would like to say, but the way things are, I can't. I don't know how it will be for me, for a while, and I couldn't burden anyone with that kind of outlook."

"Do the best you can, Levit. And I'll think of you every day."

He drew her close, burying his face in her hair. Then, silently he nudged her, and she backed into the hotel.

MacAshen rode west in the early dawn, fording the river at the foot of the avenue. Across the Colorado, the trail wound through the draws, then up the limestone cliffs. The road was fairly well defined this close to Austin and, when he surmounted the near heights, a vista of low, rolling blue ranges opened up far in the distance. The clouds seemed to rest upon the earth, and in the direction of the river, stark, uneven ridges marked the foothills stretching toward the falls of the Colorado.

In a small grove of spreading live oaks he met an old settler from the Flat Rock country, pushing for Austin with a load of hides. "How goes it on the ranges?" Levit asked.

The settler nodded his head toward the country of the falls, in the north. "Moochakah Comanches have been busy up there," he said.

Eight miles west of the ridges, Levit halted again in a little grove of pecans. When he had rested, he turned north toward the Bee Caves. Redbud and mountain laurel—the mescal bean— were everywhere. The maroon and yellow of the bachelor's button colored the open stretches. MacAshen passed a deserted stone house, its white and mortared walls spectral-like upon the pathway. Occasionally, he noted rainwater in the stone pools close at hand.

The Bee Caves were as he remembered them, some twenty miles from Austin, and he turned west as he passed them. Two miles onward, he crossed the Little Barton; around the Shingle Hills, he pointed toward the Pedernales country. The terrain grew rougher. The winding road, with occasional ascents, offered frequent panoramas of the distant rises, slopes of dark bear grass and cedar covered mesas. He came upon a sudden sweep to the north that gave a view of more than fifty miles, range on range of dark hills, each higher in the background. Closer at hand the shimmer of tiny streams knifed through the rolling valleys.

Suddenly, near the end of day, Old Warrior halted abruptly.

The scudding, white clouds seemed to move back, the ground ahead fell away, and MacAshen again looked down upon the canyon of the Pedernales.

The river was clear and sparkling, inviting the traveler, as it had invited the Redskins for a thousand years. The path declined steeply toward the floor of the canyon. Spruce, cypress, and cottonwood reared their heads to great heights. Vast root formations spread out among the stones of the channel and the water splashed in deep pools between the shallow rapids.

Levit made his camp for the night under the spread of a huge cypress. His tiny campfire cast fitful shadows upon the heavy walls close at hand, but he slept the assuring sleep of the returning wanderer and Old Warrior stayed close beside him. He was on his way again at dawn.

North of the canyon, he was in the ranges, but he kept the course of the river in sight on his left. It was higher now, and the terrain was vastly greener. Except for the post oak and occasional scrub cedar, the country was open. For the first time, Levit saw again the lemon yellow of the mesquite blossom. Thorny branches of the legume caught once at his boot top, and he plucked a cluster of pennate leaves, pressing them between his fingers as he rode along. There was tannic acid in the mesquite, decay resistant.

He topped a rise in the prairie, from which the far ranges became visible again. In the distance the chains seemed endless and, upon the northern extremity of his vision, the cylindrical perfection of Round Mountain stood against the sky.

Warrior shied, and Levit saw a rattlesnake beneath a fallen tree. He wheeled the horse away. Further on, a deer skitted from the path, bounding off into the draws.

Once he saw a plume of smoke atop a faraway promontory, and he wondered if it might be a signal.

Two days out of Austin, a sudden range of low, sharp peaks developed in the south, the markers he sought. He turned to swing back across the Pedernales.

"We're above the mouth of the canyon, old fellow," he remarked to Warrior. Here the river flowed through a gentle valley, lined with willows and occasional cypress. A log house lay back in the trees.

"Hello, there," a man called to him from a pole corral. Levit dismounted and threw his bridle over Warrior's head.

"Well, if it ain't MacAshen!" the man boomed, pushing his way out to greet him.

"Howdy, Elledge." MacAshen smiled at the settler. He gripped the big hand warmly.

"I knowed you'd be showing back in the valley, Levit!"

"It's been a long trail, Elledge, but the fighting is over among the white men now."

"Did you get my letter, Levit?"

"Sure did."

"Well, come on in the house."

Mrs. Elledge was a plain woman with a kindly smile. "I know you're mighty glad to be home, Levit," she welcomed him.

"You can be sure of that," he acknowledged. "And I'm glad to see you're still here, Mrs. Elledge. Anything left of my place up the river?" he asked the homesteaders.

"I don't know, Levit. I haven't been that far in a long time. Never can tell when the Comanches will show up. Or white bushwhackers. Not many left around here now but us."

When dawn came the next morning, Levit was already following the road up the bank of the river. The emerald green of young pecans marked its course. The valley was broad in the west; it fell back on either side, its gentle undulations stretching on and on.

He noted a few of the Pedernales' particular variety of cacti, the tall white blooms sentinel-like in their solitude. In the far distance he could make out the adobe walls of what had once been the little hamlet of Pleasant Hill, and in mid-afternoon he halted Warrior on the crest of the river slope.

There it was, off across the stream, exactly as when he had ridden away in the romantic surge of 1861—his home. Thank God for that! The ranch house stood a hundred yards or so beyond the churning rivulet, outlined by the shade from a great live oak. And there was no sign that other wanderers had tried to take over.

In the broad yard, when he had crossed the ford, MacAshen swung from the saddle and looped the reins across the pommel. He slapped his horse across the shank and grinned understandingly as the horse charged back toward the old stalls and feedbins, in search of the grains and hay that once had been there.

Levit slowly mounted the steps, the sound of his passage echoing. There was heavy dust upon the verandah and window sills. Apparently it had been a long time since men passed through the door. Memories crossed MacAshen's mind as he wandered through the silent rooms. He laid a hand for a moment on his mother's dusty old piano. In the hallway, he lifted his father's sombrero from the rack and turned it in his hand. Then stiffly he threw his war bag across his shoulder and mounted the stairway.

11

West of the Paint Rock country flows the Concho, "the River of Pearls," twisting back and forth until it blends its waters with the rolling sweep of the Colorado. Southward lies the Brady, then the San Saba, and eventually the Pedernales.

This was the country of the Singing Hills, the legendary hunting ground of the Paneteka and the Tonk. For two hundred miles, north to south and east to west, there spread a vast and bloody battleground. It was a battleground far removed from the populated lands, and certainly one unsung amid the greater drama of the eastern conflict. But it reached down to the valley of the Pedernales—almost to Austin—a last defense line against the maraudings of the savages in the fateful year of 1865.

MacAshen lost no time. He hired a pair of sandy-haired youths; a middle-aged settler named Lubbock; two recruits from Buck Barry's old frontier militia, named Meadows and Torkin; a Mexican, Pepito, to handle the camp and cooking chores. Lastly, from the Palo Alto valley north of Fredericksburg, he hired a young German wrangler, Herman Nusser.

MacAshen resurrected his father's old branding irons from the smithy. The parallel lines of an inverted double S, which suggested the tiny spill in the river, had given the name to the

MacAshen spread, the Ranch of the Falling Water, and he meant to preserve the name. He saw to it that the bunk shacks were made comfortable, then he moved his own few personal things into a room off the main hall in the big house. Quickly, too, since there were no evidences of longhorns still ranging the valley itself, he sent his waddy along the barrier walls, searching the thickets for wild cattle even as he screened the valley for Indian sign.

The gnawing fear of Indian atrocity preyed on the countryside, and even as MacAshen went to work another such horror shocked the settlements of the upper valley. Two little German girls were seized right on the outskirts of Fredericksburg, one of them mutilated and burned to death at the site, the other carried away.

MacAshen supposed the settlers were defenseless against such maraudings. The Germans had made treaties with the Comanches, but the treaties did not stop the atrocities, at least where other tribes were concerned. Henrich Stahl had been killed in sight of the town, too, and a man named Grobe on Landrum's Creek. Another, Arhelger, had been scalped right in Fredericksburg; then the Meckel brothers at Loyal Valley; and a man named Berg.

But what was worse, at the moment, was the warning flashed down through the frontier grapevine that even now Santanta and five hundred Kiowas had returned to raid along Elm Creek, north of the Concho.

Smoke from burning ranches mottled the horizon. Travelers buried the mutilated bodies of victims where they found them, then moved hurriedly on, eyes cast over their shoulders. At some point along the way, MacAshen reflected, the Germans who had tried to settle this hill country would have to learn that the natives played no favorites on the frontier, regardless of treaties.

Contingents of Yankee troops moved westward from Houston on July 25. When they marched into Austin, there came with them the Union ex-brigadier, A. J. Hamilton, a former Texan, now named provisional governor of the state.

Karryl Newcomb stood with the Whipples on Congress Avenue, watching the arriving column. The soldiers hoisted their flag over the capitol, then raised their tents on the green lawns.

What would Hamilton do? How far would he go? He had once made his home in Austin, and he had refused to support the Confederacy. Forced into flight, he left all he had behind him. Now he was back in Austin, and supported by an army of blue-coated Yankee troopers.

The people who were present in the capitol when Hamilton arrived spread the word on what happened there. The new governor had laid his presidential appointment on the desk. "I am here as provisional governor of this state," Hamilton said to Stockdale.

Stockdale studied the Union appointee. "I remember you well, Hamilton," he said. "You were one of the few Texans who threw up everything to stay with the Union. I recall that the secession committee raked the countryside for you, but you escaped."

Hamilton nodded. His achievement in eluding the rampaging secessionist committee appeared to stir recollections. "I hid in a cave above town," he answered. "After a while, with help, I made it out of the state."

"And now you're back again."

"Yes, I am back again."

"I think you will find everything in order here, as far as this office is concerned, Hamilton. At least, I have tried to leave it so."

"I expected that, and I am sure there will be no difficulties for me in assuming the responsibility. I know this is a trying moment for everyone here, and I have no wish to prolong it for you. Is there anything else, before you go, that you wish to say to me, Stockdale?"

"For myself, no. For the state, however, I will say that I hope you will deal as kindly with Texas as you can, considering everything."

"Considering what Texas did to me, you mean?" Hamilton drummed his fingers on the desk. "I bear no grudge for that," he said, turning to gaze directly at each of the men present. "Let me set everyone straight on one thing, right from the beginning. A man fights for what he believes to be right—I did, and I presume you did. But the fighting is over. Texas has been my home; I consider it so today. It has nothing to fear from me if it now keeps the peace. I plan to call a constitutional convention, and I hope the people will attend it. My ambition

[116]

is to see this state again a strong, active, faithful partner in the Union."

Stockdale had no reply to that. Hamilton had indeed been a respected figure in this community. Did he mean what he said now?

Slowly each man turned away, one by one going out the door, down the steps of the capitol, and into the street beyond.

Devers had seen Hamilton at Houston earlier. Sometime after General Granger's entry into the state, another courier had arrived in Houston, and when he was through with his basic mission, he hunted out Devers, delivering a letter the swarthy man had long been awaiting.

Devers had then called on Hamilton, finding the provisional governor in General Granger's quarters. He showed Hamilton and the army officer his letter—a fresh commission as Treasury agent in Texas.

"Well, it's not entirely unexpected, sir," Hamilton acknowledged. "The government is beginning to send out people everywhere."

"I'm glad you favor it," Devers replied.

"I didn't say I favored it. I don't express an opinion on what the Federal authority elects to do."

"I assume further instructions will come forward to all of us in time, Mr. Devers," General Granger said. "Such orders as this are always implemented later on. But until then the collection of all public property will be carried out by the military alone, as it has been in the past, if that is what you came to talk about."

"Do you mean cotton?" Devers queried.

"I'm referring especially to cotton."

"But what else is there for a Treasury man to work on—like the government's expecting him to?"

"I can't answer that, sir. In fact, I don't even care to try, for it's not my problem. I've told you the way it is, at least for the time being. And you will be careful to abide by my admonitions."

That had been some weeks before, now, and Devers still chafed over his reception from both the new governor and the army commander. Despite the fact that he had heard Granger predict possible changes, he wanted to get on with things.

Besides that, he was bitterly angry for other reasons. Storm was one of those, and although the gunman had gone on west, he managed before he left to dig at Devers again about his blood. "You just want to stick around where there're plenty of people, seeing if you get yourself by," he laughed. In the exchange that followed, Storm needled the swarthy man until Devers dropped his guard, divulging a hint or two of his advances toward Karryl Newcomb.

"Sure. I knew it was something like that again," the gunman laughed. "I've had you pegged right for quite a spell, and I'd just as soon shake you till you get this woman-stuff out of your mind. You're not safe to be with till you do. The Newcomb girl!" Storm laughed again. "No wonder you didn't take to me grabbing onto her, back there in front of old Fall's inn, that day. Well, good luck, Devers. I'll wait for you out west somewhere, for you'll be along in time. Somehow, a breed never gives up hoping; but don't say I didn't tell you. That Newcomb woman ain't one not to recognize the blood in a party."

Storm had left after that, and Devers stalked the floor in his anger, turning over and over inside. When he was like this, he hated all people.

Yes, Karryl Newcomb had gone again—she'd disappeared because Devers sought to make up to her, as any man would do. Next time he ran into her . . . well, the Union troops were here now and only he knew who the girl really was.

But Devers had no idea of the direction she had taken in her flight. Maybe back to her old home place, he thought at first. But the thought was foolish. The Yankees might still be looking for her in Mississippi. Maybe she'd managed to tie in with one of the wagon trains heading for California.

He tried to extract something from her Aunt Betsy, but that lady wouldn't even talk to him.

Late summer came, and along with it more political vultures. But to accommodate the newcomers new orders did arrive on Federal procedures, as the commanding general had expected.

"Granger's rules on the handling of cotton no longer stand," Devers told one of the new men who had teamed up with him. "There are orders out of Washington, and the soldiers don't have anything to do with it anymore."

"What's the scheme?"

"The rules say now that anybody's goods 'actually or constructively' in the hands of the Confederate states at the time of surrender are to be picked up. That covers cotton. Any person wanting to sell cotton, or ship cotton, has to prove that the Confederates didn't have any claim on it. It'll be hard to prove most claims."

"Well, how soon do we get busy?"

"Right now."

In the plantation country around Houston, the Treasury agents made their first collections. People with only modest farm lands. like Mrs. Newcomb, were just as badly scourged as the others. In Mrs. Newcomb's instance, she appeared to be picked out as a special target.

Late in August, she wrote Karryl, telling her how things were going. "Everything in our part of Texas is mighty bad right now, especially for the farmers along the rivers," she said. "Almost all of the cotton in Houston—from last year's crop—has been taken away. There are so many of these terrible government people around, and every one of them makes the farmer prove the cotton belongs to him before he can sell it. If he can't prove it, well, the cotton is just hauled away, and we never see it again."

Her letter continued. "The Yankees are all backed up by soldiers now, and people say that even the Union officers are helping to cheat our planters and merchants out of their cotton. A lot of the money is going into their own pockets, it's said. This man, Devers, whom you'll remember, is a Treasury agent now, and we hear some very bad things about him. People think he was a Federal spy all the time."

General Granger worried more over the plight of the Negroes than the plight of Houstonians or the bayou farmers. As the heat of the deepest summer began to settle upon the Gulf country, he noted apprehensively that labor in the cotton fields had ceased. He advised them to stay at home and work for wages. "Whether they will or not remains to be seen. But on one thing I am determined. They will not congregate at military posts. The army cannot support or feed them."

On August 6, Granger was relieved by General H. G. Wright and late in the summer, Negro soldiers began replacing the white troopers in the Federal garrisons. As a result, the blacks from the cotton fields swarmed into the towns by the hundreds.

12

Summer burned into autumn. The yellow blossoms became mesquite beans, and the meadows were golden with sunflower.

MacAshen made plans for his first cattle drive. He wanted to get in at least that much work before taking off for a quick trip back to Austin, but he would have to rake the upper river valleys, if he expected to find any cattle left anywhere. He assigned the care of the rancho to the Mexican, put together his gear, then led the rest of his waddy out and up the south bank of the Pedernales. With him were all of his newly recruited hands except the Mexican: Lubbock, whom he named foreman; the two teens; the German youth, Nusser; and the former Rangers, Meadows and Torkin.

The route was due west across the South Grape, to the headwaters of the river where it branched into the Wolf and the Bear, then north. The abandoned army fort, Martin Scott, lay on the river's bank below Fredericksburg, and scattered, well-kept fields of alfalfa spotted the landscape. MacAshen swung wide upon the hills to avoid the little town. It was here that the first Germans who came with Meusebach from Nassau had settled in 1846.

Across the Live Oak, they came to a rocky land, rising and falling to the contours of the shale draws, and spotted at irregular intervals with scrub shin oak. The waddy camped on the first night above Fredericksburg in a gentle meadow looking north across blue, hazy ranges, for perhaps fifty miles.

Next day the going became rougher. The thin, reddish brown soils of the Tishomingo became grayish friables, and then shallow, stony, calcerous chalk. The waddy camped at Cherry Spring, the old rock houses of which appeared to have been long deserted. Beside one, a thick feathered shaft, cut from ash, was buried half in the soil.

"Kickapoo," Lubbock said. "But it's had a season on it."

There were live oaks on the Beaver. The water in the stream ran clear and cold, and a mile beyond its crossing, the men came to the deep shelved banks above the rushing torrent of the Llano River. They threw their reins and, dismounting, plunged their faces into the refreshing water. As they came up they saw their first wild cattle in the thickets on the far side of the stream.

"They're comin' down to get water and likely they're meaner'n hell!" Lubbock warned.

MacAshen went back into the saddle. "Meadows and I will cut across and get behind them," he called out. "You, Lubbock—and Torkin and Nusser—cross the Llano farther up, then come down from there. Stampede anything you see east, toward the basin." He motioned to the Monhall boys. "Slip downstream a ways and cross. And make sure the cattle don't head back toward the Brady once we get them running."

He motioned his own partner alongside, then spurred into the water, and just as he did so the animals on the other side appeared in the open.

"Nothing but mustang cattle—'black cattle,'" he yelled at Meadows.

"'Mestenas,'" the other called back.

"Where the hell did they come from?"

"No telling!"

"Well, we'll take anything we can get," MacAshen yelled again, forcing his mount across the shallows. "Cattle are cattle when you haven't got any at all."

Black cattle—or "mestenas"—were scarcely what Levit had hoped to find, but, as he had indicated, beggars were scarcely to be choosers, and they'd do at least for meat. Most of the blacks had been killed off by cattlemen in the fifties, but apparently the strains had cropped up again during the war years. It was not hard to distinguish them, once they were in the open. The first marks of identification were the lined backs—stripes of white and brown and yellow—the "lobo stripe," it was called. Blacks and browns predominated, but there were duns and brindles, reds and whites, and strange unbelievable tints of mulberry blue. They kept their heads low, horns extending outward from their square foreheads.

"Look, MacAshen!" Meadows yelled once, and when the former followed the direction indicated, he saw other cattle, a half-dozen of them, and this time they were, indeed, longhorns—scrub animals running with the blacks. But even as such they stood out. The longhorn somehow was a saner-looking beast, even in his wildness. Besides the vast spread of horns which swung horizontally from his skull, the longhorn's body sported narrow hips and flat ribs; high, thin shoulders and pinched-up flanks.

"Let 'em go, so long as they're headed south toward the Cave Creek draws!" MacAshen shouted to Meadows. "That way, they'll work on toward the Pedernales."

"I'll let 'em go, all right. But they may not stop even that far down," Meadows answered.

When breakfast was over and camp chores attended to next morning, MacAshen said to the Monhall boys: "This is as far north as you two will go. I want you to work out of the Llano bottoms and drive whatever you run into straight on toward the southeast. There's plenty you can do between here and the Enchanted Rock."

"But you're going farther up, and there won't be no Injuns on this side," one of the boys grumbled.

"I hope not, but don't be too sure. Anyway, you sweep this valley clean. And afterward, ride back to meet us where the Sandy and the Hondo mix, just west of the Cedar Mountains. When we come down that pass we'll need help—if we have any luck at all."

The next day MacAshen and his remaining riders rode on until they reached Fort Mason. MacAshen found a nostalgic burden in the loneliness of this second deserted army post.

North of the post, they were in San Saba country. The gentle rolling hills gave way to long stretches of large red boulders.

Suddenly, the warm, languid days changed, the nights becoming cool. MacAshen made camp on the San Saba, and then he went to work in earnest. He ranged the cowboys far upon the prairies pushing what stray wild cattle they could find before them to the river bottom. One day late in the month, the northern thickets had been cleaned out and there was nothing left to do in that area.

"What we've got will stay close enough to drive," MacAshen declared finally, "and Lubbock and Nussar and I will do that driving. While the cattle are moving, we can also scout a piece up toward the Brady. Torkin, I want you and Meadows to drop back south now to Katemcy Creek and work that section out. But don't go past the mouth of the Bullhead. Wait there till we come down. We'll herd whatever we've been able to keep together along there then, and throw them in with any you and the Monhalls have held onto. Then we'll see if we can push them all on to the Pedernales."

"O.K., Boss." Torkin and Meadows packed their gear and headed out. Then MacAshen and the other two started the herd eastward.

"They're driftin' well," Lubbock said on the morning of the third day after leaving the range camp. "If you'll take off just a mite of time, there's something down to the south over the ridge I'd like to look at once again."

MacAshen glanced at him in surprise, but he nodded his acceptance.

It was not far. West of the Shin Oak range, Lubbock turned into the East Deep, following the course of the little stream until it opened into a broad meadow. The brook meandered against the escarpments, and he skirted it until a small tributary cut into the pathway. Lubbock reined up suddenly, and MacAshen stared down at the blackened remnants of a cabin. Off to the rear, the clearing extended to reveal what had been a log corral, and a few corn cribs.

"Homesteaded here in 1860," the man said haltingly. "They burned me out two years later. Got the old lady here. What they done to her before she died was terrible."

MacAshen swung slowly off his horse. Lubbock did not dismount.

"I was down the glade over there." The latter nodded his head. "I saw them, when they came sneaking down on me.

Had time to break across the Deep and lose 'em behind the hills there. Guess they knew I'd circle fast, but I got back too late. Saw the smoke as I come up, and they were gone."

In a week, MacAshen and his full waddy were teamed again on the Sandy, and they pushed southward. The wide, flat plains resolved into sharp low peaks and heavy red granite cliffs.

Once, back in the distance, a cloud of dust rose and then out of it appeared a small herd of stampeding black animals. They were shaggy, and odd humps rose above their backs.

"Buffalo!" MacAshen yelled, "and they're a long way down."

"May be running from Indians," Lubbock warned. "We'd better hole up here for a spell, and watch that trail back there."

They did halt, protected from sight by the brush of the hillside. After a time, however, MacAshen said: "No Indians behind that herd, Lubbock. Something else—maybe lightning, or an animal—scared them."

"Reckon so, boss."

They rode on, traversing slowly the narrow valleys and rock-studded passes, and pushing the blacks and hybrid longhorns they'd been able to assemble along before them. "I've seen Indians run buffalo close-up," Lubbock said suddenly, as he and MacAshen rode along side by side. "It was quite a while ago now, though. I woke up on a rocky little butte out Palo Duro way one morning and the buffs were all around below, maybe a million of them. A half-dozen Plains Indians were on the flank of the herd, too, close enough to knock me down with a rifle ball if I moved, and if they saw me. I didn't, and they didn't. I just watched.

"Those Indians worked in on the side of the herd, and the buffs didn't seem to mind at all. One was carrying a lance. He rode right up beside a young buff, and then he swung his arm and drove the lance right through the fast-running buffalo's heart. It was not till then that the other buffs began to run.

"Saw something else, too. One Indian got in the middle of that herd with a bow and arrow. But he didn't have time to use it, because the herd clamped down on him when it started moving. He saw he was trapped—those buffs really stampede when they go—and he slid right off his mustang's back on top of the buffalo nearest him. Then onto the next one; and I swear if he didn't scamper right across those shaggy backs till he hit the side nearest me. It was rocky ground, and when he was close, he jumped straight out and beat it into the rocks, right under the knoll I was on.

"I could have killed him easy, for the rest of the savages were far away by then, and that stampede had the roll of thunder. He turned around and saw me. Had my rifle in my hand. I'll never forget the look in that Redskin's eyes, MacAshen. He figured his time had come, and he made a funny little moan. But he was game, and for some reason or other I didn't have the heart. We just looked at each other, him down the slope, and me sitting up there staring down my gun at him. I recollect he was wearing a bone whistle in his scalp lock, and a beaded necklace around his throat, and there was an old Mexican locket tied to the beads. He had a long scar on his face, from over his left ear, clear down to his nose.

"After a while, I shook my head and nodded him back into the valley, and since it was clear out there now, he could make it that way. He backed away a piece, unbelieving, but then he got the idea. I saw him look back once, a long time, studying me; and I let him go."

Carefully they worked the herd they had put together south until at last they came once more to the defiles pointing downward toward the pastures on Cave Creek.

"They'll stick, what with winter in the air," Lubbock had prophesied.

"Let's hope so," MacAshen answered, "for this is where we're leaving them. Drive them on into the thickets, Lubbock, then call in the boys."

Two nights later, back at home on the Pedernales, MacAshen stoked the fire and wondered if he could make a go of it, considering the scrubbiness of the stock he had been able to herd on the first drive. He went to his room, lighted a lamp there and placed it on the table. The lamp was a primitive utensil: a large saucer containing tallow, in which was suspended a tallow dip. "I've got to find some of the new sperm-oil lanterns somewhere," he thought. He sat for a moment on the side of the bed, looking around the room. A call from off on the northern rim, a gray wolf howling its doleful, wild concert interrupted his memories of childhood.

MacAshen's thoughts now were on Karryl Newcomb. Would

[125]

a rugged ranch like this appeal to her? The loneliness of the prairie beast's cry penetrated the night, and even the tragic plight of the little German girls rose to cross his mind. He yearned for even an hour with Karryl again. And he meant to have it. But somewhere, out there beyond where the wolf had howled, maybe other sharp black eyes were trained upon this valley tonight, too. He couldn't bring Karryl back here with him yet, and he couldn't leave this spread to run itself, either.

He drew off his boots and blew out the lamp.

In Austin Karryl set about the task immediately of finding some way to earn her keep. There was a little boarding school in the city, a seminary for young ladies, and she saw possibilities in that. One day, after several visits to the school, she was able to say delightedly to Mr. Whipple: "I've got myself a job as a teacher."

The seminary was described in its folder as standing just off the Avenue, at the intersection of Pecan, boasting "hill and valley, lawn and umbrageous forest trees, amid bracing mountain air," and she pointed out the claim that "these advantages give robustness of constitution and consequently the vigor and elasticity of intellect which is necessary to success."

Mr. Whipple followed the pages with her. "It's a wonderful opportunity," he smiled. But then, "You must remember, of course, that the way they speak of it here was before the war. They have had a hard time of it, not only because of the usual troubles most of us have experienced, but because of the Indians, too."

"Indians in Austin?" Karryl asked, startled.

"Well, not exactly here, Miss Newcomb. But you see, a great many of the girls come from ranches in the farther counties. Many of their homes have been destroyed by the Indians during the war. Often their parents have been slain. You've met the headmaster?" he asked.

"Oh, yes." She told him about her interviews with The Rev. Mr. Smith. He boasted a mien like a Shakespearean actor, a wing collar, and a vast enveloping black frock coat.

"I know him well," Mr. Whipple smiled.

There were several others on the faculty. One of the women teachers had conducted her about the school, showing her the microscopes for studying flowers and the magic lanterns with slides. "They've got studies in waxwork and shells and embroidery, too," Karryl marveled. "But good heavens, Mr. Whipple! How did I ever find my way into such a task, my life having been what it has?"

The old churchman smiled again. "The ways of the Lord are hard to understand, my dear," he answered. "Just don't worry about it."

After that, summer resolved into autumn in Austin, too, the hot, dry days gradually becoming cool and pleasant again. Cool weather made the task of teaching little girls a lot easier, Karryl explained, for they didn't fret so much and think up mischief when they were comfortable. Mr. Whipple chided her that perhaps it was the teacher who fretted most—and was the more uncomfortable—when the seasons were taxing. "We look for ease and contentment more and more as we grow older," he warned.

Karryl applied herself to the task she had assumed. She went early to the school and stayed late. It was good to be close to children again. She wanted to hug every single one of them up close to her, even the naughtiest. Almost startlingly there came to her the realization that even greater than her own need for understanding and comfort was the yearning in each little girl under her care for whatever she could bestow of these same emotions, herself, on them. Suddenly yesterday's troubles seemed far away and she prayed they would remain so.

13

Two hundred miles north-northwest of the Rio Grande village of Roma-Los Saenz—at an undermanned, understocked horse and cattle spread between the Nueces and the Frio—the head wrangler and owner, Rand Connaught, stopped work in the corral to eye a rider slowly coming up the lane toward the ranch house. Actually, he noted the horse first, dun in color, but richly dark and outlined by a deeper stripe around the legs and above the hocks and the knees. When they were closer, however, it was the man himself who took all of Connaught's attention, a lithe young fellow thorn-snagged and obviously travel weary—the inevitable identification of those returning north from out of the forbidding Brasada.

"You going some place, cowboy, or just lost," he asked bluntly as the rider halted and swung slowly down from the saddle.

"Just going."

"That figures. Most folks pointing up out of the Brasada keep on going if they can." Connaught was a tall, spare westerner, his long mustache waxed to sharp points. He was a discerning man, however, whose eye was always directly upon the face of the individual with whom he was talking and he liked to talk. "Where you from, young fellow?"

"All over. East of the Mississippi while the war was still going on. Just lately, south of here, toward the border. Around San Isidro, and Longorio."

"Reckon it wouldn't do no good to ask if you was running or just drifting, so I'll put you down as just drifting. You eat this morning?"

"Not yet. I've been low on provisions."

"Uh-huh. Most folks are. Go throw your saddle over there close to the watering trough and look to your horse. You can wash some of that alkali off too, if you want, while you're at it down there by the well. Then come on up to the house."

The newcomer complied with the rancher's suggestions, looking first to the needs of his horse, and then to his own. Then he turned back to the house. Connaught met him on the back porch.

"You don't look so road-blistered now." He grinned. "That cold water that comes in from under the Frio can put new life in a body when you put your head in the trough." He led the way indoors. "Had some wolves around last night, and I like not to have got to bed at all. Still sleepy myself, and I could do with some strong coffee, too. Grab a chair here in the kitchen and I'll pour us some. Then I'll rustle up some grub for you."

The traveler eyed his host attentively as the latter moved about the kitchen. Then the rancher sat down across the table. "My name's Connaught," he said. "You got a handle?"

The other did not answer immediately, and Connaught spoke up again. "Not that it makes any difference."

"I've got a name," the black-haired man said. But he did not offer it, at least at the moment, and Connaught did not mistake the meaning. A man could ask too many questions in south Texas. Approvingly, however, he watched the young fellow dig into the food that had been set out on the table before him.

The loneliness of the prairies had different effects on men as everyone in this part of the world knew, creating a gnawing appetite for talk and fraternalism in some and total silence and inscrutability in others. The Brasada, in spite of all its wild and primitive attractions, was like the Lipan or the Comanche who rode down across it. It could be protective and strong and concealing. Or it could be cruel and treacherous and deadly. The men who traveled its brakes were only too aware of that.

"Did you see any savages down Brasada way, as you was

coming through?" Connaught asked.

"No."

"Well, maybe you was lucky. They sure have been bad a-round here the past year. Worse than any time I can recollect. Sometimes coming in from all directions at once—the Lipans and Kickapoos from south of the Rio Grande; Mescaleros from clean out past the Pecos; Kiowas from north of the Red; and the Comanches from wherever they might happen to be when they got ready to hit us."

"And you've been able to stand them off here?"

"Oh, they ain't too eager to get plugged themselves, so mostly they lean toward running off the horses, stealing stock, killing what they can't eat. During the war they hit Uvalde once real bad, though. Took over the church to keep their horses in. They're after a mite of hair sometimes, but not too often. Did get a whole family over on the Devil's River, not more than a month ago, and a couple of Mexicans since then, right close to Uvalde."

The conversation shifted again.

"Ain't been worried so much about Redskins as about Mexicans. The boys are with the horse herd right now, but when they're in we can make a pretty good show of it, far as the Indians are concerned. It's different with the Mexicans. So we have to be careful."

"You got anything left to lose?"

"Not much, no, but what I do still have I'd like to hold on to."

"How many hands have you got?"

"Three. Just three. And just boys, at that. They're from up country, never been close to the Tornillo before. Hard to hire hands that'll stick for long around here. Most of 'em slope off after a spell, and I'm used to that now."

"You say most of your trouble starts on the other side of the Rio Grande?"

"Usually, I reckon. Plenty of small-fry politicos on the other side, and some big ones, too, and they cut loose ever so often. But I spent a year down in the Tornillo myself, and I know most of the outfits on this side of the river. They usually let me be, seeing as how I haven't got too much to take anyhow."

Connaught wiped his face with a bandana, and returning to the earlier subject, stared at the man before him. "You look

[130]

young, fellow," he said. "But them lines around your eyes didn't come from no camp meeting. Don't reckon you'd be hunting a job?"

The other sat silent for a time. "The fact is, I am," he said.

"You're not headed for some place already, like up on the Sabinal, or maybe even the Bosque?"

"No. But I wouldn't want to put you wrong. I'd like to have a stake again that would get me clean away from the Brasada country, and I would work to get it. Truth of the matter is, I didn't just happen by here today, Connaught. I was looking for you."

"Looking for me?"

"Yes. A fellow by the name of Kalmbach told me you'd likely take me on for a spell, if I could find your gate."

"Waddy Kalmbach?"

"I never heard any name but Kalmbach."

"White-haired fellow, older than me, with part of his ear missing?"

"That's the man."

"Why didn't he come along with you?"

The visitor fell silent for a moment. Then he said, "He's done his traveling, Connaught. I buried him a week ago at Realitas."

"Ah."

"Once he said when I wanted to put some ground between me and the Brasada I ought to hunt you up. Said he'd sent a fellow or two your way before, but didn't know if they found you."

"They found me." Connaught changed the subject. "What brought you down into the Brasada to start with, cowboy?"

"I was in the army. Escaped from a Union stockade just before the war ended. Had to shoot my way out, with a smuggled pistol. Figured the Federals would be after me, once they moved in on Texas, so I headed for the border."

"Well, it ain't unusual for young fellows from the war to head for the border. But you ain't told me about Waddy Kalmbach. We rode together in earlier years. How did he die?"

"From a bad going over by a couple of mean hombres. He didn't have anything they wanted, and he was pretty old, even to shove around. But they tried to stomp him in the floor, like it was some kind of sport. And they would have, if I hadn't just happened along. Even then it was too late to keep him from folding up a couple of days afterward."

"You just run them off?"

"No." The black-haired man paused. Then he went on. "They tore into me as soon as I showed, and—" He did not finish the sentence, but his abrupt halt was eloquent. "Kalmbach said you were on the level here, and that you always needed a hand, but not for rustling."

Connaught smiled grimly. "A lot of ranches in Texas today— even some of the big ones—were started with a few rustled cattle," he said. "But the trouble is, young fellow, I don't know all there is to know about you. How come you're looking for a place to light? Why don't you just keep on riding?"

The other answered quickly, and even Connaught was startled by his frankness. "I could be wanted up in central Texas."

"You been into something?"

"I never took a dollar from any man that didn't belong to me. Or anything else. But trouble has a way of riding along with me, or it has been that way ever since I got back to Texas. And I've had to stand up to some people here and there. I've been lucky, but the way things are now, a lot could have been saddled on me since I've been out of touch that I never had anything to do with. I've got to set down somewhere until I can find out, but then I want to go on."

"Young fellow, when you first got down off your horse, I figured it was something like that. I'm a pretty good judge of men, just like I am of horses. Seeing as how you was geared up, and how you carried that right hand, I had you pegged, and I figured you'd left a few hombres a lot wiser." He halted only momentarily. "But I'm soft for a horse, that dun of yours, he sure took my eye. Always figure a man by his horse. Reckon you can throw your saddle here for a while at least—or until you get ready to move on—and I'll find you something to do to earn your keep."

"I'll be beholden to you for that."

"Well, maybe you ought to start off around here by hitching that six-shooter up off your shank and onto your belt. And get a glove on that right hand. My boys ain't been around much, though they ain't so stupid either." He twisted the ends of his mustache. "But we got to have something to call you by, son, while you're working with us."

"My name is Ord."

The rancher started, but quelled any other reaction he might have had. "Ord. I've heard the name, as most everyone in south Texas has. Story is that a man named Ord may be the fastest gun on the border now. Don't get me wrong on what I have to say to you, but we ain't got a private cemetery around here, and we don't want one. Beyond that, me and the boys will be proud to have a fellow like you alongside. Even for just a spell, if you figure to move on later."

Wholesale confiscation of plantation cotton came to an end early in the winter. At Houston, Devers prepared to move on westward.

"We're through here," he said to his men. "You can stay, or you can go with me." He lit a cigar. "Nothing left around Houston to keep us anyway," he went on. "The government tells us not to fool with cotton raised after 1865, because the Confederates are working out ways to prove they own the new crops that have been planted."

"You got something else in mind, Devers?"

"Yes, and in a business we know more about." He turned to one of his cronies. "We'll need horses. Good country horses that the Federals have taken in. See if you can get some. I'll look to the rest."

In Austin, Karryl threw herself into her work at the girls' school. Protected as she was in the cloister of the seminary and the quiet tranquility of the old pastor's home, she felt none of the weight of the after-war burdens—at least in the same degree as other people. The dangers which had followed her to Texas— the threats which had hung over her—seemed far away now. One pronouncement, coming from the Union commandant in Austin, did nettle her, however.

"Texas," wrote Major General Stanley to the Reconstruction Committee in Congress, "is worse than any other state, because she has never been whipped. Her women are still universally rebels." Someone in Washington—or perhaps on General Stanley's staff in Austin—saw to it that the message was made public. It spread among Austin women like wildfire.

"He's just being picayunish because we won't be as sweet as he'd like us to be to his soldier boys," Karryl had said to Mr.

Whipple, "but I'm not worried about that. What does concern me is something else—the silly rantings some of those northern people are making about how we run our schools."

"Working where you are, it's natural that you would react to that sort of thing more quickly," Mr. Whipple smiled.

"Well, it's all because of the blacks—and I guess that's to be expected, since the war was fought over them, anyway. Did you know, Mr. Whipple, that Negro children have been applying for admission to our schools?"

"Yes. At Brenham, the Northerners have suggested teachers be selected from among recently freed slaves. Schools are closing in some places, they tell me."

"That's silly," Karryl responded. "Why don't they just let them go on and enter, if they want to?"

At about this time, MacAshen—on the Pedernales—picked up a message left for him at the Elledge homestead down the river. It was from Stockdale, back in Austin.

"Stockdale's sent for me again," MacAshen said to Lubbock. "And I was planning to ride in, anyway."

"Got any idea why he wants you?"

"Not exactly."

"When are you going?"

"He said to be there just before Christmas."

"Well, you'd better play it foxy, with all them Yankees in Austin."

"They've just moved out of Austin, or at least the soldiers have. There was some word on that. They've gone to San Antonio. And one of the things Stockdale said was to be prepared to go on to San Antonio with him, myself. So I guess whatever he's got in mind is tied in with the army. Going to San Antonio sets up another matter, Lubbock.

"We've got to get some better stock here at the Falling Water than we've been able to, so far. We can't keep going with the kind of cattle still left in the brakes hereabout, even though we've gone as far north as the Brady. Strong and meaty strains are all that will keep us alive, if we stay on the Pedernales."

"What do you figure to do, boss?"

"I want to buy some stockers—if they're still to be had—from down in the south, along the Guadalupe or the San Bernard. You can look to that for me, and then meet me in San Antonio when you're through. I'd planned to handle it myself, but with this call from Austin, I guess I can't. I want you to make that buying trip for me, Lubbock."

"How many head would you want?"

"Up to two hundred."

"How'll we get 'em here?"

"They can be driven north around the headwaters of the Guadalupe, and then back down along the river to the Cave Creek pastures."

"Pretty risky. The Comanches are apt to be watching. And there are plenty of white men who'd grab a herd, too, if they could."

"We'll have to take the chance, Lubbock. But I guess every hand will be needed to be sure it doesn't happen. I can meet you along the way—at San Antonio—during the last few days of December. Or right after the first of the year. That will give you and the rest of the outfit a Christmas in San Antonio."

The foreman grinned. "Not a bad idea, boss," he said.

After Lubbock had left, MacAshen went to his room. He took from a drawer a colorful little shawl, bought from a Mexican trader. He hoped Karryl Newcomb would like it; it was all he could take her in the way of a remembrance for Christmas. Carefully, he folded it and returned it to its place.

Some days later he rode down the Pedernales toward Austin, choosing the road this time that ran by the Mathews grinder, six miles outside the city. He crossed the Colorado at an upper ford, then went past Bull Creek, where the Texans had maintained their powder mill in 1863. He reached Austin late in the evening.

A boy was waiting for MacAshen at the hotel. "Mr. Stockdale wanted to make sure you got in," the boy explained.

"He said to be here tomorrow."

"He still says tomorrow. Ten o'clock in the morning. But he thought you might rather bed down at his place while you're here, instead of the hotel."

"Thanks, but I guess not. I've been in the saddle more than two days now. I'm dog tired and dirty, and I'm turning in. Tell him I'll be on hand when he gets here in the morning."

MacAshen did retire immediately, but he was up again at daylight. He had breakfast as soon as the dining room opened.

Then he headed directly for the cottage on the hill.

Karryl was ready to leave for the school when he got there. "Oh, Levit," she cried. "Where in the world did you come from?"

He elbowed the screen aside, pulled her up to him, and kissed her soundly. "Why, right out of the brakes," he said. "I told you I'd be back."

"But you didn't even let me know you were coming. Why didn't you write?"

"Wouldn't have done any good. There's no way yet to get a letter back here from the Pedernales." He stepped back. "You look good," he said, "splendid!"

"I'm fine, Levit. Really, I am. But do come on into the house." She led him into the parlor. "When did you get here, Levit?"

"Last night, late. And so done in that all I could do was fall into the sack. Everything appears to be about the same as when I left. Tell me, how has it gone for you, Karryl?"

"I'm a school teacher."

"A what?"

"A school teacher, and don't you laugh, either. I have a job, looking out for a lot of little girls. What's more, I love it."

"Well, if you say you're a school teacher, you're a school teacher."

"I told you I'd get a job," she said, "and I did. Are you pleased?"

"Of course, I'm pleased."

She pushed him onto the settee and sat down beside him. "Now, tell me everything that's happened to you, Levit."

"That won't take long. I've been trying to get set up again."

"But your home—was it still there?"

"Yes, it was still there. At least the house and barns were. Nothing else. I've lined up some help now, though, and a few head of stock."

"And you?"

"Me? Oh, I'm all right. Lonesome, but otherwise well."

"Well, it's something to hear you admit you've been lonesome. I've been lonesome, too, Levit," she said.

"Then I came back just at the right time."

"You certainly did." She looked at the clock on the mantle. "I'm glad you came back, too, Levit." Then she thought for a

[136]

second. "I can get someone else to take care of my little girls this morning, and we—"

"No, don't do that yet. Go ahead and look after things as you usually do. I've some other matters to take care of, anyway; that's why I came out here so early. I wanted to see you before I got started. But it won't take long to get through with what I have to do."

"I'll be home in the afternoon. And don't you keep me waiting, Levit."

Stockdale was in the hotel downtown at the hour he had set. A half-dozen other men were with him. Some of these Mac-Ashen had known personally in earlier years; the rest he knew by reputation.

"Where do you want to talk?" MacAshen asked Stockdale.

"Here, if it's all right with you."

"It's all right with me. Shall we use my room?"

"Yes."

In that location, after the men had seated themselves, Mac-Ashen said, "All right, Stockdale, from the people you've picked here today, I'd say you had something important to toss out. And it must have to do with us out on the border."

"It has to do with you, certainly, MacAshen. Most of the others here are already filled in—fact is, it's what's happening in their counties that has finally just forced the matter to a head."

"Go on, Stockdale."

"Guess the Indians haven't hit you yet since you've been back on the Pedernales?"

"Not me, personally, no. Some of the German districts have been hit, but they don't say much about it. I've heard reports, though, Stockdale—or at least a lot of them."

"The country north of you, and to some extent down below San Antonio, is being scourged, and has been for the past six months, worse than in the recollection of any man familiar with the frontier. The slaughter has suddenly become unbelievable. And nothing's being done about it by the Union soldiers, or any of the Yankees that have been sent in."

"What did you think they would do about it?"

"Knock them off the prairies, or else help us to do it." Stockdale tossed a sheet of paper on the bed. "There's a hundred names on that page," he said. "Men, women, and children killed by the Indians on the Texas frontier just since the Yankees came in here and took over. And so far as any of us know here, not a single horse has been saddled by the Unionists to go out after them. You've been lucky up till now on the Pedernales, MacAshen."

"I know that." Levit looked at the rest of the men in the room. "Since you've already been talking among yourselves before I got here, I gather you've got some plan in mind."

"We have," Stockdale answered. "Once you told me to count on you, if you were ever needed. Does that still go?"

"Of course. What I can do might not amount to much, but I'm in the gun-sight as much as anybody else here. What is it you're trying to set off, Stockdale?"

"Just this—or, I should say, two things aimed at just one result. First, we've got to lay it on the line before the Union army authorities. Second, if they don't take the bit in their teeth, then we'll have to put together the Texas Rangers again, ourselves."

"Who will?" MacAshen asked.

"A bunch of us, all of us gathered here now. A committee that will step forward and take that responsibility, secretly and under cover."

"Have you been in touch with the Union command?"

"Yes. They'll talk to us in San Antonio. That's why I said to be ready to head that way," Stockdale replied.

"You think we'll have any luck with them?"

"Frankly, I don't. Philip Sheridan made a quick trip from New Orleans to San Antonio a while ago, but he went right back to Louisiana. I've been told he wrote Washington from there that all was peaceful in Texas. So likely they'll stick to that line."

"And after we've seen them in San Antonio? What then?"

"We'll try to find the old Rangers—they scattered after the break-up—and at least get some of them back in the saddle again."

"Where are the Comanches holed up, Stockdale?" MacAshen asked.

"The best we know, they're mostly up on the Red River, right now. But they could be anywhere tomorrow, from the Missouri in the north clear down to the Bolson de Malpini in Chihuahua."

"Are they teamed up now—all together?"

"We've been told the Yapparikas are north, on the Kansas border. The Kotchatekas are on the Canadian River. But the Noconees and the Tanimas may be together on the Pease. The Tenawahs, too, east of there. The Panatekas usually go it alone."

"The Quohadas?"

"Strangely, they've not shown much, just here of late. So far as we know, they haven't moved out of the Palo Duro in recent weeks. But if they should, with things like they are now, there'll be hell to pay! There were a thousand men in the Ranger force we had on the line from the Red River to the Rio Grande in '61. They scattered quick, when the South went under, and the big job now, if we take it on, will be to get them back. That means we've just got to find someone in the field to head them up. Somebody who knows the prairies. Somebody they'll close up behind, and who'll take the risks. A man smart enough at the same time to keep his head down—MacAshen?"

"Are you talking about me?" MacAshen demanded.

"Somebody has to do it. And those of us who've had the chance to think on it figure you're the best man we know for the job."

"When's this pow-wow you've got set up due to be held in San Antonio?"

"Two days before Christmas."

"*Before* Christmas?"

"That's what I said. Maybe that don't fit in with your plans, but it didn't fit in with the rest of ours, either. It was the best the army would give us, so I took what I could get."

When the others had gone, MacAshen spread out on his bed, reflecting on what they had asked of him. Christ in Heaven! Here he was, right back in the middle of it again. But how could he say no? He got up, put on fresh clothes, and went downstairs. At mid-afternoon, he headed slowly toward the Whipple cottage.

Karryl was sitting in the swing on the verandah, but she rose quickly when she saw MacAshen and hurried down the pathway to meet him. "I've been waiting for you, sir," she scolded.

Levit rolled the brim of his hat in his hands. "I'd have come earlier if I could," he answered.

"What's happened, Levit? What's the matter?"

He told her how he had spent the morning, leaving out, of course, those matters related to the purpose and proposals arrived at in his meeting with Stockdale and the others. "I can't stay in Austin to spend Christmas with you, Karryl, like I expected. And I've spent weeks—months—counting on it."

"Why not, Levit?"

"Some things have developed that slapped me right in the face—things related to Stockdale and others who were here before the Yankees arrived. And now, I've been told suddenly I have to be in San Antonio, not here with you in Austin, at Christmastime."

"Are you in danger, Levit?"

"No. Nothing like that. It's just some matters that have to be worked out."

"Can't you come back to Austin when you're through in San Antonio?"

"No. I can't do that, either, now. If I'd had any idea of how all this would shape up, I would have. But I sent my men south for a herd of cattle, before I left the Pedernales. They are to meet me in San Antonio. Look, Karryl, there's nothing I want so much as to spend Christmas with you. It's likely to be pretty empty for me, too, if I don't. But I can't. They'll have that herd in San Antonio when I get there, and those longhorns have to be driven home. What's more—because of the way things are out along the headwaters of the Guadalupe now—every man among us will have to go along to guard that herd."

Karryl said nothing.

Levit took a parcel from his pocket and opened it, bringing forth the little shawl. Quickly he slipped it over her shoulders.

"Oh, Levit, what is it?" she asked.

"It's called a serape saltillero. They're made like this only in one place in Mexico—Saltillo. I found it in a Mexican's trader pack as he came up the valley a while back, and I wanted to bring it to you for Christmas."

"It's beautiful, Levit, but you didn't need—I mean, just coming back to see me for Christmas was present enough." She ran her hand along the colorful fabric. "It's beautiful," she repeated. Then, turning to him, and putting her hands on his shoulders: "Things never seem to work out just like we'd like to have them, do they, Levit?"

"It seems that way." He put his arms around her. "But listen to me, Karryl. You've got to go on for a while just as you have been doing. I'll get back sooner or later. You will, won't you?"

"Of course, Levit, of course," Karryl answered. "What else could I do?"

14

San Antonio, in the year of 1865, was a gaudy city, exciting, feverish, bustling with the business of the frontier. As Levit returned to it—the first time since his boyhood—it was a city filled with cattlemen and their families, and soldiers.

Presidio de Béxar, the Spanish had called the place. It spread from the headwaters of the San Antonio River down across the cold, exploding floodlets in the sudden valley of the San Pedro. Narrow streets wound tortuously upon the tracks of the ancients, twisting, bending, and twisting back again from the broad plazas to the tiny patios of the grandees. Just now, in the dusk, it sparkled as with the garnish of brilliants on an extravagance of green. Adobe houses spotted the rolling hillsides, clustering sometimes about the fallen masonry of old missions.

MacAshen and his companion directed their horses between the trains of canvas-covered two-wheeled carts, some of them drawn by twenty yoke of oxen. Swarms of *mubros*—the Mexican mule-men—beat their charges along the thoroughfare, too, the tiny animals struggling under great bundles of sticks as their masters screamed out at the ox-drivers clogging the streets. Everywhere was color—orange, gold, red, blue, green—but the beauty, the spectacle, were not all-impressive to MacAshen. He could visualize the scars, too. San Antonio was a city that had spawned not only the tragedy of the Alamo, but the Anglo massacre of the Indian chiefs in the truce of the Council House as well. Against the adobe walls of the Plaza des Armes, Arredondo had executed a thousand men in 1813 and had driven their wives into the sordid place called the Quinta to provide sport for his troopers.

It was a city with a Spanish atmosphere and heritage, but overrun now by blue-clad troopers. Maybe it still sang to the cadence of the Mexican guitar, but it listened, too, for the sharp, rocking blast of the six-shooter. Even as MacAshen and the others pulled up before the hotel, there was meaning that could not be mistaken on the faces of the men who clustered near the doorway.

The meeting with the Yankee army officers, on the morning after MacAshen and his friends arrived, was held at cavalry headquarters in an old building just off the Plaza. Colonel Merritt had instructed his adjutant, Roman, and Colonel Badger of the Union's Second Louisiana Cavalry, to sit in with him while he listened to the visiting delegation.

The Texans quickly opened the meeting by stating the purpose of their visit. Stockdale outlined in detail the scope of Indian depredations all along the frontier, concluding with an urgent appeal for Union soldiers to halt the red atrocities.

"We've got to have relief, Colonel, and quickly," he said.

Merritt heard him out, but he did not answer immediately. Instead, after a time, he nodded to Roman to take up the issue.

"The colonel's desk is always stacked with appeals like this from the frontier settlements," Roman observed. "But we've said it before and we'll say it again: Most of it, to our way of thinking, is just plain hysteria."

"Seeing your children mutilated and murdered right before your eyes isn't hysteria, Major. And that's what's happening— everywhere—all the way up to the Red River. There was a time in this country when civilians didn't need to argue for protection against this sort of thing—soldiers took care of it, at least to the extent they could."

"You Texans never thought much of army help."

"We worked with the soldiers, and they worked with us— what there were of them, of course. There never were many in Texas."

Merritt broke in now. He rose and stepped to a map on the wall. "I think there were, Stockdale," he contradicted. "A fort was set up here at Camp Verde, west of Fredericksburg, in the middle forties; another at Fort Worth. And there were others, making a line straight across the frontier. I'd say the old army did pretty well by Texas."

"There were never more than three thousand soldiers in all those posts, Colonel, spread across a thousand miles."

"Well, you people always claimed you could handle things by yourselves. You ought to be sufficient at least for one tribe of Indians."

"A single tribe! Sir, you can't be that misinformed on Texas. Why, we're facing up to thirty thousand Comanches alone right now. But there're a half-dozen other tribes native to this state, too: the Tonkawas, Karankawas, Coushattas, Quapas, Wacos, Lipan Apaches. And there are the 'adopted' bands—the Delawares, Shawnees, Caddos, Ionies, Anadarkos, Kickapoos, and the Wichitas. Even still more than that, we have to put up with the ones just passing through, like the Creeks and Seminoles, the Cherokees, Osages, and the Toways. The Comanches are the worst, of course, but we've got no less than eighteen tribes to worry about, and many branches of several individual tribes."

"You make it sound pretty bad."

"It is bad, Colonel, considering how few hands we've got to try to stop the Indians."

Stockdale's presentation appeared to make little impression on the Union colonel. The meeting had been under way almost two hours. "Have you men anything else you wish to say to me," Merritt queried eventually.

"We've said what we came to say," Stockdale answered.

"In that case, we'll make a record of your remarks here." Merritt glanced toward Badger, the cavalry officer. "You handle it," Merritt said. Then he turned toward the door, striding out before even a final protest could be registered.

Badger gazed after him, then directed his attention to Mac-Ashen. "I think I remember you," he said to Levit. "I was with Schofield in Tennessee. What the colonel wanted me to tell you, I guess, is that United States troops are moving on to the Mexican border. Those who stay behind are posted for protection duty for the Negroes. That may not set well with your people, but that's the way it is. Merritt is in command here." He was silent for a moment, then asked, "How far from here does the real trouble begin?"

"North of San Antonio, and west, the whole country's open," MacAshen answered. "Not a hand to stop the red devils but those of the settlers themselves—what're left of them—and that's damned few!"

"What's the answer, considering that soldiers are needed elsewhere?"

"A frontier police force of our own, again."

"Could you put it together without government money? Quietly, maybe?"

"We could if we had to."

Badger rapped his knuckles gently on the table, studying the grain in the smooth wood. "I'm afraid you've not gained much out of this visit," he said quietly at last. "Personally, I'd like to say we'd help, but there's no use misleading you."

"Then we'll have to work it out for ourselves."

The officer raised his eyebrows. But he spoke again after a moment. "Maybe you will," he said. Then he added, "And perhaps you should."

Lubbock had to go no farther down the Guadalupe than the Holbrook ranch in search of the stocker cattle Levit wanted.

"We'll let you have a few," the rancher told him. "I can draw a hundred first-grade stockers from my own herd. Mr. Bartlett, south of here, might add fifty more to that. Some of the others will pitch in, but I can't say with how many."

"We'll be glad to get what we can as long as they're prime stockers."

"My family spends the Christmas season in San Antonio," Holbrook continued, "and that's right around the corner. We could drive the herd in then, ourselves. We've got to be taking some stock to market when we go, anyway. Seems like the past five or six months have just raced by, and we need to be at it again."

"Good! That would help things along."

Holbrook passed the word on to the other ranches after Lubbock and his cowboys had gone back northward. Standifer Wayne, Holbrook's closest neighbor to the south, was one of those who agreed to provide a dozen head for the stocker herd.

"Why don't you go in with Holbrook and those cattle, boss?"

Grippa suggested to Wayne. "You've been wanting to see San Antonio. And a spell somewhere besides a workin' cattle ranch for a few days would do you some good."

The suggestion was instantly appealing to Robella. Just to sleep in an honest-to-goodness, factory-made bed again! And certainly the others would do with such an interlude as well, Burr especially. He wasn't cut out for the solitude and loneliness of the Texas prairies, Robella was beginning to recognize. She was wearing badly, though she kept it hidden as much as she could. But the beds in this house! The large one in her room was affixed to the far corner. A hole had been chiseled into the floor and a pole planted firmly in the crevice. Horizontal beams ran from the pole to the walls to make a large rectangular frame, and core and rawhide strips were attached to the beams to support the bed itself. The frightful mattress rested on that. She took up Grippa's suggestion.

"I agree with you that the visit would be wonderful for all of us," she said to the old range hand. Turning to Standifer, she continued, "I think we should do as Adam suggests."

"All right," Standifer agreed after a time. "If you and Margaret wish it, Robella. And Burr can go along to help take care of us."

The gratitude was apparent in Robella's eyes, but she did not speak of it. A little later she went into her room. She sat for a while, looking out the dark window, then she went back across to the washstand. She held the candle level with her face and stared at herself in the mirror, raising a hand to touch the lines in her cheeks.

The Bartlett foreman, Ham Orgain, was selected to boss the trail herd, and it was put into movement ten days before Christmas. The cavalcade followed the Houston-San Antonio road northward to the point where it joined El Camino Real, ancient Spanish communications route from the border to San Augustine. "This road was blazed in 1691 by Domingo Terán de los Rios," the rancher Holbrook informed Standifer Wayne.

In the distance, the faint blue smudge of the rising hills blurred the skyline, and there were thunderheads up there. But the voyagers reached San Antonio without difficulty. The stock was herded to the south, beyond the jacales along the Salado. Burr was driving the Wayne wagon, and now he steered it into the heart of the city. The leather braces groaned when he hauled up with a shock of the brakes before the Menger Inn.

The Waynes were quickly established. Robella, once in her room, reveled as she had never before in the comfort of a hostelry. The Menger was a half-dozen years old in 1865, and she could recognize immediately its old world service and splendor— the reason for the fame it already enjoyed. Noting that game dishes were featured on its menu, she had food brought to her room. The influence of Teuton ancestry was quickly detectable in the flavor of the hotel's cuisine, too.

Robella lighted her night lamp, a long section of wick appearing through a slit in a piece of stiff cardboard. The night lights of the Menger, once ignited by a guest, were never extinguished until that visitor's departure.

Burr and Margaret walked upon the plaza adjacent to the hotel, both of them startled by the odd spectacles around. The myriads of birds appealed to the girl and there were even pepper trees in the courtyard. The musical cry of the candy-vendor, "Carmencillo-de-leche! Dulce! Dulce!" tempered the strange notes of the city; and Burr was astounded to observe a coach-and-four passing down the avenue. In it was a gentleman in silk hat and with him a white-satined lady.

The Waynes were made welcome by the innkeeper, himself, Herr Menger. Although of German extraction, Herr Menger spoke English well.

"This city, it is my delight," Herr Menger told them, "and I try to see that my guests here enjoy it, as I enjoy it."

"Sure, it's different," Burr said. "Even from a place like New Orleans."

"Perhaps, at your convenience, you would let me show you about, and tell you of San Antonio. Each day I walk the streets, the weather permitting. It is my sole recreation."

"We'd like that, Herr Menger."

Lubbock was bunked up in one of the range hands' hostelries, waiting for MacAshen to arrive. That day now also having come, the plainsman found Levit at the hotel. "The cattle you wanted are here, boss," he said.

"Good. When can I take a look?"

"Tomorrow. They're in a big herd which is mostly culls. But there are two hundred prime stockers for us. They'll have to be cut out. Fellow named Orgain is bossing the outfit. But the ranchers came in, too."

"Glad to hear it, Lubbock. I've got to pick up some money first. Then I'll want to see the cattle. What ranchers came in with them?"

"Fellow named Holbrook put up most of the herd. And he's here at the hotel. There's another one along who just kicked in about a dozen stockers. But he's only getting started out on the Guadalupe. Fellow named Wayne."

"Wayne?" Levit felt a slight constriction in his throat as he repeated the name. Lubbock nodded.

"I know one of the Waynes, I think," Levit said. "That is, if it's the same family. And, Lubbock," he pointed out as an after-thought, "we've finished the other job we came here to do. I want to get home now as quick as I can."

"Just give us the word."

The bank to which MacAshen hurried immediately after parting with Lubbock was one headed by a French resident named Leroux, a man who had come to Texas from Alsace with Henry Castro in 1844. The floors of his establishment were finished in hardwood, and he pointed out the window glass with pride to his visitor. "Imported," he said, "from New Orleans." Levit smiled, and Leroux went on, "You would avail yourself of our services, sir?"

"Yes." Levit told the banker his needs, gave his signature to drafts on Raymond's firm in Austin.

"It's a pleasure to accommodate you, Colonel," Leroux continued. "We knew of your father, but you were young when he came to San Antonio. It is good you now associate yourself with us, and it is a relief to be able to serve a cattleman again who knows where he stands."

"Texas ranchers have been hard put to stay on their feet, I guess."

"They have, indeed. Early in the war cattlemen prospered. Longhorns driven to New Orleans brought forty-five dollars the head. But that played out quickly, when they all tried to drive that way at once."

"I was gone then."

"Perhaps you are fortunate that you were."

MacAshen returned to the hotel. In the richly appointed

Menger bar, the first person he encountered was Burr Wayne, there with his father. Burr greeted MacAshen with a vigorous handshake.

"Didn't realize, nine months ago when I met you at Houston, that we'd be selling you cattle in Texas before the year was out," Wayne observed loftily.

MacAshen smiled. "No, neither did I. But I'm glad you've made your start."

"We were lucky enough to get at least one good range hand to help us. You spending Christmas here, Colonel?"

"No, I think not, Wayne. Once we cut out those cattle you brought us, the only thing we can do is start them up the trail."

They talked awhile. As MacAshen was leaving, he said politely to Burr, "I hope I'll get to meet your mother and sister while I'm here."

"You certainly shall. I'll see to that."

MacAshen met Mrs. Wayne and her daughter in the lobby as he prepared to start with Lubbock for a look at the cattle. Burr made the introductions.

"Oh, Colonel MacAshen," Margaret exclaimed, "Burr told us about you. I'm so glad to meet you."

"It's also quite a pleasure for me, miss," Levit responded. "I've heard of you, too, and you do credit to the description."

"You've heard of me?"

"Yes. From a lady who knew you well—Miss Newcomb."

"Oh, Karryl."

As soon as he had spoken, Levit realized he had unwittingly brought up the one name that would be of interest to both him and Burr. He sensed a sudden alertness in Wayne's manner, too.

"This your first visit to San Antonio?" Levit asked Margaret.

"Yes, sir."

"I think you'll like it. You must try to see all of this old Spanish town while you're here."

"We'll do that, Colonel MacAshen," Robella broke in. "And I hope to see you again," she added, nodding goodbye to him as she and Margaret moved on.

MacAshen and Lubbock found Orgain with the herd of stocker cattle. Levit inspected them carefully and liked what he saw. He paid Orgain in the gold he had obtained from Leroux.

"We'll take them over as soon as I get back with my pack and the rest of my men," he said. And then to Lubbock: "Round up the others and meet me here. We'll move out today."

Burr inquired about Levit again, but he found that Mac-Ashen had gone. "I think the colonel is driving his herd out already," Herr Menger informed him. "These hill country people, they do not stay too long in San Antonio—they are always hurrying to get back to their own preserves in the north again. In San Antonio, we do not hurry," he smiled.

"I've noticed you don't," Burr agreed, laughing. "And since there's nothing else to do, I think I'll take my sister for a stroll about the city today. Just to get in the spirit, you might say."

"Would you and your sister care to avail yourselves of my poor guidance in your sally? I've not had my own exercise yet today, and I am always intrigued by the excitement occasioned in the first glimpses of those who seek out our city's attractions."

"We certainly would."

"Then call her, if you will, and inform me when you're ready. We shall then be on our way."

When Margaret appeared in the lobby alongside Burr a short time later, Herr Menger said, "Seldom do I have the privilege of conducting one so young and beautiful about our gardens and our plazas."

Margaret smiled sweetly. "And it's almost never that anyone speaks so nicely to me—or of me—as that," she came back. She took the older man's arm. "Not even my brother says such things to me," she confided.

Burr shepherded them toward the door, and then out onto the sidewalk. "In due season, Herr Menger," he informed that gentleman, "if you had a sister as I have, you would become cautious in the way you speak."

"I am never cautious," the German laughed. "But now, shall we get along?" He indicated the street beside the hotel. "This is our main thoroughfare," he pointed out, "and we can go this way if you like. It is called the Alameda."

"That's a beautiful name," Margaret said.

"It is related to the Alamo. The Alamo means a place of

cottonwood trees, while the Alameda refers to a row of trees with a path between."

"Could we see the Alamo, too?"

"Of course. I will direct you there first, if you wish, but I think you will not be pleased. The Alamo is only a jumble of stone now, despite its exalted history." He led them along the sidewalk in front of the hotel. Then he pointed out the Alamo in the Plaza beyond.

It was, indeed, only a ruin, and they could not even get very close. But the park around was pretty, and to that extent she was placated. Close up within the shade, the *Pagarias*—women trappers—displayed their little cages of singing birds for sale, too, and she clutched her brother's arm.

"Oh, will you buy me one, Burr?" she implored.

"Later, Sis, later," with a sidewise smile at Menger.

"Let us move on," Menger counseled. "There is much, much more to see."

"I've heard of the gardens in San Antonio." Margaret spoke up, "Gardens that they say run down through arbors to the river. Are there such things, Herr Menger?"

"Indeed, there are." He conducted them along the avenue westward. "They begin here," he said finally. In the distance, he pointed out a great stone mansion. "That is the home of Colonel Erasmo de Seguin," he explained. "Its zaguan, or entrance hall, is supposed to be the most ornate in Texas. And there are the gardens about which you asked, behind the house."

Margaret gazed at the picture plots. "Oh, how delightful," she murmured.

"I, too, am fond of this part of San Antonio. Beyond Seguin's home you will see the residences of other Canary Islanders like him—the Trevinos and the Navarros."

"Do these families still live here?"

"Yes, indeed."

Herr Menger, in their slow jaunt, appeared to most enjoy the German establishments, which they came to now. "The Braunfels folk like to have their *kalter aufschmitt* and beer in this setting," Menger pointed out. He waved a cherry hand to a passing couple, and patted a chubby blond boy on the head.

Burr noted the broad-breasted Teuton matrons, smiling at him as they set their trays of little aromatic nut cakes in the open window sills to cool; but Herr Menger shepherded the three of them rapidly on. Eventually they crossed the river, stopping momentarily as they did so to watch the Indian washerwomen chattering and splashing in its waters.

Then they were among the bustling wayfarers on the Plaza des Armes. The big square was filled with cattlemen and Mexican vaqueros, eating from long tables. Fat, tawny materfamilias dished up scalding black coffee, eggs hot with red pepper, and beef steaks fried with onions. Margaret marveled that people were able to swallow any of the food, but apparently the heat deterred no one.

Back in the hotel, she could scarcely be contained. "It's such a wonderful city," she exclaimed to her mother. From her window, even as she said so, she noted a trio of Mexican caballeros in pantaloons trimmed with silver buttons, spurring their horses along the avenue. She leaned far out to see if she could get a better look at their faces.

"I'm glad you're happy, dear," Robella said.

"I've never been so happy or so excited in my life, Mother."

The romance of the setting, the fragrance of the San Antonio valley—the languor on every hand—these things almost intoxicated Margaret. But for Burr it was different. How could he really enjoy any of it with only a young sister alongside.

Burr wished Karryl Newcomb was in San Antonio with him. He had not been able to get her off his mind. Already he should have been back to see her. A vague misgiving penetrated him because MacAshen had spoken her name so easily. Was MacAshen interested in Karryl, too?

Herr Menger, the hotel proprietor, said to Burr: "You are a young man, and young men seek excitement. Have you been to the Plaza des Armes in the nighttime?"

"No."

"Then you should go. It is completely different at night."

"Different how?"

"Go there and see for yourself. But have a care, when you do. Although one may look at our fräuleins, it is verboten to go beyond. On the Plaza, at least."

Burr did go to the Plaza that evening. He found it illuminated by flaming lamps and scores of small campfires. The plaza was filled with visiting cowhands, soldiers in dark blue uniforms, Mexican caballeros—and senoritas.

An aroma of chile con carne, tamales, tortillas, enchiladas, frijoles, and sopa de arroz, came from the cooking fires; and there was shrill laughter on occasion—contrary to what Herr Menger had said—from the shadowed recesses.

"The devil take it," Burr exclaimed angrily. "Why the hell am I going through all this alone?"

Christmas came quickly and was gone. Holbrook gave notice thereafter that he wanted to leave for home as soon as possible, and Standifer Wayne hurried to find a banker he could talk with. As it happened, that banker was the same Leroux MacAshen had called on.

"I'm worried, Mr. Leroux," Wayne said. "And that is why I wanted to talk with some of you business people. I do not understand the country folk in Texas, or just how they go about making a success of their ranching. How long do you think it will take me to get on a solid footing—if I ever do?"

"Well, if you have a stocker herd, you have a good start. A herd will double itself in four years, today, granting that the Indians and rustlers leave you alone. And if the weather does not destroy you. Perhaps the weather is more to fear than other things. A bad norther, Mon Dieu, it is a terrible thing. Bulls go first, then the yearlings. And if it's bad enough, then the strong three- and four-year-olds are stricken, too. What you need most, M'sieur Wayne—or at least this is the way I see it— are experienced hands to take care of you, since you do not know your way yet."

"I realize that, and my son does, too. We hoped we'd be able to find some men here in San Antonio. But I haven't run into any, and I don't know if I will."

"Try at the Silver King. Boys who want work can generally be found there."

Wayne thanked the banker and left. That same afternoon he and Burr went to the Plaza des Armes, as Leroux had suggested. San Fernando Cathedral looked down from the west, and a line of one-story adobe structures circled the area. On the north stood the building which had served as headquarters for Santa Anna; and adjacent thereto was the Silver King. The two entered the saloon.

Booted dusty riders were gathered about the tables of eucher, and a folksong rose from the group clustered around the saloon's battered piano. Burr's spirits were lifted a trifle as they stood inside the door and listened to the words:

> *Coffee grows on live oak trees;*
> *River flows with brandy-o;*
> *Go choose someone to walk with you*
> *Sweet as molasses candy-o!*

Burr and his father found a table and ordered drinks.

"We're looking for some good cowhands," Burr Wayne said to the bartender, when they had been served. "Do they check in with you?"

The man inclined his head toward a pair of youths leaning against the rail at the back of the room. "Always two or three hangin' out in the Silver King."

Burr swallowed his drink, then walked toward the boys indicated. "You fellows looking for work?" he asked.

Slowly, they turned: "Depends, mister. Where?"

"Middle Guadalupe."

The two boys mumbled to each other. The first—a tow-headed boy—turned back to Burr. "As long as it's not way off down the Brasada way we might be able to go along," he said.

"Then you're hired. Where do you fellows hail from?"

"Up on the Leon River. But we've been around."

"All right." He told the pair of his plans and where to join the wagon on the morrow.

"We'll be there," the others pledged.

Burr returned to his table. He had raised his glass for the last drop, when a touch on his shoulder brought him around. A dark, slender youth in blackened leather chaps and linsey-woolsey was behind him. "I heard you asking about peelers," the youth said. "You got all you need?"

"Are you looking for work, too?"

"I am, mister."

"What's your name?"

For a brief instant, the youth hesitated. He glanced downward, his eyes fixing themselves finally on the rawhide strings through the corner of his chaps. "Lacing." he answered. "Ben Lacing."

"All right, Lacing. We could use at least one more. Be ready to go by daylight. We're riding out with a couple of wagons." The youth accepted quickly, attentive to the further instructions. When the interview ended, Ben Lacing nodded his head in understanding; then he turned quietly and walked out the swinging door.

At the hotel, Robella and Margaret finished their packing and went downstairs for dinner. After they had finished, Margaret drew her mother out through the hotel entrance for a last look at the spectacle of the prairie fireflies coming in from across the river. The Plaza was aglitter in the dark.

Every time she had stood here in the evening, Margaret had felt strong urges filling her bosom, for this was the hour when one sensed the heartbeat of the city.

There were young men always at that hour in the Plaza, and when she saw them the yearning to live coursed through her. The handsome Mexican gallants passed strange messages with their eyes—warm, intimate messages. She found herself exulting, too, as the lanky, curious American cowboys followed her with their gaze.

Back inside, Margaret said to her mother, "We'll be going home tomorrow, but this is the most wonderful Christmas we've had, or ever will have!"

They were under way early next morning. At noon, when the wagons had halted and the preparation of a midday meal was begun, Wayne called the trio of new riders up to the wagon and introduced them to his mother and Margaret.

"Here are the new cowboys, Sis. Say hello to them."

The two companions whose services he had first engaged broke into broad smiles and doffed their sombreros.

"Mighty pleased to meet you, miss."

The third man, Ben Lacing, stared for a moment, then removed his hat. But his eyes remained on her face. Margaret met the expression with a puzzled glance of her own. Maybe he had never before seen a girl like her. Maybe he didn't know just how to act.

She gave him her hand. "You—you've come to ride for the Waynes?" she asked, noticing that his hair was thick and dark, and his eyes clear and cool and questioning.

"Yes, miss, I hope so."

"Why, I think that's mighty nice." Quickly she added: "I'm glad to meet all of you." Then she turned, and retreated into the wagon.

[155]

Late in the afternoon Margaret moved over with the Holbrooks, and sometime afterward Standifer Wayne switched to his saddle horse. Burr sat with his mother on the wagon seat. They followed the road down out of the hills and pointed toward the Comal.

When they had ridden for perhaps an hour in that fashion, and were not far southwest of the German community of New Braunfels, he said: "I think I'll leave you folks when the road turns toward the Guadalupe, Mother."

"Leave us, Burr?"

"Oh, you'll be all right now, Mother. There are plenty of hands with the wagons. I've just been restless as the devil—I'll have to confess—and I want to go in to Austin to see Karryl again."

"But Christmas is over now, Burr."

"I know that, Mother, But she's been alone over there all during the holidays. It's not likely she's been very happy. She's got nobody there really to turn to."

"I . . . I wish you wouldn't go just yet, Burr," Robella protested, almost pleadingly.

"Well, why in the world not, Mother?"

"I'm afraid. Oh, not afraid just like it sounds, Burr. But, well things haven't been too good for me just lately. Or—or for your father, either, as he told you before we left. You've not noticed those things, but . . . well, couldn't you wait till we get back home and are settled down again, Burr?" Her words were almost feverish.

"You're tired, Mother," Burr placated her. "This trip's been hard on you."

"Yes, I'm tired, Burr. But the trip has not been hard on me. I'm afraid it might be more than that. I've been wanting to talk with you, but I've not known exactly how to say it." She faltered for a moment, reaching hesitantly for words. "This country we've come to, Burr, it is rich and beautiful and it offers a person many things. I have hoped that in time you would come to love it, though I'm beginning to doubt that now.

"But Margaret will become a woman here, Burr. She's that now, by the standards of this land. It may be good for her; perhaps she will be good for it. But I'm terribly frightened, Burr. She's my little girl, and if anything should happen to your father and me . . . oh, Burr, won't you please, please stay close and look out for her?"

"But nothing is going to happen to you, Mother," he said.

She sighed. "One never knows. The past few years have told on both of us; your father as well as me. It's the little things you haven't begun to notice yet that are meaningful. Your father is no longer capable of the things he once was, and certainly I am not. I'm desperately afraid, Burr, for all of us."

"Mother, you're gloomy today. Of course, I'll always look out for Margaret and Father. And for you, too." He chucked her under the chin, attempting to cheer her. "But you look fit as a fiddle to me."

She rested her head for a moment against his shoulder and was silent. Then she raised her eyes and faltered: "I—I didn't mean to try to spoil your chance of visiting with Karryl, Burr. It's just that—"

"Forget it, Mother," he muttered shortly. "I'm not going off and leave you when you feel like this."

15

There were new wagons along the Pedernales that winter. They came singly, bringing only a man at a time, or perhaps one family. Luckily, these were undemanding people, seeking only cabin space close to the river, a plot on which to plant a few acres of corn and vegetables. But the Pedernales was MacAshen cattle range.

Levit was in the saddle almost constantly, and he was at home on the Pedernales less and less. Attempting to set up some kind of system into which the old Rangers might be attracted again was no easy chore. Others were at the same task elsewhere, but the primary effort rested solely upon Levit. It was only by keeping his cowhands riding the valley up and down the river from the Falling Water that he was able to advertise his property right to the immigrants while he worked at his new obligation.

"We've got to have a damned tight organization—there's no other way to put a Ranger force together we can depend on," he told Lubbock when his foreman urged him to take out a spell and look after the needs of the Falling Water.

"Well, let 'em build on us here. There's eight at this ranch alone to start with."

"What good could eight men do, in the job that has to be

done? We've got to have a lot of pockets just like this—places around which the old-timers could be clustered—and where we could reach them when we needed them."

"You settin' up such places?" Lubbock asked.

"I'm trying to. Roberts, up on the Llano, is coming in. And Swanson, at Mason. There are others, too—not many yet—but they know what they're doing. And, God knows, they're willing enough."

"The Federals may ride in on you."

"Not if we're careful. The idea, Lubbock, is to try to get jobs for the men we need on ranches close by, where we could call them together quick. And since we can't place many in any one spot, we've got to have a dozen—maybe two dozen— such outposts."

"How long do you think it'll take to put this army together, MacAshen?"

"It won't be an army, Lubbock. But I can't answer that, anyway. Those of us who're in it will just have to do our best."

In one of the rare intervals when MacAshen was at the Falling Water, however, his wrangler, Herman Nusser, corralled a two-year-old golden buckskin stallion. "I've been hoping for something like this," MacAshen said to Nusser. "I'll have a mistress for this animal someday here on the Falling Water." To Lubbock, he said: "I'll break the horse myself."

"You sure you want to, Levit? That's no range donkey. That's a wild stallion, wilder than any I ever saw before."

Levit laughed. "You don't think I can, eh?"

"I didn't say that. It ain't my job to think. But there's no sense in getting your neck broke. Let Nusser ride him. That German knows how."

Levit looked about at his men. "Anything one of my outfit can do, I ought to be able to do better," he grinned. "Besides, all of you men are peelers. How about you, Meadows?"

"Boss, I'm a cowhand, not a wrangler," Meadows hastened to point out.

"Tie the stallion up," Levit ordered.

"Don't do it, boss," Lubbock urged again, unsuccessfully. Meadows started the buckskin on a gallop around the pen.

Torkin, near the gate, watched the horse's red-rimmed eyes carefully. After the buckskin had circled the corral twice, the lariat swept out to catch both front feet. Torkin then jerked backward on the rope and looped it around a corral post. The buckskin fell heavily on his side. Meadows came up from behind and seized the horse's head. He twisted straight up, a knee against the horse's neck.

Working fast, he looped the front feet and attached the lasso to the hind. Then he tightened, and three of the buckskin's feet came together. In a second, the horse was unable to rise. Carefully, Meadows slipped on the bridle and made it fast. Next, he belted the saddle straps, and finally tied a kerchief across the horse's wildly rolling eyes.

"Throw off the lines," Levit said to Meadows. When that was done, the big stallion came to his feet. Levit tightened the cinches. "Now grab the blindfold, and get out of the way," he shouted. He vaulted into the saddle.

For an instant, the animal appeared dazed by the light. Then, suddenly, recognizing the unexpected burden on his back, he came explosively to life. He hunched frantically, burying his head between his hoofs and bawling out in anger.

"Look out, boss!"

The buckskin whirled and spun. He leaped abruptly, legs stiffening. Again, back arched, he shot a half-dozen feet into the air.

Levit stuck to the saddle, his knees like the clamps of a vice, but the maddened animal's gyrations shook him almost out of his senses.

"Ride him, MacAshen!" Meadows yelled.

The buckskin suddenly leveled out, scattering the men by the gate and driving the rest hastily over the bars. Then he ran, bucking and bellowing out his rage and anger. But eventually he slowed, and when the buckskin passed the gate again, MacAshen threw a leg across the saddle and slid off. "How'd I do?" he demanded of Lubbock.

"Reckon all right, boss, not to get killed," Lubbock replied gravely. "I told you that wasn't no ordinary bronc." MacAshen rubbed his side. "You ready to let somebody else take over, boss?" Lubbock inquired.

Levit grinned. "I am now," he said. Then to Nusser. "But gentle that horse like you never gentled one before."

The weather was raw and cold in January—the days short and bleak, and the nights long, dark and forbidding. Men kept close to their fires and entertained themselves with stories and songs.

MacAshen, home for a few hours, heard the heavy, agitated pounding of the hooves even before the dogs raised the rider coming down the valley road. So explosive was the man's arrival that he was almost upon the compound before the yelps and barking drowned out the abrupt halt. MacAshen sat up in his bed, shook the sleep from his eyes. There were voices from the corral, and a sharp order that quelled the barking. He swung his feet down upon the floor, reaching in the darkness for his boots. Through the window, a cold star hung low upon the ink-marked skyline, and the brassy illumination from the heavens silhouetted the southern wall in jagged outline. He stood up and struck fire, lighting the tallow dip before he reached for his clothes.

In the big room adjacent, he stoked up the coals in the fireplace and threw a log upon the glow. The sparks showered, and he stoked again, feeling the cold pinch of the air upon his back.

Lubbock came in quickly with the man. The expression on his face telegraphed the intelligence to MacAshen all too clearly.

"Savages?"

The rider's jaw worked, and for a moment the words did not come.

MacAshen shoved a chair forward. "Sit," he ordered.

The man hesitated a moment, staring at MacAshen and turning a face raw from the weather toward the blaze in the hearth. Then he twisted the chair forward, spread his hands out over the fire and settled violently upon the rawhide seat.

"He's running the line, MacAshen," Lubbock furnished. "Name's Kaspel. There's a war party behind the Bullheads."

The door opened again and Meadows came in, pulling his coat about him; then the Monhalls. From the kitchen quarters in the rear the Mexican too slipped quietly into the room.

"Bring coffee," MacAshen ordered, "and food."

Suddenly, the newcomer moved impulsively.

"I was coming in from the Putnam Mesas," he whispered, hoarsely. "East, down the Cottonwood, where it hits the big wash. I'd trailed a straying horse, my pie-bald, to the Seven Hundred Springs on the upper South Llano, and caught him; and I was moving back in north of the Bullheads toward Blount Mountain, calculating to hit the settlement and bed down for the night. The Cottonwood and Prairie Mountain Springs come together halfway between the Bullhead peak and Blount Mountain, two miles west, and old Coppinger lives in there. Homesteader, with a spring and a few acres of winter oats.

"They saw me first. They were coming up the Cottonwood—that's south—and they were driving a hundred head of horses. Rode right into 'em close enough to look straight over their heads at Coppinger's cabin."

"How many?"

"Twenty-five, I reckon. Mostly Kiowas, but they were led by Comanches. I could see the lances."

"Quohadas?" Levit demanded.

"Reckon so, but I didn't try too hard to make out what they was. The pie-bald smelled 'em. When he plunged, it brought me up, and there they were, coming on in double file, the caballado in the middle, and the young bucks just moving up to set a forward scout. I cut the pie-bald loose, and cleared back like hell across the Prairie Spring branch. Got a rifle ball through my stirrup strap, and the arrows cut across my bridle, but I beat 'em out. Rough country in there. A dozen of 'em rode my tail for the next two miles, maybe more, then turned back to join the others. Figger they thought to catch the pie-bald and maybe they did. I circled wide to the east after that, back behind the shank of the Blount and up the ridges to the summit, where I could see. They were gone, but west of there the birds were rising, so I figured they'd moved that way. I rested my horse, and when it was clear, I rode back to the Coppinger cabin."

The Mexican brought in a pot of coffee and poured a tin cup full. It was warm, but not hot, and he set the pot on the coals. The man drank deeply and gratefully, wiping his sleeve across his face.

"Worst I ever saw," he burst out violently. "Coppinger was penned up inside the cabin with arrows. Dozens of 'em, and deep. But they didn't kill him then. They let him die, slow I guess, so he could see."

He reached for the pot and filled his cup again. Again, he drank and set the cup down. He rose suddenly and turned to face the men.

"Guess they held Coppinger's wife till they had him nailed up good, then they went to work on her. She was a young woman, twenty or so; maybe you've seen her. Long yellow hair, and they wanted that hair. But not too quick.

[162]

"What they done to her was awful. You could still see it in her face, fresh dead. Coppinger was tore up bad, but the arrows didn't do it. He tore those holes in his body trying to get loose.

"They cut his wife's clothes off, and then they really worked on her. Heated arrowheads—that sort of thing. Tricks with knives they learned from the squaws."

Perspiration stood out on the man's face, in spite of the cold room.

"That's enough," MacAshen said. "Were there any others?"

"Coppinger had a kid, a little girl. She wasn't there. They got her."

A slab of beef was on the table, and a pan of bread. Mac-Ashen gestured toward the food. "You'd better eat. You'll need your strength." He watched the man fall upon the food. Then he turned toward Lubbock, standing tense and granite-cold in the shadows. "How far has he come?"

"He rode in by Crab Apple Creek, and down the Palo Alto to the Pedernales."

"Which way are you going, Kaspel?" MacAshen asked the man.

"Down the river, and across to Round Mountain. My wife and kids are in there, unless . . . " The thought brought him sharply to his feet, turning toward the door.

"Give him a fresh horse Lubbock, the best you've got." MacAshen motioned to the Mexican. "Wrap that beef in a saddlebag and pour the coffee in a canteen. Tie it to his saddle."

The rider pivoted, his hand on the door. "The Germans are gathering up above the river at Bell Mountain. I got word to them. I'll check on my own, and pick up what I can, if everything is all right over toward the Colorado. Then I'll cut your trail above the Llano."

MacAshen nodded. "Tell the others we'll be away from here by dawn," he said, and as an afterthought: "Be careful." The meaninglessness of the caution struck him as soon as he had spoken, but the man was gone. MacAshen turned to appraise his riders, lined stiffly against the wall in the flickering light of the fire.

"So they've come at us again," he accepted harshly. "I'll want both you Monhalls," he decided. "You stay at the ranch Meadows, and Nusser as well. You, too, Pepito. You've got

[163]

guns and ammunition. But send word both ways up the valley. See that pickets are put out to the north. If the savages are moving this way, let the people send their families here. A half-dozen of you could beat away a hundred warriors. Check the provisions, and be sure the water barrels are filled. I'll leave it to you, Meadows."

Meadows left the room, the cowboys behind him, and Lubbock returned.

"Has Kaspel gone?"

"Yes, boss, and he's moving fast."

"Lubbock, you can go or you can stay. You've had your share of this kind of thing already." Lubbock's eyes were cold, and MacAshen had no need to hear his reply, but he waited.

"I'll go."

"All right. Check the gear. The Warrior is rested, and I'll take him. We'll wait three hours, since we couldn't gain anything in the dark except tired horses. Meadows can leave now."

Elledge came in with the German, Grobecker, during the dark hours, and later Ramsdale from the South Grape, with one of his two riders.

"Moon's high, Levit," Elledge muttered, shaking the leather coat from his shoulders and working his hands over the fire. "I saw it for a minute before it hit that cold cloud bank. It was a red moon tonight, most like the color of blood."

They ate, and drank of the freshly made coffee. MacAshen brought out his old army bag. He took a square of soft deerskin and folded meat and bread in it, then filled the round canteens. Outside, the saddled horses stamped, and the wind freshened, bringing with it the intimation of harder weather.

Daylight billowed upon the land in clay-cold, ash-like swells that shrouded the hills and fogged the hollows. Above the Round Head, the route was upward and west, to the point where the Burnet road joined the north-south trail. Lubbock rode abreast of MacAshen, and behind them came the Monhalls, the eagerness on their raw young faces in sharp contrast to the steel-hard earnestness of their companions. A low escarpment ran to the right of them, and an abrupt valley to the left, and Elledge and the others held the drag close and compact. Schist and sandstone fractured under the heavy hoofbeats, but there was rainwater with a crust of ice in the rocks. A layer of fine, frozen mud on the path held down the usual splatter of limestone dust; and the parched, penetrating bittersweetness of burdock weeds, still fighting the winter, assailed their nostrils.

"It will be cold today," Lubbock warned.

They dipped into a coulee, followed the winding defile down until it crossed Willow Creek, and then ascended rapidly once more.

"Redskins on the warpath in winter. They must be hungry." MacAshen muttered once.

"Splinter bands. Young bucks breaking down from across the Red, or coming in from the Estacado. Kiowas, likely, chopping for horses and scalps, before the Comanches move in and sweep the season's crop."

"There were Comanches in the band."

"Maybe just enough to watch the Kiowas, and hold 'em to the smaller drives. And to let 'em know who's master. When the Comanches come, they come like Comanches."

MacAshen held up his hand, and the column halted. A small cluster of horsemen flanked the trail ahead. Spread out a bit, they had pulled up their mounts and were watching MacAshen's riders carefully. They were lean, trailworn men, marks of wind and snow chiseled on their features.

"Strangers," Lubbock observed. Levit walked the Warrior a few steps, and one of the riders detached himself to prod his mount forward. The man was dark and heavy set, and a two-day growth of black beard was splotched with the evidence of heavy riding.

"Good morning to you," the man called out.

Levit nodded. He glanced ahead at the other horsemen. There were four of them, one a leather-clad blond giant of perhaps thirty-five, with a heavy pistol strapped low on his thigh. All were motionless, eyes attentive.

"Guess you're the Pedernales rancher, MacAshen," one queried, his eyes probing for something. "At least, I'd gather as much from the descriptions I've heard of MacAshen."

Levit nodded. "And you?" he asked.

"Name's Devers. I've taken over a cattle outfit down on the Blanco. Been riding this way in search of strays and drifters."

Levit nodded again. There was something vaguely familiar about the man, but he could not bring the image into focus. He relaxed a trifle and motioned his men to dismount. The group ahead kept to their horses.

"Devers," MacAshen considered. "Seems I've heard the name. But I don't place you. You're new to the hills?"

"Yes. My country is southwest of San Antonio."

MacAshen shook hands, and the gesture seemed to produce just a trace of relief in the other man. MacAshen put it down to Devers' newness on the range, and he nodded his head toward his own group.

"Lubbock, my foreman," he said. "The Monhall boys—."
He called each man in his party by name, and each nodded. Devers motioned his own riders forward. The blond man's name was Castlerod. MacAshen again noted the way he wore his guns; he did not remember the others' names.

"You're riding fast," Devers remarked.

"Yes. The Redskins were in north of here yesterday. A pursuit is mounting."

"Redskins?"

"Comanches, or Kiowas. Likely they've swung west now, but they'll circle north, since they're driving a herd of stolen horses."

Devers turned to his cowboys. "Did you hear that, Castlerod? Indians!" Castlerod nodded coolly. Devers turned back to MacAshen. "I guess we'd better join up with you," he said.

"We can use every hand." MacAshen pulled the Warrior's head around now and stepped back into the saddle. Lubbock and the others followed his action. As he swung astride, he called to Devers, "We're headed for a rendezvous on Bell Mountain."

"I'll send a man to the Blanco and follow you," Devers said.

Eight men were assembled in the shallow basin south of the ridge below Bell Mountain, and a ninth was poised on the summit above. The ridge ran west and then north, breaking the perspective. MacAshen studied the waiting group as his column wound downward. The horses trailed their reins, and holding the center of the posse was a tall bearded giant, Lenneweber, from the country west of Loyal Valley. MacAshen knew the man. His heavy, big-boned frame was clad in thick corduroy, and a black sombrero rested low on his shaggy brows. He wore a Colt's .45 revolver on his hip, and a Sharp's carbine rested in the crook of his arm. His air was that of a man confident of his action: estimating, evaluating, appraising. He stared hard at the approaching horsemen, his gaze lingering for a moment on the faded butternut pack behind MacAshen's saddle. Then Mac-Ashen and his hands reined into the circle and swung aground.

"Herr MacAshen?" the German asked.

"Yes."

"I know you. But you're older, yet."

"Time has a way with men."

Lenneweber's restless gaze moved on to Warrior. "Ach, so! That is a fine horse you ride; indeed, a charger."

"He's old, but he's earned his keep."

The dark stare returned to MacAshen, deep, discerning, but revealing none of the thought behind it. "It is well you come. We need you." MacAshen inclined his head a fraction in acceptance. Lenneweber continued: "These men, they have asked me to lead. You can ride with us or, if you wish, we can ride with you."

"You know the land, Lenneweber. It's not important at the moment. You take command, and we'll follow."

Lenneweber turned toward Levit's men, studying fractionally each rider in turn. He raised an abrupt finger. "Elledge, it is glad I am to see you again." He halted a moment before Lubbock. "I know your face but your name I cannot remember."

MacAshen supplied his foreman's name. Lenneweber paused a moment in thought.

"Yes," he said softly. "It comes to me now."

He looked searchingly at Devers, and the three riders who had by now followed him in. "Mr. Devers," MacAshen called out in introduction. "A rancher from the Blanco basin to the south." Lenneweber considered him wonderingly, but he accepted the outstretched hand, and then he turned back toward his own band. He signaled the lookout, and the waiting horsemen tightened the cinches on their mounts. "The Indians are moving west," he said. "We are more than a day behind, already, but—" He turned to Ramsdall. "I will ask you to go down the Cottonwood to the Coppinger place and take care of things there. When you are finished, we will need you, if you can catch up."

The rancher from the South Grape nodded. He crooked a finger toward a rider standing across from him. Then he stepped into his saddle, raised his hand in a half gesture, and wheeled his horse down the basin.

Forward, Lenneweber set the pace and the direction, and MacAshen rode beside him. They rode hard, but the movement did not dull the raw, biting edge of the cold wind in their faces. West of the Enchanted Rock, the horsemen marked a more northerly course, swinging wide around the base of the Putnams and leveling again above Cherry Springs. They forded Marshall Creek and Bear Springs Branch without delaying the pace.

"Many pursuits like this we make," the German said to MacAshen. "But mostly with no success."

MacAshen did not answer, and after a while the German turned toward him again. "You have been away." He did not press the question, but MacAshen understood its import. Again Lenneweber's eyes dwelt briefly on Levit's trappings, the old and tattered cover on the saddle canteen marked with a faded C.S.A.

"Yes," he answered. There could be no advantage in evasion. "I've been with the army—the Confederate Army."

"This, I had heard." Lenneweber's eyes did not falter. They continued to sweep the countryside. MacAshen studied the great, hulking figure of the man, so expressive of the vibrant, driving force of this shin-oak empire, and oddly enough he could detect no bitterness about him. But it could have been nurtured deeply; the site of the Confederate massacre of the German boys on the Nueces was no more than a hard day's ride from the spot he was traversing at this moment. Lenneweber's son had died there.

"War among civilized people, a tragic thing it is," Lenneweber declared tonelessly.

"Men find that out too late."

The German stared again, but he apparently had made his point, and he changed the course. "It is your first Indian scout since your return?"

"Yes, but I was in the Cave Creek wars, and in the troubles around the South Grape as a boy. North across the Red, too, in 1858."

"It is much the same, but since 1863, these raids have been smaller, more often and worse. Most of the raids have been on the Bosque or Concho. Also, north of the Colorado and Brazos, but settlers there are few, and most who stayed are dead."

[168]

"The way I've heard it, you've had plenty of trouble here close to the Pedernales, too."

Lenneweber raised his eyes. "We must admit that, Herr Mac-Ashen, though we do not like to. But especially since the Confederate troops left the frontier posts, and the Rangers disbanded, there has been nothing to stop the Indians. They steal and kill despite their treaties with us; then back across the Red to Indian territory they ride."

In the mid-afternoon, Lenneweber spread the scouts farther afield, and they rode bent over the saddle, eyes on the ground. Once, MacAshen happened to look behind him, noting a thin spiral of smoke far back to the east and the south. He called to Lenneweber and indicated the blot against the sky. The German studied it; then he nodded understandingly and went on.

For a time no incident occurred to slow the march, but late in the day, as the riders wore with the constant movement, the flanker off to the north signaled a rendezvous. Lenneweber called out to the horsemen to dismount and rest; then motioned MacAshen to his side. The two rode wide of the file, across a terrain slashed by weathered gullies, to the plateau where the outrider waited. MacAshen recognized the sign before Lenneweber spoke.

"This is the trail," Lenneweber said finally, "and a large band it is."

He bent low over the hoof tracks again, raising a blade of grass here and there, watching it droop again. "Early in the morning. Very early," he decided.

Ramsdall and his partner came up behind them when they reached the far side of the Llano. They called out, and the column halted to wait. Their horses heaved, and Ramsdall pulled off his hat to run a tired arm across his brow.

Lenneweber said to Ramsdall: "The smoke, we observed it from the prairie."

The man's face tightened, deep cords rising in the sinews of his neck. "I fired the cabin," he said. "No one should ever see it again."

The Indian trail led directly north now, and the land was flat and even. They camped on the headwaters of Salinas Creek in a dry gully that ran back a thousand feet to the west and ended abruptly in hundred-foot cliffs. Twilight fell like a cold mantle upon them, and Lenneweber conferred with MacAshen.

"I think they are still far ahead," he said. "Hot food will do us good."

MacAshen agreed. He opened his pack and took out bacon, coffee, and bread. "Stay here and you won't have to open your saddle bags," he said to Lenneweber. The German considered a moment, then accepted with dignity.

"That is kind of you. I had no time to select wisely of rations."

The smell of bacon frying floated over the coulee; afterward, tired men opened their blankets and fell upon them. Lubbock came to sit on the other side of the tiny campfire, and Lenneweber went to talk with the lookout. Levit refilled his tin cup with coffee and drank slowly. He rested his back against his saddle and watched the sharp stars break through the darkening sky. The low, throbbing murmur of the creek and the intermittent stamp of the horses lulled him, but sleep refused to come. Once, MacAshen noted that the newcomer, Devers, was eyeing him with a strange, probing expression, but turned away when his stare was detected.

He moved about and found Elledge, also nearby, gazing quietly into the blaze.

"It's something new, ranches down in the Blanco basin, is it not, Elledge?" he asked in tones that did not carry beyond the two of them.

"Yes. Never been many people in there. I hear stories about the Blanco country, Levit, but nobody really knows much about it. New outfits down in there for sure. If I was running the kind of spread you've got at the Falling Water, I'd keep an eye on the pass to the south. Don't figure the longhorns would drift off the Pedernales by themselves; but they might be persuaded."

Levit saw Lenneweber when the German returned to roll into his blanket. The horsy smell of the riders around, the quick rising crescendo from the tired, sleeping westerners, the job before him tomorrow—and maybe the day after—stirred heavy recollections out of the past, of lonely patrols and midnight advances, of sweat and dirt, and sudden death all around. The earthy aroma of the open prairie, borne in on the north winds, added dimension to the contemplation. MacAshen recognized the aching throb of his own tired muscles—the absence of relaxation upon the hard, unyielding earth, and he wondered if the life he had set for himself made him, too, as unyielding as that soil. He was a man still riding alone, though not necessarily because he wanted it that way. But the prodding of a thought of months ago came back to him: that an army without a symbol was an army without a purpose. Could the suggestion apply to man as well? The question troubled him. Did he really have a symbol, or anything like that? For what was he striving? He recognized a void, like the black expanse up there above him; and he knew in that moment, too, that there was only one way he could bridge that void. He knew he would someday, but how and when? Karryl Newcomb was heavy upon his thoughts; this night as never before he wanted her near him.

Elledge moved away to his own blankets, but Levit saw that Lubbock was still there, gazing into the dying coals. Levit pushed himself up. "I've got some tobacco, Lubbock," he said, "in the pack behind you." The man tossed the fold across to him, and he drew out the wrap. He rolled a cigarette and passed the weed and the paper to his foreman.

The smoke warmed him, but it did nothing to dispel his morbidness. Something weighed upon his mind, and he sought to remove it. He thought of Kaspel's story on the tragic fate of Coppinger's wife.

"It is a hard, unhappy country for a woman, this country of the hills," he said finally.

Lubbock's eyes mirrored recollections, but his silence was the silence of discernment. "It is better here than on the Pease and Wichita, or west along the Double Mountain Fork of the Brazos," Lubbock answered finally.

"It's no different anywhere."

"The wars will pass, and men will lead peaceful lives here, because it is a good country. Some must go before." MacAshen thought he caught a sigh, but Lubbock spoke again, quickly. "Homes can make this land, and homes there will be."

"Why do men force their women into such a life?"

A trace of sorrow infused Lubbock's words, but his eyes across the firelight drilled into MacAshen's face. "Why do women allow it? I think you are restless and uncertain yourself tonight, MacAshen. But the time will come when you'll have a family here on the frontier, too. A woman will want to come to you. Maybe one already does, and you're holding back."

The blood coursed in MacAshen, but he did not answer. Finally, in total weariness, he slept, aware of the men around him and of the dim cedar-crusted cliffs above him, but oblivious then to the tension of the moment and the task to come.

A firm, but quiet grip awakened him. He was conscious that the hours had passed; it was the blackness before dawn. Around him, the men were rising heavily to their feet. It was cold, very cold, and with their blankets rolled into saddle packs again the men shivered in the mountain air.

Lenneweber had built a fire, and the aroma of bacon sizzling in the pan wafted over to MacAshen.

"With your father, I trailed like this once, MacAshen," the German said. "A good man he was, and he made friends with my people."

"I want to keep up that friendship, if I can," Levit responded quickly to Lenneweber.

"I think you can."

Dawn brought out the perspective of rough country ahead. The sun came up, but it was scarcely visible in the ground fog. At midmorning, Lenneweber raised his hand, beckoning to MacAshen and Lubbock. A small depression lay before them, and there was evidence of recent occupancy. Here the Indians had camped. The raiders had killed one of the mustangs, eating the sides of ribs and the hindquarters. In the darkness before day, after they had moved on, the wolves had come down out of the brakes and torn the rest of the carcass apart.

The posse crossed the San Saba a dozen miles west of the old ranger camp, and at noon they were in the foothills of the Brady Mountains. Lubbock studied the sign, carefully going over the ground again with Elledge and Lenneweber. The German came back to MacAshen. "We have gained. Tomorrow we strike them."

In the afternoon, they came to the Colorado, wide here and shallow, studded with granite rocks and cold upon their legs. Across the great river, they found themselves at the entrance of a ravine, and as they approached it, the dull sun sank toward the rim of the hills in the west. Lenneweber signaled a halt.

"Again we rest," he advised, and a moment later, "we camp here tonight." He wandered a few paces up the incline, Mac-Ashen at his side and Lubbock close behind. Lubbock bent down and breathed the vapor rising from horse droppings in the dust.

"Fresh," he confirmed. "Not many hours ago."

"Yes," Lenneweber replied. "We are close. They will pass east of Santa Anna peak in Coleman County and make for the Callahan Divide beyond. We cannot let them reach it."

They camped well back from the stream in the protection afforded by the shale walls of a low depression. The saddle packs were thrown on the ground and opened, and the men sat eating silently of pemmican and jerky and cold canteen coffee.

Lenneweber sent one of his men forward a half-mile to the summit of the canyon wall to watch the trail for rear guard scouts. "They have not discovered us yet," he surmised. They led their horses back to the river to drink. When they returned, they tied the stake ropes to their wrists and settled themselves on the ground. MacAshen placed his rifle beside him, rolled in the blanket and laid his head far back. Lenneweber came to sit beside him.

"They do not yet know we follow. We must attack before they move once more," the German repeated. Suddenly he halted and leaped to his feet. Levit heard him utter a harsh curse. "Mein Gott, man! The blaze!" he shouted furiously. Devers seized a blanket and beat hastily at a campfire he had ignited. It was well aflame. The German rushed forward with his own blanket and scattered the embers. The cowboys stamped upon them.

Lenneweber fumed at Devers; then he glanced apprehensively upward at the ball of smoke that drifted slowly above the draw. The cold expression in his eyes when he looked down caused Devers to spread his arms wide in apology.

"That was a fool stunt, I guess," he admitted. "But I didn't think. I haven't been on many Indian trails before." Levit's eyes focused on the man Castlerod, standing at the far side of the circle. He sensed rather than actually saw a short-lived smirk on Castlerod's face. Something told him to watch Devers and his outfit more closely in the future.

The darkness lay like a cold blanket upon them. While Mac-Ashen slept, Lenneweber called to Lubbock, speaking his instructions quickly, and the cattleman nodded, inclining his head afterward toward the rider who had come with Ramsdall.

"We'll be back," Lubbock said.

MacAshen rose after midnight, going forward with a second man to relieve the lookouts. There was no alarm, and at the appointed time, two hours later, he came back and shook the man nearest at hand.

"Wake up your partner and take the watch," he said, and the rider rolled slowly to his feet. Lenneweber was astir.

"They should be back soon," he said. "I sent Lubbock and another to locate the savages."

MacAshen pulled his coat tighter about him, but Lenneweber inclined his head toward MacAshen's blanket roll. The latter turned back and lay down again. The mountain air was sharp, almost numbing, and MacAshen's eyes closed again, responding quickly to their training.

A little later, Lubbock and his second returned. They alerted the lookout and slipped silently down into the camp. Lenneweber heard them coming, and rose to greet them. Lubbock spoke low and quickly, and the German listened carefully.

Lenneweber frowned upon receiving the report. "Bad, that is," he said. "You are sure?"

Lubbock nodded. "There's no doubt about it."

"You have done well, nevertheless," Lenneweber whispered. "Now sleep. An hour it is before dawn," he said, and rolled up in his own blanket.

The gray forerunners of day had cut into the dark eastern sky by the time they reached the upper rim. The Texans kept to the grass now, muffling the hoofbeats, zigzagging behind projections and dodging the graveled swales. Lubbock led the way. Little more than a half-hour beyond the cold camp, he raised his hand. Lenneweber motioned MacAshen to join him, and the three men dismounted and climbed to the summit of a small knoll.

"They're a little beyond, under that black wall," Lubbock said. Lenneweber accepted the warning, his studious eye running back and forth along the rocks.

"It is only the horse herd," he told MacAshen.

MacAshen swung toward him. "But there was a big party!"

"They moved on in the night without halting. They have

broken now into small bands, and each is fleeing for the river. Lubbock found this out last night. He followed the horse herd, but there is only a handful of braves with them."

"This all happened in the night? Why?"

"They found out that we follow them."

The Indians had chosen a sheltered spot. In their sleep, they held their own mounts close to their sides with lariats, and they had hobbled the half-dozen bellwether horses of the herd. The warriors were on the far side of the herd.

"Maybe we can still get to them," Lenneweber told Mac-Ashen. To Lubbock: "We will drive between the Indians and the herd. That will push them back against the wall."

Lenneweber watched the sky. The white men walked their horses almost upon the Indian camp, coming eastward around the extension of the mound. The savages were then directly to the north, and the black wall bulged down to block out the vision to the east.

Suddenly a horse snorted.

"Move out!" Lenneweber shouted.

They hurtled toward the encampment. The savages came up with spears and rifles in their hands and hit the backs of their mounts in a single movement. It was perhaps a hundred yards from the entrance of the defile to the camping place, and even in the short moment required for the ranchers to sweep out into the open, the Indians broke swiftly for the open valley. The white men plunged after them.

The whine of a rifle ball burned MacAshen's ear. There were no more than five or six of the Indians, and he thought he could pick out the Comanches. A fusillade from his own men bombarded MacAshen's eardrums.

The herd ran west, and the Indians pointed north. When they had passed the shoulder of the wall, the redmen spread apart, each setting a course for himself across the valley. Mac-Ashen saw a Kiowa go down, and farther away, an Indian pony. Off to the left perhaps a hundred yards, a savage deflected, then closed up swiftly again behind a Ramsdall cowhand. The pounding hoofs and the shrill cries of the other combatants smothered the sound of the Indian's advance. He raised his lance, the colored streamers of bright bird feathers flashing in the thick light. The savage thrust from his right side, forward and down, and the lance passed through the rider's body, driving him to the ground.

MacAshen dug his spurs into old Warrior. The slug from his own revolver knocked the Indian from his horse.

It was over. If there were others, the last of the dark forms had disappeared into the cedars on the ragged slopes, and Lenneweber pulled up beside MacAshen. His steely gaze, roving across the landscape, counted the riders, and as they turned to watch for a signal, he motioned them back into the circle.

Off to the west, a half-dozen of the men had headed up the stolen caballado, crowding it back upon the company. Two others brought in the body of Ramsdall's cowhand.

"Five dead" Elledge fumed, "against one white man. It ain't enough."

"We'll run the rest of them down," MacAshen snapped.

Lenneweber shook his head, eyeing the sky. "Even if we tried," he explained, "the trail would soon have disappeared in the rain and snow that cloud will bring."

"White men have turned back too often, Lenneweber," MacAshen countered angrily. "Sooner or later somebody's got to keep on going."

"Perhaps," the German answered calmly, "but that is a job for the future, MacAshen, when there are men enough here to do the job. Beyond this point one faces not just an Indian band, but an entire Indian nation. Someday that nation will strike at us in full force here, and when it does we must be ready to meet them."

Slowly the cavalcade moved out and down the valley southward. Now Lenneweber rode in deep thought. "Last night we were upon them, before they split," he said finally. "But quick, they ran."

"Somehow they marked us," Levit threw out bitterly.

"Yes, MacAshen. They marked us. But I think the word 'somehow' is not appropriate. I know how they discovered our presence, and so should you. The thing that puzzles me is something else: Could that 'somehow' have been deliberate?"

16

By the start of 1866, all provisional governors in the South had been displaced except Hamilton in Texas.

Hamilton ordered the election of delegates to a state convention be held in January, and it was held on schedule. Delegates were selected through that process for a constitutional convention, to be held early in February. The convention was to renounce secession and slavery, repudiate the Confederate war debt, and eventually to elect new state officials. After all of this, the legislature would ratify the Thirteenth Amendment to the United States Constitution which provided for the end of slavery, and Texas would take its place again in the Union.

Austin prepared for the occasion. The capitol boasted a new shingle roof, and newspapers informed the delegates they could leave umbrellas at home. Madame Coss, the concert artist, also arrived about that time to enliven the social atmosphere.

Karryl attended Madame Coss's concerts, as did every Austin woman who could. The rumor had gotten around that, somehow, merely by listening to Madame Coss a person improves on romantic competence. Some people thought the idea funny, however, and viewed from their angle, Karryl could agree. Editor Raymond was one of these; and just to help such matters along, he thought he ought to report on a brand new contraption of which he had heard called a "palpitating bosom." He observed that since patents were already in use on hoopskirts, corsets, hats and waterfalls, "If our inventors cannot manufacture emotions, they at least can produce the means of simulating them." Everyone, he presumed should certainly be so equipped after hearing Madame Coss.

"The notions people get!" Karryl murmured roguishly moving back and forth before the mirror in her room. She cast an appraising eye upon her own breasts and decided against any such necessities.

The Constitutional Convention, when it met in early February, had an optimistic outlook in spite of a sudden and alarming new internal danger. Cholera appeared in many places. Delegates from San Antonio believed that people got the disease by drinking bad water out of irrigation ditches, and they considered withdrawing, in order to remain close to their families. But they saw opportunities in the convention. San Antonio, largest of all the Texas cities, had voted against secession, but she had paid her own way, nevertheless. Now the San Antonians wanted to be heard, and the place to be heard was at the convention.

Two men of German descent, J. A. Paschal and E. Degener, were to represent San Antonio. From the hill country, a Mason man named Ranck, and MacAshen's neighbor Farnsworth, were the delegates.

"I'm going in, too," MacAshen told the latter.

"Good. You want to travel with us?"

"If you leave soon enough."

"Ranck and I are going by way of San Marcos Springs. He wants to see the German delegates from San Antonio before we get to Austin, and I'd just as soon myself. We're more or less teamed up along the same lines. So we'll get together there at Judge Blossom's, and ride on from there. That way we can talk."

"All right, Farnsworth. I'll go with you—if Ranck doesn't object."

"Object, hell! We've got to cross the Blanco Basin to get to San Marcos Springs. Ranck's just like me. He favors numbers crossing that stretch."

The early rains were already beginning to turn the landscape green beyond the passes in the southern wall by the time Mac-Ashen, Farnsworth and Ranck set out. Spring seemed to be in prospect earlier this year, and a few mountain flowers already were indicated. Spiderwort and lilies flecked the lower inclines, while here and there pinkish primroses colored the countryside. Levit's horse stirred a grasshopper mouse from among the rocks, and once a fox squirrel scurried across the trail.

"I was down this way last year, MacAshen," Farnsworth said. "It's wild country clear across the Blanco Basin."

"I know that, Farnsworth. That's why we always kept out."

"The country's jumbled and brush-covered, barren on the ridges but fertile some places in the valleys. It's a tricky place to pen cattle, and too broke up for the homes of settlers."

"They're bound to move in, sooner or later."

"Maybe so. I've heard there're some in already. What their business is—if any do live down on the Blanco—I'd have to guess. A man can lose himself in the Blanco country, and nobody'd ever find it out. Even the Indians keep away."

Herr Ranck broke in: "Biberstin, at Fredericksburg, he was around by the springs; it is sometime ago now. He hears a good deal about new cow outfits on the Blanco. Some even have it that there is a headquarters, stuck back somewhere in the ridges of the Basin."

Below the pass, the country fell away to the southeast through truncated cones of limestone and clay. They crossed the Blanco, and at sunset made camp beside a brook feeding northward. Farnsworth called to MacAshen from down the stream. He pointed toward a broad sign on the bank where a small spit shallowed the flow. "That's a cattle trail, all right," Levit acknowledged, "and they were herded when they passed this point."

Near dusk of the third day the three horsemen reined up on a high elevation. The basin was behind them now, and from this point the landscape dropped abruptly to the black prairies. Directly below, the great springs of the San Marcos erupted, hurling torrents of crystal clear water out into the river bed, and long green reeds swept back and forth beneath the surface. All about were scattered the stones of old missions. San Francisco Xavier de los Dolores had been here, Nuestra Señora de la Candelaria, and San Ildefonso.

To the west, a few fences and the irregular outline of buildings marked the site of a big homestead. Down the San Marcos a couple of miles in the other direction, another great compound was visible.

"That far one, the one off toward Austin, that's the Nance ranch," Farnsworth said. "The big one south, that's Judge Blossom's."

The San Antonians were waiting at Judge Blossom's, having arrived only an hour or two earlier. Ranck greeted them warmly, and introduced MacAshen and Farnsworth.

"MacAshen," Herr Paschal mused. "I think I have heard of you. Could it be from my friend, Herr Lenneweber of Loyal Valley?"

"I know him."

Judge Blossom made them welcome. "I could have been a delegate myself," he said. "But just now I am faced with a journey to Houston and then to New Orleans."

"You'll miss a lot of excitement, Judge."

"I'm not averse to missing that. At my age, one attempts to avoid such things."

Judge Blossom suggested everybody dispense with discussions on the convention for the time being. "You will have plenty of time for that as you ride along tomorrow," he said. "My only recommendation is that you urge people to try to restore themselves to normal lives, accepting—where they can—such conditions as have now been imposed, and to hope for better things in the future. Here, tonight," he went on, "let us arrange for ourselves a social evening, rather than an evening of serious talks. Just a few days ago, I obtained a new quantity of Madeira from a shipment that had just arrived in your city of San Antonio. Very old, and very good. I should like to have you join me in trying it."

The Germans laughed. "You flatter us, Judge," Herr Paschal said, "and in hospitality you outdo us. We will be glad to partake of your benevolence. And we, too, favor an evening of relaxation. A long ride, it will be, tomorrow."

The social evening passed rapidly. The entire group retired early, and at daylight they were up again, to find Judge Blossom awaiting them.

"We'll think of you when the clamor begins in Austin," one of the San Antonians said in parting.

"And I," MacAshen added, "I thank you personally for putting up just another traveler."

"Glad to, sir, glad to. I'll hope to see you down this way again someday, as well."

The quintet of travelers made the thirty miles to Austin in twelve or thirteen hours, talking among themselves as they rode along. MacAshen took no part in the portion of the conversation related to the convention. He had no say in that upcoming event, and it would be just as well if he kept out of it now, too. He had had no chance to report back personally to Stockdale and his little group since the ill-fated journey to San Antonio, and he was overdue in Austin. By the frontier grapevine he had been able to keep them partially informed on what he had been doing, but that was not enough. Most of the people he needed to see would be in Austin for the convention, and no better time would offer for another quiet meeting. And there was always another impelling reason why he wanted to come to Austin, of course—perhaps a more compelling reason.

MacAshen and the Germans reached Austin an hour before dark and found rooms at the Mansion House. MacAshen freshened himself, changed clothes, then headed immediately for the white cottage on the hill.

The door resounded under his knock. Karryl opened it.

"Levit MacAshen," she cried. She thrust the screen outward, impulsively pulling him down and kissing him. "Don't just stand there," she exclaimed. "Come on into the parlor . . . don't act like you're surprised over my excitement."

He grinned. "I'd ride in every day for a welcome like this."

"I'll bet you would! Why I haven't even heard a word from you since—since before Christmas. Do sit down, Levit, and tell me all that's happened. You can't imagine how I've wanted to know."

"I've been busy. And things have been going along tolerably well, I guess. But you . . . you look great! Are you still teaching?"

"Yes, and I like it very much. Besides, with all the things that are going on in Austin right now, and with all these people coming to town for the convention—well, I'd just rather stay up there at the school than anywhere else. Tell me, Levit, did you come here this time to see me, or to attend the convention?"

"I've nothing to do with the convention. But the time was right, while it was on. I came mainly to see you."

"Well, I'm glad. Where are you staying, Levit, with so many people filling up our little capital city?"

"Oh, I got in at the hotel. But the town is stacked. I was lucky to get a place to sleep, I guess."

"I know." She laughed. "Burr Wayne told me the same." She hesitated as he straightened up more attentively. "He's there at the hotel, too. He and his father came to attend the convention, like everyone else."

"I see."

"Burr told me he'd met you in San Antonio. He was quite puffed up that he and his father had had to let you, a Texas rancher, have some cows for your ranch less than a year after he'd seen you in Houston."

"He did that, all right, and we were glad to get them. Where's Wayne now?"

"At the hotel, I guess. He came to see me earlier this afternoon."

"Then it looks like I've arrived in Austin too late, after all."

"What in the world are you talking about? Of course you haven't. Burr is a childhood friend, Levit. I've told you that before. As a matter of fact, I was lucky that he could even come by. He's overwhelmed with meetings and all that sort of thing. You seem displeased, Levit."

"I'm not. I just hadn't planned on having to share you with someone else while I was in Austin."

"Share me, Levit? Why Burr couldn't even come back to visit me tonight, even though he wanted to. They've got him and his father all wrapped up in the things those people at the convention are doing. He has a buggy rented from Mr. Miller and he said he'd come and drive me to school in the morning, but so far, it seems like that's about all I'll see of him."

"Well, can I have you to myself this evening?"

"Of course you can."

"Then put on your frills and feathers. We'll go out for supper, at the hotel."

"Frills and feathers! I wish I still had some of those things.

But don't you fret. I'll find something to wear, you can be assured."

The lobby of the hotel was jammed when they reached it later in the evening. They hesitated for a moment in the center of the big room, gazing about. Levit pointed out one of the delegates around whom a group of Texans had congregated. He was a heavy-set man with a great mop of black hair and a square-cut beard graying at the edges.

"Mr. Throckmorton," Karryl acknowledged. "I've seen him in the streets. They say he has been selected as president of the convention."

MacAshen nodded. "James W. Throckmorton. The Indians call him 'Buckskin Coat.' When a buckskin coat has been turned out right, not even a bullet's supposed to be able to go through it." He pointed to another individual. "That's Edmund J. Davis," Levit disclosed. He's a rising politician, but on the other side of the fence. He was a district judge at Brownsville when the war began, and he ran off to Mexico when the shooting started. Spent most of the war down there—even tried once to capture Laredo but failed, so they tell me. Lincoln made him a brigadier just before the war was over, and he turned up in Texas again."

They walked toward the diningroom then, and a guest, glancing at a newspaper in his hand as he emerged, brushed against MacAshen. He raised his eyes with a quick word of apology and started on. Then he halted and turned back. "Colonel MacAshen!" he exclaimed. "Why, how are you, sir? My name is Holbrook. We met in San Antonio at Christmas, in connection with the sale of a small herd of cattle, if you remember?"

"Of course," Levit responded, holding out his hand.

"I'm glad to see you here at the convention," Holbrook went on.

"I'm not at the convention, but I'm just as glad to be here."

Levit drew Karryl forward and presented the rancher to her. "Newcomb," the latter mused. "Could it be that you are the Miss Newcomb the Waynes, our neighbors on the Guadalupe, speak of so often?"

"We're old friends," she replied.

"I am glad to have seen you," he said to Levit. "But don't

let me keep you from your dinner.''

They bowed to each other and Karryl and Levit moved into the dining room.

"Wayne, again," Levit remarked when they had been seated. There was a needling at him inside.

"Don't pick at me, Levit," Karryl said quietly. "For you've no reason to. And let's not spoil this wonderful evening, just because someone's name is mentioned.''

"I don't intend for it to be spoiled. But somehow here lately I can't stand the idea of some other man chasing after you.''

She placed her hand on his. "Then stop thinking of such things, Levit," she said tenderly, "for no other man is chasing after me. Not that they haven't in the past though," she added with a toss of her red hair.

When the meal was concluded they went back outside and walked slowly up the avenue. In the dim light of the street lamps MacAshen drew her close to him as they walked along. "How soon will I see you again, Levit?" she asked, when they reached the doorstep.

"I'll be at Bull Creek most of the day tomorrow. That's a little way out of town. I need to see Stockdale again, but there's nothing this time that will take me out of Austin in a hurry, like before. I'll be back about dark, then all the rest of the time I'm here will be ours.''

"I'll be waiting for you," Karryl said.

17

Burr Wayne arrived at Karryl's house early the next morning, as he had said he would. "I've tried every way I know to shake the folks we came to Austin with," he fretted as they drove along to the school. "But something new crops up every time I start out of the hotel. They've got me booked up for one get-together after another right up till the time the convention opens its doors."

"You are becoming an important man out in your part of the state," she smiled.

"I doubt that. There just aren't many people along the Guadalupe. It is my father, I think, they really want in the sessions. But he wants me to go along with him, as well. I'm going to break away at least for a while tonight, though, Karryl."

"Don't do that just on my account, Burr."

"What do you mean, just on your account?"

"I just can't be with you tonight."

"Why not?"

"I have another engagement."

"You mean with another man?"

"Of course. And don't take that attitude with me, Burr."

"You expect me to be pleased?"

"Well, certainly you've no reason to be cross."

"Guess I ought to know there'd be others beating a path to your door," he admitted. "Pretty girls like you are bound to have plenty of admirers. Who's the man you're favoring, Karryl, or shouldn't I ask? Some Austin rustic, or maybe one of those Union officers?"

Karryl stiffened. "Certainly, you've no right to ask. What's become of your manners, Burr? An Austin rustic, or a Union officer! How could you say such things? The people here aren't rustics to me! Maybe once they would have been. But not any more. They've been kind in every way, Burr. And I've had no cause to complain about the Union officers, either. They've been as courteous as one could ask, at least so far as I'm concerned, which I'm beginning to think is more than you are. Colonel MacAshen is calling on me, the rancher from the Pedernales Valley, whom you know."

"MacAshen, eh? He seems to keep cropping up. What's he to you, Karryl?"

"You've no right to ask that either—and no reason to. Besides, I told you all about him back at Houston."

"He was only resting up over a bullet wound or something, and you and your aunt were doctoring him. Now it looks like the treatment's stretching out."

"Burr! Stop trying to quarrel with me! And stop jabbering all this nonsense, too."

"It's not nonsense to me. And I'm on notice too, now, that I'd better look to my own interests around here. How about seeing me a little more in the daytime, then—today even. A buggy ride in the afternoon, when you've finished at your school? I'll take off, whether they want me to or not."

"Would you like that, Burr?"

"I'd like it better than nothing at all. I want to talk to you, Karryl, seriously."

"Well . . . I shouldn't. And you must bring me home before dark. Pick me up in the buggy at the seminary about two o'clock, if you wish."

"I'll do that."

Stockdale's small ranch a few miles north of Austin sat back some distance from the post road itself, screened by huge oak trees. When MacAshen rode up at mid-morning the former

[186]

governor met him on the verandah.

"Tate and Woodworth will be along in a little while, Levit," he said. "They couldn't make it quite so early, after all."

"It's all right, Stockdale. I'll be glad to sit around and talk a spell."

"We can do that here without anybody bothering us. That's why I decided to get us together out here at my place. Thought it would be just as well if we stayed apart in town. You've been going pretty hard, haven't you, Levit? From the meager reports you've sent from here, there, and yonder, by one person or another, I'd say you'd been around a good many places."

"I never knew Texas was as big as it is, Stockdale."

"Nobody does." The former governor grinned. "Well, come on in the house for a cup of coffee. Also, I've got a couple of fellows back at the bunkhouse I want you to talk to. If you like their looks, maybe you can use them."

"All right, Fletcher. But be careful about who you talk to back here in Austin."

"I am. I know the families of these boys, and they were raised in the border counties. They've got an idea something is up, but they don't know anything else about it."

"Let's go on then and see them now."

They walked through the house and across the ranch yard to Stockdale's log bunkhouse. The youths were sitting on a bench out in front. Stockdale called their names to MacAshen and the latter shook hands with each.

"Done any scouting—or met up with Indians?"

"No. But we've rode, and worked with cattle, plenty."

"Can you handle guns?"

Both boys grinned. "Want to see for yourself, mister?"

"No. If you're sure of yourselves you don't have to prove it to me. Stockdale tells me he's already filled you in on how it is shaping up out in the border counties. And some pretty hard, rough work. Maybe dangerous work, too, ever so often."

"Like in the old border days?"

"Maybe worse. Are you looking for real range action?"

"Well, we missed out on the war, and we figured that if the Indians still want to fight us Texas folks—or some of them white renegades start acting up—we could take a go at 'em."

MacAshen smiled at Stockdale. "You men stick around for the rest of the day here with Stockdale's hands," he said to the cowboys. "I'll talk with you again, when we're through with other things here."

"All right, mister."

The other men whom Stockdale had expected arrived about noon. As soon as dinner had been served all around, he led the way out onto the verandah, then into the yard where a huge oak provided shade for a half-dozen benches.

"All of you know what we're here for," he said then. "Since we got together last, after the San Antonio trip, plenty has happened, so MacAshen tells me. You want to take over now, Levit, and spell it all out?"

"Yes." MacAshen sketched the steps he'd undertaken first. "Quite a few people already in the act," he said. "But trying to bring men together when you've got no way to keep them up hasn't been too easy. We've hit on something, now, however, and things are beginning to shape up better. We're getting men spotted down near ranches blocked out as rendezvous points. Some ranchers close to us are taking on men as cowboys who'll be on call to us. We've still got a lot of blanks to fill in, of course. So far, when you figure in numbers, we've been able to locate only a handful of the old riders. But we've got some new ones."

"Some of that we already knew, of course," Stockdale said. "And like you asked us to, we've lined up places here and there in these men's counties, too. We'll give you a tally, and map out spots you've not been in touch with, Levit, before we quit here today."

MacAshen nodded. Then he went on at considerable length, speaking of places, and people, and how they had pledged to help, particularly in the hill country, and southwest of San Antonio.

"But now some other decisions have to be made, and this may be even more important than what we've been talking about," he said finally. "No single citizen, however good and worthwhile his purpose, can—or should be allowed to—establish an armed outfit like this answering only to him. It's dangerous even under present circumstances, and given the wrong turn somewhere—well, you know what could happen. If we succeed in getting the Texas Rangers back together as a real fighting force, then some kind of real authority—some responsible man or group legalized by government—must sooner or later call the shots. From the top, of course."

"We've realized that, MacAshen," Stockdale agreed. "Direction must, of course, in time pass to somebody higher up, as you infer. But not yet."

"Who would you turn a Texas Ranger organization over to, Stockdale? Hamilton, maybe? From what I've heard, he'd simply get us broken up."

"I'm not too sure of that. But we won't take the chance, even so. I think there'll be somebody else, soon."

"Who?"

"Hamilton means what he says about a new constitution, and returning the state to its own people. There'll be an election in Texas by summer. When that occurs, whoever heads the slate will be our man, and he will head the Rangers again, too. Between now and then, we'll just go on as we are now."

"All right, Stockdale. And maybe together we can turn over to him at least a passable frontier outfit, by then."

When the meeting had broken up, MacAshen went back to the bunkhouse and talked with the two young cowhands again.

"If you really want some border action, I think I can set it up for you," he said. "At my spread, we're full up right now. However, those of us with ranches on the edge of the Indian country pick up hands for everybody when we run into them. There are two or three good places needing help, and you'll like the surroundings. Mind you, the work will be hard. And you know what they pay is for riding herd. But every now and then there's some excitement, and they can use you."

"Well, if Mr. Stockdale says it's all right, you can count us in."

Burr Wayne called on Karryl at the seminary at two o'clock in the afternoon, as she had told him to. He helped her into the buggy and they drove up the river road, idling along as they visited with each other. It was a pleasant afternoon, and Karryl thought how silly it was for anyone to think she should not be happy to be with an old friend like Burr, whenever she could. Besides, he was a perfect gentleman, too.

"You're more like the Karryl Newcomb I remember now back in Natchez," he said once.

"I'm glad you approve of me today, Burr." She laughed.

He was pulling the horse to a stop at the Whipple house as the sun dropped behind the distant hills. Burr tied the horse at the edge of the grove on the side below the arbor, then walked Karryl slowly up the path. They halted by the arbor benches.

"You've been so much nicer today than you've been on some occasions," she repeated, smiling. "And I'm grateful for that, Burr."

"I still don't like to think of you going out with someone else."

"Now don't talk like that again, Burr."

"I've something I want to say to you, Karryl."

His sudden seriousness startled her, and she halted in the path to look up at him.

"You haven't encouraged me a lot to say what I want to say . . . I want to ask you to marry me."

Karryl's eyes went wide.

"I should have asked you right at the start, that first day at Houston," Burr said. "Oh, I'm not working up to it with a lot of fuss and fiddle like a man usually tries to do when he's asking for a girl's love. Not like you'd probably have expected of me. But I'm asking you to go back to the Guadalupe with me. I'm in love with you, Karryl, and I want you to be my wife."

Behind them, the sun had dropped completely under the far hills, and the heavy shadows were settling all about them. She stared at Burr. He was, indeed, offering her his hand, his love, and everything he had. And not only these things, but security, freedom from anxiety.

But she couldn't marry him. She simply couldn't and she'd never tried to make him feel she could.

"Oh, Burr," she whispered. "I don't know how to answer you without hurting you, my dear. But, Burr, I can't marry you."

"Why not, Karryl?"

"Because I'm in love with someone else. And I have been for a long, long time."

She put her arms around his neck and kissed him. For a moment she clung to him, refusing to let him go. "Won't you try to understand?"

"Am I supposed to?"

"I want you to. Oh, it's a heartless, cruel thing to do to a man, to refuse an offer of marriage. I know that, Burr. And my dear, my very dear Burr, I can't even begin to tell you how much it means to me that you really do want me. But you'd not want me if I couldn't feel in my own heart I wanted to come to you."

She started to say more, but in a startling instant the words seemed to freeze completely in her throat. Burr saw that she was staring at something over his shoulder—that she had become white as a sheet. He swung about to follow the direction of her gaze.

Levit MacAshen, his foot on the lower level of the steps to the verandah, had halted abruptly, staring unbelievingly himself at the scene in the arbor a dozen rods below him.

Burr snapped: "What the hell!"

"Wait, Burr," Karryl whispered frantically.

"What are you talking about?"

"Don't you understand, Burr?" she pleaded. "Please, Burr, go back to your buggy and leave. Oh, don't you understand?" she sobbed.

He stared at the figure poised before the steps to the verandah. "MacAshen all the time," he intoned. "I guess I do understand, Karryl." Then he turned swiftly and stalked away toward the grove below the house where the horse was tethered.

MacAshen watched Burr Wayne until he had disappeared in the duskiness. His glance shifted stonily back to Karryl. Then, stiffly, he swung around on his heel.

"Oh, no, Levit," she cried. "Levit . . . please . . ."

He did not stop, and she stared numbly at him until he reached the end of the pathway. In a moment he, too, had passed completely from her sight.

18

Politics seethed within Texas in the spring of 1866 though most of the survivors of the war itself had little time to indulge in such activities. The specious reasoning which characterized many of the tirades had its effect, of course, but people still had to go on living.

Farmers about the settled regions of the state did their best to get the crops in again, but because of the wholesale exodus of Negro field hands—often now openly encouraged into movement by itinerant rabble-rousers—most of the plantations remained bare and untended.

Beyond the Black Belt, however—along the lines of the frontier—this particular problem was slow in making itself felt. There were no crops in the remote districts requiring immediate care. On the Guadalupe, as on other western rivers, spring brought out the fragrance of all natural things, just as it always had—like the wild honeysuckle, for instance.

At the Wayne ranch the black-haired cowboy, Ben Lacing, who had been seated on the bunkhouse step, rose to his feet and walked toward the grove before the big main cabin. By the log bench under the live oaks he halted momentarily. He glanced toward the open doorway a dozen rods away, but detecting no movement, he wandered slowly on toward the far end of the clearing. The corrals were there, and the raw, aroma of trampled manure came to him.

He halted to listen to the faint yelping of a distant coyote, loping toward the sand dunes. Caution was habit to him, for there were men who also used such signals to relay intelligence to their kind. But the call was repeated from farther away, and he walked on, relieved.

He circled, passing by the orchard and came slowly back toward the grove. Margaret Wayne was on the bench under the live oak when he came abreast this time. She was studying him intently, and he thought he had never seen such bright eyes and heavy lashes. A strange glow seemed to emanate from her. He rolled the brim of his hat in his hands.

"Chill in the air tonight," he said. "Don't you have a wrap, miss?"

She moved a trifle on the bench, tucking her skirts about her trim ankles. "I'm going inside soon. Won't you sit down?"

His hand touched hers as he carefully lowered himself beside her, and she did not move her hand. Lacing's arm tingled from the contact, the blood moving up into his neck.

"We haven't seen much of you lately," she said.

"Oh, Grippa's had us busy."

"Fiddlesticks! You boys wouldn't let Grippa, or the work either, stop you if you wanted to do something else."

"What else would we want to do?"

"Ben Lacing! 'What else would you want to do?' Why, a lot of things. I'd think you'd want to come up to the house and see all of us once in a while, just for fun. Sing and hear music with us, even. Don't you like things like that, Ben?"

"Haven't given it much thought, I guess."

"Well, you should."

He again rolled the brim of his hat in his hand. His discomfiture seemed to please her, and she commenced to hum a soft little tune to herself, just to emphasize it.

"What are you singing?" he inquired after a time.

"It's called 'The Laura Waltz.'"

"Well, it's a pretty song. And I like the way you hum it."

The yelp of the coyote sounded suddenly again in the distance, and instinctively Margaret moved. They were very close.

"That was a lonely cry," she whispered. "You know, Ben, sometimes I think I would like to run away into the prairies and live a lonely life just like the savages. I don't know why, but I just think like that."

"You'd miss the comforts of home."

"Oh, it isn't the comforts—I know I'd starve to death, or some wild animal would tear me apart. Really, I'm frightened to death when I'm alone, but sometimes living here on the edge of the real West is like living on the brink of a canyon. The urge to leap is always there. You've been all over the prairies, haven't you, Ben?"

He considered the girl's query before answering. "I guess I can't deny that, miss," he answered.

"Deny it? Why, I think it's wonderfully thrilling. All those strange-sounding places like the Llano Estacado, the San Saba, the wild Brasada."

"You think they're thrilling just because they've got names?"

"Of course."

"Well, don't ever go running off toward them. The Brasada's a far piece different from the Guadalupe."

"Oh, fiddlesticks, Ben!" she came back impatiently. "Of course I'm not going to run off anywhere. I only said it to see if you'd say you'd miss me when I was gone, and look how you answer!"

The statement surprised him infinitely and he responded: "I guess I don't know much about girls, or how to talk to them, either, Miss Margaret."

"You certainly don't. But then you're no worse than the rest. You cowboys are all alike; I'm finding that out."

"All alike?"

"Of course you are. When you have a chance to say something nice to a girl, do you say it? You certainly don't. In fact, Mr. Lacing, I can't get any one of you to talk about anything that's the least bit interesting to me. All you know anything about is Indians, and riding, and those far places."

Ben laughed. "Don't be too hard on us, miss. We don't get much chance to talk to pretty girls, much less figure out what's going on in their heads." She smiled at that and he went on, "But don't think we're not interested in girls a mighty good bit; and we talk about 'em, too, among ourselves."

"Then why don't cowboys speak right out? Oh, I'm always trying to get them to. But no, they just stick their heads under

[194]

their arms like chickens. Or else—they try to talk and play big to see if they can make an impression. Boasting about wars, and outlaws, and savages. Wearing those heavy black guns and acting like they knew how to use them. Calling out names like Cortinas—and Helm—and Storm!"

Lacing reacted instantly. The mention of the gunman, Vanner Storm, had an unexpected effect on him. But Margaret did not notice. "Of course, I should say that that's the other boys, Ben. Not you. At least, not all the time. Oh, I'm not excusing you any, merely because you're not entirely like the rest, Ben, but it's the one thing I think I really like about you. You're just as hard to get to know as they are, even if you don't wear one of those pistols. I've heard Father and Burr and Adam talk about these wild gunmen out on the prairies, and I hate to see our boys trying to act like them."

In the shadow, his face was a study, and thinking that perhaps she'd intruded on something personal this once, she was quiet. She slipped her hand into his, then pulled it slowly away.

"I'll have to go in now, Ben," she said. She left him standing in the shadow.

Lacing was still there beside the huge live oak when Burr walked into the yard with Grippa sometime later. The evening was well along now.

"Something bothers me, boss," he heard Grippa say.

"What's that, Adam?"

"We've penned down plenty of longhorns, and branded a sizable passel of calves. I've had the boys on the back passes and trails to keep them in close."

"Yes?"

"Well, I've been trying to count. We ought to have a whole pasture full, stumbling over each other, in fact. But when you try to run 'em by, the count runs mighty short."

"What do you mean?"

"We haven't got all the cattle we drove in here. I don't know why. The boys haven't let many drift back out. But that herd's not half as big as it ought to be. Something's happening to those longhorns, and I don't know what."

"That's strange, Adam. We'd better check again. Don't worry Father with it just yet."

Grippa nodded understandingly. "The old man looks like he's weathering," he said. He turned and headed toward the

[195]

bunkhouse, and Wayne walked back into the house.

Undetected by either of the men, Lacing remained where he was, drawing deeply on his cigarette. He exhaled the smoke slowly in a white cloud. Eventually, he dropped the tobacco on the ground and pressed it into the earth. Then he turned, stared thoughtfully at the low black rim of hills off toward the San Marcos country, and walked into the bunkhouse.

19

Andrew Johnson had taken the Presidential oath in April of 1865. His proclamation, on April 2, 1866, a year later, that the Rebellion in the South was over except in Texas did not satisfy the radical abolitionists. The position espoused by Senator Sumner, in contrast to Johnson's liberal views, was that "a state resisting the Union has committed treason, forfeited its constitutional rights and destroyed itself as effectively as if it committed suicide." In the House, Thaddeus Stevens was proclaiming that the southern states, as such, had ceased to exist, that they were "conquered provinces."

Sheridan seldom concerned himself with Texas, and he gave it almost none of his time. At the height of the chaos created by the Indians, he informed a congressional investigating committee that army occupancy was still a necessity.

"There is a lawless class which cannot be controlled except by the military," he reported, avoiding almost entirely the matter of Indian atrocities.

In comparison with previous years, however, the early months of 1866 gave hope for fewer depredations in Texas. Most of the Comanches, except the Yapparikas, were camped in Eureka Valley, in Indian territory, above the Red River. The Yapparikas had gone north again with the buffalo, and there had been reports of only a few war bands in the winter months.

But early in the spring, the frontier staggered suddenly from new outrage that matched in horror the savage episodes of the fifties. Seventeen painted Indians, sweeping down on Legion Valley, surprised a tiny settlement empty at the moment of male defenders, and brought terror to the women and children there. Besides the victims left in the ruins of the settlement itself, neighbors found two mutilated children on the trail, and later, the ravaged bodies of two women.

A hundred miles above Legion Valley, another band of Indians massacred still more settlers. Indian agents beyond the Red reported that a war party of Noconees and Kotchatekas had returned from a raid even as far down as Montgomery County of Texas, bringing three young white captives with them. But the Union Army did nothing.

The Texas state convention closed during those anxious days, and Hamilton ordered a further election to be held on the fourth Monday in June, 1866 to select Texans for the state offices. The Confederate faction nominated Throckmorton for governor. But there were many problems, and not all of them actually related to Indian attacks. White men were finding themselves in constant friction with black troops. Cholera struck again, too, as warm weather advanced. It moved unseen and disastrously among the coastal cities, approaching the peak of its own devastation just as summer began.

And news from the North was ominous. The political steamroller that had won its first victories in Congress in the spring moved inexorably on. With crops approaching harvest time, the Yankee victors laid a destroying tax on cotton production.

Throckmorton took over the governor's office in Texas on August 9, 1866. On August 20, President Johnson issued a proclamation declaring that the insurrection in Texas, too, had come to an end; and with the proclamation, the war between the North and the South was, theoretically, over.

But the intricacies of national politics were not the major problems clamoring for settlement by the new governor when he took office. Before Throckmorton were dozens of petitions from the settlers still trying to hold their homes. One of these was from Lampasas County:

For more than one year past the frontier has received no

protection from the general government. The Indians have been encouraged, and their raids have increased in number, boldness and violence.

Whole settlements have been broken up, families reduced from affluence to want, the rewards of a lifetime of industry passed off before their eyes. Up to this point the cries of suffering humanity have not been heard. The frontier is falling back. Give us protection, and you will give us peace and security.

Assailed from the prairies by Indian tribes and from the civilized regions by the new hordes of carpet-baggers, cattlemen on the frontier began now to shield themselves by driving their longhorn herds completely out of the country.

The cattle frontier—when the Indian would allow it—ran along an advancing-retreating line approximately from Uvalde on the Frio to Doan's Crossing on the Red River. But summer saw the advance guard of more than a quarter of a million head of longhorns pass northward across the Red River. The Kiowas attacked those herds and the settlers of southern Kansas rose up to block the Texas trail drivers, but the herding still went on.

From the Palo Pinto Mountains, where six thousand longhorns had been assembled after the close of the war, the Goodnight riders now drove that stock a hundred and fifty miles westward. In the summer, they herded nine thousand additional head, too, by way of the Concho up the Pecos to Fort Sumner. A man named Duffield even came down out of the Iowa cornfields, buying twelve hundred longhorns close to MacAshen's range; then he drove them back through the Indian territory into the Chicago market. And in the wake of these great cattle efforts, designed in part, at least, to checkmate the thieving ambitions of some of the new arrivals, vicious outlaw gangs appeared on a schedule, seizing upon other men's property wherever it was to be found.

Elledge returned to the Pedernales from a trip to Austin late in August, 1866. He rode on to the Falling Water to talk with MacAshen.

"Stockmen up in Wise County are selling what they've got left for a dollar a head, just to get out," he reported. "Around Gainesville, they claim white men are behind the Indian raiders now."

"Anything said about help from the army?"

Elledge snorted. "With Sheridan running things? He stalked away a step, striking a fist into his palm, then returned.

"Get ready for a shock, MacAshen."

"What're you talking about?"

"Sheridan. When Throckmorton asked for soldiers, Sheridan said there were troops enough in Texas now to keep the peace. Only thing is, these soldiers have to be kept over in East Texas to look after the Negroes."

"Well, we've known since the start that if the border counties were ever straightened out again it would have to be a Ranger job."

Again Elledge snorted. "Sheridan said he'd allow no home guards or armed bands to be raised."

"The hell you say! He thinks he can even rule out a man's right to protect himself?"

"Yep, and that's not all. He's ordered that even though you couldn't have people of your own to guard your homes, places overrun by renegades and guerrillas are still going to be held responsible for those outlaws' acts."

"That's about as ridiculous as I've ever heard."

"That's Sheridan for you."

"To hell with Sheridan! If he'd wanted the job of fighting the Comanches, he could have had it. But since he doesn't, we'll do it our way. Throckmorton's taken over full responsibility for the force we've been putting together out here, Elledge, as you know. He'll not stand hitched by that kind of an order. And neither will we, along the border line."

In December 1866, the new Congress, by a two-thirds vote, excluded the representatives from the newly reconstructed states. Immediately thereafter a joint committee of the Congress was appointed to work out a new plan of reconstruction. The move carried ominous implications.

But the primary threat before the Texas frontiersmen outweighed the impact of any political intrigue. West of the farm regions an assorted party of Noconees and Wichitas, led by Panateka Comanches, hit near Spanish Fort south of the Red River in July, leaving a trail of horror behind. Thirteen of them caught a settler's wife in her home and ravaged her, and her four children.

Over across the blue hills in Austin, Throckmorton was

[200]

signing a bill ordering up what now constituted three battalions of Texas Rangers, in defiance of Sheridan—and this time into the open if necessary. He did not issue the order immediately, but his close associates knew that it was ready for instant implementation, should the need become imperative.

A courier rode into the Falling Water. He had come from Austin, by way of the Bee Caves and the Pedernales Canyon. Levit met the man when he threw his reins at the hitching rail. The messenger voiced a few short, terse statements while he tied his mount, whereupon Levit turned quickly and led him into the house. The man brought the saddle pouch. When he was inside, he opened it and produced a dispatch. Breaking the seal, Levit studied the message.

"All right," he said. The man was gone again quickly and Levit called to his Mexican.

"I want Lubbock," he said, "and Steve Meadows and also Torkin."

He went to the old roll-top desk and opened it. He drew out the yellowed frontier maps, opening them on the big table. Later, he went into his own room for additional sketches. When his associates came in, MacAshen went over the message with them.

Lubbock reached out a hand and placed it on the rancher's arm.

"You've had something eating on you for quite a spell, Levit. You haven't been yourself. There's a big job going on and a lot's depending on you."

MacAshen did not answer. He turned toward the fire. A cold-edged blade had been driven deep into his heart, and he felt like saying: "To hell with all of it!"

"Let's get on with it," he said finally. He strode back and forth across the room. "You'll go north, Meadows, up in the Llano and San Saba country. Find Buck Barry. You know what to do and say. The men are to stay close, now, to rendezvous points, where we can get them instantly if we need them. Lubbock, your route is west and northwest. Your men are Swanson and Jones, at Mason, near the old ranger camp. Torkin, it's the Uvalde for you. That's a long way, but Richarz is waiting down there." He struck his knuckles together. "Play it close to the table," he said. "We'll have our own work to do, if the worst comes. And remember: nobody moves, nobody talks, unless Throckmorton sends on the further word. I'll let you know, by one means or another.''

"You be foxy yourself," Lubbock warned. "Those Yankee scalawags'll bear watching now. They'll be after anybody they can get anything on.''

Steve Meadows and Torkin left quickly. Lubbock tarried only a short while and Levit came down to the bunkhouse before he left.

"I'll ride part of the way with you, Lubbock," he said.

"Where to, boss?"

"It's time to have it out with the Germans," Levit declared. "They're in this, too, whether they want to be or not. But they've got to be asked—polite like, at first—and I want to be the one to ask them.''

Levit felt better as he headed across the ranges. He had had a bitter shock back there in Austin. But he knew he must put it out of his mind. The conviction that he had not handled himself well with Karryl Newcomb suddenly dug at him, despite the implications no man could avoid. Maybe he should at least have waited to hear what she had to say.

The men approached the German settlements by way of the Cave Creek pastures, cutting across open land toward the little valley where Lenneweber made his home. The house was finished in mortar of a delicate pinkish tint. It was a big house, its basement of three rooms laid low in the ground and provided with gun slits. Levit was surprised to note the number of people around the place. When he rode up toward the corral, he saw a large man detach himself from the gathering and approach the newcomers.

"Herr MacAshen! It is glad I am to see you. Herr Lubbock, also. Get down, my friends, get down.''

"Looks like you're having a fandango," MacAshen said.

"Only a few of the young people. They all meet at some home once a week and tonight it was the Lenneweber's turn. Let me have your horses looked to." He turned and called to one of his ranch hands.

"We can go on, Lenneweber," Levit interrupted.

"When it is dark, yet?"

"No matter. We could camp along the creek.''

"No, my friend. Believe me, you both are welcome. Come with me to the house. You will be well received by our people."

Although it was not yet dark, the young Germans were already around a campfire in the grove. The odd melody of German folk songs rolled from across the way. There were instrumentalists in the group. Levit noted a violinist, and later he heard a zither and a clarinet. When the voices died down at times, the young people rose and danced their strange Old World steps before the fire, their brass-toed shoes striking brash notes upon the hard stones just beneath the thin dust.

"This is our *gesangverein*," the German said. "In English, you would call it our singing club." He smiled.

Inside the house, the coloring of the walls followed the outer pinkish hue, and the entrance boasted fanlights on either side. It was an elaborate entrance for a frontier house; there was glass in the door, tiny panes six inches square.

Lenneweber presented MacAshen and Lubbock gravely to his wife, a broad-breasted, smiling blond woman who spoke no English, and smelled of freshly baked bread.

One of the young people left the circle about the fire and approached the house.

"My daughter, Hilda," Lenneweber announced. In appearance the girl was much like her mother, and Levit guessed she was older than the usual frontier maiden, perhaps twenty or twenty-one; she offered him her hand in a frank manner that momentarily surprised him.

"You will make ready the sleeping quarters for the gentlemen," Lenneweber admonished the girl. "They will be our guests tonight." Her smile of welcome somehow warmed MacAshen as he had not been warmed for a long time.

"Let us be seated a while, gentlemen, for a visit," Lenneweber went on. "Later, we will have supper, but maybe now you will try our German beer?"

Lubbock grinned appreciatively, and Levit nodded his acceptance. From the direction of the kitchen in the rear of the house came a serving girl, carrying a tray with three huge steins, and each man reached for his portion.

"A grand brew, Mr. Lenneweber," Lubbock exclaimed.

Lenneweber beamed with pleasure.

When Lenneweber's daughter returned, she approached the

group. Without hesitation, she reached forward and took Mac-Ashen's hand, drawing him to his feet. Still smiling, she indicated the melodious turmoil across the yard beneath the trees, and began pulling him toward the door.

"Ach, Herr MacAshen, I did not think," Lenneweber exclaimed. "I look upon you as an older man. But our young people do not. You're not much older than they."

Levit hesitated, but Lubbock gave him a push with his hand. "Go along with her for a while. We can talk later," Lenneweber encouraged.

Levit took the girl's arm. In the dim glow cast from tapers within and the flare from the distant fire, she looked like a Valkyrie. She had the strong, heavy bosom of her German mother, a waist too slender, and sturdy hips.

"Most of our people cannot talk with you, but I speak English," she said confidently. "Still, you will like us, and we have music." She beamed up at him, and now he managed to return her smile. But he looked at the circle a little dubiously. Hilda took his arm, and he felt a gentle pressure from her fingertips. The young men and women eyed him questioningly, and Hilda lifted a hand gaily, speaking in German. Then she turned to him and said: "I tell them your name."

She pushed him forward, and several of the Germans clustered about him, then drifted away to their games and dancing. Hilda stayed close to his side, and when the music began again, she turned to face him, putting out her hand and raising his own. Before he realized it, she had forced him into the steps of a polka. He felt awkward, but Hilda pretended not to notice.

Levit had not danced in a long time, but as the memory of the steps came back to him, he skipped as nimbly as he could through the routine. Once, in the proper passage, she came close to him, her body resting against his, and Levit felt a tremor where she touched him, a tremor followed by a slow warmth. He thought he caught a glimmer of surprise in her eyes; then she swung out and on with him, and the music suddenly halted.

Someone handed him another stein of beer. Then he wandered at Hilda's side from group to group, listening to their laughing remarks in German, trying to piece them together from the words he had learned at school as a boy, and suspecting that many remarks were aimed humorously at him.

Another youth came up to claim Hilda, and as Levit turned

to go the flicker of interest in the eyes of the girl did not escape him. He hurried back into the house.

MacAshen could see by the faces of his companions that they had not entirely wasted their time; they greeted him jovially. "More schnapps, Mama," Lenneweber called out. Frau Lenneweber appeared from the kitchen, then retreated for replenishment.

Suddenly, a man hurried into the room. He spoke a few sentences in German into Lenneweber's ear. The big man rose abruptly, started toward the door and hesitated.

"You will be interested in this, gentlemen, if you wish to join me," he said soberly. MacAshen and Lubbock followed.

"One of our men has brought in an Indian," Lenneweber said.

They hurried across the yard and toward the outbuilding below the ranch house. On the far side was a small stone corncrib and the door stood open. A sperm-oil lantern had been lit. MacAshen noted one of the German hands just inside the door and another in the further shadows. On the ground, the dark outlines of a body were silhouetted.

"He is dead?" Lenneweber demanded. The cowboy nearest the door nodded.

"It was above here," the man in the shadow cut in. "Two savages, driving horses, and heading for the San Saba. The other, he gets away."

Lenneweber knelt and turned the body over. A fresh scalp, the blond scalp of a man, dangled from the string around his torso.

"A German scalp!" Lenneweber said harshly.

"Ja!"

The Indian's face was covered with a pattern of painted lines, purple and gray and yellow.

"Wichita!" muttered MacAshen. The German rider said, "The one who escapes, he is painted black and red, and he carries a lance."

"Quohada!"

"Take the body away and bury it," Lenneweber ordered finally. "Then say no more of this." The ranch hands nodded, and he motioned MacAshen and Lubbock to return with him to the house.

"You may wonder about our silence on such matters," he said. "It is because of our colonizer, Herr Meusebach. A grand old man, he is. The Comanches call him 'El Sal Colorado'—the Red Beard. He dislikes punishment of Indians. We shield his feelings. In early years, he gives Buffalo Hump and Mopechee-cope presents worth three thousand dollars. The Comanches honor him. They do not honor all Germans, but Meusebach they honor. They make no raids upon Fredericksburg, or upon Meusebach, north at Loyal Valley. But they kill many others. We strike back, but Meusebach does not know."

"All this is exactly what we came here to talk to you about, Lenneweber."

"About Indians?"

"About trying to stop this senseless killing of white people. And how to do it."

"And who, Herr MacAshen, will be the men who will do that work?"

"Rangers."

"But Rangers are verboten."

"That's why we came to talk with you."

"I see." They had reached the verandah. Across the way, the music and laughter about the campfire had heightened with the darkness.

"Come in the house, gentlemen." They followed him into a little room off the parlor. He indicated chairs and invited them to be seated. Then he went back to the main salon and issued brief instructions in German. He returned and closed the door behind him.

"Let us talk, my friends," he said.

The conversation ran long into the evening.

"Your hesitancy in even speaking of new armed companies, that I understand," Lenneweber said. "For from your words, I gather three companies again are banding. But our purposes are not in conflict. Rangers in the hill country? That is not new. Since 1850, we have them. Back in 1855, James Callahan was made captain of a company, and he chased the Kickapoos from Bandera Pass. There were others, always with Anglo-Saxons for captains, but the Rangers are mostly hill country Germans. It causes no bad feeling. That feeling, it comes from something else.

"Some Confederates argued that Germans blocked slavery in the hill country. But there were maybe thirty or forty slaves

[206]

right in Fredericksburg in 1860, yet.

"When the war began, we could get no powder or bullets here because the Confederates looked upon us as enemies. If the Redskins had known this, they might have destroyed us, regardless of Meusebach. So we make plans. We have a gunsmith here named Krauskopf, and a silversmith, Lungkwitz. They need material for an explosive charge, so they use saltpeter from the bat caves at Fredericksburg. Krauskopf, he finds quicksilver at Galveston. They make a device to roll out copper sheets, and another to stamp percussion caps from strips of copper. From the fusion of saltpeter and quicksilver, they get a charge for the caps. So we have cartridges. It saves us. The people who used those guns were 'Rangers,' if anywhere is such man as a 'Ranger.'"

Levit nodded. "We've all heard something of your troubles. But mostly your people kept to themselves so much that I guess a lot went on we never heard about. I'm afraid you were hurt pretty bad by some of the things the soldiers did."

"Yes, we were hurt. Part we could expect, I realize. Some Germans stayed loyal to the Union, always, but not all. And some Confederates were outlaws, no less. Once, four Germans were hanged down on the South Grape, where they were only herding sheep."

"There are things on both sides which would be better forgotten, Herr Lenneweber. I didn't come here to fight the Civil War over again. Our job now is something a hell of a lot different."

The German's bitterness eased instantly. "I agree with you, Herr MacAshen. And I realize your job is to fight Indians, not Union soldiers again. I say to you that I am pleased you come to me. I will see what we, too, can do. We will speak of it again."

MacAshen prepared for bed with a feeling of grim satisfaction in the results of at least this much of his effort. But before sleep came, his satisfaction was diluted by a vague sense of failure from elsewhere. He could handle his tasks with men; why had he let a woman so destroy his ambition to live just like any other man?

At daybreak he was up again, as was Lubbock, to find a bountiful breakfast, and Lenneweber waiting to join them.

"Good morning, gentlemen. A fair day it is for your journey." The Lennewebers offered them an array of pork and eggs and white biscuits, with cups of black coffee and dishes of sweets. MacAshen and Lubbock attacked the food with vigor.

Afterward, Lenneweber strode with them to the corral. In a walled enclosure nearby, a small flock of sheep crowded close to a rock fence, and Lenneweber reached across and laid his hand on an animal's coat. He gestured to MacAshen to follow his example.

"These sheep are merinos," he explained. "You feel that wool? Soft, yes? Far silkier than wool on any other merino sheep in America, even back in the Pennsylvania hills."

"It's a good product," MacAshen agreed.

The German turned to face him squarely. "You come here, Herr MacAshen, for two matters, I think. Not only to talk of Rangers, but to make friends so there might be a chance for your Rangers. And especially when there are Union soldiers in these hills again. This," and he nodded toward the shaggy animal, "is another barrier, even so small though it is, which always stands between your friends and mine."

"How do you mean?"

"The Germans in these hills are cattle raisers. That is our large interest. But we herd sheep, also, and we have proved such planning is right. Anglo-Saxons do not approve of sheep because they do not understand sheep culture, nor how to mix sheep with cattle on the range. It will come in time, but you could serve your people and ours, Herr MacAshen, by trying your hand at such."

Levit was taken aback. "As a suggestion," he said finally, "it doesn't leave me with much of an answer. But I get your point," he answered shortly.

"What you need is to get a small herd and prove the truth of what I say to yourself."

"That's a big mouthful to throw at a cattleman, Lenneweber."

"You think it could be worthwhile, considering the many kinds of good results that might come?"

"Well, I don't know. I sure never thought of raising sheep. And I've not had a chance to be at home on the Pedernales much anymore."

"I ask you to try. If an Anglo-Saxon would try sheep culture along with cattle, and prove it would work, then others would follow, and much of the unfriendliness in the hill country would end."

"Maybe. At least it's worth thinking about. But I don't know anything about sheep, and neither do my cowhands."

"I make you a proposition. That is, if the Comanches leave us alone long enough to try it. I give you some sheep, and a herder. You could put them there at least while you are away, and by that means you could prove to yourself the value of sheep."

"You've got such a man?"

"Yes, an Anglo-Saxon, yet. He is a fine herder, and he has a homestead here. But I would buy that from him, for the effort is important to us all."

"All right, Lenneweber. I damned sure didn't come here to talk about anything like this, but send the sheep on. My horses may run off, but they'll come back in time, I guess. I'll let a few of those sheep run in the higher draws for a while. Then, if it won't work, I'll send them back, unless the dogs have killed them."

Lenneweber laughed. "Sheep are hardier than longhorns," he warned.

Levit put his foot in the stirrup and pulled himself up.

"Of the other matter, we will speak again soon, Herr Mac-Ashen," the German said. Levit nodded. He started his horse up the path, followed by Lubbock.

"Also, Herr MacAshen," Lenneweber called out, "you will need a cabin for the herder. He will bring a wife with him."

"A wife!" Levit pulled on the rein, ready to call the whole thing off. But he had given his word to Lenneweber, and the colonists were strong upon that nicety. It would not do to hedge now. He nodded somewhat gloomily to the rancher and rode on up the hill.

20

Three hundred miles to the north of the Falling Water, across the gradations on the tributaries flowing down into the Red, the Prairie Indians held their grand council in September. All were there: Ten Bears; Iron Mountain; Horseback, the Nocones chief. From the far Llano Estacado came Mah-to-chee-ga, the Little Bear; and Nau-ce-dah, the Strong Shield; and the one whom they called A-Man-Not-Living. The villages along the Washita sent Lone Wolf, the Kiowa; and Tau-ankia, the son of Lone Wolf; and Ton-ne-un-co, the Kicking Bird.

Asa-Toyeh saw them come. His tipis were first upon the scene, surrounded by the timber near the flowing stream, in the manner of the Comanches. His heart was filled with misgivings; the signs were ominous, and he was an old man.

He had been to the villages of the white men. He had seen their power and their perseverance. It was a vigor that equalled the resource of the Indian. This much he knew, and he was no longer young enough to lead men in battle himself. He had been born on the Plains, hunting throughout these hills a thousand miles to the north, and equally far to the south, for more years than he could remember. The Indians were many, but the white man was strong; and Asa-Toyeh was deeply troubled.

He sat before his *tipi* and watched the clans as they arrived, making their camps and erecting their lodges.

Chewing Elk, the Yapparika, set his shelters in the glen behind Asa-Toyeh's *tipi*, and came to make his greetings; then he moved back to the business of his tribe. The travois were broken down by his women, and the poles raised to support the skins of the lodges. Some of the skins were gray; others boasted weird and colorful design; and the tops of each were blackened by smoke from within.

More of the bands arrived. The warriors, painted with the pigment of the march, squatted before their shelters, blowing clouds of smoke into the air from k-neck k-nick, the Indian tobacco, and exchanging salutations with the new arrivals.

It was a routine Asa-Toyeh had witnessed a thousand times, and his troubled thoughts took comfort from the routine. The Indian women moved silently about their work, or argued over the division of their duties. Their smoked buckskins, especially those of the Panatekas, were tanned almost to a delicate lemon yellow. A few steps away, a young squaw, kneeling beside the stream, was running a comb made from the quills of a porcupine through her dark, coarse hair. Beside her, on the ground, was a buffalo pouch for carrying water, and from her belt hung a drinking cup made of buffalo horn.

Some of the women were collecting baskets of buffalo chips for fuel. The Indian women preferred them even to brush tree limbs because they burned hotter, when ignited, and retained the heat in a coal-like glow. A wrinkled crone touched Asa-Toyeh's arm and motioned to the food spread out behind him on the skin that stretched below the *tipi* poles. Asa-Toyeh smacked his lips upon sight of a bowl of cooked Sego lily bulbs, and the huge container of mush made from buffalo marrow and crushed mesquite beans. There was corn too, though kiln-dried, and powdered; and with it, the squaw laid a pouch of honey on the skin. A long strip of barely warmed horsemeat also was suspended from above, and in a decorated rawhide box at his elbow a fragment of pemmican.

All this was Asa-Toyeh's way of life. His spear was retired now to its place of honor before his lodge, and his people knew that he would never again carry it into the prairies of Texas. But there were a hundred *tipis* on the banks of the stream below, and the younger men who filled them were eager to be on with the business that had called them here.

Every clan had its representative at the Grand Council.

The white man had fought his war, and the Indian had cautiously played one side against the other, taking what he fancied from either. Now, he must make a decision. The soldiers of the Great White Father in Washington were pressing him, and the Texans were moving into his valleys. He must accept the white man's ways, or he must face this rugged settler upon his own ground.

The council began at twilight. Tosawi sat upon the southeastern rim of the great circle, and the firelight reflected from the bright color of his skin. A narrow line of white paint ran horizontally from each extreme of his broad forehead to join and move down his strong, aquiline nose. His face was intelligent, but his thin lips and knife-like black eyes reflected a deep and sinister cruelty.

In the background flashed the wine and scarlet war bonnets of the Cheyenne and Arapahoe. Beyond them were the Wichitas, the Caddos, the Anadarkos, and the lesser bands; and in the center sat the strong echelons of the Comanche nation. The minor chiefs had begun their orations first.

They were of the tribes who lived nearest the reservation compounds, through whose villages the soldiers must pass first if they struck at the Plains Indians. They were suspect, for they maintained contact, treacherous though it might be at times, with the white man.

They were afraid, and they said so.

The Kiowas ridiculed such fears; the lesser family bands of the Comanche nation had stormed their defiance for all white men, and for all Indians who trafficked with the white man.

It was the turn now of Asa-Toyeh. He was the first of the chiefs from the mighty Prairie clans to speak. He rose with dignity—mindful of the dangers to the Wichita bands and careful of the feelings of his brittle cousins from the Llano Estacado—his deep chest slowly expanding and deflating as he marshaled his thoughts.

"I have known the frost of a hundred winters," he began. "My heart is grieved to see our brothers, the Panatekas, driven from their lodges and their valleys. I have ridden the trails which belonged to the Panatekas in seasons before many of the fathers of our strong men here this day were born. I knew the white man when he first came to the hills. He came with his hand raised in greeting, the words of a brother upon his lips, and we made treaties and respected him. Behind these Taibos came others of their kind, and they scratched the soil with the sticks they call plows, and they killed the buffalo from the southern plains. There were those who kept the treaties, and we honored and respected them; and there were others who, crowding upon their heels, seized the prairies, and they drove us from the meadows where our horses grazed. And so we met them with fire, spears, and with war clubs.

"There are many kinds of white men, and all of them seek the hunting grounds of the Indian. But our greatest enemies are the Texans, and though they fought for the people who have now been vanquished, they are not vanquished themselves; and they come against us now with ever-increasing fury.

"The Bluecoats press us from the North to adopt their way of life, which we do not understand. They tell us we cannot ride down into the prairies where the Texans live and kill the buffalo.

"When I was young, we scorned the thought that the white man could grow strong, and we let him move upon the prairies. Today, he is spreading over our hunting grounds like the prairie fire. In my youth, I would have raised my voice in the cry of war. But I am an old man now, and I must recognize the dangers to which the Wichitas point, though my heart likes it not.

"The Bluecoat has not yet gathered his powers to strike at us. The Bluecoat is tired, bitter from his own war. But if he should at last decide to turn that might against the tribes of the Great Plains, these streams might run red with the color of our own blood.

"I am an old man now, it is true, and I am alone as I stand before you urging in this hour that you look again with new eyes upon this danger. The white men are as the leaves from the sycamores; they spread across the face of the valleys, and they accumulate about the springs that flow from the earth; and though you touch them with fire and destroy them, while you have turned your back they are there again in greater quantities, each year adding to the numbers that came before. And I fear we face no alternative but to learn their ways."

A deep guttural sound came from the rim of the circle, and Asa-Toyeh turned toward Mowway, the Kotchateka, whom the white men knew as "The Shaking Hand." The frown on

Mowway's face was hardened by the huge bear claw, his only ornament, which he wore in his scalp lock. Mowway had won the claw in hand-to-hand combat with a grizzly; and now his bull-like voice slowed Asa-Toyeh's words. The Kotchateka said:

"Asa-Toyeh speaks like the Kia-hi-piago—the Tonkaways— who grovel before the white man."

The drum rolled. Asa-Toyeh sighed and sat down.

Tosawi had risen, too, and now he moved inward from the circle of warriors. Mowway stood aside and Tosawi struck the rim of the drum sharply with his war club, catapulting it beyond the outer braves.

"I am Tosawi, war chief of the Panateka," he shouted. "Are the Panateka old women that they must bow their heads in shame before the weaker tribes of the Wichita? The Caddo counsel caution; but their young warriors still ride down upon the settlements in the dark and gather scalps of settlers and their women. This, because they know the Comanches must stand the blow if the Bluecoats come to punish the Indian. The Comanche can meet the Bluecoats; the Caddo cannot. And the Comanche must defend his own hunting ground, for the Caddo will not defend it for him.

"The Panateka has faced the white man oftener than any other Comanche. But the Panateka has brothers upon the prairies who are great, as the Panateka are great, in war; and I wait now to hear the word of my prairie brothers on what their course will be."

It was late, and many had spoken. Parro-o-coom, the Quohada, slowly came to his full height. The drummer had retrieved his instrument, and when he saw Parro-o-coom rise, he struck it sharply, cutting into Tosawi's oration. Parro-o-coom was powerful, commanding, even in an assemblage of strong and commanding chiefs. His black hair was parted, long queues reaching almost to his waist. Silver pieces flashed in the braids, and a scalp lock hanging from the center of his forehead supported a single black feather. A streak of white pigment ran down the part in his hair to the scalp lock, and a heavy gold ring hung from his right ear.

The circle became silent; Tosawi sat down; and the chiefs waited for the words from the old Bull Bear of the Antelope band. There were no warriors like the Quohada. Parro-o-coom stared majestically about him. At Tosawi, cruel, virile, ambitious. At Asa-Toyeh, inscrutable and beyond his hours of leadership.

"The Quohada come to few councils of our Plains brothers in these days," he began heavily. "Perhaps we shall not come again, for I hear words that we of the Antelope band cannot understand. We are not good talkers, but we are great warriors. The Quohada have no friends among white men, and they will accept none. They are sworn to destroy the Texans. We have waited to hear your counsel here; and now I tell you that the Quohada will kill the white man wherever he can be found, and use the white man's women and children for the Quohada's own comfort; and the white men's cabins will be burned from the prairies before us. Thus I speak to the Panateka and to the other Comanches. There is no other way for the Quohada.

"I am Parro-o-coom, and long have I, as war chief of the Quohada, faced the white man. But today I, too, grow older, though the Quohada are greater now than they have ever been.

"I have heard of a white man on the Pedernales, a rancher, strong among his people, and young, who leads them. We will destroy the white men's homes on the Pedernales and drive those white men back upon the farm lands. Beside me here is White Eagle, a warrior new to these councils. He is the war chief now of the Quohada, strong and young enough to meet these young new white chiefs, and he will lead Quohada war parties tomorrow. Hear now his words."

The warrior who had sat nearest Parro-o-coom rose swiftly and came forward. His tall, muscular frame carried few garments, a deerskin breechclout about his middle and moccasins upon his feet. But a great buffalo robe covered his copper shoulders, and he dropped it on the ground as he stalked from his place.

Only a thin line of white paint crossed his forehead; his eyes were black and brilliant, and his chin unyielding.

"I am White Eagle, of the Quohada," he introduced himself coldly, even to the Comanches. "When I came here, there was a grove of apple trees in the orchards of the white man along the Brazos. Those apples will ripen in season, and when they are ripe, the Quohada will be there to pluck them. The Quohada will never cease to be there when the moon is high. Beyond the Brazos lie the Llano, and the San Saba, and the Peder-

[215]

nales. The prairies belong to the Comanche, and this we will teach the white man.

"The Quohada do not make long speeches, and I have finished."

At departmental headquarters in New Orleans, General Sheridan read over again a digest of intelligence reports from the West. They worried him. He did not like Texas, and he was certainly aware of the fact that Texas did not like him. Washington, too, appeared to be disapproving of his methods of governing conquered states.

"Damn it," he muttered to his adjutant, "You can't please everybody." He glanced through the window at a Freedman's Bureau official, dozing comfortably on a bench in the shade from a huge azalea.

His adjutant eyed him sympathetically. "What you'd like to do, I think, sir, is go along with those frontiersmen," he dared to suggest. "Why don't you just tell a few of the others to go to hell?" the officer continued. Sheridan opened his mouth to blister the man, but the words would not come forth. Candor was a thing he understood. He turned back to the window, staring at the figure outside in the shade.

In Austin, Throckmorton received a telegram. Troops would be sent to the frontier in the spring. But he had begun to question anything attributed to Sheridan. He did not reply.

The governor received a second telegram. Sheridan would do what he could for the outlying settlements; he had received authority to concentrate his whole available cavalry force on the frontier. Word was sent to MacAshen on these two messages.

"Hold off until we send you orders again," MacAshen was instructed.

The advance units of Sheridan's Fourth Cavalry, when they did come, passed up the Pedernales road toward old Fort Martin Scott at Fredericksburg. The cowmen at the Falling Water watched the Negro troops go by.

Elledge and Ramsdall rode up the Pedernales to the Falling Water. They threw their reins, dismounted to greet MacAshen, and stomped into the house.

"Feller named McClaren shot to death by Indians just a little ways north of my place, at Cedar Mountain, last week," Elledge reported.

"I know. Ingram's gone after the killers. But Ingram tells me McClaren's horse was not taken, or his other stuff. The Indian sign was poor. Likely there's no trail at all."

"What's that mean?"

"The Comanches never killed McClaren. White men did."

"Which white men you talking about, Levit? The Germans?"

"Of course not."

"White men from the south, maybe? The Blanco basin?"

"Most likely."

"Well, a whole army couldn't cover all the corners down there. Did you see the soldiers they sent to Fort Martin Scott, Levit?"

"Yes."

"Those black fellows won't even try to tangle with Comanches, much less outlaws."

"Don't bank on that, Elledge, and don't blame the soldiers. Government policy has got them strapped anyway. The government says they can't even chase the Redskins unless they show up off the reservations. And once back across the Red River again, they go right back under the Indian agent's protection, so the soldiers have to stop."

"They've got soldiers on those reservations up in Indian territory, too."

"Yes, but just to keep order, not to punish. And they're under a different commander. He's got orders to protect the Indian the same as the white man."

"Who thought that one up?" Elledge asked grimly.

"Parker, the Indian commissioner. An Indian himself. He was a colonel in the Union army. He's a Seneca, a member of one of the Eastern tribes—and a sharp individual, I've heard."

"Well, he must be, to get away with what he's getting away with."

"I don't know if he's aware of what's really going on, but there's beginning to be hell to pay everywhere because of it."

Fall paid Levit one of his infrequent visits a few days later. Levit met him at the step and pulled him off his horse.

"You're a sight for sore eyes," he said. "I was halfway planning to ride all the way down to Houston and see if the

Yankees had got you."

"They wouldn't have me, MacAshen," the old plainsman retorted. "Eat too much. That's why I have to hole up with my friends ever so often."

Levit led Fall inside. "You're looking mighty spry for an old fellow—how do you do it?" he asked admiringly.

"Well, I've had tolerable treatment, and I dodge work as much as possible. You're lookin' fine, yourself, MacAshen. Being home agrees with you."

Fall gave an account of the troubles of the people around Houston; the affairs, insofar as he knew them, of Mrs. Newcomb; and the latest troubles with garrison troops.

"But you're still on the same job?" MacAshen interposed.

"Yep. Traffic gets heavier every day between Houston and Austin. The riding is not too good for an old man, though. And the railroad is building."

"When did you leave Austin?"

"Yesterday. Bedded down at a nester's in the valley last night."

Levit turned to stoke the fire. Fall's eyes questioned him.

"Things have been a little jumpy around here," Levit said finally.

The old man scratched his thin locks. "So I hear," he remarked dryly. "Down around Austin there are rumors that folks are putting Ranger companies together all through here. Got the army some worried. Had a feeling I might just join one of those Ranger bands. I'm getting tired of the bayous."

Levit laughed. "You stay where you are for a while, Fall. Such business can't be straightened out overnight. This country's been running wild for a long time now."

"Well, I'll be close, and don't you ride off to any new wars without me."

Levit studied his visitor affectionately. "I'd feel a lot better if I did have you alongside. You've fought the Indians before. I hear old Parro-o-coom has his eye on me. He's got the idea the Comanches will have to clean out this valley if the Indians want to stay on the Plains. I've got something to settle with the Quohadas myself some day," he added grimly.

"MacAshen," Fall began with some hesitation, "I'd like to ask something—not too personal, I hope. Any reason why you haven't asked about Karryl Newcomb?"

MacAshen hesitated. "Of course not, Fall. I was wondering if you had any news of her."

Fall stared at him, and finally said, "Reckon she's well—and busy."

The two men had supper. The Mexican came in and cleared the table, and returned with a fresh pot of coffee.

"Maybe I'm getting old and just plain unmannerly," Fall blustered. "But I had it figured you took a high interest in the Newcomb girl. I'm gathering things have changed a bit. She was lonely when I brought her to Austin."

"She had plenty of friends the last time I saw her," MacAshen said, with some coolness.

"You're referring to that young Wayne," Fall said. The accuracy of the remark took Levit by surprise.

"So that's it," the old man concluded. "Never would have figured it that way myself, though."

MacAshen rose and paced up and down. "Look here, Fall," he said finally. "The Pedernales is no fit place to bring a girl like Karryl Newcomb. It never has been, and it may never be!"

"Other men have wives here."

"Yes, and plenty of them have died—in the most horrible ways."

"That won't stop people, Levit."

"Well, I'm afraid it doesn't matter much, anymore. I just wasn't the man to match up to those oldtime friends of hers, Fall."

"What gave you that idea?"

"I'd rather not go into it. But it's not me she wanted to marry."

"Oh? Fall cocked an eye at Levit. "And when did you learn that?"

"Quite a while ago now."

"Well, she's still lonely, the way I look at it. And though you don't ask me, I'll tell you that when she heard I was coming out here, she spoke like she wanted you to know she hadn't forgot about you."

Levit did not respond to that. After a while, he banked the fire and handed a tallow dip from the mantle to his friend.

"Sleep well," he advised, "but don't unload your shotgun. This is Indian country, remember."

Fall prepared to depart soon after breakfast. Levit helped him saddle his horse, and tied a heavy bundle of food on the pack behind him. The old man stepped astride and stretched out his hand.

"Fall, I don't know what to say," Levit confessed soberly.

Fall put his hand on his friend's shoulder. "Reckon I don't either, Levit."

The year of 1867 ran on and MacAshen, busy over a vast region, was almost unaware of the days as they slipped by. But suddenly, on one of the occasions when he was at home, his troubles multiplied in a manner neither he nor anyone else would have expected.

Lubbock heard the strange, low murmur from up the river first. He strode to the entranceway, staring curiously toward the distant pecan groves. Suddenly he understood the cause of the odd refrain. "By God!" he shouted. "Hey, boss!" he yelled. He rushed to the ranch house, thrust open the kitchen door, plummeted past the startled Mexican, and leaped at MacAshen.

"Boss—they're here!"

"Who's here?"

"Those damned woollies! Take a look out that door."

MacAshen hurried to the verandah. Slowly breaking out into the open, on the ranch side of the river, was a herd of some twenty or twenty-five of Lenneweber's merinos.

"He really sent them," MacAshen murmured, almost spellbound.

Lubbock clutched his arm, whirling about to gaze toward the compound. "Listen to the horses, Levit," he entreated. The mustangs had caught the scent of the sheep, and the unfamiliar odor had thrown them into panic.

"Send those varmints away, Levit, before they ruin this spread."

Levit interrupted his foreman brusquely. "You know I can't do that. I gave my word."

The herd came slowly on, and Levit noted a shepherd following some distance behind, a rifle over his arm, and a sheep dog close beside him. Just then, a shabby gig drawn by an aging horse appeared through the underbrush some yards behind the herder. Even at the distance, Levit recognized a woman on the seat. The gig was piled high with household goods.

"Damned if Lenneweber didn't carry out his promise to the last gasp."

The herder saw Levit. He raised an arm in signal to the dog, and the dog charged around in front of the herd. The man walked ahead and motioned to the woman to bring the cart on. He traveled the hundred yards or so, Levit going slowly down the path to meet him.

"Guess you're Mr. MacAshen," the man shouted. "I'm Jake Hamlin. Lenneweber sent me over to herd these sheep for you. Finest bunch in the whole flock."

Levit nodded glumly, staring at the fat little animals. He shook hands with the herder, his eyes moving to the woman on the seat of the rig.

He noted how carelessly her blouse held together. She was a woman of perhaps twenty-five, with a mouth full and expressive, and she looked at Levit with a bold appraisal that startled him.

Levit turned back to her husband.

"Well, you're here for better or worse, I guess. We've never run any sheep on this ranch, and I don't know how it will go."

"Aw, don't worry about that, Mr. MacAshen. Sheep are easy. Don't cause no trouble. You'll be glad you're in the sheep business when the herd begins to grow."

Lubbock came forward at MacAshen's beckon, and the rancher raised a thumb in his direction. "This is Mr. Lubbock, my foreman," he said. "Your name is Hamlin, I believe you said, and this is Mrs. Hamlin."

Lubbock nodded skeptically to the man. When he saw the woman close up, he drew in his breath sharply.

"We're not set up for womenfolk here," he pointed out. "But it looks like you've got your own gear."

"Got what we need," the herder returned.

"Those woollies will work the ridges in the south passes, up there," Lubbock directed, pointing to the hills, "and off the cattle pastures. Plenty of water and forage there, maybe the kind sheep like."

"That's sheep country, all right, at least it looks like that from here," Hamlin remarked, squinting in the direction Lubbock indicated.

"We've got an old line shack squared up over there, at the mouth of that choked draw. It's not much, but it's close to the pass. Guess you can fix it up," Lubbock continued.

The herder nodded. "It'll do."

The woman had not spoken, and now MacAshen apologetically addressed her: "You've had a long trip. You must be tired."

Her bold eyes accepted his civility, and she nodded lightly.

"I'll have my cook fix up some food for you, and you can make yourself comfortable for a while. Hamlin, you start those woollies across the river and point them up that farther creek bank. It will take you to the range cabin. Lubbock will show you the place. When you get your gear unloaded, you can come back here for food."

The herder nodded. Lubbock brought up a horse from the corral and tied it behind the rig. Then he mounted the plank seat and whipped up the dray horse. The cart crossed the river behind the herder and his flock.

MacAshen turned to the woman beside him. "Come on in," he invited. "They'll be back after a while."

He showed her into the small room off the big main hall. "There'll be water and towels on the stand," he said. Then he went toward the kitchen to give his orders to the Mexican.

MacAshen did not return to the main hall immediately. He walked through the kitchen and out into the yard beyond. He went on thoughtfully to the corrals and looked at the restive mustangs, slowly settling down and watching him with baleful eyes. Steve and the others were north along the Cave Creek, and Nusser had gone into Fredericksburg on a ranch errand; MacAshen could not expect companionship or sympathy in the bunkhouse. He sat for a while on the log in the workshop, turning the handle of the forge slowly and watching the glow rise.

He was aware, however, that he must return eventually and so, somewhat curious, he started back toward the house. He went in through the kitchen, stopping to watch the Mexican at his chores, then continued on into the hall.

The woman had deposited herself comfortably on the smaller chair in the main room, close to the hearth. She looked up when MacAshen came in.

"I hope you found what you needed," he offered by way of welcome.

"Yes. You are good to us."

Her voice was deep and husky, and her answer aroused a suspicion she had not been a frequent guest in a master's abode. He noted that when she took her eyes away from his face, they ran to the fixtures, rough and used though they were, and to the modest, but solid, comforts of the big room.

The dress she wore had no particular grace; it was a simple one from a trader's pack; but it hung about her rounded, evident curves, and it was drawn in the middle to outline the full breathing contour of her bosom.

"I hope you won't find it too lonesome down here. We don't have many women in this country. Our nearest neighbors are almost a day's ride down the river. The settlers there have wives, but they never come this far up the Pedernales."

A flicker of interest touched her expression, but it was gone in an instant.

"We always live alone. That's the way with sheepherders."

MacAshen rose and walked to the door, searching the terrain beyond the river for a sign of Lubbock and the herder. His lanky frame worked with the muscular control born of military training, and a glimmer of satisfaction passed over her face.

MacAshen turned back from the door to find a confident smile awaiting him.

"Don't know as I should be imposing on you like this, Mr. MacAshen. I should have gone on to the cabin," she said.

"Lubbock and your husband will have to fix it up before you can use it, and you won't need to bother about food tonight. There's plenty here."

"I'm not complaining, Mr. MacAshen. I've not seen many houses like this. You must hear plenty of echoes around here."

Levit laughed. "It is a big place, isn't it? We don't use the upper floor, though, anymore."

"You live inside here all by yourself?"

"Yes."

She seem unconvinced.

"Would you like to look around?" Levit suggested, suddenly feeling sympathetic. "Go ahead, if you want to."

She rose slowly. Levit followed her as she wandered self-consciously from room to room, examing each little object, sometimes turning questioning eyes to him. He explained the items that seemed to puzzle her, and it pleased her when he talked. His gaze traveled over her. She was voluptuous. To call her a rarity on the frontier would have been putting it mildly, he thought.

He shook himself, turning hastily to look through the door again. To his relief, Lubbock was sloshing heavily through the stream. The herder followed, driving the gig.

"Here they come," Levit announced brusquely. "We can eat and then you can get on to your cabin."

21

Karryl's first year in Austin had long since passed, and with it at least a part of her fortitude, but she still tried to do the best she could.

Here in 1867 Austin, people did not sit around grieving over their troubles, although the situation in Texas was often chaotic. She marveled at her new state's stoicism while striving to assert a measure of her own.

It had been a turbulent year, a year not only of disorder, for others, but one of acute sadness for her. In that year, though, Karryl had matured beyond her own realization. She had come to recognize the meaning of real friendship, evident in the solicitousness of the people who were close—the Whipples, the headmaster, the Millers, the Raymonds. She had found a job to do. To her surprise, she had come to realize that she wanted more than ever to do that job well—to do whatever she could to help others accomplish what they sought to achieve.

Tragedy more poignant than anything she had ever known had overtaken her. Two men, each in his own fashion, had wanted her, but in the welter of life's strange complexities each had gone his way, and neither had come back. Once she might have handled such a thing with quick dispatch. But she was older now, and she recognized the changes in herself.

At first, the knowledge that the Wayne family had settled on the prairie below Austin had been exciting to her. But Burr had wanted her for his wife, and when she could not accept him, he had gone away.

Levit MacAshen also had come and gone. In the deep of the night, alone in her room at the Whipple home, she prayed that Levit would come back, if only to let her explain. Sometimes she became terribly angry in the thought, but always she ended up sobbing instead. The hours turned into days, the days into weeks, and the weeks into months. She saw no reason to believe he would ever return now.

The winds were brisk, and Karryl hurried along the path to the white cottage. The winds that came down out of the hills never ceased to pierce her. Levit MacAshen was out there, somewhere. He had left her without even so much as a goodbye. He had been so obviously hurt, so angry and with it all, so immovable. And yet so foolishly so! Something in the very thought of him always inspired her, even while she fumed. Sometimes though, she wondered if only an illusion stood between her and Burrell Wayne, depriving them both of happiness.

But the thought of MacAshen would not leave her.

She stopped suddenly, staring off across the distance and asking herself if she really believed that MacAshen would never return. Then, angry and oppressed by the obviousness of the answer, she hurried on into the cottage, her red hair a flag of frustration.

Mrs. Whipple met her at the door. "Law, child, you must come home earlier these nights," she scolded. "There's so much trouble around, a pretty young woman like you can't afford to be out on the streets alone this late in the day."

Karryl gazed into the older woman's face. The smothering grip of trouble, indeed, the weight of the whole world, seemed to settle around and upon Karryl like a shroud. Suddenly, everything that was bottled up inside of her broke. She burst into tears and threw herself into Mrs. Whipple's arms. "Oh, what is to become of me—of all of us?" she sobbed.

Mrs. Whipple held her tightly, patting her gently as she did so. "There now, my dear, do not let what has befallen you destroy your fortitude. All of us realize how much you have gone through. But you have been bearing up wonderfully well. I did not mean to frighten you, only to speak a word of caution."

Karryl quieted. "I'll be careful," she promised, pushing the hair up out of her eyes and slowly pulling herself away. She went on into her room and sat down on the side of her bed. It occurred to her suddenly that her life had grown a little too orderly, that caution and regret were the only emotions that seemed to be in her mind anymore. Angrily, she wondered if some gesture more in keeping with the vigor of this land was not overdue if she, as a woman, must cope with it alone, and become a part of it. She was tired and slipped off her shoes. Then she loosened her garments, one by one, dropping them on the floor, until she stood completely unclothed before her mirror.

"I won't be this young forever," she snapped. For a surprised moment, she wondered if her troubles had stripped her of the last vestige of decency. In this frontier city, who cared?

She slipped into her dressing gown, but did not turn back to the mirror. After furiously plumping her pillows, she stretched out on the bed again and closed her eyes to rest. But they would not stay closed. She lay and stared at the ceiling, angry again, and tremendously unhappy.

There was a hue and cry in Austin that week. A trader had bought new guns and ammunition, and before the army could question his motives, he had disappeared into the wilds.

"Those guns will be pointed at white men," Throckmorton telegraphed to General Sheridan. But little could be done to prevent it then.

The army quartermaster was ordered to put the frontier posts in order, however, for the arrival of the main body of troops. Sheridan had four thousand men in Texas now, and Fort Chadbourne and Fort Stockton were reoccupied.

But north of Dallas, white outlaws were robbing and burning and killing in a wave of brutality that equalled the savagery even of the Comanches. The bandits came into the towns in packs, defying peaceful residents. Law enforcement by scalawag governments, forced on the isolated communities, seemed seldom able to stem the lawless tide; indeed, often there was evidence of active collusion. In a city even as large as Galveston, far down on the coast, the Yankee chief of police absconded with all the city's funds. His clerk was arraigned for embezzlement, but it did not bring back the money.

Quiet, earnest men came to the ranch to see MacAshen daily. They came from the distances, conferred briefly in the house on the Pedernales, and rode away again.

But in Austin, Governor Throckmorton's own relationship with Sheridan was worsening fast, and that spelled alarming new dangers. Then, on July 30, 1867, the army commander angrily removed Throckmorton from office.

"What a hell of a time to have this happen, Steve. But I was afraid of it," Levit snapped when Meadows rode in from the lower settlements with the unhappy revelation.

"Reckon all we've done, we'll have to do over again. Or at least sit tight now until some new kind of a Texas government comes out of the mess," Meadows said.

"I don't know about that. But it may rest on me—and some of the rest of you around me here—to see we don't get five or six hundred men marked down again as rebels—or plain outlaws." MacAshen went on: "Not only Sheridan, but General Griffin, too, has been after Throckmorton a long time. Griffin's claim is that the governor wouldn't punish outrages against Union troops. The charges were ridiculous, but that does not mean anything to the Yankees."

He walked a step away, Meadows slowly following.

"I guess Sheridan never considered the past," Levit muttered. "I was at the secession convention in January of 1861 when Throckmorton earned a place in a little group of men some people called the 'immortal seven.' They were the handful that fought against secession. I remember Throckmorton's words, Steve. When they called his name for the vote, he said: 'In view of my responsibility, in reverence of God and Country, unawed by the wild spirit of revolution around me, I vote no!' And once, when they hissed him from the galleries, he shouted out: 'Mr. President, the rabble may hiss, while patriots tremble!' But none of that would mean anything to Sheridan, either. Did you hear who would succeed him?"

"Yep. It's Elisha Pease. Heard Sheridan offered it to John H. Reagan first, and that's strange. But Reagan was plowing and told him to go away."

"They could have picked somebody worse."

"Not much worse. Pease has been hand-in-glove with the carpetbaggers."

"That's true. But Pease can't be as bad a governor as some

[228]

they've put in over the other states. He's had his good days in Texas. Pease was governor twice, you know. I don't think he'll really try to harm the state."

"But what'll he do for us out here?"

"I don't know. Once, he did a lot. When he was governor, the frontier line moved a hundred and fifty miles westward. We'll just have to wait and see."

Meadows spat on the ground. "Hate to see a scalawag in the Governor's Mansion in Austin," he said.

Now MacAshen smiled. "Pease built the Governor's Mansion, Steve. He's lived in it before."

In Washington, Congress adjourned in July, to reconvene in November. President Johnson decided to rid himself of Stanton, the secretary for war, but Stanton refused to resign. Thereupon, he was suspended by the president, and General Grant was ordered to take his place. When the congressmen returned on schedule, the president, in accordance with the "Tenure of Office Act," submitted his reasons for removing the secretary. The Senate refused to concur. Stanton returned to office, only to have Johnson remove him a month later. Immediately, the House voted to impeach the president. The trial was set for March 15, 1868.

Frustration was torturing Levit MacAshen, but he couldn't put Karryl out of his thoughts, no matter how he tried. Should he go back just to see for himself again?

Lubbock and Elledge answered that question: "If some of those carpetbaggers spot you on the streets of Austin right now, they'll cut you down. Seeing as how you're needed out here, it's not worth it, whatever your reason for wanting to go. You never know what Sheridan's cooked up. Wait a while and see how the wind blows."

Fretfully, Levit accepted the admonitions of his friends, and thus it was that Lubbock instead, while delivering a string of horses to Austin for Miller, first learned of the President's latest action. He couldn't wait to get back to the Falling Water with the news.

"They finally got him!" he reported to Levit then with great satisfaction.

"Got who?"

"Sheridan. The Federals finally got enough of Sheridan's doings down this way. And he's been moved out. Moved out of the South, at least."

"You mean he's been relieved of command?"

"Yep. Relieved of the command in Texas, anyway. The President did it himself."

Levit drew his foreman into the house. "Get on with the story," he urged.

"Happened a spell back, as I understand it. I guess the military kept it quiet as long as they could. The word got out while I was in Austin. Must have been on the telegraph wires. Sheridan's been sent clean out of the Confederate country—he's gone north to head the forts in Missouri. Guess he'll learn up there what it means to face up to real Indians, because he sure didn't try to find out down here."

Levit strode to the window, working his hands behind him. "This news is more important than you can even imagine, Lubbock. It probably means at least one thing: if someone with any real gumption is sent in to replace Sheridan, then the Rangers won't have to worry about tangling somewhere with Union troops. You and I and every damned man among us knows what that would have meant, and it had begun to look like we had no choice. Now, maybe we will have."

"Maybe so. But don't you count on us not having any more worries, at least not yet."

Nearby, in another corner of the central Texas mesquite brakes, another man also followed the course of events. Further, he was pleased over an unexpected bit of luck that had occurred to him.

Devers had found Rhoda Hamlin, too. Or, to be more exact, he had just rediscovered her. Sudderth brought him word of her presence at the sheepherder's cabin. He informed Devers about her at the saloon in the cluster of cabins on the Blanco.

"A woman! Out here? Devers exclaimed.

"Sure is, boss. What's more, it's a woman you're acquainted with."

"What're you talking about, Sudderth?"

"Remember that sheepherder and his wife you ran into down Houston way, back when we was picking up the cotton? The fellow that drove the sheep herds to Hockley?"

"You don't mean that woman named—" he hesitated, recollecting, "—Rhoda something or other?"

"Rhoda Hamlin? That's her, boss. She's living right here on top of us."

Devers eagerly pressed his crony for further details.

"Saw the old coot in the pass, herding woollies, first," Sudderth said. "Had just a small herd. He's driving for that MacAshen. Can't figure it out, either; MacAshen's no sheepman."

"And he's living up there—his wife, too?"

"In a line shack. He's crazy as ever."

Devers ran over the singular experience he had enjoyed at Houston. The man and his wife had wanted attention and excitement, and he had undertaken to provide both, especially for the woman, for that kind of a woman seemed never to resent him.

"You say they're herding in the pass itself, Sudderth?"

"Right smack-dab. Range cabin, though, is down the slope, in the canyon on the off side. Pretty well below the pass, and east a little, in a boxed draw. That trail over the ledge don't go through the pass, though, Devers. It drops down just east of the road that runs by that range cabin. And by the way, that fellow Hamlin is spending all his time with the sheep right now. Says there are varmints in the rocks."

Devers listened attentively. A short time later, he saddled his horse and rode off alone toward the north.

It was late in the afternoon when he halted at the cabin. Hamlin was in, awaiting supper. He remembered Devers from Houston, and the big man's appearance sent the sheepherder into great exaggerations of welcome.

"Don't get to see many people up here," he volunteered. "The waddies down at MacAshen's spread stay close to the river. Don't get to talk much, me and the wife, except to ourselves."

They were amazed to find Devers had become a rancher, right at their door, and the sheepherder dwelt on it. But Devers was more satisfied to observe that the same expression he could call up so agreeably still played on the woman's face even while her husband ran on. She remembered well.

"It's getting along," Devers said finally. "I'll be moseying home."

The herder raised his hands in protest. "Well, now, it's not far till suppertime. Rhoda here will be fixing some vittles, and you're sure welcome. She's right glad when people come by."

Devers accepted the invitation to remain that long. After the meal was over, he said, though, "Glad to run into you people up here in the hills. But now I will have to be hurrying home."

"You'll stop back by?"

"Sure. Whenever I'm up this way."

From Fredericksburg came Lenneweber, also back to the Pedernales, finding Levit MacAshen once more at the Falling Water.

"I'm glad you've come," Levit greeted him. "Get down and come on into the house."

The German followed. Levit placed the man's small pack in the room adjoining his own and called out to Pepito for refreshments. Lenneweber sat down. "I felt it important that I come. I have wanted you to know that I have not been idle," he began. "Biberstin, he took as I did to your thoughts. I think we can promise you some help."

MacAshen listened carefully. "I had hoped for that," he said, "but I was afraid to expect too much."

"The time has come when every man will have to stand up and be counted again on this border."

Levit nodded. "Tell me," he said earnestly, "you Germans have some friends among the carpetbaggers. Do the people in Austin intend now to get out of our way and let us Texans tackle the job that's got to be done on the prairies ourselves?"

"I think not, Herr MacAshen. Sixty-eight citizens of San Saba County have asked Governor Pease to permit a company of minute men. Perhaps it was only a blind. But he has not replied. It could have been because of what happened at Fort Mason. Had you heard of that?"

"No. I've been on the back trails."

"The Commander at Fort Mason, a Captain Thompson, interfered in a fight between Negro soldiers and cowboys. I do not know how many soldiers were shot, but the captain was killed."

"That's a hell of a thing to happen right now."

"Yes. But the big mistake is for the army to quarter Negro troops in Texas at all. I am afraid it will get worse. A visitor in my home a few days since tells me of a man named John Wesley Hardin who has caused much trouble; he can't tolerate black soldiers."

"I've heard of him. A marvel with a gun. They say Hardin's is the fastest hand with a pistol the West has seen."

"It could be true. Perhaps he is a more deadly shot than even men like Helm, down in the Brasada. But probably not so much so as Storm, or Ord."

MacAshen sat up stiffly. "You mention this man Ord. Have you ever run into him up this way?"

"No. But our people they know him by reputation."

"I wonder about him," Levit said. "I knew Ord once, long ago. He was a trooper under my command when we rode with Bedford Forrest. He did, indeed, have a matchless skill with a gun."

"You have special feelings for the man?"

"Frankly, I do. We were close—as close, I guess, as a private soldier and his commander can be. But there was something else. He had a personal loyalty to me, I felt—and I to him. Ord was only a boy then. I wasn't much older myself. Guess I never completely understood him, but I fought beside him then, and I would fight beside him now."

"He has achieved a deadly name on the frontier since the war."

"Maybe so. But I've watched those reports on Ord. He's killed men. But so have others among us. And so far as I know, nobody has ever accused him of an outright crime."

Lenneweber listened silently. Eventually, he countered: "That may be true. It would not be the first such case I have heard of. Gunmen are a strange breed of people, and those who live by the gun seem inevitably to die by it. They hunt each other out . . . the fastest of them do, at least. With respect to this man Ord, no one seems to have heard about him in more than a year. If he had been killed, such news would have shot from Louisiana to the Rockies overnight."

Levit made no further comment and Lenneweber changed the subject abruptly. "I have wanted much to sit down again and discuss with you the things of which we talked before, MacAshen. But a report on our people at Fredericksburg is not the only reason for my visit here today. I have some information you should know. The Germans have connections, as you point out, in the state capital. We hear many things. A few weeks ago, a report came to my ears that gave me great concern."

"This movement to revive the Ranger companies again—it must be progressing rapidly."

"Why do you say that?"

"Rumors are afoot, and broad things like that can't be kept secret. Unfortunately, the government officials have knowledge of the effort and Rangers are banned. Some men have already been seized."

"I know."

"Here is what I have come to say, MacAshen. The army officers realize that most of these men they have arrested are only the small people. They have not indicated as yet whether they know who is behind the movement, although they realize now that it is suddenly burgeoning into something big. When you came to see me at Loyal Valley, we talked only of a Ranger company at Fredericksburg. But in that effort, MacAshen, it was apparent to me, as it has been to all of us, that one man is directing the program everywhere. I have a feeling you are that man, although you have not told me so. I do not want you to tell me now. But if I am right, I urge you to be on guard."

MacAshen's grip on the arm of his chair tightened.

"I'll remember, Lenneweber—and I thank you."

Lenneweber smiled. "Further," he added, "I think it would be helpful if our friends, the government officials, do not learn that the Germans are willing to serve in these Ranger companies of yours, at least not as yet."

22

Southward, on the Guadalupe prairies, the Wayne ranch gradually ceased to hold Burr's attention. He longed to be away from it all. He could have made it different, had Karryl seen fit to accept his suit. But she had not, and the daily routine now dragged more heavily upon him than even he would ever have believed. He often thought of moving on—to California, perhaps.

But he had admitted this only to himself, struggling against the longing to break the news to his mother and to be on his way. He had almost come to such a decision, when Grippa brought a report that forced him to reconsider any such notion, for the time being, at least.

"That bunch of prize longhorns we been workin' to separate and build up for choice beef, it's gone," Grippa said gravely.

"Gone!" Burr echoed.

"Nothing else. Disappeared. They're not on our range. And they sure didn't stray. We had 'em on good grass and water in that pocket, and it's only rocks and briars from the mouth for a mile outward. They never walked away from there on their own."

"Our best longhorns have been stolen?"

"Looks like it. Rustled. And every one of them branded.

[235]

I've been afraid it would come. Strange goin's-on here in central Texas. Anyway, I've been all over the valley. That herd hasn't just scattered. There's not a choice beef left on the home pasture of the whole spread. Only the second graders and wild cattle. And after all our work."

"Did you find a trail?"

"Not much of one. However way they got out of there, somebody was right foxy. You can't follow longhorns easy on rocky ground. But it's pretty easy to figure where they went."

"All right. Let's go. But don't tell the folks. No need to worry them."

Grippa and Burr Wayne headed straight for the sheltered draw where the building herd had been bedded. The spot lay some miles northeast of the ranch house, on the lowering side of the plain's contour, and the draw itself was enclosed on three sides by twenty-foot cliffs. Only at the entrance, some quarter-mile in width, was there an opening, and they halted when they came to it.

"Look across there for yourself," Grippa said.

Burr stared. Then he swore angrily.

"Not a critter left," the foreman pointed out. Then he indicated the soft soil just at the mouth of the draw. "Easy to see they headed north and east," he said.. "But after that, it'd take a Comanche to follow the trail through the wash before it hits them hills up yonder."

"We'll go up, anyway, and see what we can see."

Burr dug his spurs into the horse and galloped off in the direction indicated by the track. Two hours later, they came to the first rising ground on the edge of the plateau.

The soil had been red and sandy back on the frontier prairie. Behind that, the earth had revealed only a fine yellow-gray loam, soft, and blown by the winds. But here, consistent with the sudden shifts in the soil of the Guadalupe basin, it was dark and coarse, the calcerous marls reflecting tints of bluish purple. Glauconitic clays and hard limestone spilled back into the rock. They rode slowly along. Suddenly, the formations broke again, and the soil became black and waxy. Grippa dismounted, throwing his reins across the horse's head and looping them at his elbow. He bent low every few feet.

"Cattle went through here," he said. "Heading north, around the Blanco basin." He mounted and turned the horse's head.

After a while, they came to the base of a plateau, where the black, waxy clay suddenly ended. Terraces began here, rugged, sterile levels covered with brown and gray cobblestones, debris from the upper ledges. Grippa pulled up. "No use, Wayne. The trail's had rain on it, and it's gone on the upper plateau. But it's heading north and east. You can figure they went around the Springs, then out through the Blanco country. And from there, God knows where."

Burr found it hard to break the news to the family. "Yes, Father, I'm afraid it's true enough. Rustlers. They've taken our best cattle."

The old man stalked up and down before the fireplace. "This is an outrage. It's as bad as the Yankees. What can we do about it?"

Reluctant though he was to face such a dilemma, Burr realized that his father was not now capable of running the ranch, in any way he might have been called upon to do so. For that matter, he never had been. "I guess I'll try to go after them," Burr answered. "The herd may have had more than a week's start on us, but they couldn't have traveled too fast."

Grippa snorted, and Burr glanced at him. "Three or four men to tackle a hard-bit rustler outfit big enough to run that herd off?" Grippa queried. "You couldn't get close enough to see the color on them duns. What's more, by now that herd may be split two or three ways."

"But even rustlers will have to get rid of the stock quickly," Burr argued.

"Could be, but sure not likely. And you'd be riding this time next year trying to find out. I don't know how much truth there is to it, but range gossip has it that most of these white rustler gangs have deals with the Indians. Place out west called Valle de las Lagrimas, where Indians meet up with the Mexican traders to swap the stock white men turn over to them. Got its name, Lagrimas, they say, from the way the captive white women cry when the Comanches separate mothers and children. Likely, your longhorns are headed there now, too,"

"But we sure don't want to just sit here and let thieves clean us out?"

"Wouldn't say they'll try to clean you clear out. They always leave a breeding herd. But in Texas, when small ranch outfits like this go off across a couple of hundred miles of prairie trying to stop a pilfered herd, the Redskins sometimes wait behind them, and then you've got them to worry about instead."

Robella Wayne rose to her feet. "There will be no pursuit of the cattle," she said decisively. "We will not take the chance of sacrificing lives for the recovery of our stock. We will start over again." Her eyes were misty, but there was no doubt of the firmness in her voice.

Burr eyed her uncertainly, then nodded unhappily to Adam. The foreman stalked slowly from the room.

The loss of the herd was only the first of new tragedies to descend upon the Wayne household.

Robella went to her room and sat down on the bed. She moved a hand across her forehead and found it hot and dry. She rose and stared at herself in the mirror, touching a finger to the lines beneath her eyes. A wave of dizziness caught her just as Margaret entered the room. The latter moved quickly to her mother's side and placed an arm around her shoulders.

"Mother, is something wrong?" she asked softly. A fear that had been in her mind for weeks again clutched her heart. When she stepped from her mother's room again, Burr's eyes caught her.

"Say nothing to Father," he admonished.

Robella Wayne did not improve. Late in the month a biting wind swept down across the prairies. It killed what foliage had appeared, cloaking the countryside with an atmosphere of futility; and a week later, Robella Wayne was dead. They buried her on a little knoll in the meadow beside the ranch house. When it was over, in their grief they faced each other over the hearthstone in the old house.

Burr drew his sister close to him. For a moment, she remained motionless. Then she broke, crying out in anguish and despair. Burr held her tightly, letting the weight of her emotion run its full course. After her storm of weeping had subsided, Margaret sank into a chair, miserably resting her head on a clenched fist. Burr leaned over her and lifted her face to his.

"You will have to take your mother's place, Margaret. There is no one else to look after Father—and me—now."

Margaret raised her wet eyes to Burr, slowly nodded, then broke into tears again.

Now Burr had to put behind him any thought of leaving He knew only work, hard work, would ever change things again. He had to learn everything.

"I'll build the herd back, and quick," he vowed. "There are plenty of wild longhorns in the brakes still, and I'll get them."

He and his men took to their saddles, beating the draws and driving the unbranded stock down into the lower pastures. Burr lost even the appearance of a tenderfoot. The better animals were cut out and herded into the heavier undergrowths by the Guadalupe, where the forage was rich and vitalizing.

Occasionally, Standifer indicated a measure of interest and, though he was clearly wavering now, he remembered sometimes to ask Burr of the stock.

Ben Lacing had remained in the background during the sad hours of Robella's death, but he came forward quietly when the neighbors had gone back to their homesteads. He made no effort to utter meaningless words. He did not know the phrases men used to console women in their grief. But his heart was full of sorrow for the girl in her unhappiness and he shared in her grief, for Robella Wayne had been kind to him, kinder than any woman he had ever known. Margaret read the earnestness in his eyes. When he started slowly toward her, she threw everything aside, rushing into his arms and burying her head in his shoulder.

No words passed between them. He held her tightly, offering her his own strength. Then he went back to his cabin, leaving her calmer, and comforted with the realization that he was at hand to lend her courage.

In faraway Washington, the impeachment trial of President Johnson cast a pall over the country. Even at Austin, people were dejected and fearful.

The Reverend Mr. Whipple paced back and forth across his study. Occasionally, he glanced at the face of one or the other of his guests and frowned.

"I cannot speculate on how it will go, my friends," the minister intoned. "All we can do now is wait and see. It's so far to Washington."

Eventually however, came the news that the trial was over. Johnson had been vindicated, although by the margin of only a single vote. But four days later, in Chicago, the Republicans nominated General Grant for the presidency, and the significance of that move was lost on no one.

"What do you think of our future now?" Karryl asked the old minister.

"Nobody knows what to think," Mr. Whipple sighed. "General Grant has endorsed the radical plan of reconstruction."

23

Cold weather stayed late in the hill country but oddly enough the Falling Water prospered, despite MacAshen's long absences. The stock had multiplied, and MacAshen's wranglers were corralling plenty of wild horses in the pens south of the river, too. Miller would be showing up from Austin once more.

"Your spread looks better every day, Levit," the stable-owner applauded when he did arrive. "Guess you'll weather everything, if the rustlers leave you anything to sell."

"The boys don't think we've had any outlaws through here yet, but maybe they've been smarter than we think."

"You're close to the Blanco, Levit. Some of the small ranchers down the river swear their stock is being rustled toward that basin. You know anyone who's been in there lately?"

"I met a man up here on the Pedernales a while back who said he was ranching the Blanco. The name was Devers. Ever hear of him?"

Miller's eyes narrowed. "Yes, I've heard of him. And if it was anybody but you, I'd not be talking, Levit. He's a cattleman, all right. Leastways, he knows the West. But he's got other talents, too. Some of the homesteaders who've lost cattle aren't as tight-lipped as I try to be, traveling all around here and there as I do. Can't say that any of them actually *knows* anything about this Devers. But they've got pretty strong ideas and I've heard them say he was up to something in there on the Blanco."

Spring arrived on schedule, and buds appeared on the willows in the creek beds. The sweet scent of the bee-brush was in the air as MacAshen rode rapidly down the river bank from the Falling Water.

Across the Pedernales and back against the southern rim, a depression in the wall provided a broad, natural corral open only through a narrow entrance that fanned down toward the valley; and here the cowboys had built a high pole fence. The grass was deep within the amphitheater; a tiny brook meandered about its confines; and MacAshen had had the men set up the enclosure as a new corral for the wild horses they were snaring.

As Levit rode along, a sudden spectacle before him caused him to pull up short. The sheepherder's cart was on the other shore, the horse grazing in the lush grasses. And Rhoda Hamlin was there. He saw that the woman had been swimming in the stream, inspired by the warmth of the weather.

MacAshen guessed he had surprised her, but she raised a hand in greeting and he touched the rim of his sombrero. The woman stared from across the river, waiting as though for a sign. His breath quickened, but he did not speak to her. He turned his horse into the grove behind him. He pushed on, crossing the stream ultimately, and headed for the pen. One of the new German cowboys he had recently taken on, Reed Schreiner, greeted Levit. He was proud of the horse herd and showed Levit two especially fine roans.

"Much money, those army lieutenants down San Antonio way will pay for roans like these," he said.

Levit agreed. "I wish we had a hundred more."

Schreiner posed a question. "Herr Levit, you have been riding toward the pen lately from the south, yes?"

"No, I've been gone."

"The others, they have been working this way?"

"No, they're north of the river. Why all the questions, Reed?"

"Come with me, Herr Levit. I show you something."

He pulled his own mount in by the stake rope, fixed the

bridle, and deftly threw on the saddle, tightening the cinches quickly.

"Downstream, it is," he explained.

They rode through the pecan groves, avoiding the thickets of small sumac until they came to the base of the cliff. Here was a clear space, perhaps of a hundred feet or so, where the weathering of the wall kept down the vegetation. A quarter-mile farther on, Schreiner raised his hand. He pointed to a slight lessening of the incline, a dozen paces wide, which enabled a fairly easy passage to the next shelf above. Until almost on it, the opening was hidden. He turned into the path and Levit followed. The incline led back westward, the contour of the cliff face disguising the upper ledge from below. They pointed up a steep slope. Then, rounding a sudden corner, Levit was greeted with a splendid view of the valley: the river, winding and plunging along its rocky course; the great pecan grove, bending to the winds; and in the far distance, the Falling Water itself, like a fortress beyond the sweep of the stream. Almost immediately below was the log fence of the horse corral, and the winding shelf led back to where MacAshen could observe the entire enclosure.

"I didn't know about this," Levit exclaimed.

"No, Herr Levit. But come."

Schreiner led him to the far side. The scrub cedar ran down here toward the cliff face. The man pointed to a small area between several belt-high boulders.

"A range camp!" MacAshen exclaimed.

"Yes. And it has been used much."

"Not by our men."

"No. This park, it is not known to Herr Levit's waddy."

"How did you find this, Reed?"

"I run onto horse tracks by the corral, yet. Three days back, just before the rain. I follow. Up the shelf, and on to here. Something else: out from this park they go, back to the next cliffs. And somewhere in there there is a cut to get out, south."

"I understand, Reed. Somebody's set a watch on the Falling Water. That trail leads toward the Blanco."

Riding home, Levit picked a course close to the wall, his eye studying the cliff face for other ruptures. Near the main pass, he halted briefly, shading his eyes with his hand as he studied the terrain. Then he went on. He was so preoccupied that he rode onto the sheepherder's cabin itself, before he realized it. Rhoda Hamlin, back at home, had heard the hoofbeats of his horse, and she stood now in the doorway of the cabin watching him approach. He touched the brim of his hat.

"It's a warm day, Mrs. Hamlin. I hope you enjoyed your swim."

She nodded, a slow smile molding her full lips. Levit's eyes took in the drape of the rough garment that covered her body. If it was calico, the color and nature of its texture had long since disappeared in the lye water of the wash tub, but the woman had gathered the material in such a way as to best display her curves.

Slowly, he stepped down from his saddle.

"I guess you're finding it pretty rough here, after the comforts of your homestead?" he asked.

"It's all right, Mr. Levit. I'm getting along fine," she said pulling the bench from the wall. "Sit down, please. I'll get you a dipper of water."

Levit watched her move away. Her hips swung with the muscular precision of a female puma; there was a tawny darkness in the skin of her bare ankles, neck and shoulders.

She came back with the container of water, her bold eyes never leaving his face, as he raised the cup to his lips. He drank, and returned it to her.

"I haven't seen your husband for quite a while. How are the sheep?" he asked.

"Sheep are sheep," she muttered, her voice cushioned in the husky mountain slur.

"Does he always stay with the flock?"

"Most of the time. They're new here, and they have to be taught where to range."

"But he returns at night?"

She gave him a level look. "Not always. There are cats in the hills, and wolves."

Hurriedly, he asked, "Do you have all you need here?"

She walked a step before his eyes, then came back.

"Yes, we've got . . . what we need."

Her words conveyed one message, the tone in which they were spoken an altogether different reply. The woman's meaning could not escape Levit. In the space of a measureless moment, he wondered if his boys had beaten a path to her door.

She came close, and he felt the sudden wrench of desire. He rose to his feet abruptly. Her eyes were upon him; the invitation was there. He yanked his hat down upon his head.

A flicker of surprise rimmed the woman's eyes for a moment, then anger. She stepped backward toward the door, watching MacAshen as he pulled up his horse and climbed into the saddle.

"So long, Mrs. Hamlin," he said, drawing the words out. "Let me know how it goes here." He turned down the trail, glancing back once to give her a half-salute of farewell.

"Hasta luego, Mister Levit."

The words repeated themselves slowly in his mind, as the horse galloped onward. Hasta luego—'til we meet again.

24

Negroes voted for the first time in the new constitutional elections, and with the advent of hot summer weather, another convention began its work. The presence in Austin of the radical delegates, white and black, provided the usual incidents. Most of the responsible citizens stayed off the streets, but the disorders angered Karryl.

"They certainly won't pen me down at home all the time," she announced.

On this day, she chose the hour of noon to visit the shops. She met a few people she knew, but they spoke quickly and went their ways. There were delegates on Congress Avenue, some of them reeling under the influence of liquor, others scowling their paths from door to door.

The bold, impudent stares of two husky farmhands worried Karryl. Despite the many men here for the convention, she hadn't expected this sort of thing. She quickly turned her head to one side. The men had no intention of relinquishing any part of the sidewalk. She felt a trace of panic, but stiffened quickly. "I'll not do it," she vowed. The brazen, self-assured bluster of the two amused her, but the appraising leers they cast her way weren't funny. She held her ground, moving close against the wall of the building, with her back to the pair as they idled past. The nearer man eased close so that his shoulder rubbed hers as she stood pressed against the wall.

From the door of the shop a few steps away, another man rushed forward. Karryl stepped quickly back into the sidewalk before him.

"No, don't!" she exclaimed. "I don't want to be the cause of something awful happening."

The incident left her somewhat startled as well as angry, though, and she decided then and there to be more careful in the future. "When they're drunk," she thought, "they could do anything."

The delegates—and other convention hangers-on—wrangled back and forth, accomplishing little. The entire winter of 1869 ran by with almost nothing achieved in a legislative way, and ultimately the delegates went home without even the constitution they had come to write. That latter chore was left to a military commander; whereupon even Governor Pease—the Yankee choice for chief executive officer—threw in the towel.

"I can no longer serve as a mouthpiece for an alien army of invasion and tyranny," he announced late in the year, walking out on the very radicals who had put him back in office and leaving the state for three months with no civil director of its affairs.

General elections occurring also late in 1869 were marked by the rise of the ambitious politician Levit had spoken of, Edmund J. Davis.

"He's got the earmarks of a scoundrel," Mr. Whipple told his little circle. "He's already tried to divide Texas up into three states. If he can divide the parties, what with General Reynolds coming back to Texas to run the army, he'll make himself governor."

Troops surrounded the polls at election time.

"It is an outrage," the minister reported bitterly when it was over. "Reynolds only laughs at the fraud. In Navarro County, they held no election, because the registrar cleared out with the voting lists. In Milam County, the polls were simply closed by Davis's men. It's happened all over, and they've counted the votes—at least, Reynolds says the army has counted them. Out of seventy-nine thousand ballots cast, he says Davis has won by a measly eight hundred votes."

[247]

"Would the president of the United States stand for this?" Karryl wondered.

"Grant has refused to interfere in any way," Mr. Whipple responded.

In January, 1870, General Reynolds added salt to the already chafing wounds. He proclaimed Davis governor, and ordered the legislature to convene immediately. Then he blandly proposed his own name to that body for election to the United States Senate.

In a big stone house on the outskirts of Austin, Devers reclined uncomfortably while he talked with a beetle-browed man behind an oak desk. The interview had been a sharp one.

"I don't know if I understand you, Palland, or any of the other people who've moved in here with you," Devers was saying angrily. "Reynolds must be a fool to come out like he did, right off the bat, and you—who've been buttering him up—ought to have told him so."

"He didn't ask for advice."

"You're getting soft then, waiting for people to ask. Have you read this?" He showed his host the Austin newspaper. "Even the Republicans put it like this: 'That it is inefficacious for any United States official to become a candidate for elective office before a body over whose composition he has exercised virtual censorship.'"

"I know what they're saying, but I think Reynolds will quit. The legislature itself has already passed him the word. Even the Negroes were upset when Reynolds let it be known he was putting up his own name."

"The U.S. Senate is a private club, and even like it is now you'd better not let those people look into what's going on here."

"I said Reynolds would withdraw. He won't get any support, at least, from any of our outfit. Besides, Devers, nobody ever asked you to put your oar in on ordinary folks' affairs back here, so don't worry about it." Devers glared bitterly as the man lit a cigar. "Now tell me, how goes it on your end with respect to other matters? Did you bring the collections in with you?"

Devers opened his valise. There was an assortment of specie inside, silver and gold coin, and paper money of varying nationalities. "The boys are hollering for more on the herding end," he informed his host heavily. "And what's more, we may be in for some trouble."

"What kind of trouble?"

"We're going to have to go north of the Blanco for longhorns. The boys east from us have been working near the Colorado. But we've about cleaned that country out. And the herds have been building up too fast in the basin. North of us are plenty of longhorns, but there's something else. When we start in on the Pedernales, we've got to be ready for things we haven't run into before."

"What things?"

"Scrappy set of ranchers through there. One of them is a fellow named MacAshen. He's got a following, people who've fought Indians. And there are the Germans, too. They may look easy-going, but they've got some tough hombres in their camps."

"Well, if it's like that to the north, you've still got the Guadalupe."

Devers was silent for a moment. "Yes," he responded finally. "So far, the cattle the boys have pushed up from the stand at Paradise have kept us busy. But that's changed some now, too."

"What do you mean?"

"Sudderth was down at Gonzales a while ago, talkin' with Almazan. On the way back he stopped for water and chow at a ranch owned by a man named Wayne, and they asked him to spend the night. We've hit that fellow's herd once already but they'd never seen Sudderth, of course." Devers struck a fresh light to his own cigar.

"Go on," his listener commanded.

"Just as Sudderth was saddling up to leave next morning, a couple of hands from the night crew rode in. They didn't spot Sudderth—he was already out of the corral—but he sure took a look at them. And one of those riders he knew from back a while earlier." Devers bent forward and whispered a name in the politician's ear.

The other straightened up instantly. "The hell you say!" he exclaimed.

"No mistake, Sudderth swore. I've never seen the man myself, so I wouldn't know. But he dropped out of sight quite a spell back. I shut Sudderth's mouth about it, quick, with our own outfit especially. There'll still be plenty of prize longhorns down there, but Sudderth—for one—will never ride past San Marcos Springs again. Fact is he can't figure how we managed to get away clean in the first drive."

"Castlerod?"

"We haven't spilled any of it to him yet."

Palland rose to his feet and began to pace the floor. "We know about MacAshen," he said finally, "and right now we want to steer clear of him for some other good reasons. You'll have to handle MacAshen from your end, if he's handled at all, just now. This other proposition down on the Guadalupe may change the deal up some, as you say; but one thing you ought to keep in mind: we've had word that the Mexicans can take a lot more cattle in the summer. Mexican money is good money if the Indians don't pull out on us in the delivery. You're still hitting it off with the Redskins, I take it?"

"So far as it's necessary, but there's something about that, too, that I don't like. Indians are damned hard to explain things to, and they've been bringing white captives along that they pick up on the way to the rendezvous. Settlers will follow war parties carrying captives, where they'll stay back otherwise," Devers said.

"Do these captives see you?"

"Can't miss us, Palland. The small children don't matter, but the Indians have white women, too. We hear them scream in the night, and once one of them broke away and tried to run to us."

"So?"

"I'm not squeamish. The idea is when they get through with captives they ransom them back sometimes to Indian agents or army officers. They can carry stories."

"I see what you mean, Devers. But with all your connections out there I'd have thought you could handle it. Anyway, remember this: we're moving fifty thousand head a year now. A lot of people are counting on that, and nothing better happen to it. When'll you be back in Austin?"

"Whenever this new business with the governor develops."

"You mean the state police? Well, that won't be right off. He figures the people might rise against it just now. He'll soften them up a little first. But when it's settled, he'll have every sheriff and peace officer reporting to the adjutant general."

Devers shook hands with his host, put on his hat, and said goodbye.

Outside, he lit another cigar, looking over the view around him. The politician's home stood on a hill close to the city. Before him, a short distance away, was an old bandstand on a grassy knoll. Beyond was a girl's school, and in another direction the first cottages of the city.

He strode off downtown, eventually arriving at his hotel.

General Reynolds did withdraw his name as a senatorial candidate toward the end of the month. But he didn't arrange for any other concessions, especially to the blacks.

"I hear they're finding out some things," Mr. Whipple remarked one day to Karryl. "They're finding out just what their new masters think of them, now that the votes are in."

"How, Mr. Whipple?"

"Well, one way the scalawags got the Negro vote was to talk up what they called 'social equality.' It was all cut and dried. A great, new world for the freed slaves! But it's not working out that way."

"There's friction in the ranks of the victors?"

"Friction that's mighty upsetting to the colored folks. To tell the truth, though, in spite of all the trouble we've had with these poor, unknowing freedmen it's a shame the deal their bosses are giving them. The scalawags never did intend to give them any real rights. That's bait the politicians will throw out to the Negroes from now on—for a hundred years, maybe a thousand. They'll preach equality. But what they mean always is equality for the Negro with somebody else, not with themselves. Things have been shaping up just like folks tried to tell them they would. The state won't give printing contracts to colored printers—because they're black. Governor Davis won't let Negroes come to his parties in the Mansion—and this after all the votes he talked them out of too! But here's the payoff: they're holding the State Ball next week, and the colored legislators themselves won't get any invitations. That's the best yet, when the State Ball is held in honor of new legislators, and when the white radicals are running the plans for the ball, too. It's the same old story."

The legislature adjourned shortly thereafter, to meet again in the latter days of April. Congress passed a measure accepting the new Constitution of Texas. It seated the state's scalawag representatives in Congress and, on April 16, General Reynolds at last issued a special order remitting all civil authority to the radical officers lately elected.

Most Texans were skeptical; they had grave doubts over whether the situation had been improved or worsened.

Spring tarried a while, then suddenly retreated before a belated norther. Finally, in an abrupt about-face, summer smashed in without the benefits of a transitory season. The winds became hot, the air humid, and a charged sultriness settled upon the prairies and river bottoms. The impact of hot and cold air far above the earth spread the seams, and the skies opened.

Karryl Newcomb was awed by the severity of the deluge. For four days the water fell. She was glad the Whipple cottage stood on a hill, for the lowlands were inundated. The waters poured into the homes at the foot of Congress Avenue. Reports from the west said the mountain streams were raging. The Colorado rose forty-five feet at Austin, sweeping some of the less watchful to their deaths. Traffic for the west was completely halted; the awesome brown flood, rolling down from the hills, permitted no thought of passage, and travelers whiled away their time in the inadequate hotel parlors, the damp saloons, and the gambling houses.

Karryl could reach the seminary only along a circuitous path atop the ridges near the capitol. It was necessary to travel almost a mile due north, then to double back in a full reversal of direction through the cedar groves, to reach the school, which actually lay almost within calling distance of her home across the muddy depressions. The gutters in the streets were waist deep in places, and there was no public thoroughfare on which the water flowed at less than ankle depth.

Along the way stood the old band pavilion. The roof was supported by sturdy oak posts, but there were only balustrades around the edifice. The elevation of the park did cause the water to run off however, during the deluge. Karryl used the pavilion as a resting place on her sloshing expeditions back and forth.

Devers, on his way from a visit to the big stone house on the outskirts of the town, met Karryl face to face in the pavilion as she halted to shake the water from her cape and rest a bit before trudging on. His startled eyes froze upon her.

"Jesus Christ," he muttered to himself.

At first, Karryl did not realize that she was not alone; Devers approached from the side, and the rain on the roof deadened the sound of his footsteps.

"Well, Miss Newcomb, we meet in odd places."

She stared at him in horrified disbelief. "What are you doing here?" she finally asked.

"I might ask the same of you. But I'll answer first. I'm a rancher now. I've settled down, not far away."

She remembered that he had once remarked that he had grown up with cattle. She had not believed it then, and she didn't now. "You, a rancher?"

"Yes. Maybe not much of one," he laughed, "but anybody with a few cowhands in camp is a rancher today."

She tried to picture him in the light of a struggling settler, but could not. And she wasn't going to stand here and discuss that with him, either; that, or anything else. She glanced about her, and her intent was not lost upon Devers. The bleak, drenched landscape ran away on all sides, deserted except for the two of them.

"You haven't changed, miss, except you're prettier now." She did not answer, but continued to glance around as though looking for a way to escape. "I've been sure we'd meet again," he continued. "I'm glad it was where we could talk."

"What do you want?" she demanded.

"I tried to tell you once, and you wouldn't listen."

"It's late. I'm going."

"Just a minute. I've waited a long time to see you again. You left your brand on me, you know." He paused, then went on, gripping her arm: "I guess you owe me a little time for that." She recoiled from the touch. Should she cry out? Likely no one would hear anyway. Should she try to run away?

"Let me go, Mr. Devers!"

He stared at her. "I kept my mouth shut about you once when it could have cost you dear if I'd even said a word. But I sure don't have to, anymore."

"Let me go!"

His grasp tightened, and he pulled her back around to face him. Suddenly, she heard the crunch of heavy shoes on the gravel. The steps were behind her, but Dever's grip on her arm prevented her from turning about for a moment. Devers glanced that way, angry at the interruption, but then he released her and stared at the figure approaching through the rain.

"Well, bless my soul! Miss Newcomb. Still out in this downpour?"

Karryl could have thrown her arms about the neck of the cadaverous old headmaster. "Oh, Mr. Smith," she breathed.

"Young lady, you should be indoors." He shook himself, like a huge spaniel, spilling the water from his oilcloths on the pavilion floor. His eye fell on Devers. "Good day to you, sir."

A surly nod was Devers's only response.

"I was just on my way, Mr. Smith. This is the only path I can take in the rain."

"I know, girl, I know. A distressing afternoon to be out. But I hear there is suffering in the flats below, and I am working my way down there to help."

"This is Mr. Devers," she said desperately. "We both happened to stop in here, during the downpour. He's going on now, and I'd be grateful if you'd walk me home."

"Why, I'd be glad to, my dear." Mr. Smith glanced first at Karryl and then at the man, but Karryl stepped out into the path and he followed her. Devers watched the pair for a long moment, then he strode away in the opposite direction.

On the Pedernales, Lubbock brushed the water from his leather coat as he came into the big hall.

"You'd better have some of that hot coffee, Lubbock," Mac-Ashen said. "You look like you've sopped up most of the cloudburst."

"What're you doing there, boss?"

"Trying to figure out from these newspapers what President Grant's up to, Lubbock. Have you heard of the 'Quakers'?"

The foreman's forehead wrinkled in his effort to recall and Levit went on: "It's a kind of a church, up in Pennsylvania. The real name is Society of Orthodox Friends in America. Some of these people called on the president after he took office, asking that he appoint religious men for Indian agents. So now we've got what he calls his Quaker Indian peace program."

Lubbock was aghast. "You mean a soldier like Grant will let a bunch of preachers come out here to deal with the Quohadas?"

"That's about it. The president said: 'If you can make Quakers out of the Indians, it will take the fight out of them.'"

"The Quohadas are not about to become Quakers!"

Lubbock returned to his chores. Later, he assembled all the hands and rode off to the Cave Creek bottoms to make sure the longhorns had moved into the sheltered draws before the weather reached its worst. The waddy was gone when the Hamlin woman brought the gig across the low ford of the Pedernales and up to the step before the kitchen. "Woman come for rations," Pepito announced.

"Of course, Pepito," MacAshen replied. "Give her what they need. We should have sent their provisions down."

"Woman say she like to see you."

Levit hesitated. "All right. Ask her to step in."

She came through the door of the kitchen, closing it behind her, expecting and receiving his gesture toward a chair near the hearth. "My husband asked me to tell you that the wolves killed a ewe last night."

"I'm sorry to hear that."

"He says that he will put poison bait in the pass. But the wolves may not take it. They came down in a pack. He says they have come all the way down into the valley, too."

"Into the valley? I guess they would. You're alone a lot of the time. Aren't you afraid of the wolves?"

"I'm not afraid," she said huskily. "The cabin is tight."

He took the hide coat from the woman's hand. Then he brought a tin cup from the table and poured coffee into it from the pot. "I'm sorry we have no china cups out," he said. "But we men don't bother much with things like that."

"I know."

She coiled her body in the big chair and gazed at him from under her dark lashes. Her next words startled him, even though he knew she spoke only with animal instinct. They were simple, direct; and he realized that she had come to say them. "You need a woman here, Mr. Levit."

For a moment he could not reply. "I guess I do," he managed finally. "Like most men on the range. But I have to get along the best I can without one."

She rose and moved toward him like a creature out of the dark forest. He caught the rich, natural perfume that came from her breath, her hair.

"I don't know how your fine ladies talk. Maybe you despise me for coming here."

"I don't despise you."

Abruptly, she threw her arms about his neck and planted her soft, heavy mouth upon his. He scarcely realized it when his arms went about her. She was warm, richly warm against him, and he was hungry for love. Why shouldn't he take her? Who was to care? But he lifted his head for a moment, and across her shoulder, across the tawny richness of her brow and the billowing folds of her hair, he caught a glimpse through the window of the blue terrain off toward the south. That way was the canyon road, that way the crossing of the Pedernales, the Bee Caves, the Colorado; and beckoning from beyond—Austin.

His arms loosened and he pushed her back. "No, it won't do," he muttered.

She stared in disbelief. "You mean . . . "

"That's what I mean. Go back to your cabin, and hereafter keep away from the Falling Water."

Now the measure of cruelty touched the corners of her mouth, and her red lips opened just a line. "You think I'm not good enough," she whispered. "But I've seen the way you look at me." She was moving toward the door. "Maybe I was wrong. Maybe you have a woman somewhere, Mister Levit. But if you don't have, your words don't make no sense."

"Just go on home. I'm sorry."

He went to his room and watched through the window as she beat the old horse into a fast gait across the ford and up the opposite slope.

A Fort Sill military scout, Judson Belter, dropped off at Fredericksburg when the army teams came through from the north. The old scout, serving currently with the frontier command, rode by the Falling Water en route to his home at Austin for a brief visit.

"Likely, you and the rest of your folks have been bitter at the soldiers—what with all that's been going on—but the soldiers are strapped," he told MacAshen. "Maybe they could do for the savages, if they had the backing. It ain't the numbers. The army has plenty of soldiers in Texas. It's the way they're used.

"That Secretary of the Interior, Delano, knows all about the maraudings," the scout went on. "Army reports are full of them. But Delano's just sitting tight—don't nobody know why. Indians come back on the reservations with blood dripping from their lances, offering white women and children for sale—after they get through with them. They're even showing off the scalps before Colonel Grierson—and demanding presents. And you know what? They're getting them!"

"Why doesn't Grierson do something about it?"

"He does. He butters them up and asks them not to do it again. They go home with the presents and fit out for new raids."

"But Fort Sill is a big army post. The troops there could grab the murderers."

"Fort Sill! Christ! Not long as Grierson has his way up there. He don't believe in punishing them. Tabanica sent word in a while back he wished Grierson would come out and fight. The Indian thought it was a good joke, and some of the rest of us did, too, because Grierson sure didn't take him up. The way it looks now, the Quohadas are getting ready to start some real hell. They aim to kill all the white men they can find and steal the women for sport."

"Where are the Quohadas?"

"Camped about a hundred and fifty miles southwest of Fort Sill, last anybody heard."

"Where the Rangers could get at them?"

The question startled Belter. "Rangers! Where would Rangers come from? I've not heard anything about any Rangers. But if there are still such to be had, there'd better be plenty of them when they finally hit the Quohadas. There's thousands of those Indians."

25

Burr Wayne could not leave the Guadalupe. He couldn't even go to San Antonio or Austin, leaving his sister alone with Standifer—the old man had lost his grasp completely. Burr was tortured with restlessness. There was nothing to relieve it, either. Even travelers were scarce, and only on rare occasions did they tarry.

Margaret, though, was growing a little with each hour. She had stepped quietly into the role vacated by her mother, maintaining the house beautifully and caring for Standifer as he became less capable, less able to concentrate.

Somehow, the days dragged on. Burr brooded, and all lightheartedness was gone from him.

He summoned Possum Wear and told him to saddle two horses. He spoke briefly to Standifer, then rode away with Wear.

"We'll take another look at the longhorns up the river today, Possum," he muttered as they went along.

They rode toward the far limits of the Wayne spread. There was a new herd of longhorns in the bottom, the result of months of effort. They turned deeper into the big trees. Phlox and clematis and ironweed were here; and farther on, portulaca and winecup. The Wayne homestead was lost in the haze far behind.

A tanager warbled his mysterious note from the leaves near-by, and a cardinal angrily fluttered away across the woodland. Burr looked about him at the beautiful countryside. He had once thought he might learn to like it here, but now there was nothing in it to attract him.

Suddenly, the lank cowhand pulled up his horse. "Haven't we run over the grazing land, boss? I don't see any cattle here."

Wayne brought his thoughts back to the issue of the moment. He, too, was surprised by the quietness. The last time he had been in the bottoms, scarcely a week ago, there had been long-horns in every shady cove from the edge of the prairie to the river. "They've gone on to water above," he commented.

Wear spurred up his horse again. "Well, they'd better show quick, because we've covered most of the river ourselves," he pointed out.

Wayne reined into the lead, increasing his pace. The youth's remark charged him with sudden concern. Where, indeed, were the cattle? He rode hurriedly, the unfolding perspective offering no relief from his rising fear. Could it happen again? A mile ahead spread the last rising swell, and when it had been cleared, the bending line of the Guadalupe rose once more, green and verdant, close before them. He spurred the horse into a gallop down the slope to the bank of the river. But there was no sign of cattle along its banks.

"They've drifted farther on," he called out, but doubt was evident now in his own voice. He pulled the animal's head eastward up the path that paralleled the stream. He did not slacken his pace, and the cowboy stayed close behind him. Beyond the live oaks, they struck the sand dunes, crossed them and galloped on toward the cliffs where the river leveled north.

The cowboy called out to slow Wayne's gallop. "I've been watching the soil," he shouted. "No stock has moved up above the sand dunes."

Wayne turned the horse and headed toward the rim of the prairies, some three miles distant. When he reached it, he circled again to set a course just inside the softer soil of the alluvial slopes. Now Possum drew ahead once more, bending low in his saddle, studying the terrain. But it was Wayne who noted the sign first, after Wear had passed, and his shout brought the cowhand back. They stepped down.

"Even a tenderfoot can read this trail," Burr breathed, with bitterness choking his words. "They're herded, and they've been driven out."

"Damned rustlers again," Wear echoed. "They've cleaned that whole snortin' bunch out of the live oaks."

Wayne was desperate. This was too much. What else could happen to him? The sun was midway in the afternoon skies. He glanced toward the ranch. It would take hours to reach home, and additional hours to relocate the trail. If he returned to the ranch, he could not possibly set out on the trail again before morning and by then it would be cold.

"Go back to the ranch, Wear, and pass the word. I'm going to follow those cattle."

"By yourself?"

"Yes."

"Are you loco, boss? The men in those rustler outfits are killers. They could shoot the dust off your nose without touching the skin."

"I'll take that chance. It's the only way to get the cattle back."

"Bust me, Wayne, if you're not talking like a crazy man! You can't go after those longhorns without help."

"Then bring help. But I'll stay on the trail. If you hurry, we may be able to get them back."

"You ride back in, boss, and I'll trail them," Wear proposed quickly. "I'll make sign at sundown. A smoke signal, so you can find me. That way, you can put your own posse together."

"No, Wear. Now get moving. They're not cleaning me out again."

Wayne turned the head of his horse across the prairie. The cowboy eyed him in unbelieving consternation. He could not comprehend a man simple enough to face a rustler gang alone. Wear debated upon it for as long as he could.

"No fool like a tenderfoot," he concluded harshly, as Burr left him abruptly behind, standing across the wide trail of the cattle. Wear jerked his horse around and dug his spurs into the animal's flanks. Burr didn't look back.

Above the Capote Hills, on the roll of the Mount Selman plain, the drought had turned the short gamma grass brown. But the trail was clearly visible, leading straight toward the San Marcos. Great clumps of rattleweed and stalks of sunflowers lay broken by the passage of longhorns, and small flakes of stone were turned up and around in the loose soil. Burr had been long enough on the frontier to recognize these signs. Ahead of him, the faint breeze rippled the grass, tossing it back and forth like waves upon the sea.

At the San Marcos, a great flock of sandhill cranes rose and swirled away. Wayne crossed the ford, noting that the trail turned eastward here, obviously to circle south of the Nance homestead, and then north toward the Blanco. He realized the cowhands could not hope to overtake him. In the dark they would lose him on the prairie when they did try to follow. He ate from his saddlebag, and pushed on while the light of day still gave him sight of the markings on his path.

Possum Wear reached the ranch an hour before dusk. He did not halt at the corral, but rode straight to the bunkhouse. Grippa was busy in the lean-to kitchen adjoining the quarters for the hands, and he saw Wear before the latter pulled the heaving mustang to a stop. Grippa wiped his hands on the white apron and threw it aside. He met Wear at the step, reaching out to stop him.

"What's the idea, Possum, riding that bronc right into the kitchen?" he yelled.

"Wayne's gone clean crazy!"

"Settle down, boy! What's eating you?"

"Burr Wayne. He's gone off fighting mad and crazy as a galoot, by himself, after those rustlers."

Grippa hustled Wear into the cabin.

"All right. Start at the front."

"The river herd's been cleaned out. Gone! Every longhorn in the bunch. Couldn't have been over a day or two ago. We found the trail of the herd. It was headed toward the San Marcos. Wayne went down that tract. Fighting mad, and vowing to bring the longhorns back. They couldn't be far ahead. He'll catch up."

"You damn fool! What'd you let him go for?"

"Couldn't stop him. Unless I'd shot him. He told me go get back here and raise a posse. Tried to steer him off, but he cut the trail himself. Figured then the best I could do was try to pick up some men and run him down before he tangles with that crowd."

Grippa swore angrily. "Not a damned rider in twenty miles."

"Where's the outfit?"

"Across the river and down. Take all night to find them."
He reached for his hat. "Get two fresh horses, Possum. We'll
try to run him down." The cowboy lunged out the door. "And
keep a cinch on your tongue," Grippa admonished.

The two Wayne hands headed east until they passed the rise,
then they turned the horses north and gave them rein.

"How far to where you left him?"

"Two hours, maybe three."

The sun set quickly. Twilight turned into dusk, and the fast
mounting prairie darkness overtook them long before they
reached the upper pastures. They did not spare their mounts
as long as even a trace of glow remained, but, finally, Grippa
slowed his pace.

"No use breaking a horse's ankle and putting us all down,"
he decided.

Beyond the Mill Creek Hills, Wear turned them eastward toward the upper rangelands. "It was somewhere in here," he
decided eventually. "I'ts hell to take a sight in the dark."

Above them, the stars lit up the sky, but the illumination
served only to outline the more definable portions of the terrain.

"We'll head straight for the San Marcos," Grippa concluded.
"They had to cross that."

In the wee hours, he called a halt. "Nothing we can do till
daylight. Reckon you're wore out, anyway, Wear. We'll hit
the grass for a while. At dawn, we'll work that river bank till
we find the trail crossing."

Burr Wayne recognized the principal edifice of the tiny community ahead from its size, but there was no sign above either
doorway to announce the usual "saloon." Once, it had boasted
a main room of adobe, the outer walls varying between clay tan
and a dull gray. Now, there were squatty low additions and ex-
tensions, horizontally and to the rear, and a plank roof supported by blackjack poles stretched out to cover a sod verandah.
A hitching rail ran the distance of the building before its
entrance.

Wayne pulled his horse to a halt. He made no effort to dis-
guise his seething anger. There were no horsemen riding in the
street, but a half-dozen or more mounts drooped before the rail,
and a couple of men leaned against the wall eyeing him as he

came down. Their jeans were old and faded, and worn sombreros hung sloppily above their brows. One wore two guns, low down; the other carried a heavy derringer in his belt and a knife on his hip.

Wayne threw his rein across the rail, looped it and turned toward the door.

"You're traveling hard, stranger," one of the men suggested casually, his eye running first over Wayne's horse and then coming back to the Mississippian.

"What place is this?"

"Answers to the name of Paradise," the man grinned.

"Paradise! I could think of another that would fit better."

Wayne's anger was not lost upon the idlers. The lazy posture of the men before him tightened, and the interrogator's voice hardened.

"People hereabouts like Paradise better. You paying a visit or just passing through?"

"I'll decide that later. Who bosses this trap?"

The man stood free now. His companion had stepped a pace to the side, too, upon Wayne's flank. Beside the faces of these men, Wayne's own seemed pale, but the pallor was from bitterness, and he made no effort to conceal it.

The man by the door barked out a name: "Castlerod!" Then he jerked his head to indicate the room behind him. Burr divined that the sharp reply had been a warning to companions inside, rather than a response to his question, for the low hum of voices beyond stopped abruptly. He pushed past his informant, shoving the swinging door before him, and stepped inside the room.

A half-dozen men stood with their backs to the bar, studying his entrance. They were a hard-bitten crew, he realized, scarcely the honest frontier type, and he wasted no words.

"There's a herd of longhorns pocketed in the draw a mile below this place," he bit out. "A herd that belongs to me."

One of the men moved a step forward. He was spare, athletic, and taller than Wayne; and a thin, blond mustache covered his upper lip. He wore a black velvet vest and a gray flannel coat; but beneath the coat, his pants were of corduroy, and a thick belt supported two heavy guns low upon his hips.

"Who're you?" the man demanded.

"My name's Wayne. I've not seen you before in this country.

Are you Castlerod?"

There was no answer, but the blond giant's eyes provided an affirmation.

"What about the longhorns?" he prompted evenly.

"I said they belong to me."

"You break in here to tell us this?"

"That herd was driven off my range yesterday. Or the day before. I followed it. There were tracks of horses with cattle, and when they left the herd, they came straight here."

"Stranger, I don't like your words."

An inward flash of red blinded Burr. "To hell with you!"

Swiftly, the men broke away from the rail beside Castlerod, leaving Burr and the tall man facing each other.

"I can see you're new in Texas, Wayne."

"I've been here long enough to know my own cattle. I've heard of these range camps back here between the rivers. And I've not heard any good of them. I don't know you, Castlerod, or what you're doing here. But the horses that herded those longhorns are tied at the rail out front. And I'm telling you now: you won't rustle cattle from my ranch!"

Castlerod tensed, letting the violent words sink in. His quick blue eyes measured the man before him carefully; Wayne was like a race horse not thoroughly broken—he was eager to leap, but he did not yet know how.

Suddenly, it all became clear to Burr, as well—the poise and the posture of the man before him. Almost as if he had been reared to the wild, brittle life, Burr's eyes reflected an understanding of the cruelty on Castlerod's face. Intuitively, he recognized his own danger; he was not facing up to mere gawking rowdies. These were criminals, through and through, and deadly. Wayne made a desperate calculation of his chances. There was no time for more.

As Castlerod moved, Burr snatched at his own pistol. But the explosion of the gun in his face halted the effort. He sank. Castlerod stood above him, ready to blast again. But the light went out of Burr Wayne's eyes, and life flowed after it.

Castlerod dropped his own pistol back into its holster. "You, Larue, take a look down that trail. Can't figure this damned fool bracing us here alone. But maybe he did. The rest of you get those longhorns moving!"

Outside, one of the rustlers asked: "You planning on driving this herd clear up the San Saba, Castlerod?"

"Not on your life. Devers is the guy that can handle this deal with the Comanches. Redskins ain't too partial to me. We'll go straight to the Blanco and then back to the hangout."

Grippa brought the body of Burrell Wayne back to the Guadalupe.

It had taken him hours after daylight to locate the ford where the rustlers had driven the longhorns across the San Marcos. Once on the trail, he had run fast and straight. From an incline two miles away, he had noted the little range camp of Paradise. He read the signs unerringly. He quit the cattle trail and ran down directly upon the cluster of shacks. But he had come too late.

Wayne's body lay on the sod verandah of the saloon. Grippa saw the tarp-covered form before he jerked up at the door, and the presence of the two Mexican peons staring down at the still figure told the story only too well. Burr's horse was tied to the hitching rail. The barkeep came out the door, nervously working his soiled apron through his hands. Grippa did not speak to him. He stalked past the hitching rail and pulled the tarp back from the face of his employer. He looked long into Burr's still countenance, then dropped the cover back to hide the death mask.

"You know him?" the saloonman queried.

Grippa did not answer. He pushed the door inward and swept the empty room with his eye. Then he swung back to the other.

"Start talking!"

"I ain't in it," the man said hurriedly. "I'm just running a business here."

"You're in it now. Who did the shooting?"

"Big fellow I never saw before. There was a gang of them here. Camped down for the night. This fellow comes storming in, early, and braces the whole pack. Didn't even get his hand on his gun."

"Where's this big fellow?"

"Gone. Soon as it happened. All of 'em."

"Which way?"

"North, I think. But I'm not sure. I was keeping down."

"Don't give it to me that you don't know this gang."

[265]

"Honest to God, man. I never saw them before. But they were tough. This fellow said something about somebody rustling a herd of longhorns, and he up and called the big fellow to his face. That's all I know."

"How'd his body get out here?"

"Me and the Mexicans pulled it out of there. I didn't know what to do with it. Thought maybe somebody might be coming on behind him."

Grippa seized the bartender's shirt in his fist. He jerked the man forward. "I ought to kill you anyway. I've heard about this cesspool. The talk is that there are rustlers and renegades all through these brakes. If I was sure about this dump, I'd blow your eyes out of your head right now."

The man's face was pasty white. He made an attempt to protest, but Grippa shoved him back against the wall.

"Don't be in this country when we come back through again," Grippa hissed. "If you are, I'll string you to the rafters in your own dive." He hurled the man down and left him there.

The shock of Burr Wayne's death struck the homestead on the Guadalupe with appalling force. Margaret was unbelieving.

Only when the riders prepared the body of her brother as best they could and brought it to the house to lie until it could be buried, did Margaret begin really to comprehend what had happened. Standifer for a moment pieced the circumstances together, too, but he stood helpless and very old, watching with tired eyes the passage of new tragedy before him.

Lacing was there, understanding the horror in Margaret's eyes, yearning to offer her protection.

"Stay in the house with the body," Adam said in a low voice to Possum Wear. Then he nodded to the others to follow and walked quietly away. He went to the wash bench and poured water over his head. The others strode on. When he finished and limped to the bunkhouse, the men were silently waiting. Lacing stood in the far shadow, his eyes grim and still.

One of the cowboys from the Leon River bottoms, the one they called "Towhead", spoke first. "What happened?"

Adam gazed at the faces around him. He dropped his head, then slowly lowered his aching limbs to a bench. "The damned fool stormed into the whole gang of rustlers. Must have called them, too. He didn't even get a shot in."

[266]

Lacing's neck muscles tightened. He was glad he stood in the shadow. The towhead spoke again.

"You want to go after them?"

Grippa sighed. "Four or five of us? Against a dozen, maybe two dozen killers? I want to, all right. But there's no use our being as crazy as Wayne. Only way to go after them is to round up all the ranchers and the cowboys. And how long would that take? Three days, four, maybe more. That bunch're already past the Blanco. In three days, you wouldn't even have a trail."

He beat his hands against the worn fabric of his clothes, watching the dust and dirt rise and settle.

"We're not going anywhere," he muttered unhappily. "Can't ride out of here now, leaving Margaret alone. And something else: when a posse starts out after the kind of men holing up on the Blanco, it had better have the difference before it goes in there."

"How many men you figure we'd need?"

"More than we've got. Sometimes one man makes the difference, but I reckon we haven't got that kind of man."

Lacing pulled his hat down over his forehead. He moved slowly toward the door.

"I'll look to Margaret Wayne," he said.

The older man's eyes shot to Lacing's face. He studied the dark-haired youth carefully, watching him pass through the door. He shook his head as if in perplexity, then noting the uncertainty in the expressions of the other men, he rose to his feet. "Come on," he said. "There's a grave to be dug and a box to be made."

In the house, Lacing motioned to Possum Wear. "I'll take over," he said. "Better get to the bunkhouse and try to rest some." Wear nodded slowly.

Lacing could not get his thoughts together. He paced slowly up and down, wondering what further hell and damnation could be visited upon Margaret—this young lady, fresh out of a rich man's plantation home, tossed down on a half-settled cattle range, to live with a hodge-podge of cowhands, cut-throats and wild cattle.

"By God," he muttered, "what she's going through would kill a Comanche."

He went into the kitchen, and after a while began to prepare food. Later, he put some of it on a tray and filled a cup with water. He went across to Standifer's door and pushed it open. The old man lay on his back, staring at the ceiling. He did not look at Lacing, and now his words seemed directed to no one at all.

"My poor little girl. What will become of her?"

Lacing moved to the side of the bed. "Don't worry, Mr. Wayne. She'll be all right. Best you have a little food now. You'll need your strength."

Standifer turned his head. "Ah, Lacing. I'm glad it's you."

"Then try a little of my cooking. It's not the best, but it'll pass for want of something better."

Standifer sat up on the edge of his bed and took the plate on his knees.

"Can you manage, Mr. Wayne?"

"Certainly, I can manage, Ben. I'll be all right now." Lacing backed slowly toward the door. He took the knob in his hand and pushed gently.

"Ben," Standifer spoke up again. "Look after my daughter, please. I'm not able to do it myself now. You're a good boy, Lacing. Burr liked you, and my dear wife, she was very fond of you. I feel the same. Margaret will need many friends in the days ahead. Help her, if you can."

Slowly, Lacing came back to Standifer's side. He placed his hand on the old man's shoulder, and Standifer looked up into his face. Lacing said no word, but the grip of his fingers indicated a pledge. A smile touched the corners of Standifer's mouth, then his thoughts wandered back to the food.

Lacing halted momentarily by Margaret's door. If only he could persuade her to try to eat. Ben had no experience in circumstances such as these, and he hesitated. But he thought of the grief-stricken woman inside, frightened and alone, and he raised his hand and tapped gently on the panel. For a long moment, there was no sound. Then he heard halting steps within, and the door opened.

Ben's nails dug into the skin of his palm. He wanted to reach out and pull her to him. Instead, he counseled her, almost in a whisper:

"A little food, You'll need to eat. Could you try?"

He saw the chin go up, the red-rimmed eyes level with clear, swift determination. "Yes, Ben, of course, I'll eat. Let me come to the kitchen with you."

Lacing put his arm around her. She glanced up once at him, her expression grateful.

When Adam returned to the house, he saw she was fighting to force down at least a few mouthfuls. He laid his rough hand on her shoulder and squeezed it gently. "Good girl," he said. She gazed up for a moment and the bitterness came to the surface. "Oh, those horrible gunmen," she cried out. "I hate them! I hate them!"

Grippa's hand pressed tight, steadying her.

Margaret quieted. Then she rose slowly to her feet, turning to Adam. "We must bury Burr tonight. While it's still light enough to see." He nodded slowly.

"I'll come with you." When Adam raised a hand to protest, she went on, "Yes, Adam. It's my job, too. Ben, will you look after Father?"

Lacing nodded.

"We must hurry," she said.

26

Fall sprawled far back in the big chair before the hearth at Levit MacAshen's ranch house on the Pedernales. Levit studied him with misgivings, but the older Texan appeared unperturbed.

"Weren't nothing but a small fracas," Fall explained confidently. "The fellow won't die, though I can't say I'm glad."

"But he was a bona fide officer," Levit argued.

"Officer, my foot! One of them renegades Davis has been hiring for his state police. Nothing legal about them. What's more, if it hadn't of been for me batting him around some, he'd be laying in an alley by now, anyway, with a lead slug in his gizzard. Folks ain't taking kindly to Davis's cutthroats."

"That doesn't give us leave to kill them." Levit drummed on the arm of his chair. "I'm glad you came here to my place after you'd had your run-in, Fall. What's more, now you'd better stay out of Houston."

"Stay out of Houston? What for? That bushwhacker wouldn't no more recognize me by now than I would him. Besides, he was drunk and likely don't know even what hit him."

"Maybe not, but you'll be better off out here for at least a while, Fall."

"I was hoping you'd put me up, Levit."

Later, Levit remarked: "We've heard a lot even out this far

about Edmund Davis's new state police. But I'm sorry it was you who had to mix it up with them, Fall."

"Well, I ain't. They're a bunch of scalawags, Levit. Mostly tramps, and mean blacks. One old border outlaw, Jack Helm, was made a captain by Davis, and after that the governor fixed it so they could do their dirty work easy wherever they pleased. They've got their own way to bleed a place. When one of them—like Helm, say—moves into a town, he levies a tax of two-bits on everybody around—to pay expenses, he says. Beats hell out of people if they haven't got anything to pay with. And the governor just laughs about it.

"Davis made his adjutant general, Jim Davidson, chief of this outfit," Fall went on. "Then the carpetbag legislature passed a law saying sheriffs have to turn in the names of all 'known criminals.'"

"How many names did they get?"

"Davis says three thousand. Says his police caught forty-four murderers the first month, and killed five more resisting arrest."

"You believe that, Fall?"

"Arrest forty-four gun-slingers in Texas? With that kind of lawmen? Hell, no! But I'd believe the part about killing five while resisting. Likely, they were just simple farmers without even a charge against them. That gang even started a riot at Waco, on their own. Shot up the white folks, all over the town. In other places, it's been the same."

Levit listened thoughtfully. "It was in the books," he muttered finally.

Fall did not pursue the police matter further. Instead, he observed: "That talk about Ranger companies in the brakes is louder than it was last time I was at Austin, Levit."

Levit studiously refrained from answering, and even Fall couldn't ignore his intent.

"Well, I guess you just don't intend to talk," he acknowledged finally, "so I'll cinch my tongue on that, Levit. And maybe there're more pleasant things to talk about anyway. How long has it been since you was in town?"

"A long time, Fall. But I've had no call to go back there since the carpetbaggers took over. And there's been plenty to do here. Tell me. Fall—" MacAshen hesitated, "is Karryl Newcomb still in Austin?"

"Reckon so."

"How have things gone for her?"

The old man stiffened. "Tolerable, I guess," he answered finally. "There's been trouble for Austin folk from the carpet-baggers and their police, but I don't know of anything happening to her."

"Is she—is she married?"

"Married! Of course not, MacAshen. Leastways, the last I heard she wasn't. That was a spell back, though. Did you expect her to be?"

"Well, I supposed it might have happened by now."

"Reckon it might, at that, for all you've done to stop her."

"Stop her, Fall?" Levit frowned. "It's not so simple as that."

"Well, it's this simple: you oughtn't to be having to ask me whether Karryl Newcomb is married."

Levit said no more for a time. He went into the kitchen briefly for a word with Pepito, then came back. "Outside of your tangles with the state police, you look like you're doing all right, Fall," he said, forcing a smile now as he struck a match.

"I always git along," the other responded. "And you look right prosperous around here, too, Levit, at least from what I've seen so far."

"Things have been going fairly well, I guess. I've traveled a lot, here and there, around the frontier. But the boys look after the spread handily. The Hull brothers bought up twenty-five hundred head of longhorns on the Pedernales at seven dollars each a little while ago. They're driving toward New Mexico."

"I've got some sort of good news too, Levit. The H&TC Railroad is finally getting to Austin. There are packeries on that railroad, and they're paying twelve dollars a head."

"What'll that do to you, Fall, even when you get back to Houston?"

"Well, there won't be much more riding messenger service between Austin and the coast; you can bet on that."

"You'll just have to settle down then, whether you like it or not," Levit laughed.

The old man only snorted. "I hear the hides of buffalo bulls from out this way are worth two dollars apiece, and that people are still buying salted buffalo tongues, too. I could use some of that money, and I'd sure like to keep on the go."

Fall rode into the ranges of the Falling Water with Levit. "It makes a man feel good to get back in open land," the old plainsman said to Levit. "I saw a lot of this country in my early days."

"I know you did. But, by the way, Fall, what's happening to your grog shop while you're away?"

The old Texan grinned. "Reckon the bartender'll drink up all the stock, but we needed a new supply. Last batch in was straight poison."

MacAshen laughed. "I never expected to hear a tavern-keeper run his own booze down."

"Guess I'm too honest for innkeeping. Had to do it for a while to make a living. But I've been homesick for the prairies."

Levit led beyond the lower valleys and on into the north past Bell Mountain and Mount Nebo. "I'm glad that Karryl's been able to make a go of it," he spoke out once. "The times we've been through lately haven't been the best for people. And I'm glad, too, Fall, that she hasn't married anyone as yet."

"Uh-huh," was Fall's only observation.

On the third afternoon of their sortie, they reached the Putnam mesas, and now there was a lowering haze in the far north. "That's winter up there," Levit said. "All I wanted north of Crab Apple Creek was a last look at the stock before the cold sets in. We'd better turn back now."

"You lead the way," Fall agreed. "I'll mosey along. I'd just as soon set by the fire myself when the wind blows."

MacAshen laughed. "Nothing to worry about. It's a straight path. We'll ride a while tonight, and tomorrow we'll be ahead of the worst of it."

Darkness arrived before they reached the Walnut Springs, but they kept on. There was better shelter to the southward, and they could prepare food when they halted. The horses were in good condition, and they traveled easily.

A thin, inverted moon hung far down in the western sky, and the stars were still visible, cold though their luster appeared as the evening developed. An abrupt mesa rose ahead, like a huge oval monument, to blot out the dark line of the horizon.

"By God! I recollect that pile," Fall exclaimed. "White men used to run for it 'cause Indians wouldn't come close."

"It's the Enchanted Rock," Levit answered. He pointed toward an elusive glow, coming and going about the higher levels of the inky mass—a ghostly illumination, sometimes thin and

[273]

narrow, sometimes bright and extended.

"Indians think the rock is spooked," Levit explained. "Some white people, too. They will come this far to watch, but they won't go any closer."

"What the hell are those lights flickering like that up there, anyway?"

Levit smiled. "Nobody knows for sure, Fall. When you get closer, they're gone. Most every settler's got his own ideas. My dad used to say it was the moon, shining on water in the cracks way up on the cliff face."

"There ain't much moon now."

"But the stars are out, and they're bright enough to do the job—if that's it. Maybe it's not. I don't know, and nobody else knows. But anyway that's where it got the name 'Enchanted Rock.'"

They awakened to a raw, gray dawn. Thin, powdery snow-flakes were falling, but it was not a heavy fall. Snow stood on the bare limbs of the trees a half-inch thick, the white on black making the trees look like skeletons. It had settled on the ground at uneven places, the turfs of dead vegetation and the upcrops of soil devising odd patterns of brown upon the white. The tumbleweeds were balls of snow against the abutments. In the distance, a herd of animals drifted slowly before the weather. Levit could not make out, as they hurried on, if they were long-horns or buffalo. A hawk, silent and dismal on the limb of a stark tree, took his eye for a moment; the bird did not rise.

"We'll push all the way today," Levit declared. "It'll be cold in the hills tomorrow."

Fall nodded. He buttoned his leather coat more tightly and fastened an old oilcloth about him. And so they rode, halting only at noon to eat and rest their mounts. Sometime after dark, they came again to the Falling Water.

One of the hands met them at the corral and took over the care of the horses. Levit and Fall strode into the big house, shaking loose snow from their clothing as they went. There was ample food prepared and hot. They ate quickly, Fall going to bed immediately thereafter.

Lubbock appeared then. "Guessed you'd beat the blizzard home," he said to Levit, "'less'n the Comanches had you."

"No sign of Indians toward the Llano," MacAshen said. Lubbock was unusually calm, and Levit asked: "What's happened?"

The man hesitated. "The rustlers have made a run on us, boss. They cut the herd of longhorns working down at the mouth of the Palo Alto; drove 'em south across the rim and out by the South Grape, then on into the Blanco basin."

"How many head?" Levit exploded.

"Two hundred, maybe. We hadn't counted lately. But those were four-year-olds in there, fine stock."

"Didn't you even find a trail?"

"Sure did. Two, maybe three days old. But easy enough."

"And you didn't follow it?"

"I went south as far as the Blanco, itself. There were just the three of us, me and the Monhalls. All the rest, except the Mexican, were working over toward the canyon after the last of those mustangs. The trail showed clear at the river, Levit. Not less than ten riders in that gang. And only three of us. I turned us back."

Levit stared at his foreman. "What day was this?"

"The day after you rode out. I figured you'd be in with the snow, boss. We can get the boys and go after them now."

"Too late," Levit snapped. "The snows will already have covered the trail. Lubbock, who stole those longhorns?"

"Only one guy down there who could—Devers. And there's something else, boss. Lenneweber sent word by one of his hands yesterday. Devers is a lieutenant in Davis's state police now."

MacAshen's neck tightened. "So that's it! All right, Lubbock, I've never tried to hang a state policeman from a shin oak tree, but it's not too late to start."

"Cool off, son," Lubbock counseled. "You've got to handle this one like a fox. You've got to catch Devers himself driving the longhorns out, not his men. You've got to catch him riding with them, and bossing the show. We ain't living like in the old days. But when you tie him down that way, then you can string him up."

In Austin, Karryl Newcomb stood still in the center of her room.

The message she had just read was from Margaret Wayne, and the announcement of stark tragedy from that direction left her horrified and speechless. The letter had been a long time reaching Austin. What would become of Margaret Wayne?

And poor brave Burr. He had tackled the challenge of this raw

[275]

land, only to be destroyed by it. Tears brimmed in Karryl's eyes. The memory of young Burr Wayne swept back to overwhelm her: his easy, careless manner; his tall, lanky frame; the great mop of chestnut hair. Burr Wayne, whose entire being radiated the aura of a fading chivalry, yet a man who, without any real knowledge of his own competence, stood up to face a whole outlaw band. And now he was gone.

Karryl sank to the bed and buried her face in the pillow. Burr Wayne—a man who had wanted to marry her. The man she might have married. In God's name, would these tragedies never end? Again the thought of the girl off across the prairies horrified her, and Karryl felt old and suddenly more afraid, herself, than she had ever been in her life.

Instinctively the thought of Devers came up to stab at her again. Three men had wanted her. One was dead now, one gone. But Devers still was left, and he was frightfully close to her.

"What will I do myself?" she whispered.

Karryl's tearful concern—at least so far as it applied to the Waynes—was only a pale reflection of the actual dismay that had, indeed enveloped Margaret at the ranch on the Guadalupe. All gone—Burr and her mother, her old ties. She was left alone in a remote western prairie with obligations and responsibilities that had often destroyed even strong men.

But this never-ending sequence of horrors would not defeat her, she told herself over and over again. She would not give way to panic. For what, indeed, would happen if she did? The cattle were gone, but the land and the homestead were still there. And the men who had kept the ranch alive, they were still there, too. The cowboys! Suddenly, Ben Lacing's face was in her thoughts. No, she was not entirely alone.

Margaret went to the stand beside the bed and poured cold water from the pitcher into the bowl. She bathed her face and dried it on the towel. When she came out, Possum Wear was near the front of the house.

"Possum, will you send Adam to me?" The gangling cowhand eyed her in surprise.

"I'll sure do that, miss," he declared.

Adam Grippa came quickly. When he saw Margaret, he halted to stare at her.

"Well, now, you're my kind of woman-folks, young lady,"

he observed admiringly. "Reckon I had you figured right all the time."

She led him into the small room that Standifer had made his office. She closed the door and asked him to sit down.

"Now, Adam. You'll have to tell me a great deal. I'll try to understand everything, and what I don't, I'll have to look to you for."

"That's why you got this wore-out old foreman around, miss."

It was near sundown when Margaret and Grippa came out. He had summoned the cowhands earlier, and they were waiting now, scattered about the main room: Wear close to the hearth, two men from the Leon River near the big table in the center. Lacing was farther away, near the corner by the door.

"Boys, please come over closer to me," Margaret said. Then, measuring each word: "I've been over everything with Adam. Frankly, we haven't much left." She hesitated for an instant, but resumed quickly. "Most all of the cattle, as you know, are gone. There's a little money left at San Antonio, but not much." She dropped her eyes until she could control the choke in her voice. Then her chin came up again. "I thought you ought to know. I can't ask you to stay on here, and then not be able to pay you when your wages are due."

The men stood silent, and Adam ordered: "Keep on, miss."

"Adam says there are still cattle where our other herds come from. It's hard work to get them in and hold them for the market, and we've found that it's still harder to keep them. You know that."

"Were you aiming to try, miss?" the cowboy called Leon queried.

"I've got to try, Leon. There's no one left anywhere for me to go back to. This is the only home I have. Of course, I'm staying. I have a house, and the land on this river, and I must stay.

"Look, all of you. I can pay you a little money, for awhile at least, just a little. And I could give you each the rest that would be due you in the cattle we find or raise. I could even give you more that way than you'd earn, if we could get our stock to market again." Margaret hesitated, then hurried on: "You don't need to keep the cattle. But you could, if you wanted to. And you could run them on the pastures here until you wanted to sell them—or you could sell them back to me, when I could pay you."

She seemed to have reached the limit of her effort, and she turned to Adam for strength. He nodded vigorously and bit a huge hunk from a twist of tobacco.

"Anyone who wants to can go now," she faltered. "I wanted you to know. I can pay you whatever is due now. But after this, I can't pay you for your work as we always have. And, boys," the moisture was in her eyes, but she fought to keep it back, "thank you for helping me like you already have." She turned to go back to her room.

"Hold on a minute, miss," the towhead said. "There's no need to be in such a hurry." He looked at his partner, then back to the girl. "Reckon we ain't looking to ride off anywhere, leastways not right now. We've took a fancy to the Guadalupe."

Grippa studied the cowpoke. "Now you're talking intelligent, son," he said finally.

Lacing came forward. "You don't have to worry," he said. "Some of us will be around for sure, as long as you want us to stay." He flicked a glance at Grippa, then back to Margaret's face. "I'll be right glad to get my pay in stock. Maybe a dollar or two for gear, when it's needed, but the rest in stock. And look here, Miss Margaret—" he reached into his shirt and pulled out a worn pouch—"I'll buy up a few extra head in advance. I've saved the wages your dad and brother paid me. Been quite a while now, and I had a little before that to go on." He opened the pouch and thumbed through the currency. "Good U.S. money." He smiled. "It's not a lot, but it's something to help keep things going here till you make a roundup again."

Tears would not stay back now, but Margaret held her head high.

"Thank you, Ben, but I can't take your savings. You've worked too hard for them."

Lacing leaned back against the table. "I'm planning to buy longhorns with my money either here or down the river. And I'll still be doing that. Which way do you want it, miss?"

Margaret wilted. "All right, Ben. Adam will spell out your share of the first herd," she choked again. "And I thank you for everything."

Wear ambled slowly into the circle.

[278]

"I'm permanent," he advised, after which Margaret turned to Grippa and buried her face in his shirt. He put his arm around her shoulders.

"You see now," he grinned, "everything's looking better already, ain't it?"

27

There were Indians all along Honey Creek and beyond the Pack-saddle as the 1870 winter closed down. They were in small bands, and Levit rode with the leather-clads when they struck back. It was as though he sought to establish through such violent retaliation some new purpose, some new objective in life. When the urgent messages contained evidence of Quohada participation he became even more ruthless, resurrecting from out of the past his own mother's murder to sustain his intent. But he said nothing about the reason for these sorties to Fall, who still remained at the Falling Water, and he never took the old man along.

Fall pondered, in fact, whether he had not long overstayed his welcome, but every time he said so, Levit silenced such thinking. Further, Levit returned regularly enough to keep the old man from riding away once more.

Levit did not see the Hamlin woman again. He had the feeling that some of his hands might have found their way across the river to her cabin, but he made no effort to find out. In his mind, he determined to dispose of the woollies as soon as he could do so without offending Lenneweber. The Falling Water was a cattle ranch.

And there was something else. She had left an imprint upon

Levit. Not the sense of guilt, but a rationalization of his own circumstances. He had wanted her. Even now he could remember the raw appeal of Rhoda Hamlin. Her brazen approach had only clarified his needs, his loneliness. The Falling Water was empty without a woman to give it life.

Once he thought of the yellow-haired German girl, Lenneweber's daughter, whose very nature was an unspoken invitation to friendship. She was part of the land, a fine girl who belonged here in the hills. He had not seen much of her, but instinctively he knew that she would make a good wife. But not for him.

Karryl Newcomb had marked him far too deeply, despite the hurt. He would not change, regardless of what happened—and regardless of the time that continued to slip by. He knew no other woman would ever do.

Levit looked older now; the premature gray at the temples was heavier. But better than anybody, he knew what was putting the whiteness there. And the passage of time had constantly reasserted the question more demandingly: Should he have gone back, at least to let Karryl talk? MacAshen could not answer his own question, and because he couldn't it punished him more and more.

In Austin, Karryl herself lived now in a state of anxiety. Mr. Whipple met her once as she came in from the seminary, with a worried question on his face: "A man was here to see you," he said. "He waited a while. As the time went on, I told him sometimes you stayed at school for the evening. Then another man came to look for him, and they went away together."

"Did he tell you what he wanted?"

"No. He was a big man, very dark, and not very friendly. He told Mrs. Whipple he would be back."

She tried to turn her thoughts into other channels, as the days went by, but she could not. In her room, as she read of the people Governor Davis had selected to command his state police, she saw the name was even there. Devers, a policeman!

She tried to convince herself that he would not really turn her in to the Union soldiers but all she could think of was the fact that once he had shown he was capable of anything. She couldn't run again, and she wouldn't run again. Everything else was over for her anyway unless . . .

But she could not consider the latter possibility. It was too much to hope for. Too much time had passed. Karryl buried her head in her pillow and tore angrily at the sheets below her hands. But she could not stay in her room. She went out into the parlor, carrying the newspaper with her.

"Have you seen this?" she asked Mr. Whipple, her finger touching the account on the page.

He fixed his spectacles and read the story. "Yes," he acknowledged finally. "There are criminal names in this list of officers. It's a disgrace to civilized people."

Karryl walked to the window and stared out.

"My dear," he resumed hesitantly. "I must talk to you about all this, about our state police, I mean. I've held back because I didn't want to frighten you. There are some wild rumors about this police force Davis has organized. They've built a stockade down by the river, and the treatment they accord their prisoners is horribly severe.

"They are compiling lists—criminal lists, they call them. The names of many good people may be on those lists. Many of the state police are former slaves who will do the bidding of their carpetbag masters without question. For your own protection—" He hesitated.

"What is it you're trying to tell me, Mr. Whipple?"

"They say those lists contain the names of some women, too. I don't know, it may be just a rumor. It is supposed these ladies are remembered for their war sympathies, and that they have been added at the urging of some of the white renegades, and blacks, just to keep their interest up."

She soothed the old man, hiding her own distress. "I'll be careful. After all, I'm only a school teacher. They wouldn't know me. And anyhow, they're not about to put me in their stockade." She went back to her room, worried.

At that particular moment, however, the man who was on her mind was some miles from Austin.

Devers had gone to San Antonio to meet Storm. It had not been a pleasant interview—no meeting with Storm was pleasant— but it had accomplished its purpose. Storm had even been flattered, though not necessarily surprised. "I'll think about it," he agreed. "Had a feeling you'd be wanting me to team back up soon, Devers. But I've been doing all right on this end, and I never cottoned much to you. You're a real vinegaroon."

"It's whether you want the money, not whether you like me, that counts, Storm."

"Same old Devers." The latter chuckled. "The man that money gravitates to. I've been traveling alone, and I'm not partial to your way of doing things. But I think I'll try you again, once more. When I feel like moving back your way, that is. Right now, I've got something else on my mind, and that may take a spell."

Devers had accepted Storm's conditions. He set forth the needs and the locality involved. Then he said goodbye and quit the town. Now he was north of San Antonio again, pointing his horse toward the hangout on the Blanco. He frowned when he came down the slope toward the river. The trip to San Antonio had consumed days. He had had other things planned for that time. But he could not ignore Vanner Storm. He was glad the trip was behind him, though. He would return as quickly as possible to Austin, and settle once and for all the issue of Karryl Newcomb. And that would be in his favor. This was not Mississippi with its lah-de-dah airs and graces. She had been a fugitive woman. He had wanted her before, he wanted her now, and he meant to have her—by whatever means it took to do so.

The wide, plunging slope of the basin escarpment descended in a regular pattern of benches, and Devers's horse picked its way between the clusters of sumac and shin oak, avoiding the outcrops of coarse pink granite. Castlerod and the Mexican, Santiago, had accompanied Devers to San Antonio, and rode close behind.

Devers reined into a trail crossing a rise in the valley floor. North of the river, longhorns were grazing in the swales. "That'll be your first job, Castlerod, to clean up these draws and move those branded cattle west. Out to the headwaters of the San Saba. When Storm goes in on the south."

Castlerod grunted. Talk annoyed him. Now he dozed in the saddle and the miles fell behind.

To the east, two round knobs, bare and red in the sunlight and marked sparsely about the base with scrub cedar, rose ahead. Suddenly, Devers stood in his stirrups and shaded his eyes with his hand. A frown crossed his face. He pointed toward the draw behind the nearer of the knobs, close to the shining water. "You see what I see, Castlerod?" he demanded.

"Looks like more longhorns to me."

"You're damned right it is. A fresh herd. Right up against the stand. That bastard Sudderth! He's pulled a raid on his own!"

Above the Blanco basin, at Levit MacAshen's ranch, the Monhall boy was too excited to speak intelligently.

Lubbock pushed him down into a chair and shook him by the shoulder.

"Slow up—and simmer," he ordered.

There were dark lines of anger on MacAshen's face, too. "Tell it over," he ordered the waddy now.

"God's truth, boss," Monhall exclaimed. "Reckon there were a hundred head in that bunch. Not all we had down in there, but as many as the rustlers could pull together quick."

"Are you talking about the cattle we had set up for the drive to the San Antonio packery?"

"That's them, boss. Out by the Grape. Damnedest gall I ever seen. They went across the rim where the creek breaks out, then straight down into the Blanco basin. Tracks fresh as morning dew."

"You followed the sign?"

"Sure. Fact is, the rustlers must've lifted the longhorns right from under my eyes, this time. The trail went south, and they watered on a branch feeding south, maybe a dozen miles below the wall. Syster Creek, I think, but I'm not too sure."

"Never mind that. Go on."

"Turned them due east from there, which was sure surprising till I found out why. You know what, boss? They drove those longhorns down the Blanco itself. Ten miles maybe. And I seen 'em! They've got a hangout in there. Cabins and corrals. Saloon, too! Reckon it's not more than thirty miles south and east from here; back-trailed on us, that's what they did."

"Could you find it again?"

"Yes, sir! I seen two knobs sticking up in there, and a hidden valley behind the closest one. You'd never know it was there unless you came in from the west. And then you'd have to be just right on the rises. It's off the trail, if you were headed for the Springs. But it's sure there!"

MacAshen rose abruptly. "All right, Lubbock. Get the

horses. And don't say anything to Fall about this. Let him stay here. No use fighting with him, too, just to keep him out of this."

MacAshen's men grouped close around him as the waddy hurtled down the steep slope. He looked once at the set expressions on the bronzed faces of Lubbock and Steve Meadows. The ever-present smiles that characterized the Monhall boys were gone now; their faces too were grim.

He halted only once to call to his side the Monhall boy who had reported the rustling. Together, they studied the deceptive terrain beyond. Monhall pointed south, and they ran along the upper ledges for three additional miles, then swung east again. A cold breath was in the air from the north, but to the south it was still hazy. On a sudden rise, the cowboy yelled in exultation. His arm shot out, and MacAshen followed the direction. The shimmer of water was there, winding around and behind the nearer mesa. Beyond, he saw the longhorns in the ridge-hemmed valley.

MacAshen did not lessen the gait of his horse; he charged straight down upon the tiny, sprawling cluster of cabins. The headquarters building was evident, and he noted the sweaty horses tied at the hitching rail. Loud voices sounded from within. His riders were beside him as his boots dug into the soil; the door fell in before his hand; his eye measured the room and its occupants in a swift glance. Then he strode straight to the bar.

Devers had whirled around, his back to the bar. His face was flushed in deep anger. Three of his men flanked him on the left, bright badges shining from their vests; and another stared from a stand farther down the bar on the opposite side.

Devers had already spoken his thoughts in no uncertain terms. The fools! What had they been thinking of? Putting a herd down in the middle of the basin close enough to the ranchers for them to find—if they tried. A herd from the Falling Water! It was the kind of stupidity that brought disaster. He had been in no mood to argue the point. He had told Sudderth and the others his opinion of their intelligence. Maybe Sudderth had thought to do a little rustling on his own? Without the knowledge of the others and, consequently, without the necessity of a split? If so, just how did Sudderth and his pals expect to protect themselves? From their own outfit, and more especially from the rancher MacAshen, when he discovered his

[285]

loss? The eyes of the outlaw, Sudderth, had closed to slits. But he did not have an opportunity to speak in his own defense. Devers apparently had more to say, but his words froze in his mouth as the door swung in before the man he least wanted to confront at this moment. Devers saw the white beneath the lines on MacAshen's bronzed face; he braced himself tensely for what he knew would come.

MacAshen did not speak. He did not slow his stride. He came straight and swiftly, and when he was within reach, he swung his fist with savage speed and smashed it into Devers's mouth. The man fell, his head striking the bar and the floor as he went down. Blood spurted from between his teeth. His pain was no greater than his astonishment.

Devers's men reeled back on their heels, and one of them, the tall one MacAshen knew as Castlerod, snaked a quick hand to the butt of his gun.

"Careful, fellow!" Steve Meadows's clear voice held the room. Meadows stood free, crouched well inside the door, his fingers bent above the pistol in his own holster. Beyond, Lubbock was poised badger-like; and the door rolled in to show the Monhalls, rifles dead upon the knot of idlers at the bar. Castlerod's quick eye canvassed his chances. He did not fancy them, and he remained stiff but threatening.

Devers struggled upward on his hands. He touched his bloody lips, spat across his arm, and turned a dark, hating stare upon MacAshen. His hand suddenly wrenched down toward the bulging pocket in his coat.

"Go ahead, draw your derringer, Devers," MacAshen encouraged. Devers hesitated, then dropped his hand.

MacAshen fastened his fingers in Devers's ruffled shirt front. Almost as he might have lifted a child, he twisted the big man upward and thrust his back against the bar.

"Devers, listen!" MacAshen's voice cut the smoke haze. "You're running rustled cattle. My longhorns from the Pedernales are right on top of your hangout here. We've suspected it for a long time. Now we know, for sure.

"They tell me you're a state policeman now. I've always been a law-abiding man, Devers, and I've seen that the law was kept on the Pedernales. I've always tried to respect the authority of the state, hard as it is sometimes. But I've cut your sign, now. You're no policeman. You're an outlaw, riding under the guise of an honest rancher. So to hell with your state police."

Devers breathed hard, but he held his tongue.

"I don't know all your game, Devers. If I did, I likely wouldn't leave you here alive today. Even now, if I'd caught you pushing the herd itself, it would have been different, too. This time, I'll only take my longhorns back across the rim. That badge you've picked up saved your life. But get this—from now on, we've got you marked, and if you ever so much as set foot again on land north of the Blanco basin, I'll hang you!" He thrust Devers back roughly and stepped away. His eyes invited something more decisive from the big man. But no answer to his challenge came. Beyond Devers, the faces of the other state police shone white and uncertain against the gloom.

Levit turned. He stalked swiftly through the swinging doors, the Monhalls moving aside to let him pass, covering the space behind him with their rifles when he had gone beyond.

"Don't try for your guns," Meadows warned again softly. He tipped his head slightly, and Lubbock went out. Then Meadows backed slowly until the barrels of the carbines in the doorway were beside him.

MacAshen stepped into his saddle. He pulled his pistol from the holster and cocked it. Lubbock leaped astride, Meadows following. MacAshen put his horse squarely across the portal where his eye, above the swinging door, could cover the room. The Monhalls mounted swiftly. Then MacAshen sank his spurs into the stallion and headed up the rocky trail toward the cattle herd. The others followed close behind.

Lubbock rode abreast of MacAshen.

"Maybe I was wrong before. I'm thinking now you'd better have killed him," he said.

"No! He won't be back!"

Skepticism showed on Lubbock's face, but MacAshen did not turn to see it.

"I hope you're right," the foreman muttered to himself.

28

Seventy miles to the south of the Pedernales country, the cow-hands on the troubled Wayne ranch labored for their new boss, Margaret Wayne, as they never had before. Every one of them was in the saddle before dawn. They did not return to the compound until long after darkness had settled down.

Standifer Wayne was completely incompetent now. He could feed himself and look to his immediate needs, but otherwise, he seemed unaware of the life around him.

"You'll be the ranch tender," Margaret's foreman told Lacing.

"What does that mean?"

"You're not a regular cowhand, Lacing. I saw that long ago. The others are. You'll do the work close to the ranch house, and the rest of us will herd the wild cattle. I'm going to drive all the way from Lockhart, if I have to."

Lacing did not like the import. It meant he would be coasting while the others worked the skin off their bones to build the place again. He said as much. Grippa put a hand on Ben's shoulder.

"It's not hard to see the boss's daughter is partial to you, son, and the boys understand. She's been having a hell of a time, Ben, and you brace her up more than all the rest of us put together. She needs you close by."

Ben was silent a moment. Adam was simply confirming something Ben had long hoped was true, but he protested again. Margaret Wayne belonged to all of them, and they belonged to her.

"You're cutting a pattern I don't fit into, Grippa."

"No, I'm not, Lacing." Adam did not want to argue, but the youth was not easy to persuade. He hesitated a moment, then he repeated: "Your job will be right here. And, son—" the earnestness in the old Texan's eyes silenced another rising retort—"don't ever take your eyes off that house. Don't ever ride off and leave her alone on this spread unless the rest of us are here."

Lacing stared at the ranch foreman. But he understood now. The canny old cowman had never been deceived. He knew. He had given Lacing the role that Grippa himself might not be able to fill. The foreman turned toward the corral. He limped a step or two and halted, to bend halfway around again.

"There's always ammunition in the chest under those saddles in the lean-to," he grunted. Then he went on.

Lacing had to stay close to her now; it was his job. Every time he saw Margaret Wayne, he realized how much he loved her. He had never understood what love was before. His feeling for Margaret, since the first day he had seen her, shaded any other emotion he had ever known. If he could only take her in his arms and comfort her! But he was only a tramp puncher, and women like her were not for men like him.

He saw her worrying with the needs of her father, realizing she could not sit by the old man hour after hour, watching his rapid decline. It would drive her mad, too. But something about her changed after Grippa told her, without embellishment, that he had assigned Lacing to the supervision of the ranch. Even though she still was helpless, she seemed to take new hope.

"Work will help," Ben counseled Margaret. "Work at anything, but keep working. Dig in the garden. Wash, scrub, sew. But keep working. Try not to think of anything else."

"I am working, Ben. I'm doing all I can. But I'm so lonesome." The misery in her face tormented him. It seemed that she was about to rush him and throw her arms around his neck, bury her head on his shoulder. He stepped away, almost rudely.

"You just hold on a while. It'll be smoother after a little."

In his own cabin, Lacing dropped his head into his hands, lost in misery himself over his inability to help her more.

On the Pedernales, Biberstin bedded down in the bunkhouse of the Falling Water with Levit MacAshen's cowpunchers. It was past midnight when he arrived, on the last day of Fall's visit with MacAshen, and since it was so late the Fredericksburg man felt nothing would be served by awakening Levit before morning. But he came into the big house early for breakfast with the two of them.

"To Austin I have been, Herr MacAshen," he said. "I try to draw supplies for my men, you know which ones."

"Well, I told you when you went through they'd only laugh at you for asking. Did you get the supplies?"

Biberstin snorted scornfully. "Not even a promise of any."

"You German fellows might as well get used to that sort of treatment, too, Biberstin. Your boys are supposed to be Davis men, you know. But the carpetbag government doesn't give a hoot whether you were Unionists or not."

"Fast we are understanding that. This legislature, it gives money, but the money, it never leaves Austin. They pay the state police with the money they said would hire militia. And what coyotes are the police!"

"I know. I've met a few."

"Ach, so? At Austin, yet?"

"No. South of here. On the Blanco."

"Herr MacAshen, meet them in the country where you are strong, if meeting them you must. Judge Blossom, you know him, yet? They have arrested him."

"Why, that's a damned outrage!"

"Yes, but this Davis gang, it knocks men over right and left. That one who might have influence *against* Davis, he is a target, so! Old Confederates, they haul in quick. Even arresting women, too, they are."

"Women!"

"Yes. The word goes out they have a 'list.' Hundreds of names on it. Murderers and felons, they call the men. Of the women, I do not know. If a man argues he is killed, quick. It is said women sometimes have it worse."

"Good God!"

"It is bad, yes? And especially in Austin. But worse it will get, and out here, too. State police and the Comanches, too. And with the outlaws driving in from behind us, as well. There is much trouble both to the north and to the south of us, and it is moving this way. I come through the village of Kyle on the way back. It is around the Blanco, you know. The rustlers kill a rancher south of there, below San Marcos Springs."

"How did that happen?"

"He catches up with his herd. Rustlers are running it out into the basin. And not expecting the settlers to fight back. Peaceful it has been there for a long time. Anyway, they shoot him down in cold blood. As I hear it, he walks in on the gang and calls them. Tenderfoot! He does not even get his gun from out of the holster."

"A fool play," MacAshen said. "These outlaws are killers. People ought to know that. Why did he go it alone? There's help to be had if people ask for it."

"I do not know. Perhaps they are unaware of such help; anyway, they say this killing leaves a young girl to run a ranch all by herself."

"His wife?"

"No, a young sister."

"Did you get his name, Biberstin?"

"Wayne. He came recently to this country. His ranch, it was below Seguin."

MacAshen came instantly to his feet. Behind him, Fall did the same. "Burr Wayne?"

"I believe that was it. You knew him?"

"Yes."

"He was a friend?"

"Well, at least I knew him."

"It is sorry I am, MacAshen."

"You're sure he left no wife?"

"I did not hear of one—only the young sister."

"How long ago did it happen?" MacAshen probed.

"Months, maybe. But I am straying from my purpose in coming by your ranch headquarters here, Herr MacAshen. A message for you I was asked to deliver."

"What was it? Who sent it?"

"A man named Miller, a stable-keeper. Somehow or other he seemed to feel I was especially trustworthy to bring you the message."

[291]

"I told them that sometime ago, Biberstin, about you and others among your people."

"Ach, so. Herr MacAshen, what he asked me to tell you was that a lady whom he said you know most well is in his house. Hiding there, I think he meant."

"The hell you say! A woman named Karryl Newcomb?"

"He did not tell me her name, and I did not ask. All he said was that a minister of the gospel had brought her to his home in the night, and asked him to shield her and get word to you."

"Shield her from what?"

"The state police had put out an order to pick her up and bring her in."

"Oh, no!"

"That is what the stable-owner told me, Herr MacAshen. I think he felt you could do something about it, and I hope the information has not reached you too late. I will depart now, but should you need to call upon us in Fredericksburg, you know how to do it."

"I thank you Biberstin, and I am grateful—more than I can tell you."

When the German had gone, Fall turned to MacAshen and said, "Are you satisfied now about Karryl Newcomb, Levit?"

"What do you mean 'satisfied?'"

Fall raised himself to his full height. "I been holdin' myself in, ever since I got here, MacAshen. That was some little time ago now, an' it ain't been easy. What I'm talkin' about first is Wayne, now that he's dead. An' then I'm talkin' about Karryl Newcomb. I figure there are things a man's not free to harp on with even his near friends unless he's pressed to, and those are the things between a man and a woman."

"Are you talking about *me* and Karryl Newcomb? I'm sorry, of course, for any difficulties she might have had in Austin. And I would help her if I could. But beyond that, there's nothing between Karryl Newcomb and me anymore."

"No, I reckon not. But you better listen to me some, 'cause I see that you've still got poison in your system somewhere. And she's in more trouble now, if the German had it straight, then you've ever heard about, at least for a woman. After I left here last, I worried night and day over what you'd said to me about that Wayne fellow wantin' her. You remember it was me who brought her up that road from Houston, and I've been close to her. She wouldn't talk, never did intend to, but I've got my ways. I faced her down and near-most had to beat it out of her before I got the sorry yarn."

"A sorry yarn, Fall?"

"That's what I said, a sorry yarn. Oh, I know you saw her like you did back there that night. And I know how you took it, after all that had gone on between you two. But what the hell if you did see what you did?"

"How would you expect me to take it?"

"It ain't what I'd expect that counts, but what she'd expect. Did you ever stop to remember that that Wayne feller grew up with her, that he was more like a brother to her than anything else? Guess she never had a real brother like him, anyway. But one thing he did do, Levit, that you didn't have the gumption to—he asked her to marry him, and let him take her away from all that trouble goin' on in Austin. You know what she answered? Well, it was 'no,' and on account of you."

"What're you talking about, Fall?"

"What you saw there was a goodbye kiss—that's all, Levit. She was sending him away for good, so nobody would be in your way with her. And that's what she did. I wouldn't have said it was much to send a fellow on with that had asked a body to marry him. But you didn't even give her the chance to tell you that much." The old man's merciless eyes bored into the rancher before him. "Hell of a mess you've made of that little woman's life," Fall continued pitilessly. "And likely a hell of a mess you've made of your own, too, Levit."

The Mexican, Pepito, brought Lubbock in when Fall had gone.

"Saddle a horse for me, will you?" Levit asked his foreman.

"Where you heading?" Lubbock looked at the pack on the bed.

"I'm going in to Austin."

"Ain't that pretty risky?"

"I'm going, anyway."

"All right. I'll get some of the boys."

"No, Lubbock, I'll go alone. There won't be any trouble. I'll keep out of sight."

"Better let me or Steve go with you."

"You're needed here, Lubbock."

"When'll you be back?"

"I don't know."

Lubbock paused on the threshold. "Anything else you want to tell me, boss?" he asked probingly.

Levit halted his busy movement. He looked into the earnest gray eyes of his aide and friend. Then, soberly, he turned back to packing.

"No, Lubbock, there's not anything else to tell you—yet."

Levit's thoughts burned him like the red-hot tip of an arrow.

He had been a complete fool all the time, debauching himself away in the satisfaction of his own jealously. His damned pride! The time during which he had lost himself in the prairies, leaving her alone! Time when the drifters and plungers and renegades made life a danger for everyone. And now the state police. He prayed to God that they had not yet found her.

The miles stretched out behind him. Levit drove the horse straight through the groves of walnut trees, scorning the easier trails around. A tanager fluttered away from the path; a wild vireo darted out from the shin oaks to pace the rider.

Dusk found him at the Colorado. He plunged across the ford, the horse belly-deep in the green, swirling waters, and, on the far side, he reined to the south, behind the stores and especially the stable. Miller's house was in one of the little side streets there.

He tied the heaving mount to the rail behind an arbor, and strode swiftly around the cottage and up the front steps. He raised the knocker once and when he heard approaching footsteps, he didn't wait but turned the handle and pushed inside.

The astonishment on the face of the woman before him slowed his step momentarily. Then, when a look of unbelieving joy filled her eyes, he hurried to her.

He knew that she could read, without the necessity of words, the yearning need for her in his face. This time, it was a MacAshen different from the man she last had seen so long ago. This time, it was an unquestioning MacAshen reaching out to seize her, to pull her to him, to bury his face in her hair.

Karryl clung to him, felt his hard lips searching, smothering, as if to draw her heart out.

Miller came to the rear door of the room. He gazed in startled surprise a moment, then thrust out an arm to silence his wife.

[294]

"The Lord has answered her prayers," he muttered gratefully. He backed away, closing the door behind them.

"I thought I had lost you," Levit said huskily. "But when I heard you weren't at the Wayne ranch . . ."

"You know about poor Burr, then?"

"Yes."

"But you believe now that he never really meant anything like—like that—to me?"

"I've been a fool—a stupid fool. But I'm going to try to make up for that now, Karryl. I'm taking you home with me to the Pedernales, as I should have long ago."

She pushed back from him and turned her eyes to his. The dust of the trail was heavy on his face and neck. His jacket was open at the collar, accentuating the spare, hard lines of his neck, his strong brown chin. She had never seen him more earthy or more desirable.

"No, you haven't been a fool, my darling, but you've been so very, very long in coming back. Oh, I want to go home with you."

He kissed her again. Standing aside from her he glanced out into the night and said, "We've got to be gone from here at once, Karryl. Too many people in Austin know me, and you, too, by now. It's hard to believe they haven't found out you were here. We've got to run for it, as fast as we can. But tell me, why should these state police be after you? Just because you're from Mississippi?"

She tightened visibly, for an instant. Then she said quietly, "I'd rather not talk about it, Levit. The war was a terrible experience for some of us, much more so than most people in Texas can even imagine. And there are things that some of us must forget."

"All right, Karryl. It's not important to me, and I'll never ask you again."

A dove whistled off in the dawn toward the northern hills and Levit, careful of the fractious buggy horse up ahead, followed the line of the dove's flight with his eye. Then he turned to stare at Karryl, beside him in the gig he had borrowed from Miller, the stable-keeper.

"Oh, Levit!" She smiled back at him, drowsily. "I'm scared but so happy."

He drew her into the curve of his arm. The raw edges of the wind from the north bit at her cheeks, and she snuggled against him under the warm folds of the buffalo robes Miller had provided. The proximity of MacAshen charged her veins; she could feel her flesh beneath the padded clothing warming to his presence. Levit touched the animal ahead with the whip, and cast a glance behind as the horse ran on.

Everything had happened so swiftly that Karryl scarcely believed it. Miller had hurried in the darkness to the Whipple cottage for such of her things as he could safely carry away from there; then he had gone to the stable to pick up the horse and buggy for them.

"Bad," Miller warned, "bad for people Davis and his gang don't like. I don't know if your name's on that list or not, Levit, but don't wait around Austin to find out, for her's sure is. The river's up a little too high to ford it. Better take the gig across on the ferry. Not much movin' over the river at night, but the ferryman stays on. Once you're across, hightail it up to them hills and don't lose no time. I ain't too sure even about that ferryman. He's a kind of a shiftless galoot, and maybe he's a spotter, too, for the Davis outfit. But you can get a head start that way, and there ain't nobody likely to be able to catch up with you from here before you're in the Pedernales valley again. And I don't think they'll follow you in just now anyway, the way things are."

"Will you explain at the school?" Karryl asked anxiously.

"Of course, young lady, of course. Even now they already know why you haven't been there for your classes, and they understand. They will be happy for you, as all of us are. And as you, too, now will be happy."

Miller had one further word of admonishment. "Levit," he said, "what I said about those state police not following you into the Pedernales valley still goes, of course, at least the way things are now. But that don't mean it couldn't change overnight. The best thing you can do for both you and this pretty young woman here is to drop out of sight for a spell. See if you can't find some place to hide till you know whether they'd really try to come in there and get her—and you. Find somebody out there, maybe some of the Germans up around Loyal Valley—or one of your other settlers—that she could move in with for maybe two, three months. By then some of us could get word to you on what was in the wind here."

"I guess I could do that, if I had to. But I've waited long enough to take her to the Falling Water."

"Well, I don't blame you for feeling like that. You'll just have to do the best you can. But be careful, MacAshen."

Beyond the Bee Caves was a homesteader's cabin but Levit did not seek the hospitality of the settler's lodge. He drove the horse on until they came to the canyon itself, picking the way carefully down the slanting trail until the buggy rested securely on the level floor amid the clusters of cypress roots.

"Oh, Levit, how beautiful. How peaceful."

He lifted her from the vehicle and stood her on her feet in front of him. He turned to care for the horses, but thought better of the idea and suddenly pulled her close against his body, enveloping her again, coats, mufflers, and all, in his arms and bruising her lips with the fierceness of his caress. When he released her, pushing her back where he could feast his eyes upon her, she was weak from the outburst. "I wish we could stay here forever." He smiled. But then he became more thoughtful. "That's just what might happen to us though if we delayed any—stay here forever." He unhitched the horse and led it down to the water, Karryl trailing nearby. "As soon as the horse is rested again, we've got to go on, and fast," he said. "If they came on from behind, we'd be trapped."

He was silent for a time, looking off toward the early morning sunlight. "Sometime late today, maybe not until tonight, we'll reach the home of some people named Elledge," he said. "We'll stop there, for the Elledge homestead is in the Pedernales valley itself. We can rest then and sleep, and plan some for the future."

MacAshen was in a state of almost complete exhaustion, and Karryl was not much better off, when they finally pulled off the main route up a little roadway leading toward the southern rim of the valley. It was three-quarters of a mile from the main road to Elledge's home place, which was standing in a thick forest of shin oaks and pecan trees, completely shielded from view until they wheeled into the compound. Both Elledge and his wife rushed out to welcome them. MacAshen swung laboriously down from the buggy.

"Howdy, Elledge, and Mrs. Elledge," he intoned. "I want you to meet someone who is very dear to me," he said. "Miss Karryl Newcomb, once of Mississippi, but lately of Austin."

"Well now, we're mighty pleased to meet you, miss. And this is great news, Levit," Elledge boomed, "you bringing a young lady out here to our valley." He went around the buggy to Karryl's side, and reached up to help her down.

"We're just plain folks, honey," Mrs. Elledge said to Karryl, "but we're mighty glad to have somebody like you stop with us." She put her arm around Karryl and started toward the house, calling back over her shoulder, "you men-folks bring her things." Karryl dragged herself wearily along beside Mrs. Elledge. "Appears you are plumb tuckered out," the latter said to Karryl. You two must've come a far piece."

"We came all the way from Austin, without stopping, except for food and to rest the horse."

"Well, then, you've got good reason to be tired."

"That horse is ready to drop, Levit," Elledge said. "Who've you been runnin' from, Indians?"

"No. The state police at Austin."

"They after you, too, now?"

"No, at least not as far as I know. But they could be, and chances are they will be. It's Karryl Newcomb they've got on their list, and that's why we broke out of Austin and haven't stopped since."

"And you think they might be coming on behind you?"

"I don't know. We haven't seen any behind us as yet. But we had to come out of Austin on the ferry. The ferryman knew me. He used to work around the hotel where I stayed before the war broke out. Karryl lived there a while, too, you know. And Miller wasn't too sure about him. Fact is, he thinks the man might be in cahoots with the Davis gang."

"Well, you take an armful of this baggage and go on in. I'll put the horse in the corral and throw him some feed."

"It's about time, Levit MacAshen, that you brought a pretty girl into the Pedernales valley," Mrs. Elledge admonished a short while later when all were seated around the supper table in the kitchen. The Elledges had long since eaten their evening meal, but Mrs. Elledge placed loaded dishes on the table and clean plates in front of her two guests.

"Nobody knows that as well as I do, Mrs. Elledge."

The older woman turned toward Karryl. "This here's a real big man, and real fine one, who's brought you here, honey," she said. "And this valley has been needing mighty bad somebody just like you seem to be to help him stay in it."

Karryl, glancing at Levit with mock severity, answered, "I'm going to do my best—that is, if he really lets me stay this time."

Elledge laughed. "If he don't," he said, "you could just move right in here with us. We'd let you stay."

MacAshen said seriously, "I want to talk to you about that. That is, about Karryl stopping off here for a while. I don't like the idea of my riding in at the Falling Water tomorrow evening with Karryl alongside, without my just taking a look."

"Don't you think things would be all right up there?"

"They were, when I headed out for Austin. But even a few days can make a lot of difference. If you'll let her—and frankly—" he looked at Karryl—"I haven't even mentioned this to her yet—I'd like for Karryl to stay here with you until I can at least take a quick look around over there. Then we'll get her on over to the Falling Water."

Karryl stiffened. "You mean you don't want me to go on with you?"

"Of course I do. But I want to be careful for you, too. There are other ways to get to the Falling Water besides the road we've been traveling on. And Karryl—" he hesitated for a moment— "it's not just the carpetbaggers or state police out here, like in Austin."

"What do you mean?"

"Well, what happened to Burr Wayne is one example. Rustlers. Outlaws. Drifters cast off by the war. And they seem to be all over now. But worse than that, this is Indian country, as I've told you. We haven't seen any right around here lately, but that doesn't mean we won't sooner or later. I don't mean to frighten you, Karryl. I just want to try to make sure, in advance, if I can, that things are all right up there before we ride in."

Karryl sighed. "I'm too tired now to argue with you, Levit." But then, spiritedly, "I'm not afraid of your Indians, though. Or your outlaws."

He changed the subject quickly. "You know what?" He grinned. "We could get one of the preachers among the Germans to come down to our place to tie the knot, as soon as we're sure nobody has trailed us in here. The fact is, most of the people hereabouts would want to hold my feet to the fire if we had a wedding at the Falling Water and didn't invite them. Lenneweber would be glad to get a German parson or maybe a Lutheran priest for us. Or Biberstin, either. But it takes a little time. Would you like to help us, Mrs. Elledge," he said to the older woman, "to set up a real fancy wedding at the Falling Water?"

"Well, I sure would. Can't recollect ever attending a marriage since my own, and that was quite a spell ago. And not much in the way of frills and feathers, when it was."

"It's settled then." Levit laughed in mock relief. "And we haven't even asked Karryl what she thinks about it."

"You certainly haven't," Karryl agreed crisply, tossing her red hair in a way that fast was identifying her to most people.

"Now, now, honey." Mrs. Elledge smiled. "You'll have plenty of time later to lay things out just like you want them, and to say what you want to about anything—even like telling off this big man of yours when he needs it. But right now, the way you two look, I'd say you'd ought to be hitting the sack."

"Well, I for one at least am dog tired," Levit admitted. "It makes days now—and nights—since I put my own head down."

Elledge said: "You and me, we'll take the spare room. Couple of beds in there, and a couple of bunks. You can have your pick. The women folks'll take the big bedroom."

At breakfast the next morning Levit said, "Do you suppose, Elledge, if I send one of my men back here once I know things are all clear up there, that you could break loose long enough to bring Karryl and Mrs. Elledge to the Falling Water? That is, of course, if Mrs. Elledge would be willing—"

"You know I'd be, Levit," Mrs. Elledge spoke out.

"But you haven't heard it all," He grinned. "Just for the looks of things, granting we've got time, and the chance to do such things, I would be mighty grateful if you sort of moved in with us, until we could find out about those matters back in Austin, and maybe around us here. The sooner Karryl can get to her future home—and even start to run things—" He smiled. "The more relieved I'll be. You know what I'm talking about."

"Of course, Levit."

"Well, I don't," Karryl announced.

MacAshen smiled again. "Cowboys are big talkers," he

chided her. "They don't mean to be, but you won't be at the Falling Water a week before not a man, woman or child from the Falls of the Colorado to the head of the Concho River won't know about it. And since we plan to be around here the rest of our lives, it would be sort of helpful if someone like Mrs. Elledge was there to act like—well, like what the Mexicans call a *duenna*, until the wedding does come off."

Elledge laughed uproariously, but then he quieted and said, "Levit's talking sense, miss."

Karryl looked at each of them in turn. "Whatever you think best, Levit," she said with a trace of resignation in her tone. But her eyes sparkled.

Levit walked around to her chair, lifted her out of it and put his arms around her. "It won't be for long, any of this, you can be sure," he said.

29

In a smoke-stained *tipi* far out in the sheltered canyons of the Llano Estacado, Devers sat on a blanket before a wrinkled Quohada Comanche. The half-breed, Santiago, bringing Devers a message from his associates in Austin, found him there. Santiago had come by way of the hangout on the Blanco, and he was more than eager, considering his surroundings, to head back as quickly as he could after fulfilling his mission.

Devers had been staring at the coals in the pit near the center of the tipi, morbidly listening to the old Quohada sub-chieftain.

"My heart is heavy for you, my son," the Indian declared. "But it was bound to happen. You were born more white than red, but you grew up more red than white. When your father abandoned his family to us we sought to train you in our ways. But even as a child you would not forget your skin was mostly white."

"I just wanted to live like other whites."

"You could not understand then, and perhaps you have not accepted yet, that among white men even a drop of Indian blood within your veins makes you an Indian. Once long ago I urged you not to return to the white man's world. You did not heed my words then. Would it be futile to urge you not to go back now?"

"I'm going back, but maybe not to stay, this time."

Slowly the Indian got to his feet. Reaching down, he laid a hand on Devers's shoulder. "I am an old man now, my son, and your problems are beyond my range of vision. I would help you if I could. You have not come to us for help in recent years. Do you do so now?"

"That's what I'm here for. But you know as well as I do, it won't do any good unless you can square me out with Quee-Nigh-Tosav. He just don't cotton to me."

"Have you tried in any way to make friends with him?"

"More than once. But he's always turned his back on me. Hates all men with mixed blood, so it's said."

"I will do what I can, but that still may not be enough."

At the moment, the entrance flap was laid back and Santiago pushed inside. He wasted no time, bending over to whisper a few guttural sentences into Devers's ear.

"The hell you say!" Devers exclaimed. "You mean they let her get clear away? And after all the trouble I went to, setting it up and seeing that the general amnesties were kept quiet?"

"That's what I was told, señor. But what is more important is where she has gone." He lapsed into half-Mexican, half-Indian monosyllables. Devers jumped to his feet.

"You mean she's with that rancher, MacAshen, right up against us, on the Pedernales?"

"Sí, señor, so it was said. But no one has checked the story. The men you station in the rocks and at the pass, they have seen no woman at MacAshen's house. MacAshen, though, has returned."

"Then he's hidden her out somewhere, thinking nobody was onto them."

"Perhaps."

"What else, Santiago?"

"The way it was said to me, is that the people in Austin have decided matters would be better if MacAshen is finally now diverted from the scene. They said it would be left up to you, remembering though that what they really want is something that will indeed take his mind off such matters, but not force a showdown with the state police at the same time."

"What's that supposed to mean?"

"They said for you alone to work it out—that with your Indian savvy you ought to be able to think of some way to handle

MacAshen, and that still would never be laid to white men."

"Maybe I can," Devers said, gritting his teeth.

Devers went back to the Blanco. He had a free rein now and he would use it. But first he had to find out if MacAshen really had Karryl hidden out somewhere. She might be just hiding at the Falling Water. But he had to know some other things—everything about the Falling Water he could find out, and about the people who lived there. What were MacAshen's habits? How strong would he be for really striking back, when he got hit in his own compound? Just what were his plans for himself and Karryl anyway? Devers knew a way to get his answers quickly.

General Sherman made a quiet, unannounced inspection of the frontier forts in the spring of 1871. He traveled in a small ambulance, escorted by a handful of Federal troops. When he had rested at Fort Griffin, he struck out for the little settlement of Jacksboro en route north to Fort Sill in Indian territory, and beyond. Some days later he was in the second Texas town, and he spent the night there hearing the pleas of the hard-hit ranchers. But he had seen no marauding parties in his long tour; how could it happen, if there were so many of the terrorists at large?

When he arose on the following day, he found out.

One hundred and fifty Redskins had hit the communications road which he had traveled only a few hours before. They had destroyed the regular government train of ten wagons only seventeen miles to the southwest. Seven of the men were butchered; one of them was chained to the wheels of the wagon and roasted alive. Sherman escaped by one day the very fate of which people had been complaining so fruitlessly.

Sherman angrily ordered Colonel Mackenzie to follow and punish the marauders. But Mackenzie could accomplish little. The Indians scurried back across the Red River and lost themselves immediately among the reservation villages, even before Mackenzie could take to the trail. Sherman stormed out of Jacksboro for Fort Sill. At that post, it was not hard to determine just who the assassins were; in fact, the Kiowas delighted in boasting of their prowess while the commander of all the white man's soldiers was within their midst.

Unfortunately for them, however, Sherman did not react

exactly in the way they had expected. He ordered Federal soldiers to seize three Kiowa chiefs—Satank, Santanta, and Big Tree—and hold them to account, a command that was immediately carried out. Further, once in his hand, he consigned the prisoners to trial not before a military tribunal as they might have expected, but before the civil court at Jacksboro, in the locality where their crime had been committed.

The imposition of death sentences in that court was, of course, inevitable; and men with a knowledge of the Redskins' ways braced now for new atrocities. The reservation Indians seethed, gathering their clans in far-flung places to sharpen their weapons for greater assaults. Even the quick commutation of the sentences on the Kiowa chiefs to life imprisonment—at the request of President Grant—accomplished nothing.

The Kotchatekas were the first to retaliate. In the middle of the night they raided the military corrals at Fort Sill itself, appropriating every army mule on the post.

White Horse led another war party down the Wichita to strike at the lonely homestead of Abel Lee, on the Clear Fork of the Brazos. The man they killed quickly, but his wife did not enjoy such consideration. Before she died, White Horse's warriors cut off both her ears, then an arm; and one of the braves skinned all the hair from her head. An older daughter was subjected to violence before she too succumbed, and three other children were abducted.

In June, a few minutemen whom the counties had been allowed to raise to counter this fresh wave of violence were suddenly released from duty. But the state police force itself was augmented. The *Tri-Weekly Statesman* at Austin now openly printed its accusations against the latter system, concluding its editorial: "What a relief when these scoundrels are safely caged in the penitentiary!"

And so it went—the Indians wild upon the prairies, regardless of Sherman; and the state police, most of them with criminal charges pending, raging across the countryside.

At Hillsboro, a man named Gaithings was arrested on orders of the adjutant general and fined two thousand dollars, without even a trial. The alternative to the payment of the fine was a quick transfer to the state penitentiary without opportunity for a hearing. The people of Hillsboro were warned by the state police that if they interfered, policemen would be quartered in their homes.

Farther to the south, in the cotton county of Walker, an old Negro cited as a witness at a trial was murdered. The adjutant general sent Captain Leander McNelly to apprehend the criminals. McNelly arrested four men and brought them to trial; but in the tumult of the proceedings, pistols were smuggled to the accused men. They opened fire on the judge and the prosecutor; then wounded McNelly and his aides. A mob helped them to escape.

Davis promptly declared martial law in the country. He quartered his police on the people, forcing the payment of a tax for this occupation. Even McNelly—unique among the types on the police force—was appalled at the governor's action, for it wreaked horror on scores of innocent families.

At Groesbeck, a man named Applewhite was murdered by four policemen, and at Nacogdoches another named Harwell. Two attorneys were shot to death by state police in Tyler; then the year was climaxed by the revelation that an ex-convict, a notorious desperado named Hunter, had been commissioned to the force. Local officers at Austin promptly took Hunter into custody to answer for past crimes, but the adjutant general ordered the man released, without bail.

These were the dark hours that passed over Texas, the grim tumult of the Reconstruction ordeal. Strangely, little of this was known in the moment upon the Pedernales.

The day came when Levit sent a man up the road to ask the Elledges and Karryl to join him, and he stood on the stone porch of the ranch house anxiously watching for their arrival. Elledge's buckboard soon appeared on the Pedernales road and entered the shallow ford—Elledge was on the front seat, Mrs. Elledge and Karryl on the one behind. Levit ran forward to greet them when they halted at the hitching rail. He reached up to help Karryl down, kissing her as he did so.

"Welcome at last," he said, "to the Falling Water."

"Oh, Levit, it's all so beautiful here."

"I wanted that to be your first impression. And frankly, I wanted to have a chance to shape things up a bit, too, before you got here."

"I already love everything about your home, Levit."

"Our home, you mean."

She smiled at him. "Our home," she repeated.

"Come on in," Levit called toward the Elledges, reaching now to help Mrs. Elledge down from the wagon seat. Elledge clambered to the ground beside them.

"Everything's all right?" he asked MacAshen quietly.

"Yes."

"I'm glad of that."

Levit signaled to a couple of the boys standing before the bunkhouse, pointing to the luggage in the buckboard, and to the vehicle itself, then turned to lead his guests into the house. "I'll show you to your rooms, folks," he said. "And when we get back down the stairs, every hand on the spread likely will be here to meet the future mistress of the Falling Water." For once Karryl even blushed in her pleasure.

"I'm just as anxious to see them, Levit," she said.

The men indeed came quickly to greet her: Lubbock, grave and earnest; Steve Meadows and Torkin, both soft and gentle voiced. The Monhalls and the others, all eager, cheering, happy. The Germans, Nusser and Reed Schreiner.

They moved her things into Levit's old quarters on the floor above, renovated in the hours since MacAshen's return from Austin. The Mexican, Pepito, was a bundle of energy as he lent a hand, gleaming with appreciation when she told him of Mac-Ashen's often-expressed dependence on him.

"I'm so grateful for the way you've made me feel welcome here," she said to the cowboys.

"Well, ma'am, we'll be pleased too," Lubbock replied, "if you can just manage to ride herd on that fellow MacAshen, who brought you here."

"I'll ride herd on him all right, every time he needs it," she responded, again flipping the red mop across her head.

"I can see that already, ma'am."

The Falling Water was an idyllic wonderland for the woman from the Mississippi plantation. At Pepito's invitation, she went with him to inspect the huge kitchen. There were flagstones for flooring, and pots hung from chains in the open fireplace. She touched the hanging rows of tinware, studied the shelves of knives and two-tined forks. In surprise she noted that the household goods even included sifters and candlesticks. The huge Dutch oven, Pepito explained to her, was a sort of skillet for all purposes.

Lubbock came in through the back door to find Karryl before the fireplace, wondering aloud how she could ever produce enough bread for the ravenous men if she were called upon to do so. Lubbock saw her perplexity and said to her, "We handle our bread differently out here, Miss. You never cut the dough. When it's made up you break it off in round chunks and put it in that Dutch oven. Then you heap hot coals on top of the oven, and bank 'em around it, and pretty soon you've got bread."

Karryl sighed. In the section where the dishes were kept she noted one of the dented tin cups that the men used for their coffee. A smile touched the corners of her own mouth, and Lubbock took a box from under his arm.

"Made you some tumblers for your table, miss," he said. "Fact is, I've been workin' on 'em from the minute I heard you was comin'. Always good to have tumblers."

"How in the world did you make them?" Karryl exclaimed, as Lubbock began to lift the glass containers from the box.

"It's easy, miss, if you know how. Just take a long, thin strip of rawhide, put an old whiskey bottle between your knees, seesaw around it with the hide till the bottle is hot, then dash it in a keg of cold water. It'll break right where the rawhide strip heated it. Then you get a file and smooth it down clean, and you've shore got tumblers for your table."

Karryl laughed delightedly. But then she said, "I guess you can see, Mr. Lubbock, that I don't know much about how people live out here. But I'll learn."

"Sure you will. Levit's folks came to the Pedernales long ago, when there wasn't even tradin' posts this side of Austin. But they made this home comfortable. After you get used to it, it won't be bad. This ranch is the best there is along this reach of the frontier."

"I already love this house, and everything in it, and I'll be grateful to you all for your patience while I'm learning to manage it."

"You can count on us, miss."

In the days that followed, Karryl ecstatically explored among the things that would be her own in this frontier dwelling. She resurrected from old chests the crocheted tidies Levit's mother had made. Lambrequins which once had adorned the mantlepiece were restored to their places, as were the little displays of pretty rocks, glass ornaments and china dishes. She even brought out again a hand-embroidered pin cushion, and a mirror with an elaborate frame.

"They used to blow it, like a horn, to get the men in for their meals," Levit explained to her when she found a great conch shell. "Later, there was a bell but it disappeared somewhere while I was away in the war."

On one occasion she said to Mrs. Elledge, "I feel terrible about taking you away from your own home just to be here with me, even though I'm hoping we can settle things for ourselves quickly."

"Well, don't you worry about it. I'm glad of the chance to visit." And with that she changed the subject. "That fellow you're marrying has sure been needing a wife here at the Falling Water."

"I'm going to do my best for him."

"That's easy to see, honey. It's wrote all over you, and it's good that you're strong. The Pedernales valley's no picnic ground. It's been hard, and rough, and dangerous ever since the white man came in here. It may get worse, and the people will look to the Falling Water for protection."

"I've heard a little of that, Mrs. Elledge. But Levit has never told me much. He always said, up to now, that it was too perilous for a woman without telling me exactly why. But you've managed to hold on. And he seems to have changed his mind."

"Well, it's no more dangerous for a woman that it is for her man. But don't let none of this worry you, honey. It's never worried me, especially. If we have trouble we just face up to it and go on. And it always wears away in time."

Down by the corral, leaning over the fence and watching the mustangs, Lubbock said to MacAshen, "She's a real beautiful, real fine lady, boss. An' she's been needed on this spread."

"I guess I was getting pretty hard to live with."

"You was wearin' thin, Levit."

"Is Elledge's buckboard ready to move out?"

"Will be shortly. The boys had Elledge's team down on the grass, but they're back in now. Mrs. Elledge stayin' here?"

"Yes, she is. For a little while, at least."

Back up at the ranch house, the Elledges and Karryl came out on the porch to see the homesteader on his trip home. "I'll let you know how everything goes up here," Levit said.

"Good. And I'll keep my eyes peeled, down on the lower end. I'll get the word to some of the others to do the same, too."

Mrs. Elledge was by the hitching rack, watching her husband cross the ford and turn eastward down the valley. Levit and Karryl went on up to the verandah to stand in the shade. "Mrs. Elledge is a very nice woman," Karryl said to him. "And it is good of her to come here to help us. Tell me, Levit, are the Elledges our only neighbors?"

"I'm afraid they are, honey. The Ramsdalls are in the valley, and the Farnsworths. But they are farther away. You'll have to get used to not having women friends out here. Think you can manage with just me?"

"I'll manage," she smiled.

He turned to go, then suddenly stopped. "There is another woman, Karryl. The wife of the sheepherder." He told her of Lenneweber's mandate, how the herd had been driven in, and that the sheepherder had brought a wife. She caught the austerity in his voice when he spoke of the woman. "I don't think she will come here, however," he said, "and I don't want you to ride up to the sheepherder's cabin. But I do have to see that they're taken care of."

It seemed an odd stipulation. Why mention it at all if she was never to see the woman? She eyed him for a moment, then asked, "Is there something else you should tell me, Levit?"

"No. There is nothing else to tell." His back was stiff as he walked quickly in through the door. Karryl watched him go, a tender smile curving her lips.

The days ran into weeks, and Levit could learn of no reaction in Austin to Karryl's flight. But he did hear from his friends at Fredericksburg of other things transpiring in the city on the Colorado. For one thing, a bipartisan committee had staged a "convention of taxpayers" in Austin to expose corruption. The convention, headed by honest Republicans, found that Davis's administration had advanced the tax rate from fifteen cents on a hundred-dollar valuation in 1866 to more than two dollars. "The Germans gave me a copy of the resolution they passed there," Levit said to Karryl and Mrs. Elledge. "Listen to this: 'Violations of the Constitution and disregard of the law are frequent and numerous; but frequent and numerous as they are, we have been unable to find a single one of either class based on an honest desire to accomplish good to the people of this state, or to secure prosperity of the country. On the contrary, their apparent course seems uniformly to spring from one sole purpose, viz: to concentrate power in the hands of one man, and to emasculate the strength of the citizens of Texas as a free people.' "

"Do you think that will help to settle things, Levit?" Karryl asked.

"To be honest, I don't," he admitted. "But at least it is progress.

"I think we can begin to make our plans quickly, now," Levit said later to Karryl. "If they had been going to try anything they would have done it already. I told Lenneweber what we wanted to do here, and he said just to let him know. He would see that a priest was brought here. And he and his family also would like very much to attend."

Karryl perked up instantly. "How soon can it be, Levit?"

"Well, that's what I had to come back to ask you. And when I know, I'll go back up there and make the arrangements. That won't take me long. But it does take those folks up there a while to get straightened out so they can come down here. You know, a real wedding is a pretty big thing here on the frontier. The Germans are formal—like to take their time, and that sort of thing. Would you say a couple of weeks from now would be all right? I'll have to tell them just when. And get the word around up here, too." He smiled.

She considered for a moment. "Two weeks would be fine, Levit," she said. "But please don't make it longer than that."

"Then I'll head out for Fredericksburg again in the morning. Probably have to stay there overnight. But I'll be back by noon the next day."

"Levit," she said suddenly, " is it necessary that I stay cooped up here in the house all the time while you're away? Couldn't I just go for a little ride, close around, I mean, like just down along the river? It's mostly open there. I love horses."

He thought about it for a moment. "As long as you stay within sight of the ranch house, and where the boys can see you, too, I guess it's all right," he said, finally. "I'll tell them to keep an eye on you while you're out, but stay close, Karryl, and just ride down along the river bank."

"Oh, Levit, that will make it so much nicer. And I can ride that beautiful buckskin horse you said was to be my own."

He smiled at her, then drew her close and kissed her again.

Levit left early the next morning for the German settlement, and not long afterward Karryl walked down to the corral and asked Lubbock to saddle the golden buckskin for her.

"That's a great horse, miss," he said to her, as he led the mount out and lifted Karryl up into the saddle.

"It's the most beautiful horse I ever saw in my life," she agreed.

Lubbock told her about Levit's insistance he break in the horse himself, because of the future owner he planned for it, and how he got pretty bruised up in doing so.

Karryl chuckled delightedly, "He didn't!" Lubbock grinned over his own recollection of the corral experience.

The buckskin appeared instinctively to recognize the presence of a new master—or in this case a new mistress—upon his back, and one much to his liking. The hand was firm, but gentle, and the burden was light.

Karryl had a pleasant morning, reining the animal in and around the ranch outbuildings, and on the paths along the river bank. She enjoyed herself so much that she almost forgot to return for the noonday meal Pepito had prepared. He was on the back gallery waving when she finally turned back toward the Falling Water.

"Mrs. Elledge, it was such a wonderful ride," she thrilled, when they were seated at the table. "Do you ever ride?"

"Used to, once." The homesteader's wife laughed. "But I'm too along in years now for anything except a seat in the wagon."

"Well, if it isn't raining tomorrow, I'm going again before my horse forgets that he and I get along so well."

"It won't rain tomorrow, honey. I can tell by my bones, when it is. And I don't feel any aches now."

Mrs. Elledge was right about the weather. The next day was even more beautiful than the one which had preceded it. Breakfast was scarcely over before Karryl had persuaded one of the hands to saddle the buckskin for her again. She headed immediately for the river bank, then reined the horse across the shallow ford and rode slowly along the bank eastward. Dense clusters of violet-blue flowers crowned the thickets of mountain laurel, while the fragrance of blossoms strange to her came up from the glens alongside the trail. Suddenly she jerked the buckskin to a dead halt. A woman was standing at the edge of the pecans staring at her. She had been gathering berries or some wild vegetable in a brightly colored Mexican bowl.

Karryl knew instantly that this was the woman, Rhoda Hamlin, whom Levit had spoken to her about, and whom he had instructed her to avoid. She spoke to Rhoda, and by the woman's sullen reaction, the tone of her voice, the impudent stare, she instinctively recognized the type.

"I am Karryl Newcomb."

"I know."

"Are you Mrs. Hamlin?"

"Yes."

Karryl felt a biting curiosity, but a flash of intuition prompted her not to pursue it. "Is there anything you need?" she asked.

"No."

There was enmity in the woman's face. In a wilderness where women were so rare, Rhoda Hamlin's hostility could arise from only one cause, Karryl realized, and she certainly had no wish to prolong the meeting. She prodded the buckskin back onto the trail. "Please let me know if you do need anything."

Rhoda Hamlin did not answer, and Karryl rode back toward the Falling Water. She resolved not to speak of the meeting to Levit, and she did not return to the river bank again during his absence.

Levit was home on schedule, happy with the results of his mission and eager to impart the details to both Karryl and Mrs. Elledge.

"I just wish Aunt Betsy could be here, too," Karryl said. "But I know we couldn't let her come here now."

Someone else did ride in however. The hands raised him before he reached the ford, and when he was across they promptly ushered him up to the ranch house. Both Levit and Karryl rushed out to greet him.

"Fall, you ole son-of-a-gun! You've got a way of showing up just at the right time." Levit pulled the old Texan from his horse. Karryl threw her arms around his neck and kissed him.

"Didn't have no real business ridin' clean out here," he said,

[313]

"what with all the ridin' they got me doin' between Houston an' Austin—an' for hard money, too. Especially so soon after the last trip. But when I found out this young lady had flew the coop I knew there wasn't but one place she'd flew to—after what I heard when I was here just the other day. I figured, however, I better make sure."

They drew him into the house and introduced him to Mrs. Elledge. Karryl was ecstatic. "You'd better just stand still, Fall, and let her get it over with," Levit said. "Otherwise none of us will have any peace until she does."

"We're getting married!" she cried.

"Well, it's about time." He gripped MacAshen's hand, and then pulled Karryl in and kissed her himself. "Reckon I'm entitled to that much," he grinned.

Levit shoved a chair forward. "Sit down, Fall, and tell us what's going on back where you came from."

"Your Aunt Betsy sent her love, as always, young lady," he said to Karryl.

"Oh, Mr. Fall, we were just speaking of her. And wishing she could be here. Do you think there is any way . . . ?"

"Miss, I'd sure argue against it. She's feisty as usual, but she ain't really been too well. And other things have been goin' poorly for her, too."

"What, Mr. Fall?"

"Well, like a lot of other people, she held on to her cotton too long. It was bringin' five cents a pound up to plantin' time."

"Five cents a pound for cotton?"

"That's all. At that rate, it takes a pound of cotton to buy a pound of flour; twelve pounds to buy a bushel of corn; three pounds to buy a pound of bacon. She tries not to let it upset her, though, and I reckon there ain't much that really will upset your Aunt Betsy."

"What did you hear around Austin, Fall?" Levit asked.

"You mean about Karryl, here? Well, nothin'. Not a whisper. Kind of strange, but that's the way it was, even if she was posted. But I heard some other things, Levit. For one, people out in Lampasas County have sent another petition to Davis, asking for help. They said if they couldn't get anything else they'd take the state police—if the police would fight outlaws instead of the citizens. Five justices of the peace signed that petition, Levit, but they haven't had an answer."

[314]

"What's the matter with them? Don't they know they ought to have asked for Ranger help instead? They'll be sorry if they get the state police in over there."

"Not much doubt about that. Saw a newspaper in Austin tellin' about one of Davis's policemen shootin' a boy in the back up in Paris, on the Red River. The boy died in his mother's arms, but the policeman just laughed at her. They didn't do anything with him, either."

Karryl wanted to change the subject. "Mr. Fall, will you stay for my wedding?"

"Well, now," he said, "I'd rather do that than anything I can ever remember. But I made a promise about gettin' home with something from Austin, and I can't run out on that. I might make it back, though," he said, as if it occurred to him suddenly. "I was plannin' something new."

"Like what, Fall?" Levit asked.

"Me and another fellow been talkin' about headin' for the Concho, and I might just do that soon as I can get back to Houston. That way, I could be going this way—if I could make it."

"What're you going to do out on the Concho?"

"Hunt some of them buffs. Been a coon's age since I shot a buffalo."

30

It was dark when Devers rode through the pass from the Blanco to the Pedernales. Off to the west, the bleating of the sheep herd came faintly to his ears. The herder was there with his sheep; he would be wrapped in his blankets now, under the tarp. Devers had watched him make his campsite; he had waited until the road to the cabin was open; he knew what to expect ahead.

When he came to the small clearing, he tied his horse and strode up the path to the door. No light showed through the window, but he could not have approached unnoticed.

"Rhoda," he called out softly.

Inside, there was a sudden scurrying; her face appeared at the window. He saw the glitter of her eyes in the starlight; then the door swung inward and she stood on the threshold.

"Mr. Devers! What are you doing here?"

"I came to see you, Rhoda," he said.

"You knew I was alone?"

"Of course. Do you think I'm a fool?"

She stood clearly silhouetted against the blackness behind her. The makeshift night garment scarcely covered her breasts; the fabric clung about her thighs. She started to censure him for his audacity; then the need for him stopped her. Devers reached out a hand and drew her toward him.

"Aren't you inviting me in?"

Her red lips parted and her breath was hot upon his face. She hesitated only for a moment, then she fell back before him into the darkness of the cabin.

The morning star hung low upon the horizon before Devers came forth again. Actually, he had remained longer than he intended, but the tale the woman had angrily unfolded to him had held him much beyond the reckoned hour. There was more here than he had expected. The woman knew about Karryl Newcomb, and that MacAshen had brought her to the valley to become his wife. But she didn't know when it would be.

"She's at that house right now though," the woman bit out in the darkness. "And she's plannin' on stayin'."

He and Rhoda Hamlin had come to the clearing before the door, the herder's wife wrapped in a thick cloak. In his mind, as he talked to her, each step became easier. And she need know nothing of it, on her own account.

MacAshen and Karryl Newcomb both! Once the job was finished, he could get out of the white man's world . . . go back to the Indians, himself, this time for good. And take something along with him to make it worth his while—something he had wanted more than anything ever before in his life.

Devers studied the woman beside him. She had made her own circumstances plenty clear. She wanted MacAshen, and he had scorned her advances. She was like a rattlesnake now, interrupted in its warmth.

"I never figured you for it," he said, "but you're a jealous woman."

"I don't like fine ladies, coming here to the hills with her airs and fine clothes."

"You'd like some help with her, I take it?"

"You bet I would. I'd like to see her drove clear out of this valley."

Devers smiled. It would, indeed, be satisfying to Rhoda Hamlin to have Karryl driven from the valley. For MacAshen, so far as she could see it, would then be left just to her. And no reason to disillusion her in that regard.

"You've got a way, you have, Devers," she bit out. "You can think of something. Yes! I want you to help. I want you to run her clear out of this Pedernales country."

In the darkness, she could not see the expression on his face.

"You know the trail up through the pass," he said. "If in some way MacAshen can be drawn away from his house—and his riders with him—for a week, maybe, or longer—it don't matter where, as long as he's got his riders with him—you go up that trail. You'll have to make your husband go off somewhere, or get him drunk. I brought some whiskey in the saddlebags. But first be sure Karryl is at the house and just about nobody else. Chances are some of the other settlers are around, and it won't matter if somebody is staying there with her. Keep on the trail for a mile beyond the pass till you go around the peak. It's not far. Go up the side of that peak on the Blanco slope and build a fire. A big fire. But be sure it shows only to the south. I'll have somebody watching every night."

"What'll you do, Devers?"

"Rhoda, you just let me know when Karryl Newcomb is at the Falling Water by herself—or with just the Mexican cook. I'll think of something. It won't be tomorrow, maybe not even soon. But you let me know by the signal."

She suddenly slid up against him, letting all the full, soft rounds of her body press upon him.

"Yes, Devers," she whispered.

In the morning hours back at his own stand, Devers called the half-breed Santiago into his quarters.

"You know how to find Esa Rosa again?"

He nodded. "Sí. I know Esa Rosa. I have been to his villages. Esa Rosa never moves far unless there are the soldiers around."

Devers began to talk. His listener's black eyes opened wide, then narrowed to slits. Devers rose from his chair and poured a slug of whiskey into his glass. He swallowed it and came back to the table. He spoke up again, clearly, carefully, coldly. When he had finished, he fixed the half-breed with his stare.

"You got it straight now?"

Santiago did not require repetition. But he did not acknowledge the tense query for a moment. When he did, he answered sharply: "Sí, señor. But the boys will not like this."

"That's for me to worry about, Santiago." He scowled the man to his feet. The half-breed turned to go, but Devers had a further command.

"Tell Esa Rosa he'll not need more than twenty of those bucks for the drive. And that's a top horse herd in the corral.

MacAshen is bound to follow it. As for the other job, I want six braves. On this, he is to send one of the splinter bands from out of the Llano Estacado. One that lives away from the tribe. They're not to ride with the others, and they're not to know about each other." Santiago's expression indicated his understanding. "You make the deal, Santiago. And get that small band close quick. Tell Esa Rosa to say to Parro-o-coom that I'll pay whatever his braves want, in horses, cattle or goods. Even guns, but they'll have to wait for guns, if that's what they want."

Early in 1872 General Reynolds was replaced. General C. C. Augur was named to succeed him. But the move was tempered with a new pronouncement from Grant: "If there is any change in the Indian policy, it will be on the humanitarian side of the Indians."

Bands of Comanches came out from the canyons in April. With them rode the Cheyennes, the Kiowas, and the Apaches. In February one of MacAshen's men in the hills northeast of the Falling Water sent word that scattered war parties had begun to scourge the settlers all through that district again. One of them had taken captive a white woman, and quick pursuit had not recovered her.

Levit MacAshen, too, was confronted with a shocking atrocity at his own doorstep. They had raided his corrals and killed one of his own men, right on top of the Falling Water! Reed Schreiner dead, and the whole mustang herd gone!

Levit stared down at the youth's cold body where Elledge had laid it on the floor of the bunkhouse. The bloody scar where his curly hair had been was evidence enough of Indian mercilessness.

"Yesterday or the day before," Elledge said, "I followed the sign across the river, north, and it went out straight toward the Llano. That's where they threw Schreiner's body, just behind the north wall. Reckon it's lucky I just happened to be working that way."

"Anything to mark them, Elledge?"

"Not that I could make out. They didn't leave much; no boot tracks, no moccasins. But I'd lay it to the Comanches."

MacAshen turned to Lubbock. "We'll have to bury him here," he said. "You can pull in the men and get them ready to travel."

"Ain't you forgettin' something, Levit? You've got a weddin' comin' up in less'n two weeks."

"I'm not forgetting it, Lubbock. But we've got to try to run that outfit down and get those horses back. They were the best in this part of Texas. And it's more than that, too. We can't take it here lying down. Or they'd be back again before we knew it."

"Me and some of the boys could take out after 'em."

"You know I couldn't let you do that alone. And we'll need every hand we can get if we do catch up with them."

"All right, Levit. I'll put the boys to work on a coffin, and we'll dig a grave on the mesa."

"Make it fast, Lubbock. The sky looks bad."

MacAshen took the homesteader, Elledge, by the arm, leading him toward the house. But they halted near the front door. "Thanks for bringing him in," Levit said.

"You want me to turn out the men down the river?"

"No, we'll handle this ourselves. Chances are we're too late. They've got a long head start. But we'll have to try, and keep on as long as it makes sense. You can send word to Barry and Roberts, though, up the line. Tell them to make sure of their own hills."

"Who'll be here?"

"I'll leave Lubbock and the Mexican. I'll send Lubbock in to warn Biberstin at Fredericksburg. They can shut off the valley that way, and we'll be in front of the Falling Water north. The sheepherder can close up the path, south. I'll send him another carbine and ammunition."

"What about your marriage, Levit?"

"That's the hardest thing to swallow, Elledge," he said. "I've waited a lot of years for what we were planning here, and I guess Karryl has, too. But now I've got to put it off again. And I'm afraid she'll not understand. One other thing you could do for us, though, is get word to the Germans that the wedding has had to be set back for the time being. When I return, we'll send for them quickly."

"Well, the women-folks sure can't stay here."

"No, Elledge. I'm asking you to take them back to your place with you. And I hope—just a chance, of course—we may be able to get home sooner than I'm expecting to."

"All right, Levit. Guess you couldn't have done it any other way. But be careful when you hit that trail north."

Levit nodded again. He went on into the house, followed by Elledge. The hard mask on Levit's face told Karryl more than she needed to know, although the actual details about his wrangler's death were still unexplained.

She did not press him; at dusk she went with him, and the Elledges, and the cowboys to bury the mutilated body of the Mason youth on the mesa behind the graves of Levit's father and mother.

Supper was silent; Levit, when he spoke at all, attempted to soften his words, but the weight on his mind left little to talk about. The Elledges went early to their bedroom leaving Karryl and Levit alone.

"That conversation you had with Mr. Elledge, Levit, is it as bad as that?"

Levit looked up in surprise. He had not been aware she overheard. "There's always a problem, as I've said to you before. It's the way things are out here."

"This was an Indian raid, Levit. I know that, and that they struck the Falling Water. You are going to follow them." Levit did not answer, and Karryl came across to him and put her hands on his shoulders, looking up into his face. "When I came here with you from Austin, I knew there were dangers," she said.

"They don't show up often."

"You're trying to mislead me, Levit, and that's not fair. I'm learning fast, and I know you're worried. Mr. Elledge is more honest with his wife."

He gazed at her thoughtfully. "Maybe he is," he acceded finally. "But the Elledges have lived here during all the years of the border wars. They were on the Pedernales in the 'fifties, as we MacAshens were, and Mrs. Elledge learned to shoot a musket through the cracks in their cabin just as good as her husband could. Because they've been through so many Indian attacks, they're apt to look for an Indian behind every tree."

"I don't believe that, Levit. And I don't believe you do either. They're very level-headed people. Mr. Elledge said the Indians would come in fast in the spring." Levit strode slowly up and down. But she was not to be silenced. "Don't try to keep things from me."

He looked at Karryl fondly. There was a strength in her face that he had never seen before, and he was proud of her for it.

"Maybe they will," he admitted. "I won't hide it if you've set your mind to hear such things. But I hope they'll hold their raids to the north. The Kiowas and the Wichitas probably won't come this far south. And the Comanches would rather meet white men on the prairie grass."

"Levit, you don't believe all that, either. A part, maybe, but not all of it. You're worried, too, more than you'll stand to let me see."

He took her shoulders in his hands and looked down into her upturned face. "You're afraid tonight, my darling, and I guess I'm afraid for you, too," he confessed gently. "I have been, all along, as I told you many times. But the truth is that all will be well. Yes, there may be some trouble; there always has been, of one kind or another; but we'll weather it. The Falling Water has been here a long time, and you and I have to make sure it keeps on being here."

"What of our wedding, Levit?"

"A little while, my dear—it will take a little while longer now. It's harder than you can possibly imagine for me to have to tell you that. But I'll be back one day not too long from now, and it can be carried out quickly then." For a second he forced a smile. "With Pepito's and Mrs. Elledge's help I want you to plan a really wonderful one for us."

She felt the muscular warmth of his body close to her, the security of his presence, and in silence she accepted his judgment. They must wait, if Levit said they must. All would be well if he said it would be.

31

It was cold north of the Llano, but not cold enough to harden the moisture into ice. The paths were bogs of mud, but the men from the Pedernales continued to push on toward the north. It had been almost a week since they had left that river and they had already lost what trail of the horse herd was left after the downpours. But MacAshen would not call a halt. Somewhere, still further on, they might pick up the sign again.

Now they were above the site of old Fort Phantom Hill. The occasional settlers they encountered had seen no Indian bands go by, nor had they observed a moving herd of horses. At Fort Griffin it was the same. Fort Griffin was a supply point for the buffalo hunters and a feverish activity identified the town. But nobody had seen their animals. In Jacksboro MacAshen called at the office of its leading citizen, a frontier lawyer from the war days named Comstock, who had fought with Terry's Texas Rangers.

"Sounds like Indian raiders, all right," that man declared, "but you never know. The way things are now in north Texas, you can't tell the difference between white outlaws and Redskins."

"If it was Indians, we figured they'd make straight for the Red River," Levit said.

"Maybe they went out by the San Saba headwaters. And up the Comanche War Trail."

Karryl fretted over her forced sojourn with the Elledges. They were rough, kindly people, but the Falling Water was to be her home now and she wanted to be there. "Where are the Indians?" she demanded of the homesteader.

"Maybe back across the Red, ma'am," he answered sympathetically. "I hope so."

"Well, why shouldn't I go back to the Falling Water, then? I want to see Levit, and he should be back home by now."

Elledge cut a bit of tobacco from his twist and forced it into his pipe. "Miss Newcomb," he began, patiently, "like as not, you'd be as safe at the Falling Water as you'd be in Austin. May never see an Indian there again, leastways not in our lifetime. Even if we did, it's had raids before, in the old days, and it always came through. But Levit ain't back yet, or he'd have sent for you. There's only a couple of men up there since he left. That's not enough to hold the Falling Water when a woman's in the house. At least that's not enough these days. Down here, we can put up a dozen, maybe twenty riders if the savages come in. But we couldn't get to you there. And some of the varmints might be sneaking around. Just like when they got to that Schreiner boy."

"But you leave your own wife alone."

Elledge smiled at her. "Mrs. Elledge's been around here a long time," he said. "Reckon she knows more'n I do myself about Indian sign, and how to blast 'em if they show. You'll learn too, in time, Miss Karryl. Just have a little patience, and don't fret. Levit'll be back before long."

Mrs. Elledge understood Karryl's unrest more than her husband did, though, and she tried to turn the young woman's thoughts to other things. She showed her how to preserve butter by leaving out the salt and adding an ounce of honey to the pound, and once she said, "You've got to learn to do a lot of things for yourself out there on the Pedernales if you prosper, honey. So you mind what I'm saying and don't think about other things while you're doing it." She picked up a box. "This is soda," she said. "Or at least we call it soda. Haven't had a package of store-bought soda in the house for six years! We burn our corn cobs down to ash. Then we add a little boiling water and pour off the lye. Mix with vinegar and you've got soda."

The homesteader's wife picked at the pile of vegetables on the table. "Oh, I wish Levit would come back," Karryl murmured unhappily as she watched her. "I'm so worried for him."

"Don't you be. He'll look out for himself."

"But we've got so much to do," Karryl took another tack. "All those good things you have to eat here. We've nothing like that, and soon it will be too late to plant a garden."

"Well, you just send one of them cowboys up or down the river, then, and haul some in." Mrs. Elledge smiled. "I recollect in the early days, when I was like you," she said. "We was slow getting a garden started, too. But we just went back into the brush, and we never suffered none. Plenty in the woods to eat if you know what to eat, and sure your man knows. Things like careless weed and sour dock and parsley, growin' wild. There's poke, too, and a bush they call lamb's quarter. Wild vegetables, all of them."

Karryl walked across the kitchen to Mrs. Elledge and put her arms around her. "Thank you, anyway," she said, smiling warmly. "I'll try to remember. But I can't keep from worrying or wanting to be with Levit again."

"That's because you're still new out here. Wait'll you get a half-dozen little ones running around the place. Then you'll take life easier."

Karryl laughed now. She was embarrassed, but it was pleasant. Mrs. Elledge took a great pan of vegetable shavings from the table and stepped through the door. Karryl followed her toward the pig pens. They deposited the peelings and started back up the walk. Suddenly, Mrs. Elledge reached down and touched a stalk rising from the ground.

"This is the Spanish dagger," she said. "When it's mature, you break off the stems and boil a stewpan of 'em down into a salve. Best thing in the world for rubbing the bosom during pregnancy."

Unconsciously, Karryl raised her hands and pressed them upon her own strong breasts, and suddenly she was infused with new restlessness. She and Levit needed children, and they would have them.

The unchanging hours ran on and on. Karryl's unhappiness could hardly be contained. What could have happened to Levit?

[325]

Maybe he had been hurt. She apologized as best she could, but that did not relieve things. The Elledges refrained from scolding, but even Elledge said privately to his wife: "The Indians'll never be caught if they haven't been by now. Levit ought to be back home, like she says. Can't say I blame her for the way she feels."

In another section of the Texas frontier at a town called Salado, ranchers had met to talk of a new cattleman's association, a kind of a vigilante system, aimed at white rustlers. Prominent among the group was a man named Joe Garner. In other years, he had been called Salado Joe Garner.

As a result of the meeting, riders had been sent up and down the trails to enlist other supporters. Garner himself had headed toward the Guadalupe, by way of the Pedernales. Toward the close of the month he stopped early one morning at the Elledge homestead, unfolding the new scheme to the Elledges.

"Sounds good to me," Elledge applauded. "We've sure been needing an organization. But I wish Levit MacAshen was home to talk with you about it. He's the big man on this river."

"MacAshen? Could that be the MacAshen who fought with Forrest in the war?"

"Yep. Levit MacAshen."

"I'd like to talk to him, too, I soldiered under that Mac-Ashen, and I knew he lived down this way. You say he's gone?"

"Yeah, he's north somewhere, up around Fort Griffin. But wait a minute." Elledge called Karryl out of the cabin. "This here is Mr. Garner, young lady," he said. "Garner's a cattleman from the Salado. He soldiered with Levit." Elledge turned to his visitor. "Meet Miss Karryl Newcomb," he announced. "Her and him's plannin' to be married."

A surprised smile spread across Garner's face. "I'm real happy to meet you, miss. I campaigned under Colonel Mac-Ashen. All over Tennessee and Alabama, and part of Kentucky. Last time I saw him, he'd been wounded, though."

"He came through all right."

"There aren't many of us left out this way from that old outfit. I'd sure like to see MacAshen again."

Garner sat with them for dinner, and suddenly Karryl said: "The Falling Water is only a half-day's ride westward, Mr. Garner. Our foreman, Lubbock, is there. You could at least talk

[326]

with him. Do you think you might go that way? You could reach it before dark."

Garner reflected. "Well, maybe I ought to. I could cut across the Blanco country from there, and down the Comal to the Guadalupe."

"I'll ride back to the Falling Water with you, Mr. Garner, if you will."

Elledge came instantly to his feet. The smile upon his wife's face was replaced by a frown.

"You can't do that yet, miss," Elledge said. Garner looked inquiringly at his host. "You see, Garner, there was a raid a-while back up the river," Elledge explained. "Cowboy killed. That's why MacAshen is gone; he's off to the north hunting his stolen horses. They was fixin' for the wedding ceremony up there at the time. But there ain't many men around the Falling Water just now."

"There are three, Mr. Elledge," Karryl argued. "Lubbock, Pepito, and the sheepherder. The Falling Water is going to be my home, and I intend to be there when Levit returns."

"But he wouldn't want you to go back yet."

"Fiddlesticks! Mrs. Elledge wouldn't have left her home at all under the same circumstances. I don't believe there is any danger now, and I don't believe you do either. And even if there was, my place is there should Levit need me."

She rose before Elledge could even answer to that and went to her room. When she came out again, she had her things with her. Elledge protested, but it did no good. He finally threw up his hands. "Sure, I tried!" he lamented. He left the room and went to the corral to saddle her buckskin.

Garner said to Karryl, "You think you ought to, miss?"

"I ought to."

Elledge came back from the corral. "I wish you wouldn't go," he urged Karryl again. But she only said, "I've got to, Mr. Elledge,"

A little while later Garner and Karryl Newcomb rode off up the river.

Lubbock was north, in the Cave Creek bottoms, when Karryl returned. But Pepito was there. His flashing white smile greeted her.

"Has there been any trouble?" she asked.

"No trouble. All quiet."

"Isn't Mr. Lubbock here?"

"No, señorita."

"When will he return?"

"Soon. Tomorrow, maybe. But he not expecting you."

She turned to Garner. "I'm sorry if I've put you out," she said. "But I confess I was grasping at any opportunity. It's too bad Lubbock is gone."

"That's all right, miss. And if you're sure things are all right here, I think I'll go on to Fredericksburg instead of making it to the Guadalupe this time. I was hoping to visit with the Germans anyway."

"Levit will be so sorry he missed you, Mr. Garner."

"You tell the colonel I'll be back someday."

When the cattleman had gone on, Karryl summoned Pepito. "Go across the river, and up to the sheepherder's cabin," she instructed him. "See if all is well there, and let them know that I am back, if they need anything."

In Jacksboro, Levit gave up the search. "We've wasted our time here," he said, "and we might as well go back to the Pedernales."

"Haven't your men found anything at all?" Judge Comstock asked.

"No."

"Horse thieves are as bad as Indians, MacAshen, and north Texas is full of both."

"Well, we've sure got no help up here on either."

"State police have taken over in this part of Texas, my friend. Likely they're in league with the outlaws."

32

One of the rustlers fetched Devers from the saloon.

"Something out here you've been waiting to see," he said. His horse was still saddled and bridled, and he handed the reins to Devers. "Ride up the creek and around that knoll. Then up to the ledge where you had us watching. See for yourself."

It was a dark night, but Devers moved swiftly. He mounted the horse and spurred up the bank of the draw.

From the top of the knoll he could see the farther hills, north against the line of the Pedernales. His man had been right. There was a speck of light up on the hill. It was a far piece, and the glow was tiny in the distance, but it was unmistakable. He returned to the cluster of shacks.

"Where's Santiago?" he demanded.

"Asleep."

"Get him out."

He stalked into the saloon and poured himself another heavy drink. Then he went back outside to the sod verandah.

The half-breed came up, rubbing the sleep from his eyes.

"Get your horse, Santiago. And move out tonight. Head up the river and tell that second band of bucks we're ready. It's got to be quick. And tell them I'll see them in the usual place three weeks from tonight if I can make it. If I can't I'll send word to them."

There were six braves in the party: vicious, crafty and vividly painted. They caught Pepito as he stepped outside the door in the early dawn. One of the Redskins struck him from behind, burying the hatchet in the base of his skull. Pepito fell soundlessly. The Indian ran a quick, sharp knife around the scalp lock. Then he placed a foot on the Mexican's face and jerked the shock of hair. It came off clean, with the sound of a cork popping from a bottle.

Karryl realized immediately as she opened her eyes that she was not alone in her room. The hideous painted faces, the bare white-streaked copper-colored torsos were about her bed, two on either side. Through the open door, she glimpsed still others in the big room beyond.

Her first reaction was of violent anger, but the sinister glint in the eyes of the buck above her froze that emotion quickly. The Indian was pleased with himself. He had found other white women thus, back on the far ranches toward the Wichitas. One of the warriors by the foot of the bed spoke, his guttural voice denoting the knowledge of at least a few words of her own tongue.

"You come," he said, his arm violently indicating the door.

Karryl clutched wildly at the covers. The Indian above her reached down and in one sweep jerked them completely from the bed. Fear fastened upon Karryl, paralyzing her. She lay before them in the flimsy night dress, unable to move, afraid even to take her stare from the fiery eyes in the faces before her. The man reached down again toward her ankles, fastening his fingers in the hem of the night gown. Almost without effort, he tore it from her body, leaving her white and naked before the savages.

Karryl tried to scream, but no sound would come. This could not be happening; it was a wild, unbelievable dream, and in a moment she would awaken. Then the Indian's hands snaked forth again, grabbing her hair, brutally pulling her close to him. She thrust out frantically to force the warrior away. His putrid wild-animal smell nauseated her, and she struck out to break his hold upon her.

But then the brave at the foot of the bed came swiftly around. He grasped the painted warrior with whom Karryl was struggling and jerked him away. Then he pointed southward, and his sharp words diverted the other.

The chief's face was hard but it reflected intelligence. A long scar ran from above the left ear down across his cheek to the bridge of his nose. There was a bone ornament in his scalp lock and beads about his neck. He walked to the stand where Karryl had left her clothes the night before. He picked them up and threw them at her. Karryl grasped at the garments, covering her body from the savages before her.

On a peg of the farther wall there were coats. The Indian grabbed one, a leather coverall fringed with buckskin. There was a leather riding skirt there, too, split and sewn up the middle. He threw the garments to Karryl.

Outside the house, Karryl saw the body of the Mexican. She forced back a gushing sickness, the threatening light in her captors' eyes denying her even the privilege of tears. One of the braves brought the golden buckskin from the corral, bridled and blanketed, but unsaddled. The brave brought the saddle on his arm. The chief spoke a sharp word, and the Indian nearest Karryl shoved her toward the horse. She saddled him herself.

When she was astride, the scar-faced Indian turned again to the painted savage whom he had repelled. His eyes flicked quickly toward two more of the men, and he threw an arm to the southward. The painted warriors suddenly were gone, off across the river ford and in the direction of the southern wall.

When she saw the three savages riding down to her cabin in the early morning, Rhoda Hamlin knew that it was done. From the elevation before the cabin, she could see the distant cluster of horses west of the big ranch house. They had crossed the river, southward, and were swinging toward the barrier hills. They would pass above the sheepherder's cabin. She saw the Indian braves in the cavalcade, and she recognized that there was a white woman with them.

So that was it! That was Devers's way of dealing with people. Oh, he was smart, that Devers. He had a tie-in with the Redskins, and he'd used it. Karryl Newcomb, the intruder, was gone from the Pedernales. And MacAshen would be free.

The second line of Redskins came straight up to where she stood at the door. Hamlin was still on his bed in the corner, stupefied from the liquor she had urged on him. No doubt the Redskins carried a message for Rhoda from Devers. She would be glad to hear it, and glad when they were gone.

The Indians slid from their ponies. Rhoda's lack of concern seemed to surprise them, even to stop them for a moment. Then one of the braves pushed past her. Inside, the Indian's quick eye lighted on the sheepherder sprawled out on the bed. Rhoda looked at the savage questioningly. She did not like the expression in his eyes. Then she was afraid.

The Indian loosed his hatchet; in a terrifying instant, Rhoda saw him swing the weapon, burying it in her husband's face.

She staggered back against the doorway. God in Heaven! This was not the way it was to be! Rude hands seized her from behind, forcing her into the cabin. A warrior swung the door behind her. She pressed back against the wall.

This could not be right. They had mistaken the cabin. It was she who had sent for them, she and their friend Devers. Devers! If only he were here now. Devers would tell them!

The Indian's painted jowls curved down. How could she make him understand?

Make him understand? Something struck her wavering thoughts like a shaft of blue light.

Understand?

Suddenly, with horrible reality it all became clear. This was no mistake. Devers! The fiend! He would leave no tongues behind to speak. He had been after the Newcomb woman all the time, and he had used her, Rhoda Hamlin. She had been a fool. Her eyes darted frantically about. It was the instinct of the wild seeking an escape, but there was none.

Hands reached out to seize her again. They tore the garments from her quivering body. In desperation, she lunged wildly, writhing to break free. The mass of hair swept down across her face, and a hand threw it back possessively. She wrenched a thin, pleading cry from the depths of her aching lungs.

Suddenly, almost before she realized it, they had lashed her across her own rough table, the thongs cutting cruelly into her wrists and ankles.

Rhoda Hamlin knew now. Christ and all the Saints of Heaven! Would nothing save her? A red flush of terror encircled her eyes. She watched in horror as the thin, gleaming knife came slowly before her face. The Indian was taunting her. He reached down and touched its point to her skin. Again, she struggled, wrenching the thongs into her arms. The Indian said

[332]

no word, but a dull, brutish sound welled low in his throat. Then she felt it! The knife was biting slowly. Maddening pain came as the Indian sliced into her body. She screamed the wild, horrible scream of an animal in mortal agony.

A half-mile up the canyon, Karryl heard the scream, freezing in her saddle. The savages looked at one another. The leader grunted, and they passed swiftly on, along the southern rim toward the upper Blanco and beyond.

Lubbock rode slowly down from the north toward the Falling Water late in the afternoon. A faint drizzle was just beginning to fall as he reached the compound. Behind the far western hills, the clouds had been dark and heavy throughout the afternoon. There was a storm off there. He looked at the river. It had risen a bit. Likely, there would be a headrise, a rolling four-or-five-foot wall of dirty water sweeping down the valley as the aftermath of one of the cloudbursts in the distant ranges. But it would not reach the house itself. The spread of the valley to the south would care for the flow. Lubbock dismounted and unsaddled his horse, turning the animal into the feed lot. He took his pack and limped heavily toward the bunkhouse. Later, he moved forward to the big main building. It was always good to get home. Three or four days in the saddle hurt more than they used to.

He noted the hoof marks in the yard almost in the same moment that he stumbled over the Mexican's body. A shudder ran through him. Then he raced for the kitchen.

Inside, the house was silent. His eye took it all in quickly, the broken furniture, the scattered goods. A horrible thought struck him. He staggered across the big room and up the stairs toward Karryl's quarters.

"Jesus Christ!" he whispered. The signs were unmistakable; the torn night gown against the wall, the scattered bedclothes. She had come home! Lubbock lunged down into the big room, tearing open doors, plunging into corners and behind cupboards. He hurtled up the stairs again, his fingers clutching at door handles. A locked closet shattered under his great fist. But the Falling Water was empty. Lubbock staggered back into the yard. He knelt beside Pepito for a moment, and his eye caught the imprints of the moccasins in the damp earth. Pepito's body was cold, but he could not have been dead longer than early morning. Lubbock ran down before the house. He caught the tracks of the horses. Suddenly, his eye lifted again, and he stared toward the far grove that hid the sheepherder's cabin by the southern wall.

Lubbock resaddled his horse. When he had tightened the latigo, he leapt astride and headed for the ford. The water was higher; it was swifter, belly-deep, and his horse feared the stream, but Lubbock sank the spurs into the animal's flanks, forcing it on.

The front of the herder's cabin was shaded when he cut from the trail. Lubbock almost fell from his mount. He shoved the door inward. His eyes seemed to explode at the spectacle before him. He sagged against the wall, then turned out.

"God Almighty!" he breathed. He tried to reach his horse but could not. Instead, he clutched for support at the roof post and dropped down his head.

The river was full when Lubbock reached the bank. The headrise had come down. For hours it would be impassable, and the darkness was coming on. Up river some eight miles was a homesteader's cabin, a German farmer, on the south bank. Lubbock pushed his tired horse back up the slope and headed west through the groves. He knew the route well, but the horse was beaten. He could not travel fast.

A frenzied shout roused the farmer before Lubbock reached the cabin door. He staggered inside, where the settler was lighting a tallow wick. After a quick appraising look at Lubbock, the man reached beneath his bunk and pulled out a clay jug. A cup was on the table, and he poured a stiff drink. Lubbock seized the cup and drank. Then he whispered in low hard tones the news that he carried.

"You got a horse here?" he demanded.

"Ja!"

"One that can get me back to the lower canyon?"

"Ja!"

"Then change with me. You ride mine to Fredericksburg. He's almost done, but he'll carry you that far. Get the word to Biberstin. Tell him to do what he can. Then get another horse and go north. Find Lenneweber. Tell him I said Mac-Ashen is somewhere north of the Llano. I don't know where. But he'll be on the trails. Tell Lenneweber to send men up every trail. But find MacAshen. He's got to be told."

"That I will do."

Lubbock swallowed the rest of the whiskey. He turned toward the door. The man pulled on his pants and his boots.

"Down canyon you go?" asked the German.

"Yes. I've got to get to Elledge. Ain't no use to hope, but I've got to know for sure that it was her."

Dawn was slanting upward across the lower rim when Lubbock at last reached the Elledge home. The settler was already astir. "Karryl Newcomb here?" Lubbock asked tensely.

"No, man. She's gone home."

"You *let* her go back, Elledge?"

"God Almighty, Lubbock! I couldn't stop her. Why?"

"The Indians have got her."

A shudder wrenched Elledge. Suddenly he was old and helpless. He dropped to a bench as Lubbock glared down at him.

"Your best friend's woman, Elledge! He trusted you to keep watch over her. I ought to kill you. And sure, MacAshen will."

The homesteader's head sank further still. His body shook. "Reckon I wish you would, Lubbock."

"Where's your woman?" he queried.

"She's at the Ramsdalls'. Leastways, I hope to God she is."

His remorse penetrated Lubbock's fury. The latter stared down. Suddenly he struck his chaps with the leather glove in his hand. "All right, Elledge. Maybe I'm being a little hard on you." Lubbock walked away a step, then he came back. "I went off and left one alone once myself," he muttered, his voice softer now.

Elledge raised blank, sorrowing eyes. "MacAshen?" he asked helplessly.

"I sent him word by Lenneweber—if he gets it. You can go on down the canyon. Better make sure of your own women folk first. Then get north to Buck Barry at the Packsaddle. Reckon it's not any use now, but the Rangers there are the closest. You can give me another horse. And send somebody to bury those bodies."

Elledge rose heavily to his feet. He waited only long enough to obtain his rifle and his ammunition. "What about you?" he queried.

"I'm going west, up the Blanco. There won't be any trail now, but I'll do my best. Rained all night out there. You tell MacAshen or leave him word."

The Indians held to the wooded trails, but they did not tarry. All day they rode, halting only once for water. They took no food, and they gave Karryl none, although she couldn't have swallowed if they had. She had no idea of her route, once they had passed the rim of the Pedernales valley, except that they were pointing generally toward the west. In the dull haze, she knew when the sun had set and that she was miles from help now, the distance becoming greater with every stride of the golden buckskin. Then rains were upon them.

Late in the afternoon, the three absent braves soundlessly came up behind them. The scar-faced man heard their short, guttural words, then pushed on westward. Karryl, sick with horror, saw the full, billowing folds of a white woman's hair hanging from the painted warrior's belt. He had drawn the entire scalp from his victim. Her stomach retched.

In the darkness, they wound off against the broken limestone outcrops. Behind an almost indistinguishable shelf she discovered the mouth of a basalt cave. Apparently, the Indians were entirely familiar with the place, for they rode straight into the dark hole, shoving the buckskin forward with them. There was an area of white sand in the background. The Indians slid from their ponies. One of them reached up and pulled her to the ground. Two of the men gathered up the lines of their mustangs, and the reins from her own horse, and led them out toward a pool close by the mouth of the cavern. The scar-faced brave motioned for her to follow. He knelt beside the basin and drank. When she hesitated, he shoved her to her knees, and she submerged her face in the water.

The rain was heavier now, and they were quickly back within the cavern. The horses were tied near the wall nearest the entrance, and one of the Indians lay down across the opening. The scar-faced leader motioned her to a spot on the sand beyond him.

She tried to speak to him, pleadingly, but her voice brought a scowl to his face. He raised his hand and struck her across the mouth. Karryl tasted blood upon her tongue. She sank slowly to her knees, burying her head in her arms, her back to her captors. Tears blinded her, her muscles ached as though she had been beaten with stones, but she feared to show even an inkling of the terror that overwhelmed her. What was to become of her? Where were they taking her? For what horrible ritual had she been reserved?

Some time toward morning, the muscular distress of her body numbed the agony of her thoughts, and she slept. A rough hand awakened her in the first gray light of dawn. Almost before she could again convince herself that this was no horrible nightmare, they were astride the ponies and hurrying west.

Karryl lost track of time. The Indians made no effort to consider her. They rode fast, and forced her to maintain the pace. The vague aches of muscular exertion had become knife-sharp pains. Her skin wore from her limbs against the rough leather.

She had no thought now of the miles behind her; only of the excruciating miles still ahead. How far, how far? She dreaded the night time, for then fresh terror came upon her.

Ultimately, they were high upon the plateaus where there were no signs of life except the occasional buffalo herds in the distance. Abruptly they came upon a gorge, almost invisible to the eye from the distance of a mile away. It was a deep gorge, perhaps a thousand feet from the summit of the wall to the floor. The red abutments stood stark and foreboding, and the cedars upon the ledges were dwarfed and misshapen. But there was the glint of sun upon water along the canyon floor, and even Karryl's inexperienced eye could pick out the deer, flitting from clump to clump in the groves. The savages rode swiftly and surely. The grades were steep, but the ponies showed no hesitancy, not even the buckskin. When they reached the canyon floor, they turned west with its course again. The direction was not maintained for long, however; a short distance up the main gorge, they cut into a narrow opening that marked the entry of another waterway. They followed the new winding course perhaps a half-dozen miles, avoiding additional inlet canyons, while the contour rose moderately and the walls narrowed. At sunset, they turned into a broken jumble partially blocking another valley. Beyond the rocks, Karryl could see a green meadow speared by a tumbling rivulet. Along the waters was a cluster of gray *tipis*.

33

A man rode to Devers's stand on the Blanco. "Where's Devers?"
he demanded.

Sudderth leisurely detached himself from the idlers. He
looked over the new arrival with interest. "You got business
with him?"

"What do you think I rode clear up to this God-forsaken hole
for?" the man asked, striding up the step.

Sudderth studied the newcomer carefully, but he inclined his
head finally toward a shack at the rear. The man turned quickly.
Devers opened the door to his pounding and the stranger stepped
inside the cabin.

"What're you doing here?" Devers demanded. His gear and
other objects were scattered about as though he was ready to
move out of the place.

"I've got word for you, Devers. There's a job to be done."

"What kind of a job?"

The man took off his hat and wiped his brow with his coat
sleeve. Then he sat down in the single chair at the table. "Get
us a drink first."

Devers brought out a bottle. He set two glasses on the table
and filled them. The man raised his drink and tossed it off.

"Political, Devers, political," he answered finally. "We're

running into trouble. There's a job cut out for every man on the roll. The elections will be tough to handle this time, and we're starting now. The governor will put on special police, twenty to a county. Most of them will be from among our black brethren."

"That sounds about right for the governor."

"It's no laughing matter, Devers. This fellow Ashbel Smith is going up and down the state, speaking out for the Democrats and condemning Edmund Davis in every department he can think up. Pease and Hamilton are doing the same among the Republicans. They're making a play on the words 'high crimes and treason'—using them against the governor, of course."

"They can't hurt Davis."

"No. But they can turn out the legislature. And a Democratic legislature would throw out all but the governor. Him, too, if they could manage it."

"Well, where do I come in?"

"All over the state they'll be holding meetings. They'll be campaigning early for more whites to register as voters. Hamilton and his moderates are backing the Democratic ticket."

"You haven't said where I come in."

"You're going down in the river bottoms and get together with the Negroes. Break up mass meetings. Get ready to organize county police details."

"When do I do all this?"

"Right now, Devers. Why do you think I'm breakin' my back and bruising my butt riding over these damned mesquite brakes? Looks like you're already packed up for it, anyway."

Devers strode to the table and filled his glass again. His visitor followed suit.

"That's the story, Devers, and I'm going on to San Antonio. You can check in with the adjutant general."

"Look here. I've got business away out west of here right now, out past the headwaters of the San Saba. And it's business I was told to handle."

The man jammed his hat down on his sweaty forehead. "You've got business in Austin, Devers! Nothing comes ahead of that. No later than day after tomorrow morning. And after that, down in the river bottoms. And you'd better not be missing!" He turned deliberately and went out the door. At the rail he untied his reins, then rode swiftly up the river.

Devers watched him disappear. He went back into his quarters and threw his glass savagely against the wall. He jerked the bottle from the table and tilted it above his lips. Christ! Everything was still going wrong. Should he ignore the peremptory summons? He was planning to quit the white man's world anyway. Should he just tell the rest of them to go to hell?

No. Already they had too much on him. Too easy to direct attention his way, even in the case of Karryl Newcomb. They'd even help to hunt him down, just to protect themselves. "Santiago," he yelled. "Come in here."

When the half-breed arrived, Devers spoke sharply. The man nodded in understanding. "And tell that Redskin to hold the woman till he hears from me. It may be weeks, even months. But sooner or later, I'll send him word," Devers finished.

Santiago hurried away.

Colonel Ranald Slidell Mackenzie, as an unexpected assist from the Union Army command, drove the Comanches northwestward briefly toward the Canyon Blanco in those days. The canyon of that name was not related to the river below the Pedernales; it lay far to the west, among the red rock draws of the high plains country.

Appearing suddenly from out of the Mexican border regions, he marched his patrols from the site of old Camp Cooper, near Fort Griffin, toward the Llano Estacado. Some of the villages of White Eagle, the Quohada, and Mow-way, the Kotchateka, were scattered along McClelland Creek and the north fork of the Red River. The soldiers came upon one of the camps and destroyed its tipis, but its occupants fled before the troops could overtake the Indian band itself. The Quohadas faded back into the rolling prairies, leaving their empty lodges behind them.

Mackenzie kept on. Eventually he bore down on a vast encampment, two hundred and sixty-two more lodges. His troopers rode roughshod over the place, killing more than a score of warriors.

But again, the principal force of the band evaporated into the haze, and when Mackenzie had finished the short-lived campaign, the Quohadas were still wild within their canyons. The Indians had been scattered as a swarm of bees, and they seethed, waiting to plunge their stingers into the white men who had disturbed them.

At no hour in her history has Texas had more reason to be thankful for the Ranger tradition than in the year of 1872. As Mackenzie retired south to his Rio Grande outposts, the protection of the prairie settlements was left at least theoretically to one man alone, Edmund Davis. But that was no protection at all, for even had Davis been inclined to try to quell the bloody maraudings, he had something nearer home to worry about.

State elections were under way again, and although Davis himself still had two years in office, everybody else was up for re-election. Actually, the balloting had been delayed illegally a full year so that the carpetbag legislature could stay on in power, but now an election had been forced on Davis by his own Republican party.

Even subterfuge was abandoned. At Houston, the secretary of state struck two hundred and fifty white men's names off the rolls. He put twenty-four hundred new Negroes on the registry list. The ballot boxes from five of the largest counties were thrown out, and in one congressional race, even before the votes were counted, the governor announced the election of a friend despite the man's clear defeat.

Rumors that the Texas Rangers again had secretly banded—a force that could erupt into the open to destroy the carpet-baggers—discouraged more overt acts.

What the radicals did not know was when or where such an assault might take place. Nor did they know who would now head up the hidden Ranger bands. Levit MacAshen had been taken care of, temporarily at least. But could he be depended on to stay out of it? Nobody knew, for nobody knew where MacAshen was now, or when he might show up again.

Only the low, continuous hum of the insects and the clatter of the iron horseshoes on the shale broke the silence as a trio of horsemen rode north again on the trail. MacAshen glanced over his shoulder at Steve Meadows and Torkin close behind. They were all who were left now; gradually the others had been sent away. It did not matter, Levit conceded dully. They could not help, even though they had tried to, for there was nothing to require their help.

It was, indeed, long since anyone had heard of him. The heat of summer had passed, then autumn's cool days, and now winter was at hand again.

The crushing, paralyzing message which had reached Mac-Ashen through Lenneweber's courier in the hours after Karryl's abduction had long since torn MacAshen from every other concern.

"God in Heaven, no!" he gasped when the German youth haltingly delivered the frightful story to him on the trail. He seized the boy in a clasp of iron, almost crushing him as he tried to force an admission that all this was somehow false.

But the truth was inescapable and when at last he acknowledged that, he chilled inside. Meadows sprang to his side, fearful that MacAshen's mind would snap. He seized Levit by the arm, only to have his grasp shaken off as though it were the grip of a child.

Meadows and Torkin turned back to the German messenger, extracted the tormenting details one by one over again. Then quickly they had jolted MacAshen into a cognizance of the urgency.

"We've got a long way to go yet, boss."

MacAshen sprang into the saddle, not waiting for the others. The waddy had run southward toward the Falling Water, driving their exhausted horses at a killing gait—halting only when they had to rest their mounts—and charging blindly on when they could run again.

Yes, all that had been long ago. What had they done to her? Where had they taken her? MacAshen's mind had almost snapped on a thousand occasions when he thought of the horrors to which she had probably been subjected.

Lenneweber, Barry, Biberstin—there had been many of them at his compound when he came back to the Falling Water that day; men showing their understanding and sympathy, men silently waiting to do anything they could to help. They, too, had tried, even before MacAshen had reached home, but there was little they could do, for the Indians had left no trail.

Lubbock, who had scoured the upper Blanco basin and arrived back at the Falling Water before Levit's return, had restrained Levit's first violent efforts.

"You can't run off hell-bent for just anywhere, Levit," he cautioned. "You don't know where to go, and even if you did, you couldn't hit at the Comanches without every Ranger on the frontier. And you know you're blocked from calling them up all at once for that. With what you'd have just from here, you couldn't tackle a whole outfit of Indians. They'd kill her the minute you showed your hand; and they'd kill you, too. You've got to plan it, Levit; cover the land. If it was bucks out of the north, chances are someday you'll find her—then maybe they'll talk ransom."

"And if it was the Kickapoos, or the Lipans, out of the south?"

Lubbock averted his eyes momentarily, but then he came back. "You got to always figure she's still alive, Levit."

It had been weeks, months, then seasons without a hint of Karryl's whereabouts. Levit MacAshen did not even resemble the same man. His eyes were stark and haunted; his flesh pallid. The hair on his face hid the long chin and the high cheekbones. His clothes, his gear—worn and tattered—bore the imprint of thorny trails that had no end. He was on one of those trails now, and he swung his horse around a heavy nipple cactus.

Far up ahead lay Fort Griffin. Why was he here? The answer to that question seemed less than inconsequential to MacAshen. They said they needed him, but who could be stupid enough to think he might still have an interest in anything they might have had to talk about?

Important people were gathering at Fort Griffin, but he was not concerned with them. Answering with his presence was the most he had been able to accord their call. But while in Fort Griffin, he might find men from the far reaches who had heard of another captive white woman on the prairies. And so he had come.

A smoke haze hung on the far hills, past California Creek, but the creek itself was beyond the canyon of the Clear Fork. The trio held to the upper levels, glad that the flat, monotonous terrain lay behind them. A prairie dog village profiled the last of the bare expanse. They were close now to the woodlands again, and as they progressed the evidence of the wild life increased. The path rose higher, and the cool, pungent fragrance of the winter cedars came to them.

Presently, the great promontory lay ahead, and the military flagstaff marking the site of the old army post speared the sky above it. But there was no banner upon the staff; Levit did not know whether any soldiers were at Fort Griffin or not. They passed around the hill, and the bustling depot of the buffalo hunters appeared on the levels below.

"We may be early," Meadows remarked.

"We can rest here a while anyway." Almost plaintively, Levit added: "Maybe we'll hear something at last here in Fort Griffin."

Steve averted his eyes. He had almost given up such hope.

34

Far to the west, in the canyon where the savages could hide their tipis, Karryl Newcomb was still learning what people meant when they spoke in hushed whispers of the captive whites among the Redskins. And she had had months in which to perfect that knowledge. She was not the only captive of the band, but the others were Mexicans; there were no whites other than herself. Two of these unhappy sufferers were children—a boy of six and a girl of ten. The other was a pretty young Mexican woman. Karryl was never allowed to speak to the other captives; the one time she tried, her master had used his leather whip on her back. The little boy was driven naked about the camp and forced to herd horses in the rain and in the nights when the wind sharpened. Finally she did not see him again, and she concluded unhappily that they had let the child die somewhere in the pastures up the canyon.

The little girl was no more fortunate in her treatment; she was beaten and abused constantly and forced to grovel with the dogs for her food. Karryl had heard the Mexican woman scream out sometimes in the night, but there was no one to aid her.

Karryl was not spared the toil of the Indian squaw. Because she knew the ways of white women, the wives of the warrior required her to look to the sewing their lord and master needed, and to every other menial task at their disposal. She made shirts from the stolen dresses of her own wardrobe; cloaks from other garments they had gotten elsewhere.

The punishment she suffered from the women during her labors made the tasks no easier. The young squaws were worse, and there had been moments when she despaired of her life. But the scar-faced warrior had protected her. He was not kind; he had no feeling for her suffering. But in a sense he protected her, at least from the other braves.

There was plenty of food. A bread, called *peloncia*, was made from pods of the locust tree. It was like sawdust, but the pods had a bit of sweetness and helped to relieve the more repulsive concoctions. Another variety of bread was made from mesquite-berry meal, mashed to bits, and fashioned into tortillas, then baked on hot coals.

Terrapins were roasted alive, the Comanches breaking open the shell to eat the meat. Frequently, they drank the blood of larger freshly killed animals.

Her sufferings at least in part were alleviated one day when, having reached the limits of endurance, she seized a stave from the floor and struck the youngest of her female tormentors across the face with it. Whirling quickly, she crashed the weapon down upon the head of the second squaw, breaking the wood and driving the Indian, screaming, to her knees.

The scar-faced warrior leaped to his feet and strode between his squaws and Karryl, but she thought she noted an expression of satisfaction on his face. A torrent of guttural abuse rushed from his lips, and the squaws fell back. From that day, they stopped persecuting her, though she was still expected to perform her full share of the *tipi* chores.

One of the older squaws had lived for a time at the agency and could converse in the white man's tongue. On rare occasions she showed a rough tolerance of Karryl. From her, Karryl learned that all captives were persecuted as she had been until they showed their courage or died under the treatment. The woman disclosed that this was only a splinter band; the main tribe lived elsewhere. But Karryl learned, too, that the village chief who held her captive spoke words of both English and Spanish, although he never addressed her in these tongues, and he would not reply when she spoke pleadingly to him.

As the months wore on, Karryl could not help but learn

some of the Indians' ways of life. When the clothes she had worn on the long trek westward finally were in complete tatters, revealing her nakedness beneath, the scar-faced warrior spoke to one of his women, and the squaw ungrudgingly produced a single garment of soft deerskin. Karryl accepted it quickly, attempting to express her gratitude with her eyes, but the brave paid no heed, and the Indian woman went calmly on with her duties.

There was no restraint in the gift. When accepted as one of the tipi residents, Karryl recognized she was entitled to share with the others in all their possessions. In some confusion, she learned that the squaws also looked upon the warrior-husband as community property. She hoped and prayed that they would not insist on extending this particular portion of their unselfishness to her as well. But she supposed even that must happen in time, for why, otherwise, would the Indian chief be holding her here in his *tipi*?

They were a cleanly people, bathing at all seasons of the year in the cold water of the stream, both men and women without adornment. Required to follow their custom, Karryl, despite earlier abuses, suffered no ill effects. She became brown, and even stronger in her carriage. The men of the village had no compunction about coming close to watch her at her chores, or even as she bathed with the other squaws in the stream. But they did not intrude upon the scar-faced man's rights of priority, which seemed to include Karryl Newcomb.

Karryl slowly steeled herself to her fate, surely. But she had not abandoned hope.

The bivouac to which Levit finally made his way after leaving Meadows and Torkin at the hotel, was sprawled about the levels of a shallow depression on the eastern edge of the town at Fort Griffin. The message sent earlier to MacAshen had said the outfit encamped at Griffin would be headed by a man named Roberts, who did meet him. "We had you spotted up the valley," Roberts said. "You came the hard way."

"Yes. I don't stick to the roads anymore."

"I know."

MacAshen ran his eye over the men around. These had been his men, but he had almost forgotten what they looked like. There was none of the usual rowdiness, the devil-may-care abandon of the cowboy to mark them. Their bronzed faces foretold an exposure to the open lands for many a season. They slouched about the camp, but their attitude of indifference was deceiving.

"We've been in the saddle for months," Roberts said. Levit nodded.

On the far side of the camp were the canvas shelters of others who had come here, too. Ives from the San Gabriel, Buck Barry, Biberstin; a dozen more, even Comstock from Jacksboro.

Lenneweber was there. The big German rancher gripped Levit's hand. Beside Lenneweber was Hamilton, who had been governor of the state; and a man of whom Levit had once heard much, Ashbel Smith. Comstock was squatting on his heels, back to a pecan tree. He, too, rose to extend a hand. "Our last meeting was a happier one, MacAshen," the Jacksboro attorney said.

"Yes."

"We're glad you came. Not much can be important to you now, but we had to find out direct on whether you're still one of us."

Levit did not answer. He sank down on a log at the edge of the circle.

"Most of us received your messages about your lady, Mac-Ashen," Comstock continued quietly. "We've done what we could. We've sent your ransom offers to every band up this way we could get any trace of. Tell me," he queried, "in all these months, have you had no word at all?"

MacAshen shook his head.

"Not a glimmer of hope? Not even a rumor of her whereabouts?"

MacAshen was stoney. Lenneweber's hand pressed upon Levit's shoulder. Much had already happened in the pow-wow at Fort Griffin before MacAshen's arrival. He had not realized he was so late. Why they had come, and why they had urged him to be here, too, Lenneweber now told him quickly.

"What yet is to happen, we do not know," the German declared. "But we are determined that the thieves and murderers shackling our government must be disposed of. Whether this can be accomplished through honest balloting we cannot say. But if not, then we will take other steps.

"Almost under martial law has this election been held," the

German went on. "And for shame must I say all this has happened under our old Republican party of which I have been a member. The police have everywhere been as brutal as they could. The vote polls have been guarded by bad ex-slaves and bad whites. Honest people, Democrat or Republican, they are intimidated everywhere. All up and down the river valleys," he continued, "we hear that this man Devers has been the cause of much trouble. He was in on the killings in Nacogdoches and Tyler, and in other places, but his name never shows in the newspapers. Some of us here know Devers pretty well. He rustled your cattle, MacAshen. He is rustling cattle in central Texas even while he wears the badge of the state police."

Ashbel Smith broke in: "Devers is just one man. Why, hell, Lenneweber, more than two-thirds of the present state police force—men like Devers—have been in prison, or are under indictment right now."

"I know all that," MacAshen said, "but what is it you want of me?"

"Well, the reason why we were so urgent in the message we got to you is that these men we call our Rangers must now move, MacAshen," Lenneweber said. "If the carpetbaggers steal this election, then they must be destroyed. If they claim a victory at the ballot box, then we must overwhelm them in the capital itself."

MacAshen gazed into the German's face. He rose and moved away a step or two. Of course they would send for him in an hour like this. Of course they would now expect him to fulfill the job he had accepted back there at the start. But his thoughts were not on politics, nor on any of the other violent efforts these men envisioned. His mind was on the lone prairie oases west of here where Redskins might encamp. He might find men down in the town who would carry word to distant bands, new offers of ransom, of anything he had; and perhaps he might learn from someone of a white woman captive in some distant place.

He came back to the circle. "If you mean you want me to come back to lead that movement, I'm sorry, Herr Lenneweber—and all of you," he muttered slowly. "But it's out of the question. I've got something else to do now. It's not just a case of walking out. If I took on the responsibility again, it wouldn't be fair to the men themselves, much less to you and the other people. I suspect you all can realize that, though I know you still had to get the word from me, myself. I wish I could answer you differently, but there is no other answer. You may not sympathize with the way I feel, but that's the only way I can put it."

At that moment a man whom MacAshen did not know rose on the edge of the circle. "My name is Laurie Tatum, Mac-Ashen," he said. "I'm an Indian agent from the reservations up north of the Red. Comstock asked me to come here today and fill the people who were getting together here in on some things. I'll make it short.

"The braves have been disappearing every day lately from the reservations. They've gone back into that four hundred miles of hideaway west of here on the Clear Fork. We believe that somewhere out there the Comanches are gathering again, for something big. But there's more to it than that. Rumors up on the reservations have it that white men—outlaws—are tied in with the Comanches, especially the Quohadas. The savages think they can do in these settlements in Texas once and for all, if they can get just a little more assurance from some of the white renegades. When they'll try, nobody knows for sure, but it'll be damned soon. When they do, it will be more than disposing of carpetbaggers, for some of the carpetbaggers themselves no doubt are mixed up in whatever is going on. Does it make the proposition any more important to you, MacAshen to know that people all up and down the frontier—including your own cowboy bands, are mobilizing to meet this assault?"

Levit gazed somberly at the man. "No," he responded at last. "It would have once, but not now."

"How long will you be in Griffin, MacAshen?"

"I don't know yet."

"I'd like to talk further with you before you go. Where'll you be when you leave here?"

"At the hotel in town, I guess." MacAshen turned back to Lenneweber. "Again, I'd like to say I'm sorry," he said, "but this is the way it is."

The latter nodded. "We'll hope that you change your mind," Lenneweber said. "And when you do, you know where we will be."

MacAshen left the Ranger camp and moved on into the town to rejoin Meadows and Torkin. When he stepped through the door of the little hotel at Fort Griffin, the first man he met was Fall. Meadows was behind the old plainsman, pushing him forward. "Look what I found, Levit," his ranger announced, a grin on his face.

"Fall!" Levit seized the old man's arm.

"Figured I'd find you here, Levit. Leastways, I hoped so, when I heard about what was going on."

"What are you doing in Fort Griffin?"

"Buff hunting now, Levit, like I told you back there on the Pedernales."

"You don't know how good it is to see you." He lowered his head for an instant. "I guess you heard about what happened to Karryl? Most of the frontier has."

"I heard, Levit."

Fall did not offer condolences, but his voice was grim and his eyes dark with pity for his friend. MacAshen straightened unconsciously before the old man in an effort to put his troubles behind him for the moment.

Then he felt a hand on his arm and turned. It was the Indian agent, Laurie Tatum, who had ridden into the town from the Ranger camp directly behind him.

"I thought I'd come right on, MacAshen," he said. "I'm leaving Griffin after a while, too, but I wanted especially to talk with you."

"I was about to buy a drink for my friends," Levit answered. He introduced Fall and Meadows. "If you want to talk to me, come on in with us." He motioned to a table in the corner.

"I don't know if you've ever heard of me before today, Mac-Ashen," the agent began.

"I've heard of you."

"Some time ago, I saw some of the letters, the messages, you sent up among the reservation people. Many frontiersmen saw them." Tatum appeared to hesitate for a moment. "I'd have done whatever I could anyway, MacAshen. We've managed to get back many captives. But most of them have been children. Not many white women. It's usually too—" Tatum halted.

"Get it out, Tatum." MacAshen wished the man would speak whatever he had to say and be gone.

"I don't want to suggest I've got any good news, sir. But there is something else. I got your word through to many of the bands. By way of the Wichita tribes I even reached the

Quohadas. And I got an answer back."

Levit jerked forward. "You—what?"

"I got an answer back, MacAshen, an answer from the Eagle himself, White Eagle. He's the Bull Bear now of the Antelope band."

MacAshen's hand clamped on the Indian agent's arm. "What kind of an answer, Tatum?"

"He sent this word, MacAshen: he said to tell you he would meet you and kill you personally someday. Somehow he looks on you as the war chief of the Taibos, the Texans, who are driving the Comanches out. I guess that's because you live where you do, down there on the Pedernales. But there was a curious twist to his reply. He said to tell you he did not kill your woman, nor was she a slave of his. But the thing that was strange to me was that he did not deny knowing of her."

"What's strange about that, Tatum?"

"Well, for one thing, because the answer was from Quee-Nigh-Tosav himself."

"White Eagle! I've heard of him," MacAshen snapped. "I wouldn't believe him, damn his soul, about anything he said, even if he was speaking from the cross!"

"I've always believed him, MacAshen."

"Maybe you have."

Fall laid a hand on his friend's arm. "Easy, son," he counseled.

The agent frowned. "I'll say what I have to say and go, Mac-Ashen. I know a lot about these tribes; the way they live, what keeps them going. And from that very association with them, something mighty different has stood out about your special troubles, at least to me."

"Like what?"

"In all the months since that lady was spirited away, we've never heard a single rumor of her up on the reservations. That's what's unusual, MacAshen. We may not be able to save them, but we almost always hear, at least vaguely, of every captive, even those they won't sell back. You can be sure we tried. And yet, in all those months there was not a single clue or hint, until this odd reply from White Eagle. If he'd been wanting to deny he knew anything about her, he'd just have said that."

"Go on, Tatum."

"I don't believe it's the Indians you've got to worry about,

[352]

MacAshen. Or at least, I don't think they're holding the woman for their own purposes like they usually do. I know White Eagle's not. If he was, he'd simply have said he was. You're wrong about him. He may be a bloodthirsty enemy when he's picked you out for a target, but he does not lie. There may have been Indians in it, there may even be now—and even some of the White Eagle's Quohadas, too—but if there are, they've had a reason for keeping quiet, and not because of him."

Levit gripped the rim of the table. "What are you driving at?"

"Figure it out for yourself, MacAshen. I don't want to raise any false hopes, but maybe you've been following the wrong trail. If there were Indians in on this, maybe they've only been doing the leg work for somebody else. That's the only thing I've been able to make of it. Why not take a look elsewhere, at the people right around you, perhaps? Oh, I know you can't expect much help from the authorities—your own state police—while they ride under renegades like that man Devers. Why, hell, man! It's common knowledge up where I live that he's part Quohada, too. And he's got some kind of a strange pull even on old Parro-o-coom, as well. Not on White Eagle—he hates Devers—but on Parro-o-coom, himself. An odd one, that Devers, for a governor to commission to his police force in Texas—and the German said he'd even rustled your cattle. But though you may not be able to get any help from your authorities, you haven't made much headway in the other direction, either, and you may want to think on it."

Fall, rigidly staring at the speaker from beside MacAshen, clawed across the table to seize Tatum's arm. "Devers?" he bit out.

"Why, yes," Tatum responded in surprise. Fall whirled upon Levit.

"Devers rustled your cattle?"

"Yes."

"And he's one of Davis's state police scalawags, now?"

"Yes."

"Where'd you say he rustled them cattle, Levit?"

"Why, off the Pedernales, and down into the Blanco basin."

"Did you ever cross him, Levit?"

"I guess you could call it that. I knocked him down in front of his own men and offered to kill him."

The perspiration broke out upon Fall's face. "And Devers

[353]

has been livin' in there, behind the Pedernales?''

"I suppose he has. At least he was then."

Fall's voice was almost a whisper now, but it cut through the smoke-filled air. "Levit, did you ever tell Karryl about your trouble with Devers?"

"I don't know, I don't recall. But I don't think so. Why all the questions, Fall?"

"Did she ever speak his name to you?"

"Why, no. Not that I remember."

"I guess she wouldn't, God spare her soul. She'd a' knowed you'd kill him then, sure."

"What do you mean?"

"Levit, it was Devers who drove Karryl Newcomb to leave Houston. I know. I brought her up to Austin. He had something on her she was trying to get away from, something long ago. Something that don't even amount to much anymore now, but she didn't know that. An' I didn't either till just lately. Devers tried to pick her up first in Louisiana, then in Houston. He found her again in Austin, and he was hauntin' her there. And now you say he went up in the Blanco, Mac-Ashen. Well, Tatum here says Devers is part Quohada himself, too. Put it together, MacAshen. He was after her all the time, and sure as God he got her!"

Levit lunged to his feet.

"Figured if she ever wanted to let you know about Devers, and what was between the two of them, she'd be the one to do it," the old man whispered huskily.

Levit kicked the chair backward. He rushed blindly toward the door with Meadows close behind.

Lubbock stoked a tiny fire on the banks of Cibolo Creek. He moved the stones closer together and set the skillet on them. While he did so, the wrangler Nusser went to the stream to fill the coffee pot with water.

Lubbock worked methodically, for he had learned that that was the only way he could keep going. And somebody had to keep going, just to keep the Falling Water alive—if it stayed alive—until MacAshen came back, whenever that might be.

Possum Wear, Margaret Wayne's cowhand from the Guadalupe, saw the campfire from the ridge above. "Let's go down," he proposed to the other rider with him.

[354]

Lubbock stood up from his stooped position when he heard the crunch of hoofs on the graveled slope. Nusser moved alertly to his side.

"Howdy," Wear called out, raising a hand. Lubbock nodded, watching the newcomers slowly dismount. "Wayne waddies. From down the Guadalupe, below San Marcos Springs."

Lubbock nodded again. "You're a long ways up, son. What're you doing here?"

"Hunting the brands. They're drifting these days. Where you fellows from?"

"Falling Water, on the Pedernales."

"The MacAshen spread, eh? You're fifty miles from home, yourself."

"That's right. You punchers want to bed down for the night?"

"Was aimin' to. Been back in the brakes. But we saw the water."

"All right, throw your saddles. I'll put on some more bacon and you can set in for chow."

It was dark quickly. The rough meal disposed of, all hands turned immediately to sprawl upon their blankets. Lubbock studied the Guadalupe riders carefully as they went about their camp chores. The second of the two, a slim, silent, black-haired youth kept strangely to himself, but Lubbock thought nothing of it. Doubtless, the Guadalupe cowhands had heard, as everyone had, the story of the abduction from the Falling Water, and they were unlikely to raise the subject with men who would show the marks.

Dawn arrived finally and all were in the saddle again. Lubbock and Nusser turned east with the two Wayne men.

"Started a few head of our own back east yesterday," Lubbock commented. "With the four of us now, if a sizable bunch shows, we'll have enough hands to brand some stock, if you want to help. We can head back toward the Guadalupe then and you can turn down it."

"We'll stay with you till we hit the river," Wear agreed.

Nusser saw the strange horses first. He was a few lengths ahead as he and the others came to a corner in the bench. The horses were beyond the next low mesa, tied with stake ropes, and blankets were on their backs. Gaudy blankets. He whirled quickly back.

"Savages," he whispered. He slid from his horse, and the others followed. Nusser handed his reins to Wear. "Get out of sight behind the ledge," he whispered again.

Quickly then Nusser inched forward on his stomach. The Indians, if they were Indians, were backed against the slope of the abrupt mesa on the side away from Nusser. From where he had come around the ledge their horses were visible, but they themselves were out of sight, and the cowboys out of sight to them. Suddenly, Nusser called out, low. "Lubbock!" The foreman crawled hastily toward him, and the German leveled a hand in the direction of the horses. "You see anything?" he asked. Lubbock stared down at the tethered mounts. Three of them were blanketed. A fourth was saddled. And the fifth, a golden steed, grazed freely.

"Gawd almighty! The golden buckskin!" Lubbock choked. He made as if to rise and lunge forward. Nusser clutched his shoulder.

"Steady," he cautioned. "Get back behind the ledge." His grip stopped the older man. Lubbock dug the soil beneath his fingers. But slowly he backed his way behind the projection.

"Listen," he threw out toward the Wayne cowhands when Nusser returned. "There are four, maybe five Redskins behind that near rise. We'll leave the horses here and belly over the slope. We'll hit them from above, when we can see them." He halted for a second and looked the black-haired man over carefully. "You ain't packin' a gun," he exclaimed.

"No. But there's a carbine on the saddle, and I'll get it."

They led their mounts back a few rods and secured them. Then quickly Lubbock snaked his way up over the ledge they had skirted and into the defile below. It was a hundred yards to the slope of the mesa before him and he ran fast, the others close behind and coming silently, too. Their boots made no sound on the thick grass. They ascended quickly, Lubbock still ahead but moving slowly when they were just below the summit. He dropped to his stomach again.

There were three of the Indians in the glen. A fourth man, a swarthy half-breed, squatted nearby. They had killed a calf and gorged themselves. Now they were sprawled back against the first gentle rise, resting or sleeping.

Lubbock moved his hand ever so slightly, and his three companions eased to his side. The Indians were directly below, perhaps a hundred feet, facing away from the crest. The half-breed was farther on.

"Quohadas," Nusser whispered in his ear.

Lubbock pushed slowly to his knees. Suddenly he leaped in the air.

"Indian!" he screamed.

The crash of the exploding guns—his own and those of the others around him— drowned out whatever words might have followed.

Two of the savages fell, even as they catapulted outward. The third made the stream, but the lanky Wayne rider struck him there. The half-breed, stricken motionless for a second, now darted inward toward the jumble of rock behind him. Lubbock's pistol blasted again, the slug apparently striking the fugitive in the leg, for he stumbled as he dived for the recess.

The white men were down the rise in chopping strides. The nearer Indian was dead, and the one in the stream was face down in the water. Wear kicked the other over on his back. A gaping hole showed in the man's chest.

"Leave him to me," Lubbock shouted. "Wear, you pin that breed down in the rocks. But watch out for him!" Wear sprinted along the ravine, taking cover himself as he neared the broken area.

Lubbock whirled back to the dying Comanche on the ground before him, whose eyes were open. He could not move, but his glaring eyes passed across the faces of the white men above him.

Lubbock realized that Karryl Newcomb had not been here. He reached down and gripped the Comanche's face at the cheeks in his great hand. He jerked the savage half upright and thrust him back against the rise. His pistol was in the Redskin's face now, and the eyes were staring into his. He sighted down the barrel of the revolver, and suddenly the features beyond the steel awoke a staggering memory. The massive cheek bones! The scar that ran from the ear down across the copper face to the bridge of the nose! The bone whistle in the Comanche's hair. The beaded necklace! He had held this face in his gunsight's once before! Long ago.

In a ferment of recollection, he saw again the broken mesa far out beyond the headwaters of the Wichita . . . the Indian who scampered across the shaggy backs of the buffaloes, seeking sanctuary in the rocks below, finding it, then turning to see Lubbock's weapon in his face. The same savage!

The expression in the man's eyes! He, too, remembered. The Comanche's lips twisted in a low, sobbing wail. But Lubbock knew the recognition was there, and the remembrance.

Lubbock twisted his head over his shoulder. He thrust an arm toward the golden buckskin, leaping at its stake rope. "White woman?" he breathed.

For a slowly building moment even the pain could not erase the surprise and—as the blood began to drip from the Comanche's mouth—a gradual rise of understanding. The Indian stared at Lubbock. He understood. He dragged an inch upward on an elbow. "White woman?" he whispered. "*Your* white woman?"

"Yes," Lubbock screamed out. He did not notice that the black-haired Wayne rider was staring at the wounded savage as intently as he was.

The Indian dropped back on the grass. There was something in his eyes now, almost apologetic. His lips moved as he fought for breath.

"He is trying to tell you," Nusser muttered hoarsely.

Lubbock thrust an arm under the man's head. He placed his ear close to the failing lips. The sounds that came forth rose and fell, a guttural mixture of the savage tongue and agency English. Lubbock clung to every word.

"Where?" Lubbock bombarded.

The head could not move, but the eyes rolled off toward the north, then to the spot where the fourth renegade had found cover. The voice choked out a few more syllables. "Half-breed know." Then the fire went out, the eyes set, and the Indian's head dropped back on the grass.

Lubbock whirled on the man beside him. "You heard him?"

"Yes," Nusser replied. "I hear him say 'white man Devers.' But the rest, I do not make out."

"Come on."

Lubbock and the others snaked down the gulley toward the pile of rocks where Wear had posted himself, blocking the escape of the other fugitive. On the way, Nusser told the story of Karryl Newcomb's abduction on the golden buckskin to the black-haired Wayne cowhand.

"All right, half-breed," Lubbock shouted. "You want to get

it in there, or out in the open?"

"Wait, for the love of God!" an agonized wail came back to them.

"Wait, hell!"

"But, señor! My leg, it is broken."

Lubbock darted into the sheltered crevice, the black-haired man now close behind him. The half-breed crouched on his side, one hand holding his body up partially from the ground. "I am helpless, amigos," he pleaded.

Lubbock kicked him over on his back. "You've got that white woman!" he accused, murder clearly now his intention. The half-breed's eyes opened wide.

"No—no I haven't got her. I only go where she was, to lead Indians back with her. She was something to you?"

"You're damned right she was."

"But she has not been harmed—not yet, I swear to you."

"What do you mean, 'not yet'?"

The half-breed wrenched himself upward into a sitting position, his back to the cliffside. "I am only vaquero," he whimpered. "I do as I am bid."

Lubbock struck the man across the face, knocking him back on the ground again. The half-breed's pasty countenance turned even whiter. "Get a rope, Nusser," Lubbock ground out. "We'll string him from a cedar."

"No, señor, please God! I tell you all," the half-breed bargained frantically.

Lubbock glanced once again at Nusser and the black-haired man, then back to the outlaw. "You'd better talk fast then, half-breed!" he snapped, "and you'd better have something to tell."

"Devers," the other blurted out. "He do this. He is tied to Comanches, and he hate white men. Devers part Comanche. I am with woman only because he sends me into canyons to bring her back. Later, he will take her for himself and go back to Comanches, for good."

"You mean he's got her alone with him now out there on the prairies?"

"Not alone. He is with the Quohadas."

"With the Quohadas where?"

"Colorado Crossing."

"What're they doing at Colorado Crossing, half-breed?"

"They are coming down, señor."

"Down where?"

"Here, everywhere, I guess."

"How many?"

"Hundreds. Thousands. I do not know. Devers work this out with Parro-o-coom. Comanches coming at Pedernales again, and Devers, he is with them. When I bring woman to him as he tell me, I slip away quick with band you find here, trying then to get back to Rio Grande, myself, out of fight. Already he had quit his main gang. You let me go, please?"

Lubbock waited only an instant more. "What else?" he bit out.

"Devers, he pulls in all his old hands, but only the old ones ... big gunslingers ... Castlerod, Sudderth, Storm. He tell them to move north sometime soon now, kill rancher MacAshen at his ranch on the Pedernales. But he wanted woman first. He not planning even to tell Comanches these men come, for he say this time he make sure of something—I don't know what—one way or the other."

The black-haired Wayne cowboy thrust Lubbock sharply aside, and seized the half-breed by the shoulders.

"Where are these outlaws, rustler?"

"At the hangout on the Blanco."

"Then what're you doing with that buckskin?"

"I do not have it. The Indians, they take woman's horse as part of price for holding her."

"Come on," Nusser barked, "we have no time to lose."

They cut the stake ropes on the Indian ponies and let them run. Lubbock pulled in the golden buckskin and led it around the swell toward his own mustangs. When mounted, he recounted the broken story to the Wayne riders.

"You want us to ride with you?" Wear asked.

"No. You head back south and pass the word. Our job is north. Don't know how we'll make out with cold steel aimed at our backs, but there ain't no other choice. Haven't got anybody to send against that Blanco gang, anyway—if we figure on trying to stop the Comanches at the same time. Maybe you can raise us some men. If you can, tell 'em to head for the Pedernales. We'll need all the help we can get."

He raised his hand, then jerked his horse about and pressed the spurs. The buckskin ran behind on a stake rope, and Nusser to the side. Wear watched them go.

"God Almighty," he breathed. "What do you make of that?" He turned toward his companion. But the black-haired man was already gone, spurring his mustang brutally into headlong flight southward.

Lubbock and Nusser were above the Guadalupe, in the abrupt little canyons and arroyos, when dark came. As long as there was a moon, they continued on, but they were still a score of miles from the Falling Water at midnight. Lubbock called a halt.

"We've got to get there," he muttered. "But we won't, diving into one of these draws and breaking up. We'll hold it here, Nusser, till it's light again. But we've got to find Mac-Ashen before Storm does. MacAshen's good, but not that good, and he'd be dead before he knew he was being shot at."

They did not wait to prepare food in the dawn. The first thin streaks of dirty gray saw them in the saddle once more and plunging on. In an hour, they had cleared the southern wall of the canyon. Two more hours down the river road, brought them to the Falling Water.

There were horses at the rail, dusty and unkempt. Lubbock raised a hand to halt the man riding beside him.

"Nusser, the horses!" He threw the reins as his boots struck the ground. Then he rushed forward, thrusting open the door. "MacAshen!" he cried out as he saw who was already there before him.

35

Wear and Lacing passed the Comal Springs at dusk. They were past the Mill Creek hills at daybreak, and riding fast.

In their absence from the Guadalupe, something had happened. Salado Joe Garner, after many delays, had finally reached that neighborhood. He spent a day and a night with Holbrook. Grippa was on the verandah of the main house when he rode in to the Wayne ranch. Garner swung down and climbed the steps.

"Looking for a man named Grippa, Adam Grippa," Garner announced.

"I'm Grippa."

The newcomer held out his hand. "Joe Garner from Bell County. Been trying to get down here for a long time. I'm one of the people trying to set up a new cattlemen's association, Grippa."

"Come on in the house, and meet the proprietor of this spread."

Garner was amazed when he came face to face with Margaret Wayne. "Never saw such a young and pretty rancher before," he confessed. The girl was subdued, but Garner's outspoken admiration warmed her.

"Let's sit down and visit a while," she invited.

Grippa studied their guest. "Seems I've heard of you, but the name's not just right. Reckon I'm on the wrong trail," he mused.

The newcomer grinned. "Got another name up north of Austin," he said. "It's on account of the creek that splits my land, Salado Creek. Salado Joe Garner, that's what they call me."

The hard clop of hoofs on the river road reached Grippa's ear. As Margaret and Garner exchanged continued pleasantries, the foreman rose and walked to the door. When he saw the horsemen he hurried out onto the verandah. The cowhands whirled on past, however, to the horse corral.

Garner, his interest aroused, also came out now, and Margaret stepped to the edge of the verandah beside him.

"Something up?" Garner asked.

"I don't know," Grippa answered. "But I'll soon find out."

He started down the steps, and just in that moment Wear came limping around the bunkhouse and up toward the main dwelling. Grippa waited until he reached the verandah.

"What in hell is going on?" Grippa queried. Wear slumped to the steps. He breathed hard. But he was too exhausted for a moment to answer.

"Indians!" he jabbered finally. "We killed three Indians."

"Where?" Grippa seized the cowboys's shoulder.

"Way up, past Comal Springs. And they had MacAshen's horse. That rancher, you know, on the Pedernales. The one whose sweetheart was carried off. That horse was the one they took her on." He stopped, exhausted.

"Start at the beginning, Wear," Grippa ordered.

When the story was out, the three listeners on the verandah could only stare at each other in astonishment.

"Devers, you say?" Garner broke the silence angrily. "I know that man. He's a state policeman, living like a rancher on the Blanco. He's been suspected of rustling cattle. But to steal a white woman—and now to call in an outlaw like Storm to gun the woman's husband down! This will be the end of that sorry police force." He halted for just a second. "A real sashay by the Quohadas, too!" he burst out then. "What'll the settlers up there do, Grippa?"

"They'd better do something and damned quick!" Grippa turned back to the exhausted cowpoke slumped on the steps before him.

"What else is the matter with you, Wear?" he demanded.

"It's Lacing. Fellow's gone plumb crazy!"

"What're you talkin' about?"

"Can't say I know, rightly. But he sure did change from the man I've known after we'd heard what we had about Storm movin' in to hunt out MacAshen. Rode like a demon all the way home. And then, when we hit the dirt there at the horse lot, he didn't even unsaddle. Throwed the reins to me and ran for the bunkhouse. I slipped the latigos and started up here. And right then he came bustin' out again. I never seen a light in a man's eyes like was in his," Wear muttered. He came suddenly to his feet and pointed toward the corral. "There he is now," he continued, pointing to Lacing, who had roped and dragged an ugly black stallion to the hitching post.

"Grippa," Wear queried, "you see anything different about Lacing?"

The old man squinted through the sunlight. "What?"

"Look at his hip."

"Ah!"

"First time I ever seen him pack a gun. First time I ever seen that gun. It ain't a gun, Grippa, it's a cannon!"

A low gasp came from the lips of the girl behind them, and Adam turned quickly to her. Lacing had strapped the saddle and vaulted into it. Now he dug his spurs brutally into the shanks of the powerful animal. The horse plunged straight down the path before the door. Lacing's eyes were fixed, his face white, and if he saw the cluster of people on the step, he did not turn his head. He hurtled past and up the road toward the Springs.

A sharp intake of breath beside Grippa drew his eyes to Garner's face. The man was staring as if he had seen a ghost.

"Grippa," the Salado man whispered, "what'd you call that man?"

"Lacing. Ben Lacing."

"Lacing, huh? I've often wondered. And I'd sure hate to be standing in somebody's boots right now."

"What're you talking about?"

"That fellow you call Lacing—I used to campaign with him in Tennessee—him and this rancher MacAshen you've been talking about. The two of us rode home together, in fact. He was

[364]

close to MacAshen, close as any man alive today could be."

"Ben Lacing?"

"Lacing, hell! That man is . . . Ord!"

Salado Joe Garner gathered in the reins of his horse. There was a low sob from Margaret Wayne, standing behind Grippa, who turned and took her in his arms. Her head sank on his hard chest and her fingers clutched at his shirt.

"He's Ben Lacing!" she cried. "He's never been anybody else, and he never will be."

Salado dug his spurs into the horse, twisting the animal's head north.

Loud, angry voices sounded from the adobe building that served as a saloon on the Blanco. There were two doors, one at the center, and another on the off side, close to the corner. There was also a window in the far wall. The bar was on the right, covering half the distance of the room, and across from it was a huge fireplace. The rough tables spread out from the fire on the open end, except before the side entrance. No bartender was in evidence.

A few white men hunched at the bar. One was in the center, Castlerod and Sudderth on his right, and another man at his left. Castlerod's voice created most of the clamor.

"The whole gang's busted wide open," he fumed. "And all because of that drunken fool, Devers. He called himself the kingpin of this outfit, but he hasn't got the sense of a locoed Anadarko. I knew Devers was poison but I never figured him as making deals with those bucks to steal a white woman."

"What're you beefing about, Castlerod?" the slender man argued. "You didn't steal her."

"You think Indians can't talk? Hell! Likely they're already up on the reservations boasting about what they did for Devers, once they'd been paid for the deal. And that half-breed! The least you and Sudderth could have done was blow his guts out, making sure he didn't get the chance to spout off somewhere, sometime, himself. Wish to God I'd been around when he came for Devers. Devers was one of the gang, Storm. So that makes whatever Devers did the whole gang's doings, anytime. You ought to know that every damned man on the prairies, saddle-bums, rustlers—just the same as regular ranchers—will be gunning for all of us, not just Devers. And maybe they should!"

"You're talking wild, Castlerod," Storm warned. "Devers left you a pretty penny to help finish this job, like he did the rest of us. The woman is gone—for good. Once swallowed up in a Quohada war party, white women just don't show any more."

"I've got a hunch this one will show! And another hunch that some of the rest of us won't. You can look for a posse in here any time. You've been down in the chaparral too long, Storm. I know these people. They'll come all right, and they'll keep on coming. We couldn't kill them all, if we didn't do anything else but that!"

Behind them the half-door swung inward and a black-haired man stood just inside. Unnoticed, his gaze ran over the backs of the quartet at the bar.

"Maybe killing's the business you know best, Storm," Castlerod went on angrily, "but not me. I don't go in for it when there's no cause, no matter who it is."

"You sound squeamish, Castlerod."

"Squeamish! You don't like a man giving it to you straight. I've done a plenty in my time, killed men when they asked for it, rustled cattle, but I never took part in a rotten deal like this before—shoving a white woman off to a Comanche half-breed. For two-bits I'd shake the whole sorry mess even now and throw in with those settlers north of the Pedernales."

Storm laughed outright. "I'll mark that one down, Castlerod," he chided the tall man. "You on the side of the law . . . that'd be a sight worth livin' to see."

"Throwing a white woman to the Quohadas ain't a matter of law, Storm. It's something else. But you wouldn't know about that."

"Well, you've still got time to choose," the other went on. "Why don't you just hunt up that Pedernales outfit and tell them you'd like to join the fold, instead of bushwhacking their boss, MacAshen?"

"I'd do just that, if I had the guts. And if I figured anybody would listen to me."

"You don't have to have the guts, Castlerod," a voice from the doorway broke in.

The men at the bar swung around. "Who are you?" Castlerod demanded.

The stranger made no effort to answer. In fact, he did not

even look toward Castlerod again. He came on a couple of paces, his eyes on the other man at the bar. Storm inched forward a step now, himself.

"What's your business, cowboy?" Storm queried curiously, taking the newcomer in from head to foot.

"Look out, Vanner!" Sudderth yelled. "That fellow's Ord!"

For just an instant the name did not seem to register. Storm glanced back fleetingly at the outlaw behind him, then toward the man near the doorway again.

Ord! The mystery gunman of the Tornillo.

"Well, Devers wasn't lying after all," Storm spoke up, almost unbelievingly. He glanced at Castlerod. "I thought when he told me in San Antonio I'd meet up with you on this job that he was just using the name to get me here." He looked Ord over again. "So this is where you've been holed up so long?"

"Yes."

"Quite a spell since anybody heard from you, Ord," Storm said. "I'd about decided you'd hung up the Colt. A man like you ought to get around more."

Ord let the words sink in. Storm could not delude him. He knew the man's breed, for it was his own. To meet a gunman . . . a real gunman . . . that was Storm's passion. No matter how he tried, he could not hide it.

"What do you want here, Ord?" Storm asked.

Ord was bitter. It was as if he had never tried to shake the past. Even Storm's question was unnecessary; the gunman knew why Ord had come. With a woman kidnapped and a gang like this out to murder her husband, there could have been no question about Ord's intentions.

"You know why I'm here, and you can call the play, Storm." Ord had entered the room already tensed, and now Storm's posture changed. For a moment, they stared into each other's eyes. Then the outlaw's hand flashed down. A shock, then smoke. Ord took the blaze of the gun as the lead tore through his chest. The strength ebbed from his legs, arms, and back. He staggered against the door, still seeing Storm.

Surprise and disbelief raced in turn across the outlaw's face. For a second Storm stood there, gaping. His mouth straightened, agony showed, and he pitched forward onto the floor. Ord tried to pull himself around, but could not. Something heavy was dragging down on him—then all went black.

36

The Comanches came by daylight. They crossed the Pease, the Wichita, and the Brazos. By way of the Milburn Deep, they reached the Colorado, and eventually came up below the San Saba. White Eagle rode close to the forefront. About him were buffalo war bonnets of the first order, and full-feathered war bonnets of the second order.

Back behind the Comanches, beyond Katemcy Creek, a wall of rising smoke clouds disclosed the course of a prairie fire. From the higher swells White Eagle watched the smoke as it moved away from him. He could mark the coursing speed of the fire, moving as oil aflame on water. But it was moving away from him.

He nibbled at dried meat and pone cake made from mesquite meal. He was moving steadily, but not too fast. He would find the Taibos on the Pedernales, that was certain, and he would need his horses.

He would meet the white chief they called MacAshen this time. On that, he was assured. In the day of White Eagle's father and grandfather, the Pedernales had been the boundary line of the Comanche nation. But the father of this new white chief, MacAshen, and others like him, in those earlier years had driven the Comanches from their villages in the hills. The very name itself—MacAshen—had been the rallying word for the hill country white people.

A scowl fixed on White Eagle's face. He had seen this white man MacAshen once as a boy, at the futile peace council beyond the Red, and he had recognized the odd but deep-laid enmity that penetrated that youth as well. Somewhere here in the hills he would find and destroy him, and the hills would be safe again for the Comanches.

And what of the woman back there now in his own column, and the renegade who had brought her with him? White Eagle had known Devers since childhood, and now the scowl on the Indian's face deepened. He hated all white men, and their women equally so, but he hated even more the white men through whose veins coursed some measure of Indian blood. He would have swept the earth clean of the half-breeds as quickly as he would of any of the other Taibos. Perhaps quicker. But this particular half-white renegade, Devers, he detested more than all the others put together. For Devers had a strange grip on old Parro-o-coom. White Eagle had found that out only too well at the council when this expedition was planned.

Devers had convinced Parro-o-coom that he could pilot the war party swiftly toward the places they needed to know about on the Pedernales. White Eagle doubted if Devers was trustworthy, much less capable of being useful to the Comanches. And Devers's influence on the old Bull Bear was galling to White Eagle. But Parro-o-coom still dominated the tribal councils and White Eagle had been instructed to wait for Devers at the Colorado.

The woman? White Eagle had no interest in her. He had had no part in her abduction; and, indeed, except for Parro-o-coom's insistence, he would never have permitted even one of the splinter bands to engage in such an undertaking. For MacAshen was a chief, and the woman was his. If a man wanted MacAshen's woman, he should have had to fight for her. Ordinarily, though, since the job was now done, White Eagle would have advised to let a man deal with a captive as he wills. That was a man's prerogative, half-breed or otherwise. But Devers was not the same to him as other men. Devers's hold on Parro-o-coom marked him for destruction should White Eagle some day will it.

Back in the squaw train, Karryl Newcomb rode with the other Indian women. She rode as White Eagle had told Devers to make her ride. Her initial horror, when she discovered it was Devers for whom the savages were holding her, had passed now and she was pervaded only with gloom.

From the old squaw who had lived on the agency, Karryl had learned that she was actually held for someone other than the chief. She had not known definitely who that might be, and she knew nothing of Devers's tie with the Indians. But no Indian would hold her thus for himself, and in the dark, bitter, frightening hours, she had recognized that there could be only one person who would subject her to this horror.

She had seen the messenger when he came up the canyon finally, had seen him in discussion with the headman of the small village. Then they had brought the buckskin for her to saddle, probably realizing that she could never stay astride one of the other ponies on all of the long journey back. They had taken her away with them across the plains, the half-breed paying her no heed and giving no ear to her efforts at conversation. They had led only an old mustang along behind, and they traveled rapidly.

Near the headwaters of the San Saba, the half-breed and his Indian companions had camped with her. Then Devers had come.

He said not a word to her; in fact, he paid little attention to her at all, beyond a careful scrutiny immediately on his arrival. He seemed to be in a great hurry and once she had been delivered to him, he was ready to move on again.

The Indians appropriated her buckskin pony for themselves, obviously considering the animal now as their own property. Devers saddled the old mustang they had led along with them earlier, and made her climb astride. He tied her hands, and attached a rope to the horse's bridle. Then they had struck out overland.

Devers had scarcely halted before they reached the Quohada war party. When he spoke to her at all it was in short clipped orders, and now she was buried deep within that huge band, under guard. She had lived long enough among the savages to realize what that meant to her.

On a high ridge above the Llano, Levit MacAshen shaded a

hand across his eyes, studying the distant, advancing horde.

"Almost too late, you came," Lenneweber said to him. "The Indians moved fast until they reached the Colorado, but now they are moving cautiously. It is well for us that they slowed, else not even the scouts could have reached us in time. And surely not the Rangers. What are your plans, MacAshen?"

"I'm staying here, till we can see again," MacAshen answered. He glanced once more at the glow on the far horizon, then turned about to gaze southwestward. Twilight was coming. "They'll be closer in the morning. Biberstin and the others should be in there back of them by now."

"By morning it could be too late."

"No. The savages will bed down somewhere inside the line of the fire. And we could get at them over there if we move fast."

Lenneweber studied MacAshen carefully. "What you're thinking is that we should try," he said. "Don't play with that one, Levit. They'd kill your lady and any other white person they may have seized, the moment you did."

"I know that," MacAshen answered, "but knowing it doesn't make me like the waiting any better."

Another man stepped in closer, and MacAshen nodded briefly to him. It was Tatum, the Indian agent. Somehow, he had heard of the Indian movement at the same time that Levit spurred out of Griffin, and Tatum had ridden swiftly south, bringing with him what men he could pick up.

"Your lady will be safe as long as she is in the squaw column," he said. "White Eagle is smart enough to know the value of hostages. Take my word for that."

"She's no hostage if Devers is there with her."

"I've told you before, and I'll tell you again. There's no love lost between the Eagle and Devers. Can't figure out what Devers is actually doing there, unless he doesn't really know what plenty of other people know. But one thing you can bet your bottom dollar on: White Eagle won't do him any favors. Chances are White Eagle has already laid down some terms if Devers is to get her. And they won't be met on the march."

"I hope to God you know what you're talking about, Tatum."

"You can count on it, MacAshen!"

Now Levit stepped away from the cluster of settlers atop the pinnacle, making his way downward to another group crouched on their heels below. "All right, Garner, let me hear all of it now," he said to one of the men waiting there. "Will Ord live?"

The Salado man glanced up at him. "Reckon that's a question nobody can answer, Colonel," the man replied. "He had a God-awful hole in his chest. Strange enough, that fellow Castlerod must have plugged it up before leaving though, or so the barkeep said. Otherwise Ord would have bled to death. It was all over when I got there; the others gone. Maybe that was lucky for me.

"There was a wagon in the back, and with Ord's and the barkeep's horses, we got it moving, Ord himself stretched out on the floor. He never came to, at least while I was ridin' along. But he was still alive.

"The barkeep was scared stiff. Said Castlerod had promised to come back and blow his guts out if he didn't get Ord south to some rancho. There's a doctor at Seguin, and I told him to head that way on his own once he'd put Ord down somewhere. Most likely he will, too. I came on here fast as I could after they'd headed out."

"I'm glad you did, Garner."

"There was something else, Colonel," the other said. "The barkeep said Castlerod wanted you to know, if anybody ever got the chance to tell you, that he didn't have any part in the kidnap of your lady. And he didn't even know about it till too late."

"I'll remember that," Levit muttered. "Garner, why did Ord go in there alone? Was it on my account, or was it because his target was Vanner Storm?"

"Reckon that's another question nobody could ever answer, Colonel. Maybe not even Ord. But I'd let it stand he threw in on your account."

The men did not move from the promontory above the West Deep until daylight shot out over the land again. When that hour arrived, they could see to the farther hills as they had not been able to do in the dusk before.

The valley stretched for perhaps twenty miles in its narrowest crossing to the north, bordered on that distant side by the Shin Oaks. It reached out in either direction for thirty miles or more.

The passes to the south were through the broken country east of them.

The Comanche horde was distant but more distinct now, in the extreme western end of the basin. As MacAshen had predicted, they had halted in the far valley on the approach of darkness during the night before, but now they were moving again.

Breakfast was quick, and the horses brought up for saddling.

"Get back to Biberstin," MacAshen said to a blond-haired boy, one of Lenneweber's hands. "Tell him what you could see from here, and tell him not to come out of that Cold Creek cut-through in the Lone Oaks until the Comanches pass it this way on the other side. Not till they're past the shoulder of the mountains."

"Ja."

"Let me say it again, and you say it to Biberstin again, that he's not to hit them back there any time till the rest of us have pinned them down in front."

"Ja, mein Herr."

When the boy was off, Levit pulled in his mount.

"To which place do you go now, MacAshen?" Lenneweber queried.

"Over there," Levit said, pointing toward the rough country east. "That's where they'll go in, and that's where we'll have to be. Come on."

It was a great effort to get across the back levels of the Lone Oaks. In the distance was only the craggy, jumbled skyline of wasteland. The Comanches were to the north, around the bluffs where the Lone Oaks projected into the valley, and they must ultimately circle those projections. But they would move more rapidly now, in the center of the valley.

Three miles farther to the east was another promontory, higher than the ledges here. Levit picked his tortuous path across the rocky declines, then onward toward the distant pinnacle. His own foreman, Lubbock, reined in beside him, pointing ahead. "Magill Mountain," he said. When they reached that eminence, they swerved south completely around its base. On the northeast corner, the undulations of the mountain wall permitted entry, and Lenneweber called out, "From that height up there, we can observe again."

At the crest of the new elevation, there was indeed a clear vista to the north, all the way to and beyond the Shin Oaks. In the valley itself, the vast cloud of dust hung more clearly above the plain, coming ever closer, but it was still far to the westward and north.

"Maybe they strike toward the Lampasas, thinking to cross the Colorado at the Falls and to hit the settlements from that direction," Lenneweber suggested.

"Hell, no!" Levit retorted. "The Pedernales is the only thing that makes sense to the Comanches. They've got to hit the Pedernales hard, and they know it."

"But that would put them in the pass during the darkness."

"They won't travel at night. And they've still got too far to come. It's a full day's ride from where they are to the mouth of the pass. They'll stop again today on the water of the North Fork, and take to the gorge in the morning."

"I wonder, MacAshen," Lenneweber argued cautiously, "if your reasoning, it is wrong, then we may let them slip completely from us."

There was something vaguely familiar about this setting—the markers, the hills. "They won't slip anywhere," MacAshen said. He tried to fix the terrain in his thoughts. What was there about it that tugged at him? He turned swiftly, studying the contour of the small gorge where it left the main valley. It stretched away a few miles south, opening ultimately into the wide plain toward the Llano and beyond, to the country of the Enchanted Rock. Of course! He had studied this perspective before, long ago now, with his father. How long ago? Fifteen years? But his father's words were as clear as though they had been spoken yesterday: "When they come, Levit, they will come straight down that valley. This is the Comanche pass to the Pedernales. If I am not here, don't let them go beyond Enchanted Rock!"

He gripped the big German's arm. "Lenneweber," he said, "did you ever hear of anything called 'the Lost River'?"

The rancher considered the question carefully. "I think I have heard of such a place in the early days, from the Indians."

Levit pointed north. "This is 'the Lost River,' Lenneweber. My father showed it to me once when I was a boy from this exact ledge. You can see it easy enough, just like water was still running along its course. East of the Shin Oaks, across the path of what is now the Cherokee up there, then down around the slope of that red mountain above us. Into this valley Lenneweber, south beside Wolf Mountain, then into the open prairies and on. This is the old Comanche war trail, Lenneweber, and we'll do for the damned Quohadas here once and for all!"

Lenneweber had followed his words methodically, marking the course Levit indicated.

"Perhaps it is so," he agreed at last, since there was obviously no other way he could answer the man beside him. "And if your reasoning is correct, then we are lucky. For we have not the men to stop such a band in the open, even if we tried." He stared for a long time toward the northward. "Where shall we wait, MacAshen?"

"With Roberts, on that ridge to the south."

"That is well. The others will be in their places now."

Levit and his companion turned down the grades now toward the valley. The sun warmed them as they galloped on. In the floor of the pass were elms and mulberries, willows and giant oaks. A pool lay back against an incline, and there were migratory swans on the water. Pigeons and wild turkeys rose from their path, and a covey of quail shied upward for a hundred feet to plummet down again.

A couple of miles brought them to an abrupt slope and they halted, eyeing the heights above.

The ridge extended straight south from the higher upland plateaus, roughly triangling to spend itself in a sharp point to the south, and the narrow basin down which they had come ran north to south before opening toward the lands above the Llano. They mounted the ridge.

"They'll come through fast," Levit warned, "but they'll come through, all right. This time we'll give them what they've handed out themselves for too many years. I've waited a long time for this, Lenneweber, but I never thought I'd be trying to retrieve the woman I love when I finally squared it out with them."

The Ranger camp captained by the man named Roberts was well hidden in the high cut-backs from the floor of the pass below. Roberts gripped MacAshen by the hand as he dismounted. "I had a feeling all along that you'd show when the game was called," he said.

"Where's Barry?" Levit asked.

Roberts pointed southward toward the exit of the pass. "He's hid out there, right at the point. Ingram ought to be across from us too by now, in the shallows behind those high knobs. Lucky we got the word in time. Ingram's coming in by way of the Blounts, and Dancer Peak."

Levit signaled his own man, Torkin, to his side. "You get across there then," he said. "Let them know where we are, and what to look for."

Torkin fastened the string of his hat beneath his chin. The leather chaps he took from the horn and fixed on his legs. He raised his hand once; and Levit watched him spur dangerously down the east grade of the ridge before them.

The Packsaddle rises to the east of the Riley Mountains, and almost due north of the Granite Knobs. Ingram's Colorado River men were, as expected, in that quarter, bedded down now a degree or two to the south to support Barry's band on the far corner. This was the disposition, then, and not a moment too soon: Roberts on the western flank of the Indians' course; Ingram across the valley to the east; and Barry at the extremity, guarding the outlet. Biberstin and his men were scheduled to come in behind, cutting the Indians' route of escape.

Night had fallen on the prairie close to the mouth of the pass, and White Eagle stared into the blackness before him. He had scanned the rough surfaces of the cliff face during the daylight hours. He did not like it here between the San Saba and the Llano regardless of what the white renegade had told Parro-o-coom, and he would have avoided this route. He wondered if the Taibos had been able to gather again into the bands they called "Rangers," since their own war. He had the warriors to meet an enemy in the open or beyond the higher hills, but the passes offered sudden dangers. And surely the Texans would have been aware of his advance. He could not divide his own party to ascend the abrupt slopes themselves, and certainly he could not turn back. Or could he?

He rose and paced a step away, gazing southward again toward the dark ridges, and then at the heavens. The moon was right; it had been full and now it was waning. It was right or he might not, indeed, try the passes, despite his aversion to anything that smacked of retreat.

His principal young squaw was back there in the column, as were the women of many of his other warriors. He was especially prideful of his Indian women. Young squaws always rode with their lords on the Comanche marauding expeditions, often as far down as Chihuahua, and some of them even fought beside their masters. But White Eagle did not favor squaw-combatants, and while he sanctioned their presence for other encouraging purposes, no woman would be allowed to leave the protected squaw line while he was war chief of the party. For some reason he was troubled at this moment; some instinct warned him, and for the first time in his life he was apprehensive of his own wife's safety.

But the white woman, Karryl Newcomb, was back there too, with the other squaws, where he had ordered her to be kept and she might, in stringent circumstances, serve as a hostage. He hoped it would not come to that, though.

White Eagle supposed that Devers was somewhere close to her. He had minced no words as far as the latter was concerned—Devers would not show his face ahead among White Eagle's warriors. He would keep his distance from the squaw line, too.

Devers was a bad omen, so far as White Eagle was concerned. White Eagle had hated Devers since childhood, but it was even worse than that now. The Quohadas should have struck at the Pedernales settlements from the westward—from out around the headwaters of the Blanco where the terrain was open. And the expedition itself should have been on the trail weeks before the actual hour of its departure from the Palo Duro.

Why Parro-o-coom, of all the tribesmen, had let the half-breed renegade sell him on the old Comanche war path, and even on the timing, White Eagle could not understand. Certainly Devers could not have divulged his personal interests—that such timing was designed to enable him to reach safety among the Quohadas with his captive white woman, just as he had done. But Devers's motive in wanting to make sure of the destruction of the MacAshen fortress was clear enough now, and it certainly could have serious complications where the Comanches were concerned.

White Eagle scowled again. Yes, the moon was right or he would not try the passes after all, regardless of Parro-o-coom or Devers. Were the points on it directed skyward, then there would be water in the moon and it would fall as rain. His war-riors would leave tracks behind and thus be easy to follow when the blow had been accomplished. He fretted, though, that so long as the war party was committed to the pass before him, he could not call up the warriors into movement at once, hurrying on through the gorges under cover of darkness until they reached the open ranges beyond the mountains. But Comanche warriors had a terror of death during the night, for without the power of Father Sun to light the way there was no assurance of perpetual abode after death in the Happy Hunting Grounds, should they meet an enemy and die.

He stalked up and down before his encampment. He would study the hills again at dawn, and he would penetrate them quickly then. But hereafter, when his intuition told him other-wise, he would follow the promptings of his own intelligence, regardless of Parro-o-coom, or the other chiefs. And if this at-tack did not go well—well, Parro-o-coom was not at hand now to protect the renegade Devers.

Daylight came with spearheads of color—amber, rose, ame-thyst—dyeing the gray of dawn and painting the dark green of the cedar ridges with new transcendent tints.

To the Texans on the pinnacles in the south, the rising light disclosed the Comanche horde again in movement. The Quo-hadas were close to the mouth of the pass; they had sent the scouts forward, and the main party was not too far behind.

"They've switched to their war-horses," the Ranger, Roberts, said quickly to Levit, "which means they'll move through fast now."

Roberts cast a quick glance toward Levit's face, then turned to make sure of the others behind him. The horses of the Rangers were held down by a detail in a shallow depression, completely screened from sight of anyone in the valley below.

The forward scouts slipped quickly past. Levit, head down in the grass on the slope above them, watched one of the wiry Redskins go by.

The savage carried his spear guardedly. Its war head was over two feet in length, an inch in width, and razor sharp. The gleam from its whetted edge flashed in the sunlight. The spear was vermilion red, and the upper length was stained with blood.

The garish, spike-edged vanguard of the war party came on

behind the forward scouts. More red lances bristled skyward above that horde. A hawklike alertness gripped each copper-skinned rider, and he strained at his mount to hold the head. The Comanche war design of black pigment streaked the savage faces. Strips of otter-skin swung from their breechclouts, and strong hands held the ash wood spears, war tips skyward.

They came down the center swales, prospecting the trail ahead carefully. Even at route march, they held themselves in readiness, keeling their copper bodies to the motion of their horses, rising and falling to the movement on the trail. The round, two-foot wide buffalo-skin medicine shields hung carefully from their forearms, frail-looking protectors whose appearance belied their value.

War clubs, suspended by thongs upon the handles, swung from the wrists of the warriors. Their horses were armored about the shoulders with thick rawhide plates supporting pitch-cemented sand. Cured mats of sheepskins and softly tanned buffalo hides served for saddles, and sinewy heels gripped the flanks of the mounts with surer firmness than the rowels of the vaqueros. Behind each equipage hung a bow, ready for instant employment, and a quiver of arrows. Sharps and Minie rifles were bound to some of the Indians' saddles.

"Gott im Himmel!" The exclamation was wrung from the big German, Lenneweber. "Like Uhlans, they look."

"Lancers!" Steve Meadows corrected. "And they'll fight it out here this day."

The main body of the Comanche warriors was almost before them now, and up ahead the vanguard was approaching the end of the pass. MacAshen's eyes ran up and down the length of the column.

Steve Meadows followed that gaze, understanding the reason for it as he checked his gear—the .45, the heavy knife in the sheath at his side, the cartridges in his belt. "Look, MacAshen!" he whispered suddenly. "Back there, against the wall." Levit followed the line of Meadows's hand. "That's them, that's squaws," Meadows whispered again.

There were many of the women, and Levit could make out the protecting cordon of warriors about them. But he was too distant to distinguish individuals.

"Don't think about it now, Levit!" Lenneweber warned. "The time to seek your lady is after the Quohadas have been destroyed, as Tatum told you."

"You mean after she has been destroyed, more likely!"

"No. She will not be harmed if she is with them while the fighting lasts. It is when the outcome is evident that you must be ready, Levit."

"He's right, man," Roberts emphasized.

"I heard him," Levit snapped.

"Then let's get ready to move."

"Mount up your men. You'll go straight down this gully slope, Roberts. Straight at the side of those bucks coming along this wall. Use pistols. You've got to kill—kill fast. And dead! Don't turn your backs, or you'll get a lance through your guts."

Roberts nodded, and MacAshen went on.

"Barry'll show quick when those scouts up front get to the end there. He'll hit them first with rifles from the cliff—then he'll cut in with his six-shooters. You'll have to strike at the big party itself. It's the only way, and that'll give Ingram a chance to come off that far ridge. You've got to make it work, or you're dead. And it's got to be quick and short. Barry's sharpshooters will turn the front of the big party back from the outlet and they'll mill in the valley. But not for long. Then they'll try to knife on through—or maybe even back out. And if they do that last, then Biberstin and the Germans have got to come around that bend behind them, or it's still all up."

Suddenly, the smash of a fusillade from the cedars at the end of the valley split the atmosphere.

A half-dozen of the foremost savages tumbled, and a horse plunged headfirst.

"Carbines," Meadows called out. "Barry's going down."

The forward Indian scouts dropped quickly back into the red front, which reeled momentarily but instantly re-formed.

Abruptly, Barry came out of the cedars. His Rangers hurtled straight for the valley floor.

"Steady, steady!" Roberts called out to his own horsemen.

The full war-band was parallel now, its numberless warriors knifing suddenly forward at breakneck speed, intent on overwhelming Barry and his small handful of men.

"All right, move out!" MacAshen yelled.

Roberts was off ahead. His horse went down the steep incline, in short, sharp jumps; the Rangers close behind. They were on the Indians' flank before the Comanches realized it. The Colt Peacemakers spoke. First in short, rocking blasts. Then like thunder itself. Again the Indian front rolled back on itself.

The crash of the exploding cartridges, the shouts of the Rangers, and wild yelps of the savages charged the air of the canyon. Horses screamed; there were empty saddles before and behind. Blanketed Indian ponies reared. MacAshen pulled his own trigger as rapidly as it would work, refilling the chambers when the empties had been ejected.

But now the Indians swung around to slash back. A man beside Levit grunted, slid across the far side of his horse, dropping to the earth to hang by a toe in his stirrup. The savages wheeled back and forth at unbelievable speed. Red lances were raised and plunged as the mustangs hurtled by—meeting the blast of the six-guns as they did so.

The whoosh of a dogwood arrow sounded by MacAshen's ear, and another struck a cedar bush behind him. There were men on the ground all around him, more of them red than white. The patter of arrows sounded on the brush, and the sharp ricochet of rifle balls from the stone ledges.

One Ranger out in front drove forward too fast, plunging beyond the close-knit cordon of riders. Before the man realized it, the Comanches had folded back and let him through. They then closed again. At once there were Redskins all about. Fast, frantic blasts belched from the muzzle of the Ranger's pistol, but he could not see behind. Suddenly he screamed out in wild pain as a lance went through his body. He plummeted into the grass, and his horse bolted.

MacAshen's throat was dry. He scanned the far wall, where it resolved into small breaks and ravines that opened from above. Somewhere in there the Comanches had screened their women at the sound of the first pistol shots.

"Hold on, hold on," he prayed.

At that moment there was additional movement among the far high cedars and in the recesses below. From out of the jumble of rocks across the divide, Ingram's horsemen suddenly erupted onto the valley floor. A dozen of them—no, there were more behind, many more. A man beside Levit let go a wild cry of exultation.

Then a single Comanche came close to MacAshen, low upon

the neck of his mustang. Levit whipped up his gun, but the shock of an explosion at his elbow stopped him. The Indian reeled drunkenly, and another blast from Lenneweber's carbine knocked the Comanche from the mustang. The fallen Indian tried to rise, but failed.

From out of the swirling dust clouds two more Redskins galloped down upon their fallen comrade, leaning forward from their perches at full speed to jerk the wounded Indian from the ground. They went on, close to the slope and out toward the lower end of the valley.

On the far side of the gorge, there was no organization in Ingram's effort. His riders smashed at the prairie warriors, and the roar of the Colts echoed across the valley. Suddenly there was no form or precision in the effort of any combatant. The Colts set off a din that shook the hills, and the copper tribesmen slashed back wherever they could, lancing man or beast when they struck their mark.

Then the war party fell apart. As if with a single purpose, the Indian ponies spread out on every side, fighting for space to escape the executioners. Bows twanged, but rifles were forgotten. An occasional war club rose to strike back, and the medicine shields swept up to ward off six-gun lead; but the effort was completely futile.

In the rear, red horsemen wheeled about to scurry back the way they had come and as they turned, the line of German rangers with Biberstin and his men broke around the promontory. It became not an engagement but a rout, and afterward not a rout but a massacre. The Comanches plummeted through Biberstin's riders, paying for the passage in a frightful toll, but frantically fighting to escape the valley. Ingram's horsemen pressed behind them, and the tribesmen fleeing before Roberts's own band turned toward the broken valley slopes, striving to make their way out.

Before a slight indentation in the cliff face on the far side of the valley, White Eagle pulled up his mustang. The fighting rolled on, and now he stared down at a still figure on the ground.

The young squaw was dead. A stray bullet had done for her, or perhaps some white man had slain her intentionally.

A shudder ran through White Eagle. He had failed her.

[382]

His eyes came up to the others crouched back against the wall just inside the aperture. Behind White Eagle a maddened white man—one of the Rangers—was plunging down upon him; but he did not turn his attention from the two who were staring spellbound from beside the cliff-face. Their horses had bolted, and they were afoot against the wall.

Devers, the half-white renegade! The captive white woman too.

Devers was the man whose promptings had brought the Quohadas to this rout. His, the counsel that had cost the life of the young squaw. White Eagle brought his lance down.

From only a score of yards away now, lashing toward the Comanche, MacAshen saw the move, read the intent in it. Then he saw the white, horrified faces of the pair pinned against the wall.

"God in Heaven!" he screamed. "Not her!"

He jerked up his pistol, blasted without aim at the Redskin, the slug crashing into the sandstone. "Not Karryl!" he screamed again.

White Eagle adjusted himself. He swung the murderous warhead sharply around, point blank into MacAshen's face. In his horrible instant of fright for Karryl, MacAshen had not realized that this was White Eagle.

But the latter could not mistake MacAshen. The White Chief! The man he had sworn to destroy! The Comanche dug his heels into the flanks of his fiery war-horse. He, White Eagle, had failed his people, he had failed his own squaw, but he would not fail himself. The lance was dead upon MacAshen, and now White Eagle charged. The plunging horses came almost squarely together, swerving only at the last moment to avoid the impact itself. MacAshen snapped his revolver again and in the belching flame and smoke, he saw the frightful warhead of the lance upon him. He lunged down on the neck of his stallion, feeling the blade rip through the back of his shirt and realizing that his lead once more had missed. The drive of the maddened animals carried them a half-dozen paces apart, and MacAshen wheeled, to see the Indian already turned and coming at him again.

The Comanche rode high, his lance spiked out before him, and Levit felt the blade tear through the muscle and ligaments of his arm and side, twisting though he was to avoid its shock. Its force drove him across the saddle and his boot jerked from his stirrup.

He reeled wildly, trying to clutch the pommel with his left hand, but the arm would not respond. In a frantic moment, he toppled from the saddle into the dirt below. The crash sent stabs of pain throughout his body, but he fought his way back up to his knees, facing about, his pistol still in his right hand.

The Comanche was on him again. This time, MacAshen took no chances. He waited until the lance was almost in his face before he pressed the trigger, then he rolled, and rolled again in the same movement to avoid the stiking hoofs of the beast.

The horse went by, and Levit came back still again to his knees. The White Eagle, too, was on the ground before him. The second shot had knocked the Quohada from his horse, and there was blood on his face and chest. But he had taken the bow down with him as he fell and it was now in his hand, an arrow in the string.

He was fighting his way toward Levit, his footsteps uncertain. A terrible determination in his eyes conveyed to MacAshen the depth of the man's strength. MacAshen's side was numb and his left arm hung uselessly, but he steadied his right hand as carefully as he could, forcing himself slowly to his full height. The arrow was back, and the Indian was drawing out the last of his fading *puha* for the effort. Levit did not wait.

His lead slug struck the savage in the middle, doubling him. The Quohada pitched upon his face, and the bow flew out beyond his fingertips. Levit yanked on the trigger again, and when the pistol failed to fire, he knew he had spent his powder.

Against the wall now, Devers jerked his own head from left to right, seeking a route of escape. The pallor of impending death showed on his face, though, for there was nowhere to flee. He tugged suddenly at the pocket of his coat where the derringer lay, forgotten in the wild turmoil.

MacAshen whipped back his good arm and threw the useless pistol squarely into Devers's face, stumbling as he did so across White Eagle's ashwood spear in the dirt before him. He jerked the lance from the ground, gripped the shaft beneath his good arm pit and lunged forward in the same movement. The razor-sharp two-foot warhead pierced the bowels of Devers before him. Lance of the Quohada!

A short distance from this arena of confusion and death, a red-headed woman was huddled and sobbing.

37

Clouds still shadowed the frontier state of Texas in 1873, but there was light behind them now, a faint brushing of gold.

Voters in the state, white and black, through elections policed by the community officials, swept the radicals from office dissipating for all time the threat of new war. Davis still held on to the governor's chair, but he had lost the support of President Grant. Soon now he too was to be overwhelmingly defeated for reelection, even physically evicted from the office itself.

The new legislature terminated the state police, and dissolved the need for secret forces spread throughout the state, especially on the frontier. The countryside was growing more peaceful, and except for a few homeless scalawags, new hope and determination were abundant.

Far to the north of the Texas plains, gold had been discovered in the Black Hills of the Dakotas. A man named Glidden was soon to announce a patent on what he called "barbed wire." In a remote western corner of the state the village of Franklin was to incorporate as a city, choosing the name El Paso.

Tranquility had settled upon the valley of the Pedernales for the first time in a generation. John Levit and Karryl Newcomb were there, happy together at last, mindful of the beauty in the valley's sweep now that peace was upon the land. There were still needs and problems on the scarred frontier, but their resolution was close at hand.

A sound from up the river caught MacAshen's ear. He raised his head and listened. He knew that sound.

A file of blue-clad cavalry was chopping down on the ford. He saw the dust rise from the horses' hoofs before they entered the stream; the sudden elevation in the spirit of the animals as the cold water touched their limbs. An officer rode just in front of the detail and a standard bearer, his guidon affixed to the pole in its stirrup socket, followed at his elbow. The brash discordance of a military detail on the march came back to Levit, as of long ago.

The officer rode easily, his legs loose and his back stiff. A saber hung far back on the left of his saddle.

He rode straight to the door of the Falling Water, then he raised his hand in a signal for the command to halt. He swung down to the ground, but his men maintained their positions. He was a slight man, though tall, and bronzed from the sun and wind; his eye was keen; and a thin mustache defined his lip. His youthfulness did not detract from his natural air of confident authority.

Levit eyed the soldiers with somber uncertainty. Why were they here? The war had been over almost a decade.

The officer came quickly forward. "MacAshen?" he queried.

The rancher nodded.

"I'm Mackenzie."

"Mackenzie!"

"Yes. The name is Ranald Slidell Mackenzie, although I don't use the rest of it." By now the officer had reached the verandah and his eyes were level with MacAshen's. "I've been looking for you, MacAshen."

The latter did not answer. Mackenzie finally went on: "I rode thirty miles out of my way to call on you. I'm moving north, from Forts Clark and Duncan. The government has abandoned its policy toward the Indians. They are to be confined at last. We will check the Indians wherever they are, even on the reservations. Indians professing peaceful intentions will be required to move to the agencies and those capable of bearing weapons will be subject to daily watch."

"We've heard that before."

"Not like you'll hear it now. The orders are that we will not terminate the campaign until the last of them is on the reservation, disarmed and deprived of his mount. They will not come back to Texas."

"Did you come here just to tell *me* this?"

The soldier's face relaxed a trifle. "No, I came this way to say something else, MacAshen. The column is moving up the San Antonio road northward beyond Fredericksburg, or soon will be. Eight troops of cavalry. I'll rejoin it above Loyal Valley. We're taking a few civilian scouts with us. There are columns moving down from all directions on the Quohada villages. And we've even got a half-dozen companies of infantry awaiting us on the road, too. I thought you might like to ride with us. Not that it is a matter of great necessity. But I know something of the responsibility that you took on here on the frontier, and I thought you might like to be in on the finish. That is, if you care to ride with United States troops." The soldier smiled.

MacAshen relaxed and extended his hand. "I welcome you to the Falling Water, Colonel Mackenzie," he said. Now he smiled too. "Come into the house."

The officer started to follow him through the door, but Levit halted momentarily. Toward the bunkhouses his men stood watching the tableau in silence. Levit called out to Lubbock and the foreman came forward. MacAshen spoke briefly to the foreman. Then he turned back to Mackenzie.

"Let me offer your troop the hospitality of my place," he proposed. "A home-cooked meal never hurt a cavalry hand, and it won't take too long."

Mackenzie grinned. He relayed the invitation to his men and turned back with Levit toward the door.

Karryl met them inside and accepted the colonel's hand when he offered it. "I have just invited your husband to ride north with United States troops, if he has no objection to that," he declared, a twinkle in his eye. Karryl's face fell instantly.

"You pay me a high compliment, Colonel," Levit quickly responded for her. "And I assure you I would be honored to ride with you and your soldiers. I had never anticipated such a proposal again."

Levit caught the frightened, almost angry look upon Karryl's face which was not lost upon the visitor either. He touched the colonel's arm and led him toward the corner of the room

"I know of no inducement greater than to ride with a cavalry command again, save one," he said. He inclined his head toward the cradle in the corner, tended by a Mexican woman. "Meet another MacAshen, the next of our people on the Pedernales," Levit said. The colonel smiled, and he reached into the crib to gently pat the infant's cheek. Then he turned back, noting the change in Karryl.

"We thought you entitled to the invitation sir, and that is why I came," he said slowly. "But I sure understand your refusal. Your talents are far more in demand here upon the Pedernales than ever before."

Colonel Nelson Miles, with eight troops of cavalry, four of the Fifth Infantry, a section of artillery, and a detachment of Indian and civilian scouts, marched south from Camp Supply in the late summer. They picked up a large Indian trail on the headwaters of the Washita River. Another column, three troops of the Eighth Cavalry and a detail of mountain howitzers under Major William Price, moved eastward from Fort Union and Bascom in New Mexico. In a week they were on the Dry Fork of the Brazos.

Lieutenant Colonel George P. Buell, with six troops of the Ninth and the Tenth Cavalry and a detachment of infantry, pointed toward Indian country from a supply base at the junction of Wanderer's Creek with the Red. From Fort Sill itself came Lieutenant Colonel John W. Davidson, with six additional troops of the Tenth Cavalry, three companies of the Eleventh Infantry, and more Indian scouts.

The column commanded by Miles was the first to engage, striking swiftly at the main force of the Southern Cheyennes. The Indians had never encountered artillery fire before, and Miles drove them through the Grand Canyon of the Tule southwestward toward the Great Plains. On the Wichita, Major Price met a motley force gathered from many tribes, pressing them inward with a tightening noose.

From the depot on the Brazos, Mackenzie smashed first at the remaining villages of the Cheyennes, then at other clans near the old pow-wow landmark of Las Lagunas Quatro. An additional column from the Sixth Cavalry, led by Lieutenant Frank Baldwin clashed with Redskins on McClellan Creek; and a force under Captain Charles Veile, picking up the flight of that band, drove its remnants for a hundred miles to the west, and gradually into the trap. The circle had now closed.

The clans began to surrender. The Cheyennes came in first, then the Salt River Kiowas, and gradually the others. The Quohadas ultimately stood alone, their fate sealed. They, too, finally surrendered. The moon of the Comanches had set.

At the Wayne ranch on the Guadalupe, the rays of the declining sun moved across the room in which a man lay beneath the covers on the bed. Margaret Wayne stood beside him, watching. Outside, in the grove, a mockingbird shrilled a trenchant challenge, and a little gray-brown squirrel worked the lower limbs of a pecan tree. Cattle lowed in the near pastures, and mustangs stamped behind the log rails of the auxiliary work corral.

The girl smoothed the covers. "Oh, Adam," she sighed. "If he would only not stare so. Do you think he's any better today?"

The statement puzzled the sick man. Why should he need to feel better? In fact, why should he feel so weak at all? Something seemed to touch a responsive chord there. Pain! He could remember pain. It was a searing, splintering pain. But it was gone now.

Margaret spoke again to Grippa: "If he could only speak to me."

"Why can't I speak to you?" the sick man asked.

Grippa whirled about from his stand by the window. Margaret's hands were clutched against her breast.

"Ben! Oh, Ben!" she cried. Grippa dropped by the side of the bed and seized the patient's hands.

"Fellow, do you know me?"

Lacing turned his face toward the foreman kneeling beside him. "Know you? Of course I know you. Why shouldn't I?"

"Well, you should. And you ought to have been knowing me for a plenty long time now, too."

Suddenly, with the words, everything came back. The pain! Yes, he had known pain. A searing chest. Gunsmoke had been in his nostrils. And there had been a face, the sinister face of Vanner Storm. He had killed Storm, and Storm had done for him, too. He was not Lacing—he was Ord. And Margaret knew.

[389]

"He spoke to me! Oh, Adam, he spoke to me!" She dropped to the bedside, clutching the man's hands now in her own. Her head against them, the disarray of her hair fell across the coverlet. She made no effort to control her emotion. In God's name, what was all this? What was Margaret Wayne about?

Margaret raised her face to Grippa, crying unashamedly as she did so.

"Now, now, Margaret," the latter hastened to assure her. "He's better. He knew you. And he knew me too. Just like the doctor said, he's coming around. You wait and see."

Spring again on the Pedernales, Karryl and Levit had found a whole new world before them. They had taken time out for a long journey to Houston to visit Aunt Betsy, attending the wedding of Margaret Wayne and Ord en route. Now they were home again.

They had ridden together this day along the river. Close beside the path the little purple gentians peeked from their hiding places, and the song of a meadowlark rose from the willows. They halted briefly at a clear spot close to the southern wall and Levit jumped down from his horse.

He held out a hand to Karryl as she slipped from the saddle. In the distance, across the sparkle of the rivulet, the stone walls of the Falling Water showed almost sienna in the backdrop of the spreading oaks. Away to the north the farther pinnacles of the valley wall reflected a living shade of rose-magenta. She put her hand inside his arm and drew him close to her. "I love you, Levit," she whispered.

"I love you, too, Karryl," he said. "I have loved you since the start, back there in Houston. But I never realized at first how much. And I'm sorry for the years I cost us."

"You didn't cost us any years. It was probably through that very separation that perhaps we found ourselves. We'll never be apart again."

He gathered the reins of the horses into one hand, placing an arm around her. Slowly they started down the trail toward the river ford, strolling side by side as their mounts plodded along behind them. They stopped occasionally along the path to enjoy the spectacle. In the lower levels were dwarfed white asters. Karryl stooped for a moment to pluck a fragrant rain lily from the soil, raising it to her lips. "What a lonely note this beautiful valley plays," she said.

"Yes." He smiled. "A bit lonely, but I'm glad to say now that I can hear other sounds as well. When I was a youngster, I used to get on my horse and ride down to the valley just to be alone and to tune my thoughts—the thoughts a motherless, sisterless boy would have—to this lonely concert of the river. I suppose I felt that the Valley and I had something in common. You see, there was little music in my childhood. My mother had a piano, but nobody touched it after her death. Aside from the rowdy bunkhouse ballads, I hardly knew what the word 'melody' meant, but I had a need for some kind of music. I called this lonely little refrain from the river my Song of the Pedernales."

"We'll raise our children here, Levit," Karryl sang. "And many people—like myself—from many far places will come here to make their homes."

In the distance, the everyday routine of the valley ranch was unfolding. Lubbock was busy with some chore at the open smithy. Meadows hazed a mustang in the nearby corral. Karryl said, "It's people like you, and those men of yours down there, who have prepared this land for homes and for families and for children, Levit."

He gazed toward the compound, then off toward the hills in the north. "Like some of us, maybe," he answered. "But there have been others, too. Generations and generations in these hills and on the prairies of Texas. For hundreds of years, in fact. People ought not to forget that the Southwest already had more than a century of colonial history behind it by the time the Pilgrims landed at Plymouth Rock. Those of us who have grown up here sure don't forget it. Oh, our cowboys and Rangers did their part—maybe the most glorious part. But there were the early Spaniards as well, the Frenchmen, the frontiersmen who tried to save the Alamo, the Mexican soldiers and their colonists who came here never intending to return to their native land. The troopers out there on the Brazos in the early years, many of them buried there, unsung and unremembered, a thousand miles from loved ones. The Negro cavalrymen, too, Karryl, who fought well. Without these people to go before, this could have been an empty land."

Karryl smiled. "So much has gone on here, Levit, so isolated from the rest of the world. Most often these people of yours—

ours—have been called on to work things out for themselves. They've lived their lives alone, fought for or against each other as need be, and they've lived entirely by their own standards."

"Sure," he agreed. "Which is why they feel that maybe they're a little different in some ways. But it took individuals of every race and color and creed—I include you in this—to make the kind of folks who could live and prosper in our part of the world."

Her red hair flashed, and her eyes brightened. "I'm glad you said that, Levit. The legends of these prairies and mountains will live through the ages after a lot of other things have been forgotten. In generations far ahead, parents will read to their children about life as it was—is—here in this land. 'So those were the Texans,' they'll say. Levit, I hope I am remembered as one of them."

Author's Note

The battle of the Lost River, as such, did not occur. The last Indian encounter in the Llano country was on August 4, 1873, and it has come to be known as the battle of Packsaddle Mountain. In that final engagement of the hill country, seven Texans dispersed a band of twenty Comanches, suffering wounds themselves and inflicting casualties upon their foe. The Indians did not return to the hills.

But beyond this departure from the record, the incidence of history reported here is true. In the musty archives of the country along the frontier line of that early day there is testimony, fast being forgotten, of scores of encounters between red and white men, clashes involving numbers from less than a dozen to hundreds of agile fighters. In the early years of the decade of 1870, these battles gradually established the inevitability of the white man's incursion, breaking the power of the Comanche on the Plains as several successive military campaigns had never been able to do. Because no literary effort might properly chronicle these innumerable engagements, the elements employed by the opposing cultures have been drawn as accurately as possible into one simulation to propose honor where honor is due.

Levit MacAshen, Karryl Newcomb, Ord, Margaret Wayne, the White Eagle and all the others are of course, creations. But along the line of the Texas frontier there were many who could have been so named. The circumstances which etched their place in history should never be forgotten.

SONG OF THE PEDERNALES

sixteenth book produced by Madrona Press
has been printed on Nakoosa Ardor Offset book paper.
Type used for text is eleven-point Journal Roman, one-point
leaded, set on the IBM Electronic Selectric Composer.
Jacket design by Barbara Mathews Whitehead
Printing: The Whitley Company, Austin
Binding: Custom Bookbinders, Inc., Austin

MADRONA PRESS, INC.
BOX 3750 - AUSTIN, TEXAS 78764